PRAISE FOR

WATT O'HUGH UNDERGROUND

"Watt O'Hugh will stay with you long after you've turned the last page of Steven Drachman's **joyful, hilarious and smart** tale. Much like the dizzy feeling I have when I get off the spinning teacup ride at an amusement park, my head happily spun through time and place. Drachman, or maybe it was Watt O'Hugh, made me **an instant fan**." — Nicolle Wallace (*NY Times* Best-Selling Author of *Eighteen Acres*, and ABC-TV analyst)

"Drachman's time-traveling hero returns for retribution .... [This] exuberant novel is chock-full of fantastical elements; in addition to Watt's time-roaming ability and spectral allies ... there are demons, oracles, dragons and assorted monstrosities... Watt shines!" — *Kirkus Reviews*

"Well-researched ... amusingly discursive and rollickingly energetic. Watt evades fantastical monsters with the same self-reported aplomb he uses to confront demonic gunfighters, rob trains, and comfort distressed maidens (both living and otherwise). Four stars (out of five)!" — Bradley A. Scott, *ForeWord Reviews*

"One of the most entertaining and engaging books you'll be reading this year .... A smart and enjoyable romp where you savor every word and want to return to the first chapter the moment you reach the last page." — David Groff, author, *Clay* (Trio House Press)

"[Q]uick-reading, page-turning pulpy adventures!" — *Revolution Science Fiction*

PRAISE FOR STEVEN S. DRACHMAN
and *THE GHOSTS OF WATT O'HUGH*:

Winner, Best Fantasy Novel, Indie Excellence Book Awards 2012

Finalist, Action Adventure Category, Next Generation Indie Book Awards 2012

NAMED TO *KIRKUS REVIEWS'* "BEST OF 2011"!

"A fine writer, and a fine fellow ...." — Raymond Kennedy, author, *Ride a Cockhorse* (Knopf)

"[An] engaging tale of Western science fiction and amazing fantasy....
Drachman pens a standout lead in the character of Watt O'Hugh. The cool
hero's tale is told in charming, romping detail, from the magical
adventurer's poor childhood in the Five Points and the Tomb[s], to his
notorious, gun-toting dalliances in the Wild West and his wilder exploits
through time itself. ... Adding legitimate historical figures, such as the
esteemed author Oscar Wilde, to the fictional mix builds levels of
believability to the time-traveling romp's fast-paced flavor. ... Fast-paced,
energetic and fun; a dime novel for modern intellectuals." — *Kirkus
Reviews*

"If you gave up on the feasibility of a Western/science fiction mash-up
when 'Cowboys vs Aliens' tanked a few months back, give it another try.
On the page, at any rate. ... Drachman revives the nascent genre with his
rip-snorting, mind boggling novel ... [T]here's a lot going on in this teeming
tome!" — Peter Keough, *The Boston Phoenix*

"Blending in elements of fantasy and time travel, ... *The Ghosts of Watt
O'Hugh* is a humorous and fun adventure, recommended." — *The Midwest
Book Review*

"Quixote-esque .... With stories of Chinese emperors, legends of magical
creatures, the streets of 1870s New York and time-roaming gunmen of the
Wild West[.]" — *The Bethesda Gazette*

"... a tale of yesteryear, evocative of Robber Barons and the old West, while
ingeniously narrated from a modern perspective, courtesy of Magic and an
ability to roam Time. Watt O'Hugh is a character for sure and an engaging
narrator who will take you through fascinating worlds, meticulously
researched .... *Watt O'Hugh* is cowboy fantasy noir and worth a read."
— Mike Brotherton, author, *Star Dragon* and *Spider Star* (Tor Books)

"[A] triumph of genre bending, a fine, literary mashup of cowboy adventure
and science fiction magic that makes you wish you could meet its carefully
hewn characters in real life." — Harold Goldberg, author, *All Your Base are
Belong to Us* (Random House)

WATT O'HUGH UNDERGROUND

BEING THE SECOND PART OF THE STRANGE AND ASTOUNDING MEMOIRS OF WATT O'HUGH the THIRD

Steven S. Drachman

ISBN 978-0-9913274-1-6

Front cover illustration and book design by Mark Matcho

Chickadee Prince Logo by Garrett Gilchrist

Visit him at www.watt-ohugh.com

Second edition

STEVEN S. DRACHMAN

WATT O'HUGH UNDERGROUND

Being the Second Part of the Strange and Astounding Memoirs of Watt O'Hugh the Third

STEVEN S. DRACHMAN is a writer and critic whose work has appeared in *The New York Times, The Washington Post, Entertainment Weekly, The Boston Phoenix, Audere Magazine, The Village Voice* and *The Chicago Sun-Times*. He lives in Brooklyn with his wife and two daughters. This is his second novel.

WATT O'HUGH UNDERGROUND

Being the Second Part of the Strange and Astounding Memoirs of Watt O'Hugh the Third

Chickadee Prince Books
New York

To Lan,
Liana and Julianne

THE STORY BEGINS....

In 1863, I was employed as a clerk for the City, still a young man, fresh-faced, relatively enthusiastic about my life of respectability and about my regular pay, which required no thievery and thus no risk of arrest. Every morning I put on a tie, dampened my hair and pushed a brush through it. Then I clambered down the stairs, out the door and into the awakening dawn, sometimes whistling (sometimes not).

This was before the Federal government proclaimed the draft in Manhattan. The War was creeping across the country, unseen but greatly felt, and those of us lucky enough to be happy to be alive were all just hovering over the edge of the abyss. Life was delicious, like a drop of honeysuckle nectar, and perhaps nearly as briefly enjoyed. I was young and still alive, and I was also in love. I was in love more than I knew. And so I was bittersweetly, desperately and ominously happy.

As a clerk, I sat behind a rough, splintery little wooden desk in a large central room on the second floor of a sturdy, solid City government building, where I added up numbers and wrote things down. Though I had been at this job for more than a year, I still didn't really know what I was accomplishing and for whom, nor why anyone thought it necessary to pay me to add up numbers and to write things down, but I was nevertheless grateful to have a job.

Periodically, the administrative supervisor would leave his office and wander among the clerk's desks, peer over our shoulders, bark at us, or, on wonderful rare occasions, praise us. He was a bald man, a little overweight, with a big round face that would grow red and ripe with pride when he was pleased with one of his clerks and red and ripe with disappointment when he was angry. To-day, writing these words, seventy-three years later, I cannot remember his name, though even to this day I consider him my unofficial adoptive father, the first man who ever believed in me at all, even if it was only a little bit, and only from time to time.

On May 13, 1863, when the working day ended, I said good evening to my boss, and, upon exiting to the street, I walked Northwest a number of blocks, then hopped onto the omnibus, which shuttled me uptown to the Fifth Avenue Hotel, where heavenly Lucy Billings awaited me in the plush lobby.

"'Evening, handsome," she whispered in my ear. (I was tall and young, I had the strength of the streets, and I possessed a handsomeness that grew naturally from youth and vigor, back then, as Lucy correctly noted. This is not braggadocio. I am not handsome now; I was handsome then. And though I'd purchased my suit at one of the low-price working-man shops downtown, my tie was particularly nice that day, and so I looked the man I yearned to become, a man who belonged here, meeting the heavenly Lucy Billings in the Fifth Avenue Hotel lobby, rather than the person I knew that I really was, an orphan who'd grown up in the marshy and dark slum streets of south Manhattan.)

I was born in 1842, and so at the time I was only 20, and she was a bit ambiguously older than I. Not too much older, I supposed then, but just experienced enough to teach me a lesson or two on a number of subjects. Such as: how to impress New York society big bugs with just the right turn of phrase in just the right slightly-unidentifiable accent; how to dance the German at a society ball at a respectable address on the Fifth Avenue; the proper way to stab my fork into a bloody-red steak in the starched white stuffiness of Delmonico's stifling-cavernous dining room; how to applaud graciously from the good seats in the Grand Opera House.

She taught me about a couple of other subjects, I recall, such as abolitionism, suffragism, the free love movement, economic egalitarianism, political subversion and the overthrow of the codfish aristocracy class, matters that she shared only with certain carefully screened co-conspirators. (From this philosophical grab bag, I had my personal favorite, as you may have guessed.)

Back then I was young as the dew on a daisy, and I was excited to learn such things, especially if I were to learn from Lucy Billings, whom I loved then, and whom I love still, separated from her even, as I am, by decades. Lucy was an American girl from common blood, I thought, but she claimed to be an heiress from the old country, and at society events, she tried to pass me off as her brother. But I wasn't her brother, and I was glad of it.

A wave of nattily waxed, tail-coated and top-hatted moustaches sauntered by, knocking us to and fro, amidst the Hotel's buzzing carpeted elegance.

She slipped her arm in mine, the crooks of our elbows cohabited cozily, and we exited the Hotel together.

I cannot remember much of the ensuing early evening, although I suppose that we dined someplace Lucy would have considered appropriately classy, and that Lucy slipped me some cash under the table with which to pay the bill. What I *do* remember, however, is that either Lucy or I had a reckless and romantic brainstorm for an end to the evening, and that near-midnight I found myself drunk in a rowboat in the North River just off the Manhattan Island shore, playing the ukulele tolerably well, singing a popular song of that particular decade (less tolerably well), and watching Lucy laugh, with deep affection in her deep blue eyes.

She ran one gloved hand through her blond hair, which caught the moonlight. The rowboat cut through the black and murky waters without much urgency. Lucy was smooth as an ivory statue and soft as a velvet pillow, she had a slender waist, the kind heart of an angel, plump red lips, she wore a scarf of feathers about her neck, and I was twenty.

We splashed further into the dark distance, until the palace car that had drawn us down the Third Avenue was naught but a blurry fluttering line of light, and the oyster stores that abutted the wharf we'd just left no longer stank like a dead polecat. As we drifted from the Island, my gaze roamed, as always, to the dark swamp of my old childhood orphan home, which consumed the vitality of the metropolis like a great black hole. A mile to the north of the ghetto, like a castle on a hill, the lights of Broadway shined and taunted, a golden fairyland of joy just out of reach beyond the slum apartments.

To the West, I could see the lighthouse in the Staten Island sound, flickering in the near distance, and beyond that, the country mansions on the Staten Island resort itself, behind the heavy guns that lined its shore. Canal boats and steam ships raced along through the starry water, and the all-night gas-lit ferries, ringed by colored lamps, seemed to set the river aflame. Manhattan Island was a Christmas tree with pretty ornaments, swinging in the wind, harmless and lovely (a few of them, admittedly, broken beyond repair). My little boat bobbed on eddies and swirls as the ships passed, and Lucy smiled in the darkness.

At length I touched on a little island not a half mile across the Upper Bay, hopped into the gently lapping surf, pulled the boat up onto the narrow rocky coastline, took one of Lucy's white-gloved hands in mine and helped her ashore. It was just a towhead, really, with a few trees casting a romantic shadow, a towhead that wanted to be an island but which would never appear on any map, and which has since been washed away by the tides and no longer exists. Even as I write these words, its proud trees are long-ago driftwood. But back then it existed, and it seemed as permanent as the mansions and wide sidewalks of the Fifth Avenue, the racetrack at Jerome Park, the slums of the Five Points.

Lying on the shore of the towhead and staring up at the stars that lit the Bay, Lucy said, "I imagine you and I are staring at exactly the same star, right now," and I said that the one I was focused on was somewhat round and shiny and pretty, and she laughed, and she said she imagined that there was a planet rotating around that very star, with a young man and a somewhat young but somewhat older woman staring right down at us, thinking the very same thoughts that she and I were thinking at that very moment and saying the very same things. "What do you think will happen to that young man and that somewhat young woman?" she wondered, and I took a guess, and then she took a guess, and I admit that her guess was a little bit more romantic and beautiful, but I did my best, and I suppose that she appreciated it. I will spare you a precise recounting of our poetical sentiments, because I am pressing my luck already, but in begging your indulgence, I ask you to recall the first few months of your finest love affair, and the silly words you said, and the momentous emotions you felt.

Quiet waves tickled the shore, and the high branches of an island oak rustled in the wind, which we liked. But then came a discordant noise in the woods, which distracted us both, put a chill in the air, seemed to melt into the vapor, and made Lucy's breath catch in her throat.

I tried to shrug it away, back then, seventy years ago, and why not? I had other things on my mind. I wrapped my coat around Lucy, and I caressed one rosy cheek.

But now I wish that I had paid some bit of attention to that noise in the woods, and that I had listened to the words ringing in my ears.

Because that noise in the woods was none-other-than my older self – wiser, sadder, and more than a little translucent and fuzzy around the edges, who had traveled back through the decades to a moment in the past when my lustrous Lucy Billings might just have chosen to marry me, had I only asked, and thus changed all that was to come. The gray-haired Watt O'Hugh was roaming Time, drifting with the ancient, ceaseless wind as it wound through the millennia wreaking its havoc.

My older self whispered in my own, younger, foolisher ear, like a ghost: "*Marry me, Lucy.*"

Imploring my younger self, and nearly invisible in the night: "*Just ask her. Now. Just ask her now.*

"*Save us both.*"

CHAPTER 1

If in August of 1878, a body were to have climbed up to the top of the Sierra Nevada mountain range and stared down into the desert valley just to the east, and if he were to have squinted with a bit more than the usual level of mindfulness, he might have been able to discern a tiny black spot in the middle of miles of yellow rock and dust. My hope and expectation would have been that he would disregard it entirely as nothing more than a tiny black spot, because that tiny spot would have been the cabin where I lived back then, in that stifling August of 1878. And I didn't want to be found.

I guess calling that homestead a "cabin" is more than a bit unjustifiably grandiose. It was a sweaty, smelly little sandy-floor shack in the middle of a wasteland, with some whiskey bottles tossed in the back and chew-tobacco stains on the walls, and a rickety lean-to for my horse to hide from the heat. Sometimes, such as during this particular August, my valley was just a boundless, glimmery ocean of heat and death, but even in the daytime, in the worst, blazing 110-degree heat of summer, I called it home. A little muggy shade to lie in, read my dime novels, some of which – the more battered ones – starred an impossibly heroic version of a young man named Watt O'Hugh the Third, which is my name[*], though at that point in my life – lying on the dirt and the grit in the dark, an infamous (though framed) outlaw, for the most-part moderately or more than moderately stewed from my magical bottomless whiskey bottle, and hiding from the Pinkertons – well, you wouldn't think me very heroic, I suppose. I was still tall when I bothered to stand up, and broad-shouldered, and I had my strength left, or most of it, but I didn't look much like the heroic young buster whose features adorned those book covers. My face was now weathered and bearded, my eyes a little rummy and runny.

My little house also had the air of a temporary home long-deserted, or died-out, something that wouldn't warrant a second

---

[*] Or, anyway, it's the name I chose for myself when I emerged from the slums. I did not know my real name, or even whether I'd ever had one.

glance from that fellow at the top of that mountain range, even if that fellow were hunting for a fugitive, a slippery rascal who'd eluded the law for some number of years, through all manner of trickery.

And this was, after all, the whole point of my abode. Hiding and, of course, plotting revenge. I was an angry army of one, as I will explain shortly. I spent my days poring over maps, imagining a way to destroy my enemies and march out of their city carrying their heads on flaming spears, shock and surprise frozen to their dead-dead-dead faces. So I was angry, hopeless, drunk in the heat, and ceaselessly plotting a solo military conquest that I knew could not and would not ever come to fruition.

My existence in the desert wasn't all cruel and unusual punishment, however. Not twenty-five miles away there was a freshwater spring, eking its way out of the Sylvania mountain peaks, which I could see to the North from my back porch even on a dusty day. Sometimes hummingbirds spun about in the back, at night I could sometimes spy a meteor or two if I looked closely, in the Spring I'd get purple wildflowers, and in the winter a little cleansing snow if I were lucky. And life was occasionally tolerable in other ways, mostly as a result of a racket I'd dreamed up, which had turned out to be a good one. (I'll get to that eventually.)

So I was infamous, certainly, but I was apparently not *too* infamous for Hester Smith[*], who pounded on my door as the sun prepared to set, sweating and hollering in the still-oppressive heat. She had arrived on a conspicuously arthritic mule, which she'd bought in the little town of Penville on the outskirts of the desert, and which had trudged an admirable number of perilous miles till, as dusk loomed, men in black appeared on the horizon not half a mile from my shack.

"*Watt O'Hugh!*" she called, pounding on the door.

I shouted back at her that I warn't Watt O'Hugh, that I'd never heard of Watt O'Hugh, and that my name was Hugh Watt, who was an entirely different person.

---

[*] That's what your 20th century Harvard professors would call an "awkward segue," but as a little poetic turn of phrase it pleases me, an orphaned mudsill with only a little formal education at the Randall's Island school, in the middle of the last century, and more than a few lifetimes ago.

She kicked in the door and stood before me, five foot ten inches tall, a Colored woman, lean and muscular, and nearly thirty years of age, in my estimation. She was dressed in a blue work shirt and denim pants, and a dirty white cowboy hat, which shaded her face from the sun. The mule collapsed behind her, and her bag dropped into the sand.

Hester was breathing heavily in the heat of my white sandy sun-soaked world, and something in her face or in her eyes seemed to remind me of someone I'd known a long time ago. Then I realized that what I was recognizing was fear and desperation, which, when I greeted it face to face, seemed like an old friend.

"I'm Hester," she said, which is how I came to have learnt her name.

I sleepily criticized her for destroying my such-as-it-was door, but without much passion.

I took another swig from my bottle, and she told me that men were chasing her and were set to kill her if they caught her, and that she was sorry, but now that she was here in my home, they'd probably kill me too, these men who were chasing her.

My gut instinct was that Hester was on the side of goodness and light in this particular kerfuffle, and so I figured that I had no choice but to absquatulate and to take her with me.

"Well then," I said with a shrug.

I put on my hat, slipped my bottle into my pocket and, though I had no intention of shooting anyone to-day, I grabbed my barking-iron just in case.

I stepped outside, where I could see them in the distance, three dusty ink smudges thundering towards me from the hot-hazy far-lands.

The mule lay on his side. He kicked at the air, gasped, coughed, and stopped breathing.

Hester knelt down beside him. She shook her head. She frowned.

"I guess that mule can't gallop," I said.

"He was a beautiful animal," she said. "Not very strong. Not much to look at. But loyal and brave. A mule with a beautiful soul. He died to save me."

I nodded.

"I have a horse," I said.

"You don't want to stay and fight?" she asked me as she stood. "Protect the so-to-speak homestead?"

I pointed out that the homestead warn't much of one, and Hester pointed out that there was a principle involved.

"No reason to kill a man if there's no reason to kill a man," I replied. This was a little adage that I liked to repeat from time-to-time, usually when I was behaving cowardly like, and now it served as a countervailing principle to Hester's simplistic call to "*protect*" the "*homestead*." *Watt O'Hugh's Maxim and First Corollary*, as I dubbed it*, could give my otherwise inexcusable pusillanimity a philosophical underpinning that sounded both compassionate and paradoxically valiant, in its way, and even tended to impress the lady-folk, which was otherwise hard for a gentleman to do while he was running away from danger.

"What about your ghosts?" she asked me, and I said that my ghosts did not like taking life either. Their own lives violently ripped from them back in 1863, my ghosts were pacifists who fought only if necessary. If I were ever to pick a fight that my ghosts deemed unnecessary or unjust, they would leave me, my aim would falter, and I would die.

The distant figures grew slightly larger against a hazy ball of fire on the western horizon.

"You comin'?" I asked, and the two of us leaped onto my bay gelding, who loyally galloped east, and I realize now, as I had known then, that while I had never bothered to name him, he was my only friend, in those days. I'd bought my horse from a little ranching village in the Medicine Bow Range, right after I'd escaped from the penitentiary in Wyoming, a strong warrior beast who seemed to have sprung alive from the imagination of some painter who'd died hundreds of years ago, a steed whose coat was the color of a renaissance palette.**

---

* Of course, when I was using my assumed identity, I called it "Hugh Watt's Maxim and First Corollary," instead.

** He'd ridden with me, my horse, during that rollicking, bloody range war up in Lervine, along the Northern edge of Utah, among many other misadventures, and while some of them were successful, the most important ones were all failures, and of even the successful ones I am frequently ashamed and seldom proud.

Pounding on the desert sand and hard rocks, with the mountains looking down on me like a painted backdrop, just shimmering in the distance, the heat crushing down from above and swamping my lungs, Hester holding onto me tight, the sun scorching my skin like fire, this cracked, shimmering-hidden dream world was defined for me only by what was missing: neither the feel of the breeze nor any sounds of life, no motion of the world, of milliseconds born and expiring with each gasp. Scorpions hid beneath rocks, invisible and silent, tortoises burrowed in their burrows, and desert-banded geckos, eyes just above the hot sand, yearned to whisk through the moonlight upon the arrival of night. But all I could feel and all that existed for me was my steed's heavy fleeting hoof beats thumping together with the whack of my heart, Hester's nervous cool puffs of breath on the back of my neck, and the vigilance party, adumbral, who bore down on us. My horse was fast, but burdened by two riders, he couldn't keep up this pace for long. Without looking back, I could feel the smile of greedy anticipation on the point man's face. We were suspended, soaring, motionless, the yellow desert expanding, breathing, suffocating.

We rode past a homemade tombstone, forgotten, flowerless, cast aside at the foot of a cliff-rise, some miner who'd failed, and who had been lucky enough to have had one friend to memorialize his failure on a rotten piece of gumwood, an epitaph I knew by heart:

Chester Jordan – A Tolerable, Loyal Fellow

Just then, a little town rose into view on the eastern horizon, a slum, a few shackly old stores and houses, some splintery saloons and a dance hall at the very furthest edge, from which I could almost see the music rising, sweeping over me like the desert heat, a guiro scraping, a vihuelo wailing, and a measure of almost blissful, tuneful weeping in that language I still do not understand. This was a hopeless town filled with men from the Mexican border, the men who chased the men who chased gold to the desert. And a few unlucky women, who came along.

We swept past the little barrio, where I was not welcome (due to an incident, so to speak, which time unfortunately prevents me from relating) and then the tents of the Shoshone Indian camp just a few yards from the barrio's northeast edge, where I was a bit more welcome, albeit in small, carefully measured doses. A few Indians stood about in the sandy alleys between the tents. One was drinking, one was telling a story and laughing. One white-haired man raised a hand and waved as Hester and I passed, and Hester waved back, feigning good cheer.

After another extended stretch of empty desert, we finally hit the one-street mining town of Lida, which was composed of a shaky general store, a couple of liquor shops, a post office, and an assortment of log cabins with canvas roofs that would have flapped in the wind had there been any wind. An empty stagecoach waited at the border. If you didn't know that this town was spanking new, built on golden optimism less than a year ago, you'd swear it had been standing in this heat for a hundred years, and that the whole sorry place was fixing to collapse from decrepit old age at any moment.

I yanked on the reins, jumped off my gelding and Hester followed. I smacked my horse and off he ran. We dashed into a little doggery called Scott & Fitzgerald's Saloon[*], a little doggery with dust and sand on the floor and a rough, crumbling wooden bar crowded with sweaty miners cussing and crying with the dust in their eyes, and, as he always did at these moments, fat, old Fitzgerald, his hair and face gray like manufactory smog, tossed me a horn of his famous anti-fogmatic (strong and uncouth and so tempting, like the women who lingered in the shadows of his doggery), which I downed on credit as Hester and I ran straight through the back door, which squeaked and rattled and banged on leather hinges rotted near-through.

There my horse awaited us in a world that looked almost the same but felt off-the-reel different.

It was a little hotter, but that warn't all.

Different decades feel different on the skin, and this was a different decade.

Hester noticed it too, and in spite of her fear, she was excited. This was, I guess, what she had expected when she'd knocked on my door, something like this.

---

[*] This was really the name of the saloon in the little shit-nothing town of Lida, not a ham-handed tribute to the author of *The Great Gatsby*, a book I have not read (and I don't expect to find the time to read before I surely die on January 1, 1937), although I understand that it will go through a critical reappraisal in the years following my death.

"Are we roamin'?" she asked, her face alight. Sweat glistened frantically on her brow. "Are we roamin', Watt O'Hugh the Third?"

I nodded, and I asked her to keep her voice down.

"The desert looks yellower in the future," she marveled.

"We just need a little Time," I said. "A little Time to think, to plan. To understand how you know my name, what you know about my ghosts, what you need with me, and who that posse are. And how in the Hell you know about roaming."

She nodded, but she was still not serious, scared someplace in the back of her mind, but still giddy.

"They'll be waiting for us when we get back," I cautioned her, "still galloping after us, still thinking about doing whatever it is to you that they were thinking about doing when we left. Even if we stayed here in the future for fifty years, they'd still be right there when we got back."

I grunted at my horse, and he followed Hester and me up over the top of a little dune-like hill, and then back down to the bottom on the other side.

I stopped walking.

A paved, two-lane interstate highway lay a few yards ahead of us, and, about a quarter mile to the east, the highway forked, and a narrow side road wound north, ending at a gleaming white building, two stories, with reddish blue trim that matched the sky. In the far west, a red horseless carriage sped towards us, just a dot in the distance now, like a tiny coronal loop on the setting sun. The horseless carriage was one of those sporty little convertibles, and this was 1981.[*]

I tried to smile, and I explained briefly about automobiles, and then we patiently awaited Hester Smith's first automobile sighting. A few moments later the little red car swept past, stirring up sand and dust. The top was down, and the bald man in the driver's seat had a peeling sunburn on the top of his head. A woman sat in the passenger seat, and her hair flapped about. Her nose was red like the car.

---

[*] It was August 15, 1981, to be precise, four days after August 11, 1981, which was a rather pleasant day in the life of Watt O'Hugh, and which I had continued to visit again and again, whenever I grew thirsty, broke, over-sweaty, or lonely, and which played a role in my aforementioned racket, which I'll talk about more later.

Hester watched the convertible vanish into the east, her eyes wide. She watched and watched till it was a dot again, and then it vanished.

"When you cross the street in the future," I cautioned, "always be sure to look both ways first."

We crossed the highway and trudged along at the edge of the side road, Hester and the horse following my lead.

"Horseless carriages," Hester mused. Then she said, slowly, syllable-by-syllable: "*Aw-toe-mo-beel* ...."

And now she smiled, and just as I had recognized her desperation when she kicked in my door, this smile I recognized too, an indescribable, ineffably familiar something-or-other, a longer-ago, many-years-lost-friend, the smile of hopeful joy. *How I have missed you, hopeful joy.*

She laughed, and she looked over at me.

"*Car*," she said, and she laughed again.

The little desert resort across the road was called the "Death Spa," jarringly named for the desert valley in which it sat. A future owner was destined to rename the spa some years later, in 2003, after its bankruptcy, corporate takeover and reorganization. But I was always happy to visit the Death Spa, because this was 1981, and in 1981, I was (or rather, I *will be*) quite completely dead, and even utterly decomposed for decades, and what other establishment so heartily welcomed the long-dead as customers? This was the only one, as far as I knew, and so I was really at home here.

We passed the little one-room gift shop, the gas pumps, and the quarter-full parking lot. Hester touched a silver 1971 Pontiac Catalina, and it burned her hand. She looked sheepish, and she reddened, but then she touched it again, gingerly, and it burned her again. She looked away from me and didn't meet my gaze.

A man with a monocle and a silver-tipped cane hobbled out of the front entrance of the spa, handed me a manila envelope– such things as manila envelopes are quite common in the 1980s – and walked across the street, never speaking a word to me nor casting me a meaningful glance. In the distance, he faded into a glistening mirage. He was not a man of the 1980s and had no desire to make any pretense of it. I had never seen him before, and I would never see him again.

I folded the envelope and stuffed it into my jacket pocket.

"Do you want to see what that is?" Hester asked.

"I know what it is."

The entrance to the "Death Spa" was a long corridor. The man at the front desk was named Pete, although his nametag said "Mike."

Pete was a thin uncomfortable young man in a thin uncomfortable old tie.

Pete had the kind of beard that made him look from a distance as though he were smiling, even though he was frowning, and the kind of beard that, when he was smiling close-up, made him look as though he were frowning. So whenever I entered the Death Spa tunnel, I met a false friendliness, and when I reached the front desk, he rebuffed me with an unintended surliness.

Pete's beard frowned.

"Mr. Darcy!" he exclaimed happily and, it seemed to Hester, inexplicably. "Room for two?" he asked, through his beard's frown.

Astonishing. Without even a disapproving glance Hester's way. Times would change, between 1878 and 1981. And then more and more and more. And even more. Just wait.

Hester blushed.

I shook my head.

"Just want to tie up my horse, let the lady and me splash our faces and drink some beet juice inside. We've got some plotting and scheming to attend to. Evil is at hand."

I whispered to Hester not to worry, beet juice would taste passable with a whisper of whiskey past the whiskers, and Pete laughed, as though I were joking (which I warn't). I asked him how much credit I had left, and he quoted to me a bulger of a figure that made Hester gasp, though I noted to her that it didn't buy as much beet juice in 1981 as it would have done in 1878, and Pete laughed again, just humoring a paying customer with a bit of credit.

We settled into my regular shadowy candle-lit table overlooking the "Olympic-sized swimming pool" (whatever that means).

"Why are you known as 'Mr. Darcy' in 1981?" Hester asked me now, and I replied that while it wasn't a long story, it was a story that I was nevertheless disinclined to tell her, but I didn't even manage to spike the beet juice before Pete ran back in, his beard smiling and his brow furrowed with worry.

Well, as it turns out, the point man of the posse had swept the whole gang of soaplocks through Time and was now right out front of the spa, installed in the parking lot and determined to import to the 1980s the sort of peck of troubles typical of old-timey Western malefactors.

I hurried from the bar, beet juice clenched in my left hand, Hester close behind me.

There he was, on a black stallion, dressed in a long black frock coat, black pantaloons, black boots. He had white white skin, taut and smooth and hairless, and bright-red smiling lips. His eyes were pink and beady, plaguily evil. Between cusses, he chanted in some sort of foreign tongue. His gang sat on their horses, cackling and spitting, and every once in a while shooting into the air. Whooping, at appropriately dramatic intervals.

"He's the devil that's after you?" I asked Hester.

She said that she was afraid so. He'd tracked her from Utah, up through California, and here he was, even chasing her into the future. She had spotted him once in Cripple Creek, and he had frightened her. When she saw him again in Bodie, this worried her more. He was not a man who faded into the Western sun.

"I don't think he took a decidedly urgent interest in my actions," she said, "until I headed in your direction."

I shook my head angrily. This black-white beast was one of the chief nightmares I had mizzled to the desert to escape.

Pete put a hand on my shoulder.

"Look, Mr. Darcy," he said. "This can't go on."

He liked a bit of harmless character and a little inoffensive mystique around the Death Spa. But he had customers coming in on a charter bus in 30 minutes, looking forward to two days of carrot juice, massages, clean air, heat-cure and whatnot.

I had never heard of a "charter bus," but regardless of that, I could not disagree with his concerns, and I turned to Hester.

"I recognize him too," I said to her. "His name is Monsieur Rasháh. But he may not really be French. I suspect he's from Hell, not Paris."

A couple of kids, a boy and a girl of about ten years of age, now jumped from between two parked cars, laughing and pointing, smiles appropriately gap-toothed, not a bit skeary of the dangerous gang. Bathing-suited, shiny-greased with lotion and sloppily wet, holding their pudgy little stomachs with glee. Who could have believed such a thing in 1981 as a villain on horseback? I wished that those kids would run away, as sensible 1878 rapscallions would have done. I tried to think of a plan to pull them out of harm's way that wouldn't result in all of us dead as winter tore, but nothing came immediately to mind, and so I figured I would improvise, shoot a few bullets, maybe kill a couple of gunmen, and drag the kids to safety without incurring any mortal wounds myself. I opened the door a crack, prepared to dash into the thick of the chaos, when Rasháh pointed a finger at the children, then at his sickly white forehead. In a blur and a whoosh, the children swept through the dry air and vanished into the creature's skull.

Pete cowered.

The sun beat down.

Monsieur Rasháh began calling out again, this time in a different, heavily accented language that I didn't recognize, something that didn't sound exactly human. His face changed; became old, wrinkled, and scheming; then became very young, childlike and impish; then re-settled into his inscrutable, waxy mold.

"At any rate," I said. "He's a really ghastly lout."

"Should I just call the police?" Pete asked, I said that no matter what he did, he shouldn't call the police, and then Hester exclaimed that calling an officer of the law was entirely unnecessary given that, as she put it, "Watt O'Hugh is one of the 19th century's most acclaimed shootists!"

Pete wondered aloud who was Watt O'Hugh?; and, dodging the question, I said that one's skill or lack of skill as a shootist wasn't the issue, it was that only special extra-Magic bullets would do the trick with Monsieur Rasháh.

"And even the Magic bullets don't *actually* do the trick," I admitted. "He catches them in his left hand, and he eats them like peanuts. Exhibit A of his invincibility being, you see, the fact that he is alive out there in the parking lot. I emptied a few barrels worth of Magic bullets at that bastard back in '75. And there he is, good as gold, in the parking lot."

Pete glared.

"I give you five minutes to fix this, dude," he whispered angrily. (That's what men will call each other in the waning days of the 20th Century: *dude*. In the 19th century, this referred to a nattily attired dandy. In the 20th century, it means precisely nothing.) "Then I'm calling the police. And listen, Darcy – I like you. But fix this. Whatever you do fix this." Then, expressing the 20th century's overriding capitalist impulse, he added, "This will prove bad for business, and we cannot have this kind of thing here."

He retreated to the front desk, where he sat, tapping his fingers, doing not much of anything else, waiting to call the police. His beard beamed.

"A plan?" Hester asked, and I said that I had not only a plan, but a plan that might work. The best kind, in my opinion, I noted, and Hester said she'd always had the notion that I was drawn to the absolutely just but hopeless cause, and she looked at me significantly and with some sadness, and looking into those dark, grum eyes, I thought I could understand why, but my introspection was cut short, because just then, in the parking lot, Rasháh screamed, a loud bloodcurdling scream, and an army of red-winged demons descended from the sky. They looked just as one might imagine demons would look: gaunt, hungry, small and menacing. They had pointed ears, slits for nostrils. They laughed and smirked.* The gang spread out, Rasháh remaining out front, and the other members of the posse taking up position at each exit, a demon or two buzzing protectively above each of them. The demons screamed along in unison with Rasháh (in that

---

* I'd rather not be "pedantic," but I think it's important to note that these creatures sitting on M. Rasháh's shoulders inspired more curiosity in me than they did in the other guests – who, after all, were of the *Star Wars* generation – and so I would spend some time researching them in the decades to come. The pixies on M. Rasháh's right shoulder were 妖精, or *yaoching*, which are the nastiest Chinese demons that you might ever have the misfortune to meet, and those on his left shoulder preferred to go by their proper names and were demons of an origin that in the 1870s we would have described politely in a hushed voice as the *Eastern European* persuasion. Of this latter group one might identify Ornias, Bultala, Thallal, Melchal, and even the comparatively noteworthy Beelzeboul, who my 21st century readers would consider the Chief Executive Officer of the demons, and who popped in for only a little while for a bit of very effective and threatening shrieking.

sing-song language with its sharp cutting-knife edges that wasn't Chinese and wasn't German) bouncing off his shoulder, rippling into the angry hot air, fluttering for a moment with little, high-speed hummingbird wings, then alighting again, a thousand on his left shoulder and ten thousand on his right.

Now that we were trapped, the gunmen started shooting out the windows. The lights in the game room exploded, spraying shards of broken glass down on a middle-aged man playing chess with his teen-aged son, the father of the two missing children, unaware of their fate. This nicely lightly tanned man, with "hair plugs" that looked almost-real and thousand-dollar tortoise shell spectacles, dived under a billiard table, dragging his son with him.

I shot through the broken window at the henchman to Rasháh's left – pretty much knowing it would do no good – and a red, blistery demon caught the bullets and tossed them to Rasháh, who swallowed them. Then they both laughed.

Hester and I dashed to the front desk; I told Pete that I needed the back door, and I assured him that the moment Hester and I abandoned the spa, the Rasháh gang would leave him alone. He should then feel free to call the constable, if he wished, but I imagined the police report would reflect rather poorly on his sanity. He took my elbow and drew me behind the desk, through a narrow doorway that led to a winding windowless hallway that smelled of mold and hummed and buzzed with fluorescence, a form of future-world lighting that seemed to discomfit Hester even more than the demons had. We passed a hunched old man, a rusty guts with pallid, puckered skin, who dragged a cleaning pail and gasped and groaned as he walked. We came to a hard metal door, which Pete unbolted with a large key before sprinting away to relative safety at the front desk.

I peered outside through the keyhole. A rangy, jittery young man stood a few feet away in the hot sun, a rifle in his hand, which was peeled on the door, a red demon cackling over his left shoulder and a black demon hollering over his right shoulder. The gunman was just waiting. He had a terrible purple scar, which began at the top of his forehead, drizzled over the front of his face and disappeared behind the collar of his blue shirt. Tortoise tracks ran behind him in the sand, and the sun vanished in a slow explosion back of the mountains on the horizon.

I smiled at Hester.

"You can swim?" I asked, and she said that she couldn't, and so I asked whether she thought she could hold her breath and float for a spell if I held onto her tight, and she shrugged and nodded, though she wondered why it mattered.

"Our escape route," I said. "Along the very bottom of the ocean. Quite an idea, if I do say so myself."

Hester asked me where the ocean was, and I said, "Right on the other side of this door.

"On three," I said. "Breathe in deeply, shut your eyes, hold your breath, please do not panic and breathe by accident (because then you will assuredly die in terrible pain) and do not let go of me.

"All right?"

She agreed. I took both her hands firmly in mine.

I counted to three.

I opened the door.

A moment that felt like millennia later, all went dark, and we stood on solid ground in an airless void, ears popping, lungs collapsing. I pushed up, kicking through the water and holding onto Hester with all my strength. I could see a light far above, flickering and floating in the haze. Seaweed drifted through my field of vision. Bony-armored, jawless fish eyed us quizzically as we passed. A creature like an octopus with a coiled shell flittered above us.

Hester seemed to go limp in my arms.

After some time, we crashed up into the air like rockets, gasping and coughing, and then a while later we washed up on a sandy beach like a couple of pieces of driftwood, still gasping and coughing, though less urgently. Glistening before us was an ocean like any other, and behind us, a gentle forest of giant ferns and conifers.

"Welcome to Pangaea," I whispered wetly to Hester. "No one calls it that now, because there is no one here to call it that, but that's what it is. *Pangaea.*"

Some kind of flying insect buzzed my ear, a prehistoric sort of gallnipper, and I swatted it away, being careful not to kill it.

"My little desert valley is a dead ocean floor," I said. "It used to be an inland sea."

We lay down on the beach. The sand cradled the back of my head. Her hand still held mine tightly. Her hand was wet and sweaty.

She was still out of breath. She squinted up at the sky. The sky was blue, a little cloudy. The sky looked like any sky, except that it was birdless. And because the sky was birdless, because this beach had no gulls, the ocean didn't sound like an ocean. The clouds in the sky, like any clouds, looked like sheep, like cotton, things that didn't exist yet, but there they were in the sky.

"A great inland sea," I repeated. "This is the desert valley, which used to be a great inland sea."

"A long time ago, I suppose," she said quietly.

I agreed.

"A long time ago," I said. "Or right now. Depending on your perspective."

"What is 'now', anyway, to a Roamer?" she asked, with a laugh.

The laugh sounded nice here, in this peaceful world, and I was glad that Hester had given mother Earth her very first laugh.

Behind us, a roar, a great earth-rattling din, then silence.

"Dinosauria?" she asked.

"No," I said. "Dinosauria haven't evolved yet, Hester. It's a peaceful planet. Plant life, bugs. Some small animal life. Maybe that noise was the earth moving. Or a bit of thunder, quite a distance away."

"Good," she said, and she laughed again. The Earth's second laugh.

I propped myself up on my elbows, scanned the horizon and sighed. This land would see so much in the thousands of millennia to come, very little of it good. But right now, on this shore, it was possible to believe in a God who would know better than to create fearsome giant lizards, and then malevolent humanity.

Walking together down the beach, our feet just bouncing on the sand. Hester pointed out that we were not making any footprints, and I said that Time Roamers can change nothing, not even the sand on a beach.

"If a Roamer tries to change the Past," I said, "and there's any chance he'll get away with it, he's removed from something called the interlinear Maze, which is something you don't want to try."

"Could you always roam? Were you born with it?"

"No. Someone showed me how to do it."

This brought back a memory that I wanted to forget. Hester didn't ask me anything else about it. The sun was starting to set behind me, my third sunset of the last couple of hours.

Ahead of us was a bend in the coast and a little inlet, a pretty, picturesque thing, shining red in the sunset and descending into an inland lagoon. We zagged from the shoreline, plunged into the primitive forest, and then we climbed a small, scrubby hill that overlooked the sea and the lagoon, and we sat in the sand and small tufts of rough grass. I kicked off my boots and let my feet dry out in the arid Triassic air.

There was no sign of M. Rasháh, and I wondered what that meant. I kept looking out to sea, expecting to see him rise from the depths, laughing.

"So where is he?" Hester asked me. "When does he fly back here with his gang and kill us?"

"Watch the ocean," I said. "I assume they followed us and perhaps, not knowing exactly where they were going, they failed to grab for themselves a lungful of air. So maybe they'll come floating to the top, drowned. But is it possible to die when a body's roaming? If a Roamer cannot change the past, can he leave a corpse? I'm not so sure. When they ran out of breath, maybe they shot back to Pete's spa. Or maybe right back to Lida. Or, again, maybe they will float to the top of the ocean."

I thought.

"Maybe they'll just disappear under the depths, the moment they drown, and float off into some dark cloud, somewhere in a dream." I smiled. "Leave the interlinear Maze forever."

"And the children?" she asked. "What of the little boy and girl?"

"I am hoping," I mused, "that if Rasháh and his gang die in a prehistoric sea, their actions in 1981 will be undone, because they will have died long before they are ever born, or, in Rashah's case, *created*. (I cannot imagine such a creature having been born of a woman.) My other thought is that if they leave the interlinear Maze, perhaps they will cease to exist. It also occurs to me that if they followed me into the future – roaming into 1981 using Watt O'Hugh's frequent flyer miles, so to speak (and forgive the futuristic slang, Hester, I can no longer help myself) – then they'd be entirely unable to inflict any permanent damage."

Hester explained, quite succinctly I thought, why none of these theories held water. I nodded, but she had no better ideas, so we were stuck with mine.

I didn't really know how that worked, the Maze, but it was something a friend had said to me in Weedville, moments before vanishing into a gaping hole in space and time, perhaps forever, and so those words had taken on more than a little profundity. I thought about it a lot, that Maze.

"I wish you could have shot them, Watt," she said. "I traveled through the desert to find the world's greatest shootist in his hideout, and you haven't shot anyone."

She sighed.

"Are you a fraud? Can you shoot people at all?"

I fished into my pocket and pulled out the bottle, offered it to Hester.

"Bourbon whiskey from the future?" I asked.

She sat up, took the bottle, lifted it to her lips, took a slug.

"I can shoot people," I said, while she drank. "I'm even good at it. I'm just not particularly enamored of it."

The sea stayed placid calm. No corpses bobbing, no guns blazing.

Stars began to flicker, the night descended, the world turned a dark friendly blue, a cool wind blew off the water, and Hester and I were getting warm and tippled from my bottle of corn juice. It was nighttime, and still no one had come to kill us, and no one had washed up on the shore drowned. We were starting to get hungry, but our nerves had stilled, and we were enjoying the respite from fear.

"Look," Hester said suddenly, staring me straight in the eye. "If you want to go underground, *Hugh Watt* isn't the alias to choose."

I shrugged and took another slug.

"I never said I was creative," I muttered. "I'm just a cow herder, gone into retiracy. And you know, part-time …."

"Outlaw."

"If I was framed, am I still an outlaw?" I asked. "If I am utterly, completely innocent, am I still an outlaw?"

She nodded.

"Yes," she said. "If the jury finds you guilty, you're guilty, whether you did it or not."

I shrugged. I'd heard this before.

"Anyway," she said, "you're living off the spoils of the Lervine job, if I'm not mistaken, which was not entirely legal."

"Sure," I agreed. "But that's not what I'm wanted for. I'm a wanted man for a crime I didn't commit. No one cares about those things I really did."

I paused.

"The coast is clear," I said. "You understand, Hester? Come clean."

She had interrupted what should have been a perfectly peaceful, more than slightly fuddled afternoon, and in my view it was long-past time for her to give me some sort of an explanation.

To begin with, I wondered aloud how'd she'd located me, and Hester replied ambiguously that she'd always been good at finding treasures hidden in the sand; when I asked why Rasháh was after her, Hester surmised that it probably had more to do with me than with her, though it might have something to do with J.P. Morgan, come to think of it, as a matter of fact. (This was a name that I knew, but which I had hoped not to hear again.)

"The root of this is your skill at being simultaneously alive and not-alive," she said. "This is a supernatural wile that J.P. Morgan wants and will pay for. Quite a story," she laughed, "that one."

She lay back on the hilltop, swimming in the stars.

"You know how to do this," she said flatly, staring at this long-ago sky, not at me. "You know how to be alive and not-alive."

I grunted in affirmation. I said that there were a few different ways, and that I thought I could demonstrate all of them, if I wished it. Witnesses would swear they'd seen my dead body in the Wyoming mountain snow, and yet here I was, so the fallacious case could be made convincingly that I was now something of a ghost. (In truth, I was alive as could be, and not even a little bit dead; my death was nothing but a very good parlor trick – but more on that later.)

Still, J.P. Morgan and I had something of an unpleasant history, and I thought it unwise to help him. He had at one time promised me a fortune to run a Wild West show into New York city, but he had instead framed me for murder, shot me off the top of a tenement building (which had really hurt like a sonofabitch) and incarcerated me in a Wyoming prison, which was, to say the least, something of a breach of contract.

Hester said she understood, but in spite of all that had happened between J.P. Morgan and me in the past, he was an enemy of the Sidonians, and our enemy's enemy was our friend, and we could not afford to spit on a friend like this.

There was also the matter of a rather urgent train robbery to reckon with, she added, which she had neglected to mention earlier, and with which she needed my help, and, more to the point, the help of my ghosts, and, further to the point, the help of Mr. Morgan, but it again all came back to me. I wondered how she'd gotten herself wrapped up in train robberies and resurrection of the dead, and that crazy millionaire robber baron, and she said it was a rather long story and asked me how much time I had, and, though I no longer owned a pocket watch, I pretended to look at one, and I said that if my watch were correct, we had a few hundred million years till the dinosauria would evolve on this particular stretch of land and eat us, and she laughed again, but this time it sounded a little false, as though she were trying to flatter me.

"People die," I said, "when you rob a train."

Hester nodded in the starlight. She rolled over on her side.

"Many people will *certainly* die if you *don't* rob this *particular* train," she said. "And everyone aboard is a Sidonian."

So maybe it would not be so bad if *all* of them were to die, was the point she was making, I supposed. And I supposed I might not shed many tears for a dead Sidonian, depending on which Sidonian we were talking about.

"Foot soldiers?" I asked.

"Maybe there are a few cogwheels, but they're filthy, rusty cogwheels. They know what they're doing, whom they're serving. I don't imagine anyone who came West seeking a job as an office clerk will be on that train, Watt. They all have dirty hands; they're all ugly customers."

She paused, hesitated.

"You know all about Sidonia, don't you?" she asked. "The Sidonians?"

"I hate it," I said, "and it hates me. Of course I know." It was the reason I was hiding in the desert, I admitted. It was the reason I drank whiskey every second of the day. An ostensible social movement designed to make the world a better, fairer, happier place, it had destroyed everything I had ever cared about, and I hated it. I didn't know whether I needed to forget it or let my yearnings for vengeance rule me for the rest of my life.

She touched the side of my face, affectionately, seriously.

She left her cool hand there, and I didn't mind.

"There's more than money on that train, Watt."

As a matter of fact, she noted, a two thousand year old secret was buried in that train's safe. If it were to reach New York City and fall into the hands of a certain band of previously harmless subversives – these were gentlemen and the occasional lady who, burdened and misled by a bit of theoretical high-class education, thought it possible to construct a Utopia that included humans, and who thought that the Sidonian secessionist movement in Montana was building in earnest the theoretical Utopia they'd studied in school – if this cargo reached the innocent, well-meaning hands of that group of subversives, many people would die, devastation would reign over New York City, which would burst into flames, hatred, death, war and utter destruction, and when the smoke cleared, millions would be dead, and the city would be a Sidonian police state. As a fascistic political movement ate the continent like a swarm of locusts, the subversives would stand by, powerless and aghast, wondering what their beautiful and perfect dreams had wrought. Watt O'Hugh – of all people! – should remember the havoc the Sidonians could loose on the world, Hester pointed out, and also, by the way, the terrible anger of an unfettered New York City mob.

I was silent, mulling this over.

"If the secret on this train makes it East," she said, her voice flat, "it will bury New York, and then it will put Darryl Fawley on a throne, and then he will bury the world. Can you live in a world ruled by Darryl Fawley? J.P. Morgan will help you stop them. Will you stop them?"

Hester's eyes were sad.

"My dear," she said. "I've given you an excuse."

Watt O'Hugh, she noted, always needed to know that he was doing good. All the dime novels insisted on it.

"And your ghosts expect it, nay? If you don't do good, they will leave you. They will no longer protect you. They will no longer steady your aim."

She told me that I should feel reassured that I would be doing good, *essential* good. I would be saving many people, the way I had failed to save so many people, back in those dark days of '63.

She leaned in closer.

"You mourn the little ones you failed to save in '63, but there is one you failed to save in '75 who haunts your waking dreams."

I could feel my face darkening.

"These are the men," she whispered, "who killed Lucy Billings. They lured her with dreams of a perfect world, they played with her conscience – their leader, Darryl Fawley, even went so far as to marry her! – and they used her as bait to trap you. And then they *killed* her. You loved her so much, and this man, who loved money and power more … this man, Darryl Fawley, had the blessing to marry this jewel, this flower, this treasure that belongs to you, a blessing whose value he didn't even recognize. And he threw that away, and he let her die – like dropping the world's most beautiful and valuable diamond into the middle of the ocean – and he went on with his life without a care. She died with his child in her womb, in a lonely abandoned jail in a Nebraska ghost town.

"Lucy Billings, whom you loved, who walks the earth upon rare occasion as a deadling, a shadow of what she once was. Darryl Fawley eats ostrich *pâté en croûte* in a castle in a Montana valley, while Watt O'Hugh, the greatest shootist in the West, hides out drunk in a smelly shack and does nothing to bring Fawley to justice, nor to stop his success from growing. *Nothing*. Watt, I ask you, is that right?

She placed a locket on the soft grass beside me. I recognized it. I didn't know how she'd acquired it. I didn't need to open it. I imagined the smooth white skin that had once warmed this locket, and the heartbeat that had once enlivened it, this little locket. It made me angry that this locket had no owner to wear it and to cherish it, and to become even more beautiful because of it. The locket lay in the grass beside me, and my anger grew.

"What's in the envelope, Watt?"

I opened it, and I showed her. Troop movements, weaknesses in Sidonia's defenses, proposed or perhaps even actual maneuvers on a day not so far in the future – that is, the future back in the 1870s – when the U.S. cavalry would attack. "I know exactly what will happen every second of that day." I imagined myself there. I imagined myself killing men responsible for the death of the woman who had once worn that locket. But were I to show up on the day of battle, an angry, cursing Watt O'Hugh, whom all Sidonia recognized, I wouldn't make it one inch inside the city gates. I would die, bloody and angry and cursing the murderers within the city.

"Watt. Once the train is robbed, J.P. Morgan will send his soldiers over the Sidonian mountains, and I will put you beside Darryl Fawley. Watt O'Hugh, *right next to him.* As close as I am to you. To do as you will. To set things right. I will put you there beside him. I promise you this, Watt. This is our deal. This is our covenant. I am giving you an excuse for your vengeance, something to tell your ghosts."

Then silence.

I could feel Hester's breath. I could hear fear in her silence.

A fish splashed in the tranquil sea, and a hairless beast, the size of a dog, scurried into the baby forest behind us.

She ran a hand gently through my hair, and she brushed my brow.

"Tormented, storm-tossed, unloved Watt," she whispered. "I am the one who consoles you."

"I didn't really need much convincing, truth be told."

I told her that if she could really promise to put me next to Darryl Fawley – so close to Darryl Fawley that I could put the barrel on his skull and squeeze the trigger – then I would rob her train for her.

In the distance, a small black cloud formed on the very far horizon, casting a small shadow over our perfect, star-speckled ocean. Hester squeezed my hand, as rain and even hail pelted the far sea-edge. "Well," I whispered, "we cannot stay here forever," even though, right then, I wished that we could, and so we stood. I bent a few saplings to form a makeshift and highly temporary doorway to crawl through, and we drifted softly back to our world, where we landed with a gentle thud on the angry-hot sand of the dead valley this paradise would become.

CHAPTER 2

I am a Roamer, as I have mentioned before, and with one notable exception, Roamers cannot change anything about the past or the future. What roaming *can* give us is information, and while it is information we cannot use, it is nevertheless information that can haunt us. For example, I have recently, after much hesitation, taken a peek at my death and have learned to my chagrin that I am fated to die on January 1, 1937, which is less than a year from now. I would prefer not to die, but if I must die, I would prefer not to be forgotten forever, and so I've been rather quickly scribbling out my memories a letter at a time,[*] sitting here on the front porch of my ranch near a little town in one of those big, under-populated Western cow states, which I will not name out of respect for the citizens here, who have treated me well but would prefer to be known for their fine cuts of beef rather than the ravings of a lunatic, which the adults here all believe me to be, though harmless, in their view. The children like my stories and never doubt that they are true, which indeed they are.

This bundle of words that you hold in your hands isn't a *novel*, but rather a *memoir*, which, as they taught you at Yale, is Frog language for *memory*, which means that when I remember something, I write it down, and what I don't remember, I don't write down. It also means that it's all one-hundred percent true, though some of it's a little hazy, what with the passage of time and all the corn juice that I've imbibed over the years, and the corn juice that I am imbibing right now, as I write these words. Still, I can remember a few facts

---

[*] This morning, I woke up thinking that to-day was March 15, and that I had only 293 days to live, but a young boy from the town – a young boy named Peregrine who hangs on my every word and seems to believe my stories – this young boy has educated me as to the leap-year nature of 1936, and his facts seem to bear themselves out. So it turns out that to-day is March 14, and in fact, if you allow me to include in my calculations both the day of my death and to-day, I still have 294 days to live after all (which isn't that long, but is still better than 293 days), owing to the fact that at the end of last month, whoever created the calendar saw fit to grant me one extra day of life. So: *thank you, whoever you are.*

about myself through the whiskey fog, which might be helpful for you to know before we continue: I was a Union soldier in the War Between the States, during which I defended Fort Comfort in the battle of Plymouth, a great Confederate victory that you may have studied in school, which left me with a bullet lodged in my right leg, something I could mildly feel when it rained or snowed till I turned 70 years of age, at which point that ache was subsumed by others more painful, and I never noticed it again. In my younger years, the yellow journalists and dime novelists alleged that I was a true-blue Western paladin, almost a knight-of-the-round-table (with just a little effort, you can read all about my purportedly heroic exploits in Blue Rock, which is what spawned the series of dime novels), and subsequently and consequently the star of an eponymous Wild West show bankrolled by J.P. Morgan, which took me all the way to New York City's Great Roman Hippodrome (a grand castle, which many years ago stood briefly on Mr. Madison's Avenue and 26th Street), before I collapsed into infamy, or maybe just ignominy. By 1878, that was where I thought my story would end, before Hester knocked down my door.

There is one other thing that I think is relevant to add here before I continue. One evening out in the canyons of Utah, my traveling companion, a one-legged counter-Revolutionary, told me a story about a man named (unfortunately) Yu Dai-Yung. Master Yu was a handsome poet (but a terrible one) and a man destined to become my friend and fellow soldier in the battle against Sidonia, though I did not know it then.

He was also a man on an important but ill-defined mission in America for China's surly Empress Dowager.

And thus, not so very long before Hester Smith pounded at my door in the desert just West of Lida, Yu Dai-Yung embarked on his secret mission, because one doesn't refuse one's Empress, after all. A Peking riverboat took him south to Taishan, where he boarded the Pacific Mail steamship S.S. China, which upon departure seemed crammed to bursting with a few dozen merchants from America and a thousand illiterate commoners from the south of China, who had fled famine and looming civil war. All of them were men, and so for the coming months, Master Yu was to hear not even the hint of a woman's laugh. The last port of call for the S.S. China would be the Market Street wharf in San Francisco. The Golden Mountain of

America loomed like the Jade Emperor over the farms of Taishan.

The great smelly hulk of a vessel left the Chinese port, and within 24 hours it had slipped and wobbled through the Pacific Ocean into stormy waters. The ship lurched to and fro, yet when the storm had cleared some hours later, and the passengers found themselves miraculously alive, Master Yu felt only marginally better. For the next few months, he kept to himself, reading his books and frequently vomiting. While re-reading Volume 3 of *The Dream of the Red Chamber*, he fell asleep and dreamed nostalgically of the red chambers of home.*

After a great deal of time, Master Yu reached his destination, and the SS China pulled into the San Francisco harbor past midnight on February 11, 1878, which was a chilly and overcast night.

The Harbor consisted of a series of piers, a wooden shed for horse-drawn carriages, a row of cavernous warehouses, and a few noisy saloons that screamed into the night down Market Street, even now that the rest of the city of San Francisco was dark and fast asleep. Master Yu stepped off the ship, pressed on all sides by the crowd of peasantry, holding his small travel bag in his left hand, feeling plain and unembroidered in his simple dark surcoat, which he hugged to his body as he felt the full force of the chilly harbor wind. His face handsome, still unlined, albeit a bit wind-chapped.

Yu Dai-Yung sighed. Had not the seers of royal China proclaimed him reincarnation of the son of Yang Hsiung, the great 1st Century poet to Wang Mang, the Emperor anointed by one thousand dragons? Was not Master Yu thus born to be an acclaimed poet, to sit in the imperial court, to eat golden pheasant with expensive dancing girls in youth, and to marry well in early middle age?

How had his life come to this?

A little hint of bile tickled and threatened the back of his throat. He took a deep breath. His hat blew off his head, landed in the sea and quickly washed away. Black water thumped against the side of the steamer, and dark clouds covered the moon.

Lantern light burst through the darkness from the east. Yu

---

* How did I (a fellow who was not there) know what happened on Master Yu's journey, and what he was thinking? I would later meet Master Yu, who would entrust to me his journal, from which I would retrieve information used in this volume, and friends of his would also tell me much about Master Yu. Everything in this book is true.

Dai-Yung backed into the shadows and vanished behind a warehouse filled with Chinese silks and vases. A dozen fat white customs house officers with bushy mustaches gathered up Chinamen disembarking from the steamship, searched them, questioned them, marked them with chalk and tossed them and their baggage onto a contingent of horse-drawn express wagons, which then clattered away down Market Street.

Yu Dai-Yung waited, barely breathing, until the officers had ridden off with the Chinamen, and only the noise of the rowdy saloons still disturbed the night.

A man approached. He was Chinese. He wore a purple, silk-lined and embroidered robe. The stranger was neither young nor old. He had a thin beard, and his face was distinguished yet friendly. The Chinese man called out gently to Master Yu, wished him a good evening, called him *friend*.

Master Yu stepped nervously into the light.

The man took Master Yu's hand, offered to buy him a drink, a good old Chinese drink the way he remembered it from the homeland, just to welcome Yu Dai-Yung to San Francisco after such a long, exhausting and treacherous journey. He smiled, and he implored Master Yu to follow him. All of this would raise suspicions among most visitors to a new city in an unfriendly country, but the man spoke the northern dialect perfectly, with a flawless accent, something Master Yu had missed so terribly during the previous long months. After months breathing the stench of the common man, he indeed needed to sanitize his body with some fine moutai. And so, like a child soothed by a lullaby, he followed the gentleman from the shadows of the warehouses towards the lights of the harbor bars.

A loud, tough female voice shattered this brief moment of peace.

"Crimp!" she shouted in English, and the other Chinaman shrunk a bit in shame. "Fung, you crimp!"

Now she came into the light, a young pretty Chinese girl of about nineteen, but wrathy and fierce, the victim of a hard life, it seemed to Master Yu at first glance, and worst of all, as far as he was concerned, she spoke with a grating, goat-braying Southern China accent, which scratched and pounded like nails on the soft velvet cushion of his eardrums, even after all these months.

"You would crimp another Chinese, your own people!" the girl shouted. "But this man is not any Chinese, Fung! This man is an emissary of the Empress Dowager! And you would crimp him!"

The man shrugged helplessly, and he now seemed quite a bit less elegant than he had a moment before. Master Yu now noticed for the first time that the emblems on Fung's robe were ridiculous forgeries.

"I didn't know, Li-Ling," Fung said softly. Even his accent now seemed merely the parody of a true gentleman. "How was I to know?"

Li-Ling pinched Master Yu's cheek.

"Look at this pale skin!" she shouted.

Li-Ling grabbed Master Yu's right hand and waved it in front of the penitent Fung.

"Look at this soft, effete hand!" she screamed. "He is not a peasant, Fung!"

Fung looked down at his feet.

"Can't you see?" she added now, in a softer voice, apparently touched by Fung's shame. "He is weak and soft. You see?"

"I just wanted to make some money, Li-Ling," Fung said.

"You should have recognized this the moment you saw this man hiding at the wharf. He is not strong and hard like us. He is a little bowl of congee. Not even a man at all. Anyone with a brain would see that a specimen like this could not survive for five minutes in the world unless he were nobility, someone of importance. Someone you cannot crimp if you want to keep your head attached to your shoulders."

Clearly, the treachery bothered Li-Ling, but the stupidity seemed to bother her even more.

"My wife has not been well," Fung said, and he ventured an excruciatingly detailed explanation of the specific symptoms of this illness, which I mostly will spare you, except to note briefly that it involved pus, scabs and thick white fluid flecked with blood, and to add that it inspired some genuine sympathy even in Master Yu, Fung's intended victim, who could not help shuddering along with Fung. This was evidently a most unpleasant illness, not least for the husband of the sufferer.

"My children have the dropsy," Fung added. After a moment: "And brain fever," he suddenly remembered.

"Sit by their bedsides and do not show your face for three weeks," Li-Ling said softly. "And perhaps we will forget about this offense, and we will not have you killed."

"Thank you, Li-Ling," Fung said, and he bowed obsequiously, and he then disappeared into the night and out of our story forever.

The poet from Peking climbed upon the Southern peasant girl's lopsided rickety wagon, and she cracked the reins on the lopsided rickety mule pulling the lopsided rickety wagon, and together they descended from the cloudy starless harbor night to the tree-lined streets that led into San Francisco's business district. The lights of Davis Street blazed on the horizon in the North and glittered on the black rocky night sea, but around them, all was dark and quiet.

Li-Ling asked him a few questions, and Master Yu shook his head.

"I have trouble understanding you," said Master Yu, broaching the obvious, he thought. "I cannot understand very well the language of the peasantry. So do not be offended if I do not speak with you during our travels."

It was his view that Li-Ling should now bow graciously, and then remain silent for the balance of the ride.

"You can understand me," she said, flicking the reins a bit in frustration.

Although the poet's thoughts were arrogant and elitist, Li-Ling knew that they were not unusual for a man of his class; furthermore, his handsome eyes betrayed an intriguing capacity for growth and for compassion that seemed perhaps yet untapped. Whether genuine or not, these compassionate eyes made his handsomeness complete, and irresistible, and her anger grew at a slower pace than it might have otherwise.

So she continued speaking, giving my friend Master Yu a detailed tour of the business district, whose border they were just crossing. She pointed out the low-rent trade businesses that lined these first streets, giving a rather lengthy disquisition on the square, functional two-story gray buildings and the businesses inside, Foster & Co.'s Grocery, for example, at the corner of Drumm Street, which sat next door to Wm. Lewis and Co. Cigars, and a few doors down, the boarded up façade of the Kimball Manufacturing Company.

They wobbled along on the lopsided wagon.

"Any questions so far, Master Yu?" she asked with a smile.

Master Yu smiled back, charmed against his will, though he recognized what a loss of face this was, for a man of his stature and reputation to ride in a carriage with a peasant girl.

"I'm a poet, and a beneficiary of the Governor," he whispered gently.

"And a fine one, I am sure," she said politely, "although I am not familiar with your work."

They clopped past the aptly named "Son Brothers" business, which, according to a splashy billboard atop its roof, sold "fancy notions, stationery etc." Back then, in another time and world, the Son Brothers business used to sit at the north side of the avenue, on the corner, just past Sansome Street. But as I write these words it lives no more; unremembered, unmourned.

Li-Ling continued to speak, and, she believed, to defuse the tension of this awkward predicament, this clash of cultures, this unsought meeting of useless intellect and practical world experience on a chilly night.

Words continued to drop out of her mouth and float above the cobblestoned street on golden wings.

"You are having an easier time understanding me," Li-Ling said.

"Perhaps not," Master Yu replied.

"You still cannot understand what I am saying?"

"No," said the poet.

"Not a single word?" asked the peasant girl.

"Not a single word."

Master Yu was quite certain of this.

"But are you enjoying the ride? Do you at least find the sights interesting?"

"A bit interesting," he said, "yes."

"You have never seen anything this new in China," she said. "A few years ago, there was nothing here. This entire city rose up, as if by magic."

"Magic?"

"Yes," she said. "It is a pity you cannot understand me. It is an interesting story."

"Hmm. A pity indeed."

Across the avenue, the gold-fueled, columned castles of Leidesdorff Street finally came into view, glistening in the starlight, but neither the untalented poet nor the Southern girl noticed.

"You are a handsome man with lovely eyes," Li-Ling said, "but without a sensible thought in your head. Master Yu, only the commoners are carrying on the uninterrupted traditions of yore and saving the nation, from within and without. If not for us, China would be a three-legged dog, a monkey with no arms. If you reject us, the nation is doomed."

Master Yu did not respond for two reasons. First, he was quite convinced that he had not understood a word she said, because if he knew anything for sure it was that a man of his station could not understand even a word of the peasants' language. Second, he found her assertion ridiculous. He believed – no, he *knew* – that the ruling class, the intellectuals, had always been and would always be the foundation of the Middle Kingdom, without which the nation would crumble, and who managed to support the vast legion of country imbeciles only through the grace of Heaven. Then he smiled a bit. *I do have beautiful eyes*, he realized, as though a revelation.

Well, readers of the 20th and 21st centuries know that if my yarn were one of your romantic comedies, this conversation would have devolved into a witty shouting match, followed quickly by a passionate yet comical embrace, or at least a comical complication, but just then a few gunshots suddenly rang out in the stillness of the night. One bullet snapped into the wagon's front left wheel, and the other grazed the mule's croup. The wagon collapsed, the mule reared up, and both Li-Ling and Master Yu toppled to the soft grass of the now-neglected, overgrown garden that encircled the Bank of California building. Roses and flowering vines grew unrestrained around and over the dark, now rusting iron fence.

How did the Bank of California look to Yu Dai-Yung? A golden emperor's two-storied palace of shining blue stone bedecked by Venetian medallions, with forty-two white marble columns fronting the façade alternating with arcaded windows, a roof of burnished copper lined by a balustrade crested with finial-topped orbs, the Bank of California looked, to Yu Dai-Yung, as though it had been imagined and then sent to Earth by the Goddess of the Chinese

Moon. It looked like a beautiful woman who had just died. It looked like a supernatural blue-marble temple that lived in the night.

It looked like a place to hide.

The heavy but neglected bronze door collapsed easily under pressure, and Yu and Li-Ling slipped into the cavernous, moonlit bank. Beneath high frescoed ceilings, kneeling on floors made of black and white marble blocks, the two peered out plate glass windows into the adjoining garden. They could see five sturdy gunmen, dark in the shadows, cross California Street and take cover behind the purple-leaf plum trees that ringed the garden.

Keeping one eye on the window, Master Yu backed away, holding Li-Ling's arm lightly (gentlemanly). They passed forty mahogany desks that stood empty on the great marble floor, then they stopped beneath fierce bronze sculptures of growling watch dogs, which topped the nearest vault, whose door sat ajar. The vault was room-sized, but empty.

Master Yu checked the inside lever, which moved freely.

"Vault opens from the inside," he whispered to Li-Ling. "So no one gets stuck inside and dies. But no one can get in."

He unzipped his travel bag and pulled out two small revolvers.

"I know how to shoot and kill people," he remarked with a modest smile. "Before I came to America, I learned how to shoot and kill people."

He flipped open the cylinder, checked the ammunition.

"Stay in the vault till I give the signal," he whispered. "Open the door a crack if you feel short of breath. Don't let yourself sleep, or you will suffocate. If I have not returned by daybreak, then I am dead. Hide another day, let yourself out, and run away."

He handed her his canteen.

"Water," he said, unnecessarily. "With water, you can last without food." Then: "It's the air," he cautioned. "The air will be the biggest problem for you."

He shut the vault door, and he spun the lock.

Bird-eye maple wainscoting ringed the room, running beneath glistening black marble mantels. The Bank of California was modeled after the Library of St. Mark in the Piazza di San Marco in Venice, although Yu Dai-Yung didn't know this.

A nice, tomb-like temple in which to die, he mused to himself.

The front door creaked open. He heard the gunmen whispering to each other. They sounded frightened, which buoyed his confidence.

He scampered beneath and behind the floor desks, creeping backwards on his stomach to the office at the very farthest edge of the bank. He slid through the doorway without being seen. It was a long thin boardroom, the walls painted with scenes of an infinite canyon and a towering, frozen waterfall. In the corners of the room, stone statues of draped female figures supported dark and lifeless wall lamps. Who had designed this room? Who had loved this waterfall, this infinite canyon?

A bullet zipped through the building, shattering the wooden door, which splintered over his left shoulder. Yu kicked out one plate glass window and tumbled out into the chilly night, grabbed hold of one of the marble columns and scurried up like a squirrel, flipped onto the second floor balcony and crouched behind a great Romanesque vase.

One gunman looked through the broken window, Yu Dai-Yung shot, and the gunman's head exploded like a balloon. His body shook and teetered for a moment, then collapsed, tumbling unrestrained back into the Bank building. Yu now flipped up and over the balcony railing, slipped his thin fingers into the crack between two great blue marble blocks and tossed himself up into the sky like a bouncing ball. He caught the balustrade, hoisted himself over it, and landed with a clatter on the Bank's moon-dappled copper roof.

After that things moved quickly and bloodily. One gunman followed his colleague out of the window. Yu Dai-Yung shot him, and he died in the hydrangea bushes. A clank sounded behind him – a boot-heel striking copper – and Yu Dai-Yung spun about and shot a third gunman, who clutched his chest but seemed determined not to die, and so Yu Dai-Yung shot him again, and he expired, toppling backwards off the edge of the roof.

Master Yu sat on the roof for a long time, jumping at noises real and imagined, a revolver in each hand, pointing his guns here and there, trembling.

At length he crawled to the edge of the roof and peered over. But he saw nothing.

He dropped to the second-floor balcony, kicked in a window and descended the interior stairs in the darkness.

Li-Ling stepped out of the quiet shadows of the vault.

"I think that's it," she said. "I think you killed them."

"There were five," he said. "I killed three."

He wished that he could have said he took no pride in this, that he took no pride in killing these three men. But had he said it, it wouldn't have been true. He had enjoyed it, and it had made him proud.

"You killed three men, Yu Dai-Yung," she said. "Others ran away. I mean, they must have. Yes or no?"

She stayed silent for a moment.

"No one here, Master Yu. The Bank is dead."

She was right, and he could feel it in the air. Utter, angry lifelessness, an echoing death.

"Let's go, Yu Dai-Yung," she insisted. She took his elbow and gave him an imploring tug.

He held up one finger.

"Wait," he said.

He listened to the silence. He looked into the stillness.

"Please," she begged him.

"No."

In the corner, in the hazy-hidden umbra behind the clerks' desks lay a suspicious double-lump of shadows.

Master Yu stared, squinted, stared again, and turned to Li-Ling.

"I sneaked up on them," she shrugged timidly. "I imagine I had the element of surprise to my benefit."

"I told you to wait in the vault," he said.

"And I did not obey you," she replied.

"Hmm," he muttered. Then: "Dead?"

"Apparently so," she whispered. "You are not the only one in the world who knows how to kill people, I am sorry to say. This will be our secret, eh?"

They slipped out through the front window, and they hid beneath the plum trees, behind the bushes in the green courtyard that surrounded this empty tomb of a building.[*]

---

[*] This glorious, seemingly immortal citadel was to stand till 1906, not even a mere 30 years into the future. Who would have thought that I, Watt O'Hugh, would live longer than the Bank of California building?

Li-Ling trained a gun on the Bank. Master Yu trained a gun on the street.

"You are a good mark," she said, "for a great poet."

He shook his head.

"Don't tell anyone," he said, "but I am a terrible poet. A great gunman, it is true, but a terrible poet. I am more gunman than poet."

She smiled.

"Lucky for you, at moments like these?"

"No," he disagreed. "I am not lucky to be a gunman rather than a poet. I would rather bequeath the world even just one great poem, rather than live on a few more months or years."

"But what about me?" she insisted. "You have saved me as well. Aren't you grateful for that? To have saved a blameless life?"

"The world needs more immortal poems," Yu Dai-Yung said. "It has enough pretty girls, who are all mortal. A poem will last forever, if it is great. Even the greatest human being will die very soon, in a matter of decades at most. Where is the lasting glory in postponing the inevitable by mere moments?"

And even though she had nearly lost her life, and Yu Dai-Yung had just told her that the world didn't really need her, still Li-Ling smiled, because the terrible poet had told her, off-handedly, that she was pretty.

"Well," she said. "You have been sent by the Empress as foretold by her wise men, to save humanity, and I have been chosen as your guide. So perhaps the world needs us after all. Perhaps the world needs us more than it needs one more great poem."

At that moment, unheralded by trumpets or thunder, a great winged lizard fluttered out of the murky night sky from behind a cloud. The beast settled on the top of the Bank, stretched his great neck and looked out over the garden and the deserted streets. He seemed to smile, according to Yu Dai-Yung, who described the scene to me later, even though, as Master Yu himself realized, dragons cannot smile. A reptile's mouth is not designed for smiling. This does not mean that a dragon is never happy; it just means that, like a newborn baby, he cannot smile. Still, the dragon seemed to be smiling. The scaled beast wore the head of a camel with a demon's eyes, a cow's ears, antlers like a deer, the neck of a snake, a clam's belly, a tiger's paws and an eagle claw on each of its five legs.

"You see that?" Master Yu asked.

"The dragon?" Li-Ling said.

Now the terrible poet laughed.

"Yes," he said, still laughing. "The dragon."

"He comes here some nights, just watching over the city. Only since the bank closed, and Ralston died. Not everyone can see him. The dragon, I mean."

"I think it is safe to go," said Master Yu. "I think the dragon is an omen. I think it means it is safe to go."

Li-Ling considered this.

"You may be correct. But you might be wrong. The dragon could be an omen of great danger and our imminent death," she suggested.

He shook his head.

"The way the lights and shadows play on his face," he said, "creates an illusion that the dragon is smiling. So this is an omen that it is safe for us to go."

The mule had escaped – now the stupid creature was limping along somewhere on the city's cobblestones, in pain but filled with joy, as though true freedom were his at last – so Yu Dai-Yung grabbed his bag, and the two crept out of the deserted garden and onto California Street. They crept past Mr. Wainwright's Pantheon – the finest saloon in San Francisco, according to gourmands of the era, where, earlier that day, San Francisco's big bugs had dined on turtle soup and roast pig – which sat silent and dark and as lifeless as the corpses reposed on the blood-stained, black and white marble floors of the Bank of California and in its hydrangea bushes.

They slipped through the night, out of the lights of the financial district and descended into the darkness. To the northwest, at Jackson Street, the road narrowed, and the musty murk of Chinatown came into view. "Why would they want to kill us, whoever they were?" he asked, in a low whisper, and Li-Ling replied, "Agitation against the Chinese, perhaps, Yu Dai-Yung? After the swift failure of the Bank, and the collapse of the local economy, the locals are blaming Chinese immigration. They are rising up against us everywhere."

He raised an eyebrow skeptically.

"More to it than that, I expect."

"I expect there is," she agreed. "And I expect that there will be more to come."

He turned to her as they walked.

"But listen to me, young woman," he said. "Why did the Bank have no money? Why were the vaults open and empty?"

"We know what happened," she said. "Sidonia withdrew her support. When Sidonia smiles on the Golden Mountain, the gold flows like water. When Sidonia frowns on the Golden Mountain, the spigot runs dry."

She pointed knowingly to her eyebrows.

"Red Eyebrows," Master Yu said. "The Sidonians are the Red Eyebrows."

"The very same Hell-on-Earth," she said. "The peasant warriors from your great-great-grandfather's nightmares have returned from their graves."

The Red Eyebrows. Silent for two thousand years. Ostensibly a Chinese peasant rebellion from the countryside, in reality a demon insurrection from the realm of the damned, which came to Earth and laid waste to the land back in the days of the Hsin Dynasty, around the Year One. The Empress Dowager had warned him of this during their brief meeting in the Tower of the Fragrance of Buddha at the Summer Palace on Longevity Hill. This diminutive Empress was a tiny, volcanic terror by any subjective criteria, with a foul temper and long sharp fingernails with which to dispense her wrath with both style (of a sort) and maximum efficiency. But the Emperor of Heaven had granted her temporary possession of his Mantle, and so Master Yu loved her without doubt, and he was loyal without question. *For many years*, she had told him, *the secret of the Red Eyebrows has remained hidden, this terrible secret that can change the course of mighty rivers and make the earth crack – and so much more, terrible things...* The Palace hid a dragon, she told him, and, for the last two hundred years, a tall, green-skinned man born on a planet far away, who drank tea on occasion in the Summer Palace garden with one of the imperial advisors. But she told Master Yu that the most important and dangerous secret in the basement of the Summer Palace was the secret of the Red Eyebrows, which could never be allowed out into the world. *Never never*, she had whispered, displaying a most un-imperial fear on her regal, red-rouged face. *But it has been*, she said. *We must get it back, before it destroys everything.*

And now, here it was.

Master Yu shuddered.

A tottering, apparently drunken man appeared at the end of the street, pulled the brim of his hat down over his face. The two stopped walking. After a moment, the man waved cheerily, shouted a greeting in Chinese, and turned into a side alley.

Master Yu and Li-Ling began to walk again.

"You know a lot," Master Yu said to Li-Ling.

"I do," she said. "I've been preparing for battle for a long time. If you are preparing for battle, it is best to know everything you can about your enemies." She turned to him. "They are your enemies too, are they not, Master Yu?"

He agreed. What was his mission, precisely, in this great battle against the Red Eyebrows? *"To go to America,"* said the Empress Dowager. *"And to see what the future has planned for you. And to be brave. You will have to be brave"* So his mission could be anything and everything, or nothing at all. He would stay alert and see what he could learn. An ant crawling up the side of a brick building could be an essential clue. Nothing was unimportant.

"What happened to the men who used to run the bank?" he asked.

"Ah," the southern girl said. "Now that's an interesting one."

A man named William C. Ralston, Li-Ling told Yu Dai-Yung, built the Bank of California when he was still in his thirties, youthful, boyish, casually dapper, going a little bald. For a man with a terrible secret, he had a friendly laugh and a nice smile.

Ralston owned the thirsty Ophir Mine in Comstock, not a drop of gold or silver in it. That is, until he made a crazy alliance with Sidonia, and his mine suddenly rose from the dead like a vampire. Gold filled the coffers in his Bank and flowed through the streets of San Francisco like a great river, and Ralston's influence grew on the West Coast like mushrooms after a rain. Ralston dined on caviar served in golden bowls in a mansion that Sidonian coin had bought. Did Ralston know that the Sidonians were emissaries sent by demons from Hell? Probably not. Like all wicked demons, they had a good sales department, and they served the best wine.

Sometimes, during those heady days of wealth and power, Ralston would leave the Bank by the Sansome Street exit, mount his black horse and ride up Montgomery Street to the top of Telegraph Hill to look out over the city he had built almost with his bare hands.

Three times a week, he leapt into the frigid Bay and swam halfway to Alcatraz Island. *My body is my temple*, he would say, and he was apparently the originator of the expression. But his body was not really his temple, and maybe he knew it. The blue sandstone Bank was his temple, and the Sidonian leaders, Allen Jerome and Darryl Fawley, were his high priests.

The story ended sadly and inevitably for young Mr. Ralston, for though the banker gave the Sidonians much, William Sharon, the Bank's Nevada agent and Ralston's friend and distinguished father-figure, offered more. He offered his soul, his children's souls, the neurons in his brain.

Mr. Sharon would kill for Sidonia, and he did.

Suddenly Ralston's mine dried up. William Sharon dumped his Bank shares not a moment too soon (but not a moment too late). Crowds formed in the desperate San Francisco streets. The Bank closed its doors and went dark.

Mr. Ralston resigned his position, left the Bank alone by the California Street exit and drowned alone in the Neptune Bath House on Larkin Street. Although he was a young and powerful man, and although he swam across the icy bay three times a week, he somehow collapsed in the bath, somehow unnoticed, expiring like an old man and sinking beneath the water's bubbling surface. An attendant cleaning the pool found him dead hours later, swelled up like a baby's blue birthday balloon.

The Sidonians bequeathed San Francisco's Mantle of Heaven to Mr. William Sharon. The trim and deceptively dignified man wasted no time moving himself and his impeccable graying mustache into Ralston Hall, the mansion of his old dead friend, where he could eat Ralston's caviar, and, if he wished, humiliate and otherwise abuse Ralston's destitute and thoroughly ostracized wife and children, whom he permitted to remain in a couple of rooms off the east wing.

"He is more demon himself than man, by now," Li-Ling said. "And U.S. senator, recently, by the way. You see what we are up against? The Sidonians can do anything. And soon they will be everywhere. Under every rock, in every puddle, behind every locked door."

Now in the thick of Chinatown, Master Yu felt deflated. He had anticipated that Chinatown would look like China, and it did not. It looked like America. He sighed, and he kept quiet. They walked along Jackson Street, down a steep hill, and they neared a narrow alley, which the Chinese called 火胡同, which the peasants pronounced as "Fo Sue Hong," and which means "Fire Alley," so named for the great fire which forever darkened its name. As they passed the dreary back street, Li-Ling turned away. "Slave market," she whispered. "Where men buy slave girls. Slave girls like me." Master Yu imagined her standing in a row of young girls, in this very alley. How young had she been? He didn't want to know. A few blocks to the west they came to a similarly overcast alley, "Fay Chie Hong" in Chinese, or "Fat Boy Alley" in English. It was indeed named for a boy who had wandered its stained cobblestones a few years back, a boy who must surely have been exceptionally fat, the fattest boy that anyone in Chinatown had ever seen.

They wound up in Duncombe Alley, the site of whorehouses and opium dens, and a few haggard drug tourists were still wandering the street, even at this hour. Li-Ling unlocked a metal door set beneath a grubby, two-story brick building. Inside, she lit a lantern and led him down into a damp cellar, through a dark cave of a room furnished only with a few wooden benches and idle oil lamps, and which smelled of human failure. She unlocked and unbolted a door in the back and they sank, further, into a windowless, nearly airless alcove empty but for a flat, damp mattress on the grimy floor.

"Not a very nice dwelling," she said, "for a man sent by her esteemed majesty the Empress to save us all. But, still, a little hole in which to sleep. To make your plans."

He sat down on the mattress.

"Li-Ling?" he asked.

She nodded.

"What's a crimp?"

"Crimp gets you drunk, then slips you a little mild poison," she said. "You sleep two days. When you wake up, you're a ship's slave. You never see home again, never see family, never see friends. Never write your poems or drink your fine nobleman wine. Fung intended to sell you like a fat cow, but for less money per pound than a fat cow would have fetched at market. I saved you from that, Yu Dai-Yung."

"Thank you," he said gently.

"We both saved each other, more than once, this night," she added.

Master Yu imagined and even hoped for a moment that Li-Ling might stay with him for a while, or for the night, but she did not. With a small bow, Li-Ling was gone. The metal door swung shut.

He tried for a while to read, but the *Red Chamber* (such a passionate saga of the homeland!) burdened his heart. He blew out the lantern, shut his eyes, and he fell into a fitful sleep. He woke periodically, looked at his surroundings, became convinced that all this was certainly nothing more than a nightmare, realized with a painful start that it was reality, screamed, woke up, fell back to the damp mattress exhausted and began the whole cycle again.

Once, when he awoke, a bald Chinese man dressed in Western clothes stood in the center of the room, lit by a low glow.

The man was nearly transparent, and he looked very sad.

Yu Dai-Yung lit the lantern, and he huddled in the corner.

"Are you a ghost?" Master Yu asked.

The man did not answer his question directly.

I am sending you a message from the past, the specter replied, inside Yu Dai-Yung's mind. *My name is Tang. As a practitioner of the Dark Arts, I am not very skilled. I cannot live forever. I cannot change the past, or the future. However, I can eliminate an unneeded essence, leaving a man apparently dead. I can roam Time. I can cure certain ailments. I can talk to dolphins, which does not come in handy out West. And I can occupy your thoughts, as you see. I am not here in this room. I am in your mind.*

Master Yu nodded, though he had begun to realize that the ghost could not see him.

If you are receiving this message, the specter said, *it is because I was either killed in Weedville, Nebraska or expelled from the interlinear Maze, and thus unable to retrieve a package that I left for the management in the Golden Sky Hotel in Denver. In my absence, this package has been mailed to you, Yu Dai-Yung, care of the Donn Quai theater, in San Francisco.*

It is important, Tang said, *that you claim it.*

And then Tang, who had so thoroughly inhabited Yu Dai-Yung's cerebellum, was gone, leaving behind just a slight whiff, a little stain, on the neuroepithelial cell lining of the terrible poet's neural tube.

This inspired a poem, and so he leaned back and wrote. It was a poem of lust-stricken specters, paper lanterns floating in the wind over the Yangtze River, unwashed peasants climbing a great mountain of gold to find a hoopoe alighted on the branch of a dark brown Chinaberry tree. He was swept up in a great wave of romantic fervor, which washed over him as he wrote what he was certain would be his masterwork, a poem which, if not perfect, if not equaling the paeans of Yang Hsiung, his father in another life, would be at least marvelous.

At length he slept, his poem wrapped in his arms like a lover.

CHAPTER 3

J.P. Morgan was forty-one years of age and nearing a pinnacle of power from which he would fall neither during his lifetime nor after. He had a wife, Fanny, and four children (Jack, Anne, Juliet and Louisa) and he ran a thriving business at 23 Wall Street, down there in that "Wall Street" area that you may have heard about, doing whatever it is that people do down there, and apparently doing it well. Still, as we shall see, he was a sad, lonely lost soul.

His business was called Drexel, Morgan & Company. (In addition to Morgan, there was a fellow named "Drexel" who worked there.) As I mentioned, Morgan was only forty-one years of age, which even in 1878 was relatively youngish, but he resembled a man in his sixties. He was obese, and while to a casual observer he looked obese in the way of men who were born to be obese, he was in fact obese in the way of men who are born to be happy and loved and handsome, yet find themselves unexpectedly sad and alone and ugly. His eczema had attacked not just his face, but had recently worked its way into his soul, and now his soul itself was eczemous, puffy, red-veined and unsightly. (In my humble opinion.)

He sometimes mused that he had diseased lungs, but this was not really true. His lungs were healthy. Yet he wished that his lungs were diseased. He did not entirely want to live. There was someone with whom he wished to be reunited, someone he loved, and she was no longer alive.

He had just returned from a summer at Cragston, his barony in Highland Falls.

Highlights of his summer:

As usual, on July 4, fireworks popped and exploded and bled a reddish orange into the Hudson River, all to the joy of the financial barons (and their wives and youngsters) who'd won such a coveted invitation, and in the morning Morgan peered blearily out his bedroom window and enviously watched those still spry enough to play tennis bound about on the courts he had expended effort and capital to build. In the early afternoon, he chatted with them in a not-unacceptably-gruff fashion as they milled about in the flowering stone courtyard, wine glass in hand.

Bastards all, whom he hated, even their blameless spawn.

Through late July and all of August, he sent urgent letters to Washington and Manhattan, letters that, according to his instructions, the recipients read quickly and then burnt.

At 9:45, on this first full day back in Manhattan, he met with the firm's chief accountant – finances were "top notch," said the little man in suspenders – and then Morgan shut and locked the door of his office, lit a Cuban cigar, opened the top drawer of his desk and grasped a gold-framed photograph of his first wife.

The lovely Mimi Sturges Morgan was frozen for now and for always at the tender age of twenty-six years, seven months, twelve days, and some-odd hours, minutes and seconds, at the terrible moment when her breathing had ceased and her soft, warm hand had slipped lifeless from his grasp. Back then at that terrible moment, Morgan had sat, suddenly all alone with her lifeless body, in their lavish honeymoon suite at the Villa St. Georges in Nice, just as he was now still all alone with her lifeless photographic image in his office on Wall Street, with the door locked.

He stared at Mimi's photograph for ten minutes, at fragile eyes that seemed to sense the future, at a gentle young smile. Mimi, who would never age.

"Once a lovely flower grew near me," he whispered, "and entwined around my heart …. But it withered."

He did not love his second wife, Fanny.

He loved his first wife, Mimi.

A year or so ago, when the first sniff of Sidonian magic had wafted into Manhattan, Mimi had returned very briefly as a deadling, to hold his hand, to flirt a bit, and to stroll with him along 36th Street, just outside his mansion. And so, while he had never for a moment entirely forgotten young Mimi, it was quite understandable that since his first wife's merely momentary resurrection, she had haunted Morgan's thoughts at every moment of every day.

"How," he muttered aloud, caressing her photograph, "can one be alive and not-alive concurrently?"

He did not love his second wife, Fanny.

At 11, Morgan met with his partner, Tony Drexel, a man who, as I have noted in the first volume of my *Memoirs*, was short and fat and possessed of genuinely exceptionally gigantic nostrils. His voice was beautiful and deep, a voice so lovely that it made up for his shortness and his fattiness and could nearly (but not quite) cause one to overlook his quite unsightly nostrils, nostrils so large and deep that they seemed to present a visible tunnel into his brain, into his thoughts and deepest wishes and dreams and very being itself. Morgan had by this point in our story long since ceased to be surprised by Drexel's nostrils, though he was not yet used to them, and would never be used to them; no man born of this Earth ever could be.

Their syndicate partner Levi Morton was seeking a Congressional office in an election to be held in less than two months; Drexel updated Morgan on progress, and the two discussed what they could do to ensure success. Then they turned to financial matters. The United States was shortly to return to the gold standard, a development that Drexel expected would have a spectacular impact on the firm's financial fortunes.

"We shall shortly be rather magnificently rich," Drexel gushed, and Morgan noted without much passion that they were both already rather magnificently rich, so who the Hell cared, at this point, after all?

Morgan sighed, and Drexel muttered, "*Richer*, then, if you wish."

Drexel picked up a small ivory sculpture from his desktop, a Greek goddess with long, flowing hair. He fondled the goddess between his soft pink hands. This, with a bit of unconscious randyness, it seemed to Morgan. Morgan looked away.

As he left Drexel's office, Morgan recalled that Fanny would return from Cragston early in the evening. He felt rather guilty about the hateful thoughts that had flitted through his mind earlier in the day, and so he summoned his secretary, an eager and well-groomed young man, and asked him to have a roomful of roses delivered to their house on 36th Street, along with a sniveling note, which Morgan dictated to the embarrassed but still enthusiastic employee: *I am a beast and a louse, and you deserve better. Because of you, I am a blessed man – with all my love ....*

At that, he exited the second floor office of Drexel & Morgan, thumped down the carpeted stairway and passed into the street. The air had the new crispness of Fall, as though Nature knew that this was the day Morgan had returned to New York. In the center of Wall Street, a lost squirrel barreled through a gaggle of pigeons; the startled birds bounced into the air a bit, then returned to their places. A line of cabs and snorting horses stood before the Stock Exchange on the west side of Broad Street, and a heaving, buzzing swarm of curb-stone brokers spilled out onto the street from between the front columns of the four-story, white marble building, snarling, failing small-time businessmen in sun-faded bowler hats, fighting their way into the Long Room.

Morgan crossed Nassau Street, passed, without looking, the Sub-Treasury building, another multi-columned, shimmering marble palace, and slipped into the Bakir & Bushong Bank building on Broad Street. He rumbled down the hallway till he reached the furthest dead-end. He rapped on a dirty wooden door, whose window announced that it was the entrance to the *American Cigar Distribution Company*. A natty, muscular man answered the door, familiar smirk glued firmly to his crooked, handsome face, and Morgan entered a narrow, dim suite of rooms that bustled with visitors, but in which not much cigar distribution was proceeding. The wooden filing cabinets were cracked and fusty, and dusty sunlight squeezed its way through the office's two dirty, neglected windows.

If you have somehow managed to put your hands on the first volume of my *Memoirs* – perhaps in a shoebox in an attic somewhere – you may recall the unsavory yet officially reputable cast of characters who greeted Morgan in the cigar company's office. The aforementioned smirker was a government agent named Mr. Sneed. (I have to this day learned neither his first name, nor the specific government agency of which he was an agent.) He held out one calloused, thick-fingered hand and grasped Morgan's shoulder roughly, overly familiarly. Sneed had short blond hair, which now showed some signs of very recent thinning, a face that was beginning to vein from drinking, and a broken nose, now less attractive than it had been in his earlier youth. Beside him was Filbank, Sneed's shadow, another ambiguous government agent, but he was soft and fluffy and seemingly hapless where Sneed was scarred and rough and seemingly competent. Filbank wore an identical black frock suit, but it hung loosely in the wrong places, bulged fatly in others. He looked itchy and uncomfortable, and he hovered invisibly in the background just behind Sneed's left shoulder. In the center of the room, in a suit that had once been lovely, perhaps before it had found its current owner, stood the always groggy and always irritable W. Marley Talzek, counsel to the American Cigar Distribution Company, a man who (as he periodically reminded colleagues and clients, and, constantly, himself) had once had rather impeccable ethics, in those now golden days when he'd owned a manufactory, bequeathing lovely glassware to tasteful homes throughout New York and beyond, and more affordable glassware for the working classes of America. Before he had become a lawyer.

Finally, a young woman, blond and cheerful, attended to a balancing siphon coffee brewer in the corner, humming gently, her lovely voice an irritant to all present. A flame flickered, and the coffee bubbled.

"Gentlemen!" Morgan harrumphed, and they all sat, the banker landing in a wooden chair with a tremendous thud. The chair teetered precariously, creaked and cracked a bit, the legs nearly splintering with the great man's force.

All present inhaled nervously.

The chair then righted itself and did not collapse, and thus neither did the world's economy.

"Mr. Morgan," Sneed said. "We have a surprise for you. What I believe will be a tidy little war."

He smiled a toothy smile, but one laced with controlled rage. Sneed was in his element; brutally efficient, and angry. The others present enjoyed all this a bit less.

"After this, we're ready to take on the Oneida Community in New York, then perhaps Amana Colonies in Iowa. Then a full-scale assault on the Shakers, and then next perhaps the Amish. We'll wipe out Utopianism for you, Mr. Morgan. And while we are at it, we will wipe out Hope itself."

"It's not a joke to me, Mr. Sneed," Morgan said softly, after some time had passed.

The young woman brought the coffee, now thick, overcooked, burnt.

"Coffee," she whispered.

Her voice was like wind chimes.

She smiled.

Her smile was angelic.

Her name, appropriately, was Angela.

Sneed patted her on the bottom, and Talzek averted his eyes. His lined face pained, he was excessively and unnecessarily discomforted by this very mild display of lust. I would meet Angela in 1905 (her angelic nature yet undiminished), in connection with the Battle of Sidonia, which is how I know of the events that occurred on Wall Street in September 1878, but she is otherwise irrelevant to our tale.

Her coffee duly served, her bottom duly patted, she retreated to a stool in the corner of the room, where she sat and awaited further instructions, tingling slightly (it must be admitted) from the pat on the bottom.

On her stool, she listened to the gentlemen plot, and she pretended not to understand what they were plotting.

"It's not a joke to me," Morgan said again.

Sneed reluctantly turned back to Morgan.

"Not a joke," he nodded. "Not a joke *to you*, Mr. Morgan."

Sneed agreed icily that in to-day's United States – still suffering the after-effects of the prior decade – brother against brother, hundreds upon hundreds of thousands of faceless dead in muddy muddled fields of blood – no one could laugh at the idea of more Americans dying.

Filbank sneezed; spittle flitted nimbly through the dusty air before falling to earth.

Sneed ignored his colleague.

"You did, however, request a surgical strike on the Sidonian outpost in Montana," Sneed continued, "and I have returned to this most prestigious cigar company to tell you that the Hayes administration looks favorably on your proposal; or if not actually *favorably* on your actual *proposal* – which is, to be honest, rather ridiculous – then, at least, the Hayes administration looks highly *un*favorably on the idea of angering you, with the resulting detritus of world economic breakdown, presidential assassination, and so on and so forth. Rich men have their idiosyncrasies, I suppose, eh? Nevertheless, this news should warrant a smile and a quiet thank you. We are not, after all, asking you to join in the fighting and to risk your

life along with the boys of the lower classes. *Heavens* no, Morgan!"
he exclaimed now. "We just ask that your Majesty enjoy it from afar,
and with a smile, and a bit of useful gratitude."

Morgan nodded.

"It comes without a price, then?" he muttered.

"Of course not, my heroic Prince."

Sneed laid out the administration's demands, which included
support for the gold standard, improved working conditions on the
railroads controlled by Drexel, Morgan to help keep the recently
quelled riots of 1877 from re-kindling, and a number of favors
addressing certain international disturbances, along with a guarantee
of no further economic threats for the next decade and a half. This
was to be Morgan's one big governmental favor. The last one. No
more wars fought just to please Mr. Morgan. No more eccentricities
for the government to deal with.

Morgan waved all this away without much thought.

"And you will deliver Allen Jerome to me?" he asked.

"Temporarily, yes. If he survives our invasion. And if we
catch him. You may have him briefly."

"For a little chat," Morgan agreed. "Yes. For just a brief, little
chat."

Angela approached. She refilled the coffee cups. Then she
retreated.

The gentlemen talked politics for a few minutes, and they even talked
about sports, and then J.P. Morgan raised one more topic, as though it
were a mere after-thought.

"One other thing," he said, clearing his throat. "You may
recall a gentleman named Walt Hugbert, something to that effect.
Terrible man, horrible Wild West show some years ago, presented all
sorts of terrible ideas. A 'progressive' of some sort. Hates America.
An America-hater."

Sneed nodded. He knew that Morgan had mistaken my name,
and I think he knew as well that Morgan knew it. But it was the job of
the upper classes not to know too much about those of us who
belonged to the 99%, as you might call it, if you are reading this in the
21st century. To know our names would be unseemly, and so Sneed
did not correct him.

"You helped us put him away, if I recall," Sneed smiled. "Mr. Hugglebert."

"Where he can no longer threaten America," added Filbank, and his jowls trembled a bit as he spoke. Leaning forward confidentially, he seemed about to speak again, probably obsequiously, perhaps to praise Morgan for his patriotism and love of America, but upon raising a pointer finger to make his decisive and perhaps obsequious point, he slipped nervously from the chair and gracelessly flopped to the floor.[*] By the time he had climbed back up and righted himself, the conversation had moved on, and his moment had been lost forever.

"Dead in Wyoming, I believe," Sneed said, and Morgan shook his head.

"Dead and not-dead, concurrently," Morgan disagreed. "Remember? A most remarkable occurrence."

Sneed smiled and said that he remained a skeptic on such things.

"I might need him pardoned," Morgan went on. "No one knows whom Witt Hugleybrick actually killed in that passion crime, so there are no bereaved family members to complain." And then, Morgan added another important thing that seemed to have just flitted into his head: it was entirely *possible* that Mr. Hugglebuggle would need assistance with the transfer of a rather large amount of cash to South America, and Morgan would appreciate it if the U.S. government would look the other way. It was, Morgan said, all in the name of a good cause, and the protection of the United States from foreign conspirators.

All grunted approval.

Out on the street, in the gentle afternoon chill, the little group of men prepared to go their separate ways. Morgan shook each man's hand, and then he marched east. The others watched him. Talzek straightened his tie just from habit – his tie was not actually even slightly crooked – and he turned to Filbank and noted softly, "I was once a man of impeccable ethics. I made glassware. Fine expensive glassware for the rich. But I also made affordable glassware, so that

---

[*] Is it possible to flop *gracefully* to the floor, I hear you ask? Indeed it is. Catching one's balance upon losing one's equilibrium, and landing with a gentle flutter. This was beyond our sad Mr. Filbank's capabilities.

everyone who needed glassware could have glassware. One could hardly object to a man who makes glassware."

And Talzek walked away sadly, his overcoat unbuttoned, flapping in the wind.

Morgan arrived home in time for a late dinner, to a front parlor and living room filled with red and white roses, and lupines and lavateras in full bloom. Fanny smiled. He was glad to see her smile, and he held her hand. What had he done to warrant such a full-throated, self-flagellating apology? He had done something, of that he was sure. He did not love his second wife, Fanny, but he could still recall vividly the feelings of gratitude that he had felt in 1864 upon first meeting the sweet, twenty-two year old Fanny at St. George's Church. He had felt towards her such feelings of sweeping gratitude that they were almost exactly like love, and every bit as potent, and they temporarily – too temporarily – filled the void in his heart. And now she was like a wounded animal whom he did not wish to see suffer.

She said a few things about the trip back from Cragston, and she asked him if he had made a decision about the yacht he wished to buy.

She deserved to smile from time to time, he supposed, and a few things made her happy. Their coddled son, Jack, made her very happy, and the happier she was with Jack, the more she coddled him, and the more insufferable Morgan found him. Opium, and morphine, unfortunately, made her happy in these recent days. And, not least, seeing signs that he, Pierpont, knew that he mistreated her and was periodically sorry about it. These were things that made her happy.

They sat together by the window, the light of the moon flowing in and drifting about the room like a bit of fog. *"It is not such a terrible ordeal to be married to me, is it Pierpont?" she asked him, and Morgan said that it was not.

"There are people in the world, after all," he mused, "who have much worse lives. Boys who were shot in the head in the War, for example, and who live life with a bullet in their brains – blinding headaches, unable to think straight. There are babies in countries we have never heard of, who drown in agony in floods. No, when some perspective is put on the thing, it is not such an ordeal to be married to you, my dear."

Morgan's thoughts tended to run this way. He had not

intended to insult his wife, and not until a week from the following Tuesday did it occur to him that he might have expressed this sentiment a bit more tactfully.

Still, Fanny was used to life with her Pierpont, and given his general disposition, this was not an unusually unkind thing for him to say, and so she rested her head on his shoulder.

He put his arm about her and pulled her close, and he shut his eyes and listened to her breathe

.

CHAPTER 4

I don't really like to acknowledge it, but the villains of my story, Allen Jerome and especially Darryl Fawley, are actual human beings, and they both started out life as babies whose mothers loved them, babies who in all likelihood were charming in that way that babies tend to be, and had I been an adult at the time of their birth, their appearance – tiny and silly and adorably stupid, with little useless hands – would likely have made me smile. I hate acknowledging that they are human.

Like all adults, they had to manage their business. For me, this would have been, at one time, scribbling away in a clerk's office, or at other times, working a cattle drive across the west. For Allen Jerome and Darryl Fawley, managing their business meant attending to the demands of a kingdom poised on the cusp of empire.

I imagine that Sidonia's enemies – *counter-Revolutionaries*, the Sidonians would call them – might attempt to convince struggling little outposts that nothing like Sidonian riches could possible come without a terrible price, and they might argue that the price was eternal servitude. The businessman between our two villains, Allen Jerome, would have an easy response: *If this is servitude, give me more – I'm still not satisfied!* Harvard-educated mathematician, cold-blooded, humorless, impeccably dressed and coiffed and therefore handsome in his way, but untouchable and unappealing nonetheless.

Darryl Fawley was Allen Jerome's business partner. English, elbow-patched, less exacting in demeanor, lanky and homely but friendlier in manner, he was the more beloved of the two among the masses, but they were both acknowledged as mere political leaders. Sidonian religious leaders were known as Pharsnips (Allen Jerome's invention, which rhymed with *parsnips* and represented his contempt for religion). Along with a troupe of acrobats and clowns, the Pharsnips called the masses to daily prayer whether Fawley and Jerome were present in Sidonia or not.

Fawley had joined the movement for two reasons: first, because he had married a woman whose love he did not believe he deserved, and he wished to put her on a throne, where he thought she belonged. (Instead, he put her in a grave, albeit through gross negligence rather than premeditation.) Second, because he was loaded down every minute of every day with guilt over everything, including guilt not only over the way his genial mediocrity had disappointed his mother (the now well-known Sidonie, after whom his town and movement were named), but a more political and intellectual guilt inspired by his rather minor financial inheritance, and for this he wished to compensate by pursuing social justice. If he could leave the world a better place, perhaps he would even things out a bit. It helped that the woman he wished to put on a throne desired social justice above all else.

He was rumpled and friendly and balding, with a smile of crooked teeth, and not actually a bad fellow, all the way down deep inside of him, and under other circumstances – had he not taken a fateful trip to the far wild lands of China to discover a 2000-year-old mystery, had he not married a woman he did not rate – he would have deserved to have blokes buy him a pint at the pub in one of those little English hamlets where blokes buy other blokes pints, and he would have died with a bad liver at an appropriate age and a few people would have eulogized him briefly as a good bloke and then, I reckon, bought a few pints in his honor and staggered home and vomited on their battered copies of Wilkie Collins novels, or whatever it is they read before the advent of Sherlock Holmes. I've never spent any extended time in England, but this is what I imagine a good life and pleasant death would have been for an unremarkable and unbrilliant and not-evil bloke like Darryl Fawley.

But that innocuous end was not to be.

He did indeed love and adore and mourn the woman I also loved and adored and mourned, Lucy Billings, and perhaps as strongly as I, but although he mourned her, he had killed her, not willfully, but through inaction and through indecision and through greed and ambition, and because these were things that mattered more to him than Lucy did, which is why I hated Darryl Fawley, why I wished him dead, and why I wished to be the one to make him dead.

When Darryl Fawley and Allen Jerome traveled to their slowly growing network of Sidonian satellite cities, Fawley would invariably stake a claim for the righteousness of their Sidonian Cause, and he would think of Lucy, and he would hope, somehow, that his crusade might have earned her approval, had she lived to witness it. He still loved her, as he would ever love her. And so on these missions, as Allen Jerome appealed to the heartless capitalism within the heartless heart of the ruling class of each of his satellite cities, the glad-handing Darryl Fawley spoke warmly of the benefits to society that their movement would bring, and he would think of Lucy.

Maybe he even still believed it a little bit as late as the Fall of 1878, by which time he'd had abundant opportunity to witness the evils of Sidonism and the hopelessness of it all.

On Monday, September 16, 1878, Darryl Fawley and Allen Jerome crossed the border into North Dakota territory for a couple days fishing under cloudy skies with the mayor of the small and not-yet-growing town of Dawsey, and his cherubic deputy mayor, and on Tuesday, September 17, 1878, at about ten in the morning, Fawley and Jerome sat with the mayor and deputy mayor in a rowboat in the middle of a pond just to the south of town.

I am going to make a confession: a small bit of the following story is not fully accurate, because the mayor's name has been utterly lost to history. A bachelor or a widower, I suppose, with no children, no living parents, and no one to pay for a memorial marker in place of a grave, given that his death was witnessed and confirmed without any doubt, but his body never found, other than the very top of his skull, and even that not recovered. I have decided to call him Mayor Figg, just so I will have something to call him, although that was almost certainly not his name. I imagine he was probably a little bit overweight, and that his manner was gruff, although I don't know this with certainty – this is just how I picture him.

I have it on good authority that he had a conscience, which guaranteed his doom. I imagine that the day was probably a little bit nippy, and that Mayor Figg was wearing overalls.

The deputy mayor, of course, was Angus Weatherford, and none of us will ever forget him.

The fish weren't biting that morning.

"Why are you interested in a little town like ours?" Mayor Figg asked. "We've got about fifteen families and some not-very-good (it turns out) farmland. We're surrounded by hostile injuns getting hostiler. If we've got a hunnert people this fall, we'll have eighty next fall. We're hoping for a grain elevator but … I don't know."

"We have some pull with Jay Gould," said Fawley. "What if I promised you that Dawsey would be a stop on the Milwaukee & Waukesha Rail Road?"

Fawley wore an old sweater, which fit him loosely. His wisps of hair blew about in the wind.

The mayor laughed.

"What if you promised me a fish right now?"

Jerome mimicked the mayor's laugh, and it sounded almost friendly, although Fawley understand that to be unintentional.

Jerome put one long, bony finger to his white lips.

"I promise you a fish right now," Jerome said, and the mayor's fishing line went taut, and he pulled up a beautiful carp.

"Hark!" the deputy mayor shouted.

"This isn't malarkey," Allen Jerome said, angry, glassy blue eyes glaring.

The fish sputtered and gasped in the mayor's arms.

Dawsey, North Dakota, later changed its name to Pearce, North Dakota, named for Asa Levi Pearce, the postmaster. Sometime later, it changed its name to Freda, North Dakota, named for Freda Van Sickle, the daughter of the railroad's construction foreman, after the Milwaukee & Waukesha Rail Road did indeed bring some semblance of prosperity to the town. Around 1918, the whole shebang was destroyed by a meteorite, and so, as I write this in the 1930s, the town is no more, though a drifter may sometimes hunt rabbits in the surrounding woods and occasionally squat in one of the few abandoned buildings that half-survived the meteor. As *you* read this in the 20th or 21st century, the town of Freda is naught but rotting lumber, weeds and rusted train tracks.

"What can *we* do for you, Mr. Jerome, Mr. Fawley?" Mayor Figg asked, as the fish gasped its last gasp and expired.

"Just take advantage of our generosity," Allen Jerome replied.

The country, Darryl Fawley said, should not be run by a central dictator in Washington, D.C., periodically sending soldiers funded by robber barons to crush the ordinary man and woman of the nation, those who succeed by the sweat on their brows and the calluses on the palms of their hands.

"They will sweep in from the East, one day," he said. "We will try to hold the West, and perhaps allies from the far Winter North will be awakened after a few millennia. All we would ask is your loyalty, when the crisis comes. In the Dakotas, we will need line after line of fortifications to hold them back. People willing to die for justice, for what is right and just. This very land may well be one of the pressure points of the War. But we shall prevail, because we have justice on our side, and those who stand with us will never know want."

Well, I am sure that this little speech would have sounded to be pure craziness but for the miracles wrought by Sidonia, which were already well-demonstrated. The only argument against an alliance was that Sidonia might be the devil, rather than simply a rich uncle.

"Will we have a grain elevator?" Mayor Figg asked.

His fishing line went taut again, and he pulled up a beautiful trout.

"We can manage to buy you a grain elevator, you stupid little son of a bitch," Allen Jerome said. "Do you even have any idea of the magnitude of what we are talking about? Grain elevator, he asks! Stupid, foolish little bastard. I'm dangling the keys to the castle in front of your nose."

Mayor Figg flushed, and his slightly puffy cheeks turned a rosy red. He looked down at the two fish in his rowboat.

"It's just ... we need a grain elevator. So I thought I'd ask about the grain elevator. I apologize."

"Mayor," Darryl Fawley asked gently, "if the farmland around these parts turns fertile, and if we can arrange the railroad stop, could we count on you to put together a well-armed militia that might stand its ground in the event of an unprovoked attack from a tyrannical government? Would your men at least do their best to slow the cavalry's ascent to the northwest?"

Mayor Figg nodded.

"If you stand by us," he said, "we would stand by you. If you do right by us, we'll do right by you. We're suffering up here, but we're loyal people."

Darryl Fawley took Mayor Figg's arm, and even more gently, he said, "The government may try to infiltrate your little outpost here. They may plant a mole. You know what I mean by that? A spy. Someone who pretends to be loyal to you and to Sidonia, but who is instead loyal to Washington and the counter-Revolution. This spy could even be a friend of yours. If we could prove his guilt, we would need you to stand with us."

Mayor Figg nodded his fat little head.

"I understand," he said. "I fought in the War. I know how to do what needs to be done when a soldier's turned sour."

Then I am sorry to say, it was Allen Jerome's turn to test Mayor Figg's loyalty. Would Mayor Figg kill a mole with no proof at all, just on the word of the Sidonian authorities? Would he nevertheless stand with Sidonia and execute his brother? What if one day, Mayor Figg were to have a son, and Sidonia informed him his son was the mole? Mayor Figg nodded again and again, though his nods grew less emphatic as the questions grew more severe and morally questionable.

"It says in the Bible that a man can stone his son," Mayor Figg said, "if he's done wrong. Right in the Old Tersterment, it says that there." (This is incorrect, by the way, but I do not know if Mayor Figg recognized his error. The Old Testament says that a man *cannot* stone his son, but this mistake is often made. I remember a few things from the school on Randall's Island.)

"There may come a time when we will just ask you to trust us," Allen Jerome said. "When you will have to trust us that we know what needs to be done. You will not have the right to ask questions, to debate with us, to say no. The line of defense that runs through the Dakotas is too important. Can you do this?"

Mayor Figg thought.

"Would you do anything at all for us, for Sidonia?" Allen Jerome asked. "Anything we ask?"

Would Mayor Figg put an axe to the womb of a pregnant woman who had committed no crime and watch her bleed until dead? Would he set fire to a farmhouse and stand guard while the family inside screamed as they burned? Would he put the barrel of his rifle on the forehead of an innocent three-month-old infant and pull the trigger, if Sidonia told him to do so?

All of this was followed by a terrible silence.

Allen Jerome raised one eyebrow.

The mayor remained ever silent.

An exceptionally large and twisted coiled fish burst from out of the water, snakelike but with gills, fishlike but with limbs, light green with a white underbelly. It opened its mighty jaw and clamped its terrific fangs into the meatiest, most tender cut of the mayor's shoulder as it leapt over the rowboat, vanishing into the water on the other side, the mayor flipping headlong in tow.

The hapless politician struggled in the water even as the creature devoured him. Unfortunately, this creature was human-like in its eating habits: it savored its meals.

The deputy mayor stood and hit the creature a few times with his oar, but he did no particular harm. The deputy mayor took out his gun and shot until he was out of ammunition, but the bullets just lodged in the creature's scaly skin. A greenish pus oozed from the creature's body and floated around on the surface of the pond, algae-like, but the creature did not release the mayor, and the bullets seemed to cause it no particular pain. The beast continued to devour its meal, slurping with its great mouth, gnawing with its great teeth and licking with its great tongue.

None of the men still in the rowboat could understand how it was that the mayor remained conscious for such a long time, as the pond-beast chewed and slobbered, but he did indeed remain both alive and conscious until he was almost entirely consumed, and he screamed and screamed.

After a while, the screams subsided, and the creature sank to the bottom of the lake with a satisfied little purr. The top of the mayor's skull bobbed about on the pond's surface, but the mayor otherwise no longer physically existed.

At least five minutes passed in dead silence.

Allen Jerome turned to Deputy Mayor Weatherford.

"You didn't tell us," Allen Jerome said, "that there was a ferocious monster in this pond. I do not think Mr. Fawley and I would have come fishing with you in this particular pond had we known of the ferocious monster in this pond. This was an irresponsible oversight, Angus."

Deputy Mayor Weatherford assured them both that this was the first he had heard of it.

"I think the pond should probably be closed to fishermen in the future," Deputy Mayor Weatherford said, "in the interest of public safety."

Both Allen Jerome and Darryl Fawley agreed that this was a good idea.

"I suppose," Allen Jerome said, "that you're the mayor now."

"I suppose I am. I didn't want to become mayor this way."

"There are better ways to a promotion, you'll get no argument from me," Allen Jerome said. "No one *wants* to see his boss eaten by a ferocious pond monster, Angus. No one *plans* for such a thing. But events don't always evolve as we plan them. A ferocious pond monster – well, pretty much by definition, if it's going to eat the mayor, it'll eat the mayor when no one's expecting it to."

Whatever weapons the government of the United States might have at its disposal, the new Mayor Weatherford was quite sure it didn't have a ferocious pond monster. He felt rather uncomfortable now, sitting in the rowboat, the top of Mayor Figg's skull bobbing about in the water just two feet from the edge of the boat and a ferocious monster slumbering at the bottom of the pond.

"We can count on you?" Allen Jerome asked.

Mayor Weatherford assured both Messieurs Fawley and Jerome that he would be a good and loyal soldier for Sidonia, even if it meant committing unspeakable crimes. Shooting babies. Burning families alive. And whatnot. He hoped that these questions were hypothetical, but he was nevertheless willing to burn a family alive and shoot an infant child if it meant riches and political power, the favor of the Sidonian overlords and the assurance that he would never be eaten alive by the Dawsey pond monster. He stood straight up in the boat, shouted out, "Hail Sidonie! Hail Sidonia! I will stand by you and follow your commands, come what may!" The boat wobbled a bit but did not capsize. He held his right hand aloft in an odd little salute that he had just invented on the spot, but to which Allen Jerome took a liking.

What other choice did he have, after all?

The remains of Mayor Figg's skull fragments sank to the bottom of the pond, which surprised Mayor Weatherford, who'd have supposed that they would have floated. Now there was nothing at all to bury, and explaining all this would be difficult, indeed.

Hester and I picked up my horse at the Death Spa. No sign of Monsieur Rasháh or his gang. In fact, Pete greeted me cheerily. I couldn't let this one go, and so I asked him if the ruffian in black had returned to make more trouble, and Pete laughed as though this were just a joke. I glanced at the children's wading pool, and I saw the pot-bellied little boy and the giggling black haired girl who had so recently been occupants of Rasháh's cranium. So Rasháh had apparently vanished not only from the parking lot, but from the Spa's recent past as well, as I had hoped. I pointed out to Hester that my theory had been proved utterly correct. She smiled, glad to see the boy intact, and delighted that my confidence was returning, but perhaps still unconvinced by my quack science. Still, there it was – we drowned Rasháh in the Pangaean sea, or so I thought, and his bad deeds in 1980s America were thus erased like a footprint on a windy beach. I believed myself very wise.

I shook Pete's hand and promised I'd return soon.

Then Hester, the horse and I sped back to 19th century Lida, where there was also no sign or recollection of Rasháh or his gang. While I enjoyed another horn of fat, old Fitzgerald's famous anti-fogmatic, Hester bought herself a feisty little brown trail horse that took to her like a long-lost friend. I wanted to return to my hut, but Hester said that it probably was no longer safe, and anyway not worth the risk. "Why do you want to return?" she asked, and I shrugged and said that it had been my home, and I wanted to look at it one last time. "I suppose I would like to have been able to bury my mule," she said. "He was a nice mule. Not a lot of help, but a nice mule, and he did save my life. It doesn't seem right to leave him there." But still she shook her head and said that sentimentality would only put us at risk, and so instead, after we bought a couple of weeks of rations, we rode about five miles southwest of my hut and dug up my Lervine loot, and then we were finally off, heading north to Pyeton, where we intended to save the world and make some money, though for me not necessarily in that order of priority.

A trip that would take you – my 20th century readers – six or seven hours by horseless carriage took Hester and me a few weeks, scraping along at the foot of the mountains in the lush forest that straddled California and Nevada states. The desert shimmered through the trees to our immediate east, a near-uninhabited region till we reached Carson City.

During that time we pushed our exhausted horses during the day through the densely packed pines and set up camp inconspicuously at nighttime, which was when we plotted our pending and (we hoped) brief life of crime.

Every morning, Hester rose, faced the sunrise, and mumbled incoherently to herself for half an hour, blind and deaf to the world.

This ritual disconcerted me some, I will admit. I didn't ask her about it. It wasn't the most troubling thing I had ever seen in my life, although admittedly I had lived a particularly troubling life. It never even occurred to me to ask her about it.

About five miles north of the noisy Mammoth City mining town – an economic bubble of a town, home to 1500 burly entrepreneurs, but which would be deserted within two years – we pitched camp a little ways inland from a large pond, fed by a small stream that wound itself carefully around the forest pines. I washed myself off in the pond, while Hester sat on a log and looked the other way. Then Hester washed herself off in the pond, while I sat on that same log and looked the other way. I could hear her splash in the bubbling water, in the quiet late afternoon.

We were both tolerably clean when night fell and the moon came out, and a little mist rolled off the mountains to the west and glowed in the starry night like a cloud of diamonds. Hester quizzed me on our criminal plot, on the route in and the route out, our secret codes and whatnot. My role was really rather easy to understand, it seemed to me, but all-in-all, it seemed a good plan, especially the part where she'd gotten the sheriff of Pyeton in on the scheme, although I was not entirely convinced that we could trust a lawman ....

Anyway, apparently I passed the test, because Hester leaned back against a cedar tree, looking satisfied and more than a little bit proud both of me and also her train robbery plan. The fire crackled, struggling against the chilly haze. Hester poked the glowing embers with a stick, and they flared up a bit.

"Why did everyone call you Mr. Darcy?" she asked. "When we were in the 1980s?"

"I said my name was Hugh Watt," I replied, "and Pete looked up and said, 'Mr. Darcy?' I didn't think 'Hugh Watt' sounded so much like 'Mr. Darcy', but there you have it. I figured it would be more trouble to correct him than to just nod, stoic-like."

I look a swig from my flask.

"And it had its advantages," she said.

"In the 1980s," I explained, "it was not entirely impossible to imagine that a thoroughly respectable young woman might drive along the desert highway in a beat-up old car, and entirely unchaperoned, if she honestly wished to, a woman with what in the 20th century one might call 'a mind of her own.' A 'free spirit' who had just graduated from college, exploring America. But in spite of it all – discovering America, college book-learnin', mind of her own, blah blah blah – when she might chance to meet a man in the desert named Mr. Darcy, none of that would matter. In the 1980s, anyway. To a woman of most other eras, you know … I would assume that Mr. Darcy doesn't mean as much to them."

"So it won you the hearts of many women-folk?"

"Just one. But I won her heart over and over again."

I told her, as delicately as I could, about Julie Johnstone, who had approached me at my regular table at the Death Inn with a smile and an arched eyebrow at 6:45 p.m. on August 11, 1981 and how, as one would have said in 1981, *one thing led to another*. "But I could return to that day again and again, whenever I wanted to. And I did."

"And you never bump into yourself?"

I shook my head.

"A Roamer is only in one place when he's roaming. When he leaves the future, he's gone."

"And why didn't that kick you off the Maze?" she asked. "Didn't that change the woman's heart?"

"Not even a bit," I said. "A little romantic lark, barely remembered years from now. The world, unchanged. The woman's heart, merely tickled. And feelings of love scarcely fleeting."

Evaporating with the memory of the next morning's coffee, as the Death Spa and my own manly shadow shrank away into nothing in Julie's rear-view mirror. I thought for a moment to explain to Hester the state of future womanhood – the powerful, passionate and uniquely evanescent needs of a young woman in 1981 in a rusty car driving through the desert, but I didn't think she'd really understand, and I didn't want her to.

Well, Hester admitted, she couldn't really blame me, even though the morals of the situation were decidedly murky.

"It must have been lonely, in the middle of the desert," she said. "You must have been lonely."

"A little bit lonely," I agreed, "but that's what I was looking for. See here. Sidonia is spreading its Magic … I suppose you'd call it 'Magic' for lack of another term. It's spreading its Magic all across North America. Maybe beyond; I can't tell you that for certain. And this Magic, it has some side effects. Some things a body might find pleasant, if he didn't know any better. It feeds on our hopes and dreams and weaknesses, as best as I can figure it. But in the middle of the desert, I was safe from all that. From false hopes, and long-dead visitors in the night. You understand? No people around, no Sidonian Magic. And I could drink, and I could forget, without being reminded."

"So why leave? Why Roam to the future?"

Well, I told her, that was my aforementioned racket. The kelter from the Lervine operation in northern Utah was not a great pile of dough, not something that could buy me Monongahela forever, except I quickly figured that coin and even paper shinplaster from the 1870s might be worth something in the 1980s, and sure enough it was. The elusive owner of the Death Spa and Resort was something of a collector, and Pete kept an eye out for him, so my cache of cash was an intriguing find. I could always drop off a bit of my take at the resort, get washed-up and fed, leave some on credit for next time, and keep on going in such manner for years. As for the young lady learned in the novels of Jane Austen, it was not something planned. But there she was, waiting for me. She kept the mind steady, if somewhat perpetually repentant. I knew love, after all.

"Do all Roamers need to walk through a physical door? Before they can roam Time? Do they need to walk through a door?"

"No. That's a crutch of mine. I need to visualize the journey. So I go through a door. There is no *scientific* need for it, to be honest with you. But I cannot roam without it. One day, I imagine, I will get better at the whole endeavor."

Hester thought for a moment.

"*Blah blah blah,*" she said reflectively.

"It's a little something I made up," I said, "in a bar called Whitey's Saloon, a few years back, in a near-dead mining town in Colorado. I kind of liked the way it sounded, and it seemed to get its point across without much explanation. So I've been saying it all the time, whenever I see people. I think it could help people express themselves."

She seemed as amused by this as was probably possible, given everything, and she managed a weak smile.

"Where do you intend to hide out?" she asked. "Until the invasion of Sidonia? Until this revenge that means so much to you? I need to be able to reach you easily as soon as word comes through."

I said that I figured I'd probably go back to the homestead in the desert and bury the money in the sand.

She shook her head.

"Too dangerous?" I asked.

"I'm worried you'll get caught and squeal."

"Then what do you suggest?"

"Come with me to South America," she said. "Till the trail goes cold. And the soldiers go over the Sidonian mountains, and Darryl Fawley is in your crosshairs."

She insisted that there would be good accommodations for me, and absolute security. And it wouldn't hurt to have someone to discuss military maneuvers, in preparation for the big day.

I said I would give her offer some thought.

"All arrangements have been made," she said. "To be honest with you, you don't have a choice in the matter."

To be honest, I was relieved not to have a choice in the matter. My "choices" in "matters" generally don't work out particularly well.

The mist had settled, glimmering, in her hair, and on her eyelashes, and suddenly she was beautiful. I stared at her in silence a little too long, and she averted her gaze till I could barely see her face in the darkness.

I smiled a false, nervous smile and thanked her over-politely for her generous offer, but then I said nothing, I am ashamed to admit, because this idea – living with Hester in South America – was an unexpectedly happy thought, and it made me very sad to realize that this thought brought me so very much joy.

The next morning we packed up camp and weaved through the trees to the north, until we came to a little clearing, speckled with the last traces of summer flowers. In the middle of a patch of wild daisies stood a snowy egret, regarding us bemusedly.

"Snowy egret," I said to Hester.

I stopped walking.

She stopped as well.

"Maybe," she said, "we should shoo it away."

I shook my head.

"And keep going," she suggested.

She turned to me, her eyes quizzical.

"I think," I said, "that we should sit down, and just see what it does. It looks bemused."

I sat, and Hester sat beside me.

"Not bemused," Hester said "It looks to be a stupid bird without a thought in its head."

The bird didn't move.

"This snowy egret may be an oracle," I said.

"It looks to be a bird, a white bird."

"It could be an oracle in bird disguise," I said. "I have seen this sort of thing before. So this could be an oracle."

I watched the bird. It lifted a foot. It fluffed its left wing. It shut one eye.

"Or it could be just a bird," Hester said.

I said that she was right. It could be just a bird. But years ago, I told her, I knew a woman, someone who had protected and saved me many times. She did not have a high opinion of oracles or the clues that they could give us about our lives and the events in store for us. Everything worked out badly for this woman in the end, and I didn't know if she were even alive anymore. I was undecided as to whether everything would have been better if she had listened to the oracle. But it couldn't possibly have been worse, and so it would not hurt to listen, this time. I had long since determined that I would listen to oracles.

"Your friend ignored an oracle and something bad happened to her," Hester murmured. "That doesn't mean that ignoring the oracle caused the bad thing, or that being kind to the oracle would have prevented it. You know what they taught me in school, O'Hugh?

Temporal proximity is no proof of causation. 'X then Y' does not imply '*If* X then Y'. *Logic*, O'Hugh."

"Of course I know *that*," I said, although I knew no such thing. "Still and all. Let's wait. Just a few minutes."

We sat on the cool grass watching the bird, and the bird stood in the little cluster of wild daisies, and it never took its eyes from us.

"Oracle," I said.

The bird made a funny noise, a little peep, then a little chirp.

"Please," I said. "Oracle. I believe in your power. I will listen."

And then the bird changed, and a little girl in a blue robe stood before us. She had green eyes, and no hair on the top of her head. She had no eyebrows, and no eyelashes.

"Watt O'Hugh," she said, and I saw that she had no teeth.

"Yes," I said. "Oracle."

"I am the old woman you saw lo' these many years ago," she said, and the "lo" seemed to have some sort of dramatic effect that impressed, although it had not, truthfully, been so many years ago. "I was a wise old woman then," she continued, "and with each passing year, I grow younger and less wise. If no one solves the problems on our horizon – the problems brought by the Sidonians and their Overlord and their minions – I will grow to be an infant and wander ignorant through the land depending on pity for my life, then shrink to a helpless babe. Then blow away in the wind, and then cease to exist."

She smiled her sad, toothless, childish smile.

"Maybe most men would not mourn the loss of the oracles," she said. "Maybe most men do not think the world needs the oracles. Your friend – the one who traveled with you last time we met – this friend did not believe the world needs oracles."

I said that was true. This sounded like a threat. *You don't want to wind up like your friend, do you?; the one who did not believe the world needs oracles.* I considered pointing out what Hester had said about *causality* and *logic*, but I hadn't understood it, and I didn't think I could repeat it.

The oracle raised a finger.

"But let me tell you, the world needs its oracles. The world *does* need its oracles."

She shrugged then, a little hopelessly.

"But that is what I suppose one would expect me to say," she added. "Because I am, you know, an oracle. So of course I think the world needs its oracles."

And she sighed.

"I also think the world needs its snowy egrets," she added.

"Because you're also a snowy egret," I suggested.

She sighed again.

"I suppose," she said. "We do play an important role in the world's ecology. But maybe you are right. I imagine that you think the world needs its heroic, drunken shootists."

I shook my head.

"I do not think the world needs me," I said. "Or others like me. I wish it did. But I do not think it does."

"The world needs you to help solve the problems on the horizon," she said, "so that the oracles will not shrink to the size of babes and disappear, our wisdom lost. So if the world needs its oracles, then the world needs its shootists to save its oracles."

A little wind blew through the meadow, and the wildflowers bobbed cheerfully.

"A bit of wisdom, oracle?" I asked.

She sat down and crossed her little-girl legs.

"You will meet the Falsturm one day, in a room of gold."

"More?"

"The Falsturm may be defeated," she said, "only by the hand of the daughter of a Queen, who was born Nephila."

"And?"

"When you dig a pit," she said, "there is never enough dirt to refill it. Do not trust the Princess of Time. It is better to be lost in a forest when riding on a horse, than lost in a forest when walking on foot. Who is the master of a palace lit by fire?"

Now she was exhausted. I tried to commit these to memory, although the riddles and prophesies she'd provided me last time had not yet come in handy. She lay down on her side on the grass, and her eyelids seemed to grow heavy. I wondered who the Falsturm was. I was not eager to find out.

"Oracle?" I asked. "Could I have a bit of wisdom that I might understand?"

"There will be a terrible storm tonight," she said softly. "But I can give you instructions to a cabin in the woods at the foot of the mountain, long deserted by the old man who built it and once lived in it, and this cabin will keep you dry and safe. It will show you a few other things as well, things you do not expect, and so please keep your eyes open for these things."

She then proceeded to describe to me in minute, tree-by-tree detail, instructions for arriving at this magical cabin.

"Anything else?" I asked.

"A gold coin?" she asked. "For my trouble?"

I tossed her a gold coin, which she caught in her left hand. She then stood on one foot, and she very gradually turned back into a bird; first she grew some feathers on the top of her head, then her nose and mouth grew into a beak. The feathers continued to spread, from her head down her torso. Her legs grew skinny. Then, at last entirely a bird, she flew into the clear blue sky.

"You see?" Hester said. "Just a bird."

I said that the bird was an oracle. I said that the bird had turned into a little girl, and that the little girl had known about Sidonia, and that she had uttered words of profound wisdom (or at least words that had sounded profound and wise to me) and that the oracle had then turned back into a bird and had flown away.

Hester said she'd seen naught but a bird.

"The oracle was talking," I insisted. "Inscrutable words. Beautiful ideas."

"It squawked a bit," Hester said. "The bird. Unpleasantly."

CHAPTER 5

When Master Yu awoke the next day, he was still submerged in absolute pitch darkness, and he thought that perhaps he had died.

Then he remembered everything.

He crawled to the door at the end of the room, pulled it open, and he wandered up to the street. It was already late afternoon, and the Chinese city was alive.

He left Duncombe alley, and the breathing Chinatown of daytime passed him in a blur, the stalls selling fish so fresh they still flapped about, the fifteen cent barbershops, the herbalist on the corner, the awning that shielded the Tuck Hing meat market from the last wink of the California sun, the tea and opium piled in the wide windows of the bazaar across the avenue, the workers pouring out of the cigar factory, crowding about him and parting like the sea, murmuring in that common tongue that he disliked so much and still would not admit that he understood.

He found the theater on Jackson Street, a great crumbling old-man of a building in this newborn babe of a city, with rotting columns and peeling paint and mythic implications of past greatness.

Master Yu peered into the empty ticket office. He rapped a few times on the glass. At length, a wiry, wrinkled gentleman with an impossible, ropy mustache appeared at the window.

Master Yu introduced himself.

"Is there a package for me? I believe that you may be holding a package for me, which was sent from the Golden Sky Hotel in Denver."

He didn't explain how he came to possess that belief.

The little man turned all shades of discomfort, and he quickly vanished. Yu Dai-Yung could hear a hushed conversation in the next room. Finally, an older woman came to the window. She wore a yellow silk robe.

She smiled icily.

"Please come in through the side door, Master Yu," she said. "I am Mrs. Hong."

Inside, she walked him through a dusty, winding hallway, up a flight of creaking wooden steps and into another corridor that opened onto a narrow empty balcony, which overlooked the theater's wooden stage. A Chinese banner draped across the top of the theater proclaimed, "When Ideals Are in Harmony, the Sounds that Ensue Will be Elegant." The stage was bare and rough. Three musicians – a lute player, a zither player, and a two-stringed fiddle player – sat on wooden chairs at the rear of the stage before a backdrop depicting West Lake, near the city of Hangzhou, and the hilly green countryside beyond. Blooming peach and plum blossoms dotted the painted landscape, pleasure boats drifted lazily and motionlessly through the painted blue water, and the Thunder Peak Pagoda tickled the clouds. *Ah, China*, he sighed longingly. *To smell those peach blossoms!* (When had he last smelt those peach blossoms? Ever? No mind; their utter absence in this world of concrete made them precious beyond words, beyond rubies.)

At the front of the theater, a few actors stood about, waiting to rehearse. A woman dressed in a long white gown with long white sleeves began to sing. He knew this story, and he smiled with recognition, then frowned with sadness. A terrible snake goddess – a creature as old as the world itself – transformed herself into a beautiful young woman, who, as the opera began, was in the process of falling hopelessly in love with a mortal man on the shore of the Lake. Ecstasy bloomed; joy resulted; a wedding duet wafted through the empty theater. When her human lover died, terribly, painfully and with a beautiful, tuneful death-cry, the bereft snake goddess rose like a golden Phoenix to heaven and descended like a fiery meteor to Earth, with the antidote in her heart. Before the opera's villain, an angry monk, had the opportunity to imprison her beneath the Pagoda for all eternity, Master Yu felt a tap on his back, and he breathed a sigh of relief. He could live without tragedy for this evening. Better to watch the reunited lovers embrace and to leave the theater, pretending that the opera was over.

He turned.

Li-Ling beckoned him from the shadows.

He smiled, and she didn't smile back.

He followed her out of the theater, into the darkening and emptying moonlit city streets.

The establishment to which Li-Ling led the terrible poet bore the name Hang Far Low Restaurant, which I thought was rather unfortunate when I first heard it[*], although I understand that it was in its time a place of unsurpassed elegance in Chinatown, and perhaps in San Fran as well, owned and frequented, as it was, by the district's leading whoremongers, drug-pushers, slumlords and slave-traders.

Li-Ling brought my friend Master Yu to the third floor, marched him through a great majestic cavern of polished wood and elegantly robed patrons, until she reached a small table in the back behind a set of sliding doors.

"I have brought you her Majesty's secret agent," Li-Ling said. "May I introduce, gentlemen, Master Yu."

She pointed to an old man with gray hair in a purple silk robe embroidered with dragons. "Master Lu."

She then pointed to an older man with a bald head and dangling jowls in a blue silk robe embroidered with dragons. "Master Hu."

She finally pointed to the oldest man in the group, a painfully, grotesquely old toad of a man in a black silk robe embroidered with dragons. "Master Hsu," Li-Ling said.[**]

She bowed to each of them in turn, and then she left the restaurant.

Master Yu watched her go. He missed her immediately and painfully.

He turned to the trio of old men and smiled uncomfortably.

---

[*] This is not my poor attempt at a dirty joke. Hang Far Low was the Delmonico's of San Francisco's Chinatown, it was destroyed in the 1906 earthquake, rebuilt, and survived for many esteemed decades, even though its name sounds funny to American ears. This is a two-way street, my friends: try saying "Ronald Reagan" with an Alabama accent to a man from Fujian. He'll find it hilarious, laugh rudely and won't stop for many minutes. (If you say it to a woman from Fujian, on the other hand, she may blush, or she may just slap your face and run screaming.)

[**] In those troubled days of 1878, Masters Lu, Hu and Hsu were emperors of Little China, and they frequented the Hang Far Low Restaurant for dinner. Master Lu was the whoremonger. Master Hu was the slave-trader. And Master Hsu – the leader of them all – was the drug-dealer.

"Sit down," Master Hsu said firmly. "We have been waiting a long time to meet you."

"We were expecting you to arrive in America a bit earlier," Master Hu remarked, and Master Yu explained that he had suffered a year's worth of brutal training of the mind and body before the imperial court had deemed him suitable for the trip to America and his hazardous mission, whatever that mission might turn out to be.

"Where did you study?" Master Lu asked, and the poet said that he studied in a little village just north of Taiyuan.

"What did you learn?" said old Master Hsu. "In this little village?"

"Some things that may be useful."

"Secret things?"

He agreed, nodding.

"Things I could not and would not tell you even if you were to torture me," Master Yu explained gently.

"Then I will ask no more," ugly old Master Hsu said.

The waiter appeared with a great platter of fish fins, snails, Chinese turtle, eels, tarot root, fish brains, bamboo shoots and Chinese broccoli. Another waiter refilled the teapots, and they both retreated with small, quick bows.

Master Hsu pushed a little wooden box across the table to the poet. The box was smooth polished wood, with a sliding lid, and some sort of inscription carved into the top in a language he didn't recognize.

"Your package," the old man said. "Be very gentle when you open it."

Master Yu pushed the lid to one side, and a small shining metal sphere floated out of the box. It was about the size of a golf ball, and it hovered just at his eye level, humming gently.

"Astonishing," Master Yu whispered.

"Big problem," Hsu said. "We don't know what this is."

The sphere buzzed and quivered.

"What do you think?" asked Master Hu.

Master Yu said: "It appears to be some sort of sphere. One that can float a bit. And it appears to make some sort of indistinct noise."

Then he added: "Hmmm."

The old men looked at each other. Master Hsu seemed disappointed. Upon noting Master Hsu's seeming disappointment, the other two men then appeared to be disappointed as well.

"Well," said Master Lu at last. "It is yours, whatever it is."

"And," Master Hsu added, "we are at your disposal. Anything you need, just say the word. You are her Majesty's emissary on an important mission, and we are here to help."

"And in the meantime," Master Hu said, "we might as well eat."

The four men ate, and they drank wine, and the evening progressed. The sun descended outside the restaurant's wide windows, and shadows crept across the ornate dining room. Somewhere outside, a dog barked.

Anything you need, the man tells me. Anything you need. Just let us know. Anything at all.

Master Yu sighed. He sat on the pavement, bouncing the sphere up and down on the palm of his left hand, watching it hover in the air then descend, listening to the queer noise that it made.

He sighed again.

"Anything you need," he muttered aloud. "Could I have not said it? *I could use more comfortable accommodations.*"

Then an odd thought popped into the poet's mind. What if, he wondered, one were to bounce the sphere in one's left hand three times in quick succession, then catch it in one's right hand and hold it tight and let the vibration of the sphere rumble up one's arm and through one's body. What if one were to try that?

He decided to try it.

A young man walked by in the street, giving Master Yu a nervous look as he passed. His queue bobbed in the wind.

Master Yu bounced the sphere in his left hand three times in quick succession. It felt cold against his skin. Each time he bounced it into the air, it descended yet more quickly. On the third bounce, he tossed it into his right hand and squeezed it tightly. He immediately felt peculiar; the sphere's rumble rang like a bell inside his head. The night seemed to grow darker. Then there was nothing. Just darkness; no sound, no wind. Then he was someplace else entirely.

Master Yu stood at the end of a dock, in the light of a night sky illuminated by two moons. The weather was refreshing, the ocean breezes caressed his lungs, and he breathed freely for the first time in months. He turned and looked behind, and he saw a spired, jigsaw city of tall, golden stone buildings. It looked like an ancient kingdom but whirred like a city of science, like something from the far future. A melody rose from one of the towers, a beautiful melody played on an organ and harpsichord and accompanied by a chorus whispering lovely words that he could not understand. Beyond the crazy city, Master Yu saw a vast forest of towering trees that seemed unbounded and infinite.

He turned back to the bay, and there was Tang, sitting by the edge, right foot dangling in the water. He sat down at the edge of the dock as well. He took off his shoes and soaked his feet in the cool blue water. He looked at Tang. Same stony, stoic face, filled with sadness, same snow-white bald head.

This was indisputably the same person, but Tang was different now.

Tang was a woman! There was something slightly softer in her hard face; a plumpness to the lips and a roundness in the eyes.

How had he not seen this before?

Because when Tang had visited him in his room in the Chinatown basement, Tang had been a man! Or, perhaps, Tang had been a woman impersonating a man very convincingly. (Unless, now, Tang was a man impersonating a woman very convincingly….)

Tang wore a rough gray robe, and her ankles and feet were bare. He could see that her left foot was carved of wood. An elegant wooden foot, Master Yu was surprised to note with admiration. Most men of the 19th century would not find her beautiful, but Master Yu found her beautiful, as had I, some years before, and as would you, my readers of the 20th century, if you could see her. Her strength and fierceness was beautiful and powerful, and Master Yu wished that she could see him, and that he could talk to her.

She was talking to two dolphins. The dolphins jutted their heads above the crest of the water, and they were responding to the sound of Tang's voice, to these dolphin inflections. Tang and the dolphins seemed to be having an interesting conversation.

"Welcome," Tang said (implausibly, ridiculously), "to North Sadlareeyah."

Then, according to Master Yu, Madame Tang smiled. It was not a happy smile, but nevertheless it was a smile, according to Master Yu.

I do not believe him. I never saw Madame Tang smile, and I wish I had. I had a bit of a relationship with Madame Tang. She had healed me in the prison back in Wyoming, a miraculous healing job, sealing bones and nerves that should have been permanently ruptured. I'd accompanied her to that range war in Lervine; and she had accompanied me to Weedville, Nebraska, in our quixotic effort to rescue Lucy Billings from a Sidonian jail, an ill-fated mission that saw Lucy rise as a deadling, and Madame Tang chase Monsieur Rasháh through a great Otherworldly hole that opened in the middle of town, from which she seemed unlikely ever to return. Indeed, to the extent that Madame Tang had any friends, I would count myself among them; she was loyal, and she was innocent of the betrayals committed by my other allies in the counter-Revolution; and I missed her. After all, during the adventures that I relate in the first volume of my *Memoirs*, which I do not wish to repeat here in their entirety, she saved my life, and I saved hers, and we had once even shared an embrace, with death over our heads. And so I wish I had seen her smile.

"What is happening?" Master Yu asked.

"I cannot hear you," she said. "I do not even know if you have received this message. I don't know whether you have received the gift that I sent. The sphere I sent you, made by a gentleman of Sadlareeyahian origins named Iggs."

The moons glowed in her sad eyes as she stared out to sea.

"I have also sent a message to the dolphins here," she said. "I do not know if they have received it. I do not know if they are here with this three-dimension mirage of what I once was. Dolphins can upon rare occasions be helpful. But for the most part, they are cheerful, and during my lifetime I enjoyed talking to them, when I found my way to the sea. And so I like the idea that my voice may still reach them after my death. If, in fact, I am dead."

She scratched her bald, pale white head, then she pulled up her hood.

"Some people say that the spheres will protect you. Some people say that they are very powerful, that Mr. Iggs is a mighty wizard. He doesn't look like a mighty wizard; he is a bald, pudgy, serious little man, who most days can be found adding up numbers and balancing his accounts at the warehouse in Xiorian's southern district from whence he ships his spheres throughout Sadlo'reen. Still, not every mighty wizard must look like a mighty wizard. Where is it written that a wizard cannot know how to keep accurate books? I have not made up my mind about the spheres. Some people say they hover a bit, buzz a bit, put on a good show. These people would contend that Mr. Iggs is merely a mighty fraud and conman." Then, apropos of nothing, but perhaps an interesting fact, Madame Tang added, "Iggs' wife, by the way, Yu Dai-Yung, has the power to turn herself into a cloud of butterflies. This is an interesting and sometimes useful skill, although sometimes a bird will eat a few of the butterflies before she can recompose herself. This is not fatal, but it is disorienting."

"I wish I could talk to you," Master Yu whispered. "I wish that I could make you smile again. I hope that you are alive, somewhere, and that in the years since you recorded this message, you have become happy. What is it that made you so unhappy, Madame Tang?"

"Hold this sphere," she said. "Hold this sphere and let a veil descend over your eyes, and see the world that is invisible when your eyes are open. See the way the Red Eyebrows do. I cannot lead the way. All I can do is tell you that, if the sages have chosen you properly, you will be able to see these things."

Master Yu held the sphere; to you, it would look as though his pupils shrank away into nothing and his irises grew hazy and dim, but to him, it felt as though a strange set of translucent eyelids closed over his eyes without his willing it, and he could still see yet clearly; he was still looking out over the black ocean, but now, farther out to sea, he could spot an angry, cold fog that had not been there before, and which blocked out the moonlight. Where the fog touched the water, the ocean surface had begun to freeze over, and within this invisible icy world was a great dark ship, which seemed to be built of rock, and which bobbed impossibly on the ocean waves. Although it was very far in the distance, Master Yu could see every detail as though he were on the ship. He could even see the Captain, who stood at the bow, almost hidden in a black hooded robe. His skin was pale and scaly-rough; his blind eyes were mere slits, but they glowed red; his hands and bare feet were green claws.

"That's him, Sadlo'reen's mad sea captain, the Dark Thief," said Tang. "He is blind, and he is also deaf, but his sense of smell is strong. He has been traveling Sadlo'reen's oceans for a thousand years, and the world freezes with his touch." She paused. "This is another world, Yu Dai-Yung, but like every orbit that exists anywhere in the Otherworld, it is at risk, and the risk is the same. Here in Sadlo'reen, the risk comes through the Dark Thief. In your orbit, it comes through the Sidonians and the Red Eyebrows. But the danger all originates from the same source, a single source."

Madame Tang looked out at the water. Her eyes seemed to settle where the dolphins played blissfully.

"I cannot see these things, Yu Dai-Yung," she whispered. "All I can do is tell you how to look."

CHAPTER 6

After the snowy egret flew away, we left the meadow, and we traveled north into the woods. I followed the oracle's instructions, and when it was yet dusk, we reached the cabin, which was old, sturdy and reassuring, just as she had described, and we tossed our bags inside and tied up our horses. It smelled like an old cabin, which made me as happy as I could be, considering everything. Hester made a fire in the fireplace, and I caught a rabbit in the woods and a fish in the stream, which we roasted over the fire; I ate the rabbit, and Hester ate the fish. When night had fallen, and we had settled in to eat, the storm of which the oracle had warned me finally arrived, a ferocious thunderstorm that shook the world outside, and when Hester remarked that it was lucky that we had found this cabin, I replied that it was lucky that we found the oracle who gave us instructions to the cabin, and Hester said that if she could learn to believe in my ghosts – who had done not a whit for us up till now – then she supposed she could learn to believe in my oracle, who, after all, had found us a warm dry cabin.

One other thing about the cabin:
It had a little glass window, miraculously still intact. When I looked out the window from inside the cabin, I could see, through the storm, a dark silhouette on the horizon, a great grey city of smokestacks and tall, soot-covered buildings. The city was surrounded by a bay, and on the other side of the bay, a green forest cut through by a tumbling river, which was whipped about now by the storm. But when I stepped outside, I could see the grey city no longer. I could see this grey city only from inside the cabin, looking out.
I didn't know how such a thing were possible, or what it meant, and I didn't mention it to Hester, because, as with the oracle, I thought she either wouldn't be able to see what I saw, or she would pretend that she couldn't, and either way, it would result in nothing helpful being accomplished. So I stayed quiet, but I made a point to remember this, in case later it might make some sense.

We lay side by side on the cabin floor, listening to the quiet murmur of the night forest.

"O'Hugh," Hester whispered. "I know how I wound up in this predicament. But how does a man like you end up in the middle of the desert, hiding from the law, without a friend? I thought you'd probably have a rich uncle or two who could find you a lawyer and sort all this out?"

"A rich uncle?" I said. "Not me."

"No one to turn to?"

"I was an orphan," I said.

"In an orphanage?" she asked

"Just a lost, unwashed orphan in the middle of the Five Points slum," I said.

At that time, I told her, the very center of my childhood kingdom was at Worth Street and Park Street, where I lived as a squatter in a great dark and crumbling palace of sprawling squalor, which we nicknamed "the Old Brewery." I never even knew why, or asked. It was as bad, I told her, as she might imagine. Wet and muddy pavement beneath my feet. Street and gutters piled high with garbage. Towering tenements that creaked and trembled as their inhabitants shifted in their filth. The stench of overflowing privies drifting from the interior yards into the street and settling in my pores, on my clothing, coating me like a second skin that I lived in every day.

"But it was also better than you imagine," I added. It was a teeming, ragged neighborhood, I told Hester, but I remember it mostly as teeming with ragged men who loved their wives, and ragged wives who loved their children, and ragged chums who looked out for each other when no one else would. Back then, I had nothing, and I envied everyone.

"Sometimes, in the morning, when I was hungriest, a kindly middle-aged whorehouse Madam named Mrs. Welch would give me a bit of food or a coin or two, if I rapped on the back door. She ran the White Squall Inn (which you may have heard of), and I wished that she could be my mother. How I loved her, because she was a woman of a certain motherly age, and because she smiled at me.

"My old home has since been torn down, and a mission now stands in its place. This, I suppose, is a development for the better. Still, I sometimes wonder where my twelve-hundred-odd neighbors have gone. I haven't seen them since the police nicked me for stealing an apple and sent me away to be rehabilitated through the alleged Grace of our hypothetical Lord. So I got reeducated on Randall's Island, learned to read and write and be a useful member of society."

"You haven't seen or talked to anyone from the old neighborhood?" Hester said. "Not once, in all these years?"

In the 1860s, I told her, back when I was employed as a clerk for New York City, I took a walk south, down to the old neighborhood, thinking everyone would be glad to see me. Just on a sudden whim, and I didn't even bother or think to take off my good tie first. As soon as I set foot on Elm Street, a couple of b'hoys climbed up to the street from a cellar distillery, puffing with the effort. They were thick and tired, staggering, it seemed to me, from the accumulated weight of a day spent drinking rum that wasn't rum, not exactly, and gin that wasn't precisely gin, but which had suitably cracked their skulls open and pummeled their minds pleasantly and painfully.

They blocked my way, and they both made a commendable effort at forming an identically threatening sneer. The fellow on the left was the elder of the two, probably about thirty, though he looked a tired forty. The one on the right was a hobbadehoy not more than fifteen, and he wore a rat-eaten cap too big for his narrow, shrunken head. I could smell it on them, that rum that wasn't rum, and gin that wasn't gin.

"What did they want?" Hester asked me.

"Money, of course, so they could return to the cellar and drink more, or flop for the night on the floor of the cellar next door. It was not impossible that they wanted to steal my money to buy a paltry dinner for their families. They made a couple of mumbled threats that I could not really hear, but the younger of the two held out a knife, so there wasn't much ambiguity in this particular situation. The knife trembled in his left hand, from the so-called booze, I thought, rather than from nervousness."

"Did you fight? Did you run? Or did you tell them who you were?"

"Well, I looked like the man I yearned to become, but not the person I really was, the boy who'd grown up in those very streets and who knew how to respond to a couple of hoods who wished to jump him for money. So who could blame me?"

I didn't even really think about it, I admitted to Hester. I punched the young one in the center of his hungry face, his nose flattened at my touch and burst like an over-ripe tomato; cartilage cracked, and he staggered backwards, howling. I spun about, and I bounced the other guy off a brick tenement wall. Less than a minute after they'd first threatened me, they both lay gasping and bleeding in the street. I ran north, and I figured that I wouldn't visit Elm Street again, at least not if my luck held out.

"And then, after the big stand I took during the Draft Riots, I wasn't the darling of New York's white working class, to say the least, so I didn't ever go back."

"How did you get to the Five Points?" Hester asked me. "Where did you come from?"

I shrugged. I didn't know.

"It was as though I had always been there," I said. "No parents. Not even any name. 'Watt O'Hugh' is a name I made up on Randall's Island when they asked me what my name was. Before that, I didn't even have a name."

I smiled.

"And you, Hester?" I asked.

"And me, what?" she asked.

"Is there nothing interesting to tell about you?"

"Here is my story, then," she said.

Hester was born to two free parents in 1848, in New York city, a family of Knickerbockers since the slave ship *Africain* brought her earliest ancestors from Ghana in 1739, or thereabouts. Her grandparents were indentured, and her parents were free. All four of her grandparents came from the same village back in Africa, and as little children, her parents grew up side by side. When it was time for them to marry, they just married each other, and they loved each other as they were meant to. They bought land in Seneca Village, up in the North of Manhattan, shortly after Hester was born, and she went to the Colored school in the basement of the Village church.

Seneca Village was their Eden, a pretty little hamlet of ex-slave landowners. They grew tomatoes and beans there, and they raised cows, and they were happy.

"Well," she admitted, "children are not *always* happy, I suppose, but that is how I remember those few years. A great, warming happiness that I thought could never end."

Her father was a sailor, and he would return home every six months or so to her mother's smiles and Hester's hugs, bringing back his pay and usually a formidable haul from the trip, sometimes fruit or vegetables for the family to sell, sometimes turkeys. Once even a bull. But in 1855, while her father was at sea, Hester and her family were forcibly evicted from their homes, moved out so the government could build the Central Park, and the police gave her mother a clop on the head with his club as compensation for their house. Their Village emptied out in an afternoon, and destroyed over the following week.

"And then my father's ship just didn't come back," she told me in a whisper, "as though he knew he would no longer have a home to return to. I used to wish that meant that he had deserted us, that he didn't love us anymore, that he and his shipmates had killed their captain and taken to the high seas as pirates. Anything was better than believing that his magnificent life-fire had been extinguished by the sea, which of course is what happened. Thinking of us, he held his breath for as long as he could as he sank beneath the rocky Atlantic Ocean waves, and then at last he breathed seawater into his lungs, and he was no more, and he was never seen again."

When the money ran out, Hester's mother obtained employment in the Fifth Avenue Hotel, and she staggered along without the husband and home she loved for another two years until the tuberculosis took her, and then Hester was all alone. She went to work at the Colored Orphan Asylum on Fifth Avenue as a teacher's helper, and, after the riots, she fled New York altogether. A while later, she made it out West.

"And then a while even later," she said, smiling faintly, finally, "I broke down your unexpectedly flimsy door."

Then she changed the subject quickly, and it wasn't for a long time that I realized that she'd skipped half her life, from fleeing New York in 1863 to breaking down my door in 1878, which was the part of her life she didn't want to talk about, I reckon, and she went on for a while about her plans for the money. She said that even back on the African continent, her ancestors in their local village had already been refugees, expelled thousands of years earlier from a glorious golden kingdom at the far-fabled end of the world, which existed now only in memory and in a scribbled drawing at the very edge of the primitive map scrawled on the wall of their hut, an heirship to which they clung and which they cherished even through a hundred years of captivity in the New World, and upon obtaining their freedom, they looked again to their ancient, treasured homeland, and they continued their planning, as though uninterrupted. Upon the death of her mother and father, Hester was left to carry on the family dream alone, to achieve what had been so close to her parents' hearts, and of which her grandparents, and great-parents, and on and on, had been dreaming for millennia, longing only to travel across the sea with a great army of her fellow dark brethren and retake the golden, magical kingdom. She saw it whenever she shut her eyes to sleep. Even when she shut her eyes just for a moment, just to blink the sun from her eyes – there it was, shining in her imagination.

"And thus," she concluded, almost breathlessly, and smiling as though she realized suddenly that it all made no real sense at all, that all this was more like a particularly vivid fairy tale than a sensible plan for one's life. "I need money to restore a kingdom, and so I am robbing a train."

"I think that maybe the Sidonians were an afterthought for you."

"Yes," she agreed. "A way to convince you to help J.P. Morgan, and hence to convince J.P. Morgan to help me. I would not have cared whether the Sidonians were to rule the world, so long as I were free to live in the kingdom of my ancestors. But by now, your pain is my own, and I hate them as do you."

I am not certain why this did not bother me. But it did not. She had waited for just the right moment to confess that she had tricked me.

I said that her cause seemed an excellent one, and an excellent use of her earnings, though I didn't really understand anything she had said about her age-old quest, but most of what she said just floated a bit in the air and then evaporated in the snug darkness of the little cabin, because all the time that she was speaking, I was picturing myself sitting with Hester by a jungle stream, somewhere in South America.

Morgan returned to his home on Madison Avenue at two o'clock in the morning. I don't know the reason why. Perhaps he had been wandering the streets, hoping for a visit from a dead young woman. Perhaps he had visited a mistress on a tree-lined enclave in Greenwich

Village, on the third floor of the fourth house on the left, and he would now return to his home, pretending (if Fanny were to meet him on the stairs) that he had gone out for a midnight stroll to clear his head, to gather his thoughts on the nation's imminent return to the gold standard. Or perhaps, in truth, he *had* gone out for a midnight stroll to clear his head, and he had honestly spent the entire walk considering the implications of the gold standard. I just don't know. I can imagine all manner of interesting activities for Morgan to be involved in during those early morning hours, from political intrigue to sordid liaisons, but I cannot know everything. And if I were to hazard a reckless guess and present it as fact, that would be doing a disservice to you, my readers, to whom I have promised the truth.

Morgan had just taken off his left shoe and laid it gently in the inner foyer, caked with mud from the rainy night outside, when he heard Louisa crying out from her second floor bedroom. Morgan tossed off his right shoe and bounded up the steps, where he found little brown-haired Louisa – the shy 11-year-old who was his favorite child – shaking and shivering in the dark night. He touched her hand, and she melted into his arms.

Once she had stopped shaking, his daughter lay back in bed, and he put his hand gently on her cool forehead.

He was sweaty and a little bit drunk, and he knew that his little girl could smell the gin on his breath, but he tried to radiate fatherly dignity and balance. She did not seem to mind the gin on his breath, and he realized that this might be a redolence that would remind Louisa pleasantly of her father for many years to come, and that it might be a perfume that she would unconsciously seek out in the man she wished to marry. After a moment, he thought, *well, why not let the poor bastard drink?*

"I'm not frightened," she said, and she tried to shut her eyes.

"It's all right to be frightened," Morgan said gently. "I've been frightened for most of just about every day since I was born." And then a moment later, he wondered whether this was a reassuring thing to tell the little girl, when she was lying in the dark, shivering from a bad dream, hoping to sleep.

"You are frightened?" she said.

He nodded.

"But I will always protect *you*," he added. "There is no reason for *you* to be frightened. Let me worry about things."

"What are you afraid of ?" she asked him.

I fear always saying the wrong thing, he thought to himself, *and doing the wrong thing, and becoming a person I was not meant to be.*

But instead, Morgan shrugged and smiled, and he tousled his little girl's hair.

"Truly," she said. "Are you afraid of ghosts?"

He shook his head.

"I welcome ghosts," he said. "If ghosts are real, then we can see people who are gone, who we would like to see again. Or discover for the very first time."

He met her eyes.

"Don't be afraid of ghosts," he said, "my little Louisa."

She smiled, and she shut her eyes and tried to sleep again.

"You're afraid of dreams," he said.

She nodded, her eyes still shut.

"Dreams are just make-believe," Morgan said. "They are just you, talking to yourself. They are nothing to be afraid of, unless you are afraid of yourself."

He nudged her chin.

"Maybe tell me about it?" he asked. "Tell me about it, and we'll figure it out together."

Then she told the story of her dream, the story of a magical city in a valley surrounded by mountains, a place where all you might wish would come true, a happy land shattered by a war that came and left blood in the meadow.

"And in my dream," she said, in her embarrassed little girl's voice, "there was a young woman who wants to take you away from me. A young woman, just in her twenties, very pretty … and she was walking through the blood stained valley, calling your name."[*]

A haze came to Morgan's eyes.

---

[*] For reasons that should be obvious from this anecdote, Louisa would prove a great help to me and the counter-Revolution during the Battle of Sidonia, around the turn of the 20th Century, and she periodically told me stories about her father meant to soften my generally negative impression of the Great Man. His not-entirely-beastly conduct as a parent was one point she tended to emphasize, which I duly note in these *Memoirs*.

But he blinked it away, and he kissed his favorite child on the forehead.

"What an imagination you have," he whispered gently. "What a vivid imagination."

CHAPTER 7

We all met in Sheriff Wesley's cabin in northern Nevada, just a few miles south of the Idaho border, and a few miles north of the Central Pacific, the target of our planned crime. It was just a lean-to, nothing fancy, and we plotted by lantern light. Wesley was the ringleader. Not really, but he *wanted* to be called the ringleader, so we called him the ringleader. At the first meeting, he said, "I'm basically the ringleader of this operation." And we all nodded. "Ringleader Wesley," I said cheerfully, and I raised my flask in a little informal toast. It was better than calling him Sheriff, which seemed to make him feel guilty and regretful about abandoning and betraying his official duties and his oath of office, and so we called him Ringleader instead. It was important to keep Wesley in good spirits, as he was central to our plan of action.

There were just four men in our gang, plus a few moles scattered throughout the country, and two women, which included Hester and also another woman whose name was Anichka. Anichka was from Khabnoye, a beautiful, 15th century city in Ukraine on the banks of the Uzh River, and how she got out West she wasn't saying, and I knew better than to ask. She was the angry wife of a failed and now not-very-mysteriously deceased gold miner; she was a tough woman, but she knew explosives from her years unsuccessfully blowing rocks out of the ground, so she had a role to play. She was in her early thirties, worn down by the life out here, wiry and muscular, a little weathered, with the crookedest nose I'd ever seen on a woman, and even though I could barely understand a word she said, she had enough dash-fire in her to join our outlaw gang. (Plus, as I have said, she knew explosives. I just had to picture her husband's body blown up into the clouds and through a couple of neighboring territories to see the value she could add, and I hoped she could do the same to the train's safe, and maybe to any Sidonians who might get in her way.)

Hester outlined the division of spoils, and she briefly explained the Chapman method of train robbery, named for John T. Chapman, a Sunday school teacher who remained particularly humane when he turned to train robbery (nabbing $40,000 from an express car near Verdi), which was the main reason that Anichka had little use for him. A secondary reason for her contempt was that Chapman had failed to steer clear of prison. So he had a "method" to his name, but neither a red cent nor his freedom. Anichka preferred the "wrecking method," which doesn't require much explanation on my part, but Hester explained that the wrecking method probably involved killing people, which had the drawback of possibly killing the poor sap who knew the combination.

I stayed quiet. I was with Anichka on this one. I hated the train and everyone on it, and I wanted to kill not only every Sidonian aboard, but I wanted to kill the train. Only my ghosts, and their help and loyalty and their moral compass, would hold me back when the moment arrived. But I truly hated it, this dark train from my city of death. I stayed quiet. Maybe Hester knew anyway.

Anichka sneered, but that seemed to be the end of that for her, at least for a while. Hester described only as much of the plan as she considered absolutely necessary to reveal. We memorized our roles, adjourned, and we all walked out of Wesley's cabin into a night thick with humidity, danger and intrigue, and we rode our steeds in opposite directions, vanishing into the moonless darkness.

The next day, Hester rode into Reno, which at the time was a small, remote railroad town. She crossed the tracks, and then she rode up Commercial Row, past Reno Mercantile, The Wine House, The Oberon, and The Palace. At the end of the short street of brick and wood framed businesses, she stopped at a small hotel with a "room available" sign in the window, took a cheap room in the back, where she waited for word of the shipment.

Because I remained a wanted criminal, we both figured that I should avoid the city, and so I set up camp in the woods just to the North and tried to keep out of sight. I hunted rabbits and deer, occasionally even killed one, and roasted it over an open flame at night when the stars came out. A week later, after a visit to the market across Commercial Row from her hotel, Hester mounted her horse and galloped out of Reno to my little campsite. She brought me some coffee, a little whiskey (enough to stave off a full detoxification, with all the side effects that would likely entail, but not enough to fully satisfy my addiction, though I understood why she intended to limit my imbibing), some bread, vegetables and potatoes, a passable supply of dried meat. It was good to see her. We sat by the fire and watched the embers burn down, and we talked almost until dawn. Then she mounted her horse and rode back to Reno, and I fell asleep as the hot sun rose. After that, when Hester brought me supplies, she spoke little and stayed briefly. And so our life went, until one day three weeks later, Mr. Stanton Hugson, a clerk in San Francisco who worked for the Wells, Fargo company, skipped his lunch and ran across the street to meet Fenton Derby, a young man with whom Mr. Hugson would never be publicly associated, and to whom no connection would ever be drawn. (This was because Mr. Hugson and Mr. Derby were in love, and from the moment of their first meeting to the last, would never admit to knowing each other, even tangentially.) Stanton Hugson was tall and dark, smooth and elegant, and Fenton Derby was slender and excitable, with blazing red hair, pale blue eyes, and pretty red lips; thus, not only did they complement each other physically, but Mr. Derby would never be mistaken for Mr. Hugson, which was important to our scheme.

Mr. Hugson slipped Mr. Derby a heavily coded note as they passed each other in front of a little restaurant with yellow curtains in the window, which stood on the corner of Halleck and Sansome Streets. Each continued on his way, respective face flushed, respective heart pounding, Mr. Hugson walking Southwest to the Wells Fargo office at Post and Montgomery Streets, and Mr. Derby marching East to the telegraph office on Battery Street, where he wired Hester Smith an unnecessarily passionate love letter, which between the ardent sentiments contained in code the precise schedule of the treasure train from San Francisco, which carried a million dollars in gold shipment from the northern Sidonian mine, as well as (allegedly) the ancient secret of the Red Eyebrows.

Hester received the cable at her hotel room in Reno. The purplier passages of the message raised goose bumps on her skin, from her neck to her ankles, and for a moment she was swept up in the artificial drama, but then she calmed herself down, left the hotel without indicating anything amiss to the clerk, and she rode out of town, to my campsite, where I was asleep in the lingering heat of the day, under a tree.

On their way out of Dawsey, Allen Jerome and Darryl Fawley stopped in the town's only grub-shop, a little place off Flatt Street.

The body odors of the farmers mingled with the smell of overcooked steak and deliciously fresh eggs. Allen Jerome stuck a fork in the steak and scowled. Darryl Fawley, in his wrinkled suit, with its built-in dust, seemed to belong here; the well-groomed Allen Jerome did not.

"I wouldn't shoot a baby in the head," Darryl Fawley said. "For the Cause, I mean. Or for any reason. I would not set fire to a house with a family inside."

Allen Jerome ignored this remark. He already knew this, and Darryl Fawley knew that he knew it.

"I'm a mathematician by training, and a failed mathematician by circumstance," Allen Jerome sighed. "My specialty in academia was geometrically knotted non-closed curves, and on Wall Street my specialty was pretending that the trading models I designed actually worked, although all the while doing little more than bribe people for information. Do you believe that my trading models predicted that I should sell all my gold on September 23, 1869, because the next day the Treasury Secretary would announce sales of federal gold that would deflate the price and inevitably destroy the fortunes of bankers all over Wall Street? That's quite a sophisticated financial trading model."

"Stupid it down' to my level, Allen."

In mathematics, Allen Jerome told his colleague, 1 plus 1 equals two. Everything on one side of the equal sign equals everything on the other side of the equal sign. On Wall Street, the numbers to the right of the equal sign must be greater.

"Have you heard the sad tale of Mr. Quilford," Allen Jerome asked, "and his red rubber bouncing balls?"

Darryl Fawley said that he had.

(I imagine even you, faithful reader, have heard of Mr. Quilford's scandal.)

Mr. Quilford invented the finest red bouncing ball in the world. In its first twelve months on the market – 1861 was the precise year – every boy and girl in America who could afford it purchased Mr. Q's red rubber bouncing ball. With proper care, it would last three years. When a child grew too old to appreciate a fine rubber bouncing ball, he gave it away to his younger sibling. Every three years, sales would bounce (so to speak) then fall for two years. Mr.

Quilford found himself celebrated, then reviled, then celebrated again. Every third year, his stock price would rise, then it would fall.

When the stock fell for the third time, investors did not merely castigate him, they had him murdered, or so it was said. His body was found in the Hudson River in the wintertime, pleasantly well-preserved.

A holding company structured by Jeremiah G. Hamilton and his attorneys leased the trademark of The Quilford Red Rubber Bouncing Ball Company Incorporated, and the consortium continued to sell Quilford-branded bouncing balls. But they replaced Mr. Quilford's original design with one that did not bounce quite as magnificently but which could be constructed more cheaply. Investors saw a return at last. The company grew, and it swallowed other small entrepreneurs (who were happy to sell and retire to lives of tea in the garden), and the Hamilton toy consortium grew more.

"That's what we're looking for, when you get down to brass tacks," Allen Jerome said. "Growth. What we would call a 'return' if this were just business. If we sit in our little Montana valley enjoying the good life and do not grow, conquer more territory, win more adherents – if we focus on preservation of capital that is – we die as a movement. Eventually, the J.P. Morgans of the world will kill us and swallow us up, as they did to Mr. Quilford. They will replace us with a Coney Island version of Sidonia, and we will be frozen in the river. Mathematics creates life, and finance keeps you alive."

He tapped his colleague on the forehead, and Darryl Fawley flinched.

"So like my hero Jeremiah G. Hamilton," Allen Jerome said, "I am always thinking about return. A cheaper bouncing ball. One that is redder. One that is slightly bigger?" He was scribbling on a sheet of paper, which he eventually showed to his colleague. It was filled with numbers, and surrounded by a graph, which showed a parabola curve.

"To get our return this high," he said, indicating the highest point of the parabola, "and to keep our return from declining to here," and he indicated the lowest point of the parabola, "two elements are missing. The element of a martyr, which we have discussed. Lucy is not our martyr, as she was killed by Sidonia." He smiled sadly. "And I don't wish for the martyrdom of anyone. I love life too much."

At this he laughed, and Fawley fidgeted with his silverware.

"Lucy loved it that you stole J.P. Morgan's money," Fawley said. "You know that? I think I won Lucy's affection because of you. Because you stole money from a capitalist monster and intended to give it to the people, rather than bask in the adulation of society's gold-plated kings and queens. She didn't think you were without human worth."

Allen Jerome seemed not to have heard this, and he continued.

"Our curve inevitably therefore will not reach as high as it would if we had a martyr. We will do without a martyr." He put his finger to his lips. "But there is a sexual element here that is missing, that according to these calculations is holding down the growth of the movement and the commitment of the people. Not a lack of the act itself, which is available in Sidonia around every bend. But something unattainable. Something to yearn for, to love from afar."

Sidonia needed a princess, Allen Jerome concluded. A fearsome warrior princess with red hair, long legs, and a terrifying battle cry.

And she must of course be beautiful.

"We could have had a queen," Darryl Fawley said. "We could have had a beautiful queen who would have fought for the downtrodden with her last breath. A beautiful Sidonian queen."

Allen Jerome agreed.

"Yes," he said. "We could have had a wondrous queen, indeed. A queen can be loved; but a princess can be loved in an entirely different fashion. You are allowed to gaze upon your princess and wish that you could marry her, and to think about what such a thing might be like. That is what drives your loyalty in battle."

"When does it end?" Darryl Fawley asked.

"November 1918," Jerome said. Then he thought a little more. "Maybe October, or December. Perhaps 1919. Perhaps a delay until 1936 or 1937. Thereabouts."

"And then the Falsturm is triumphant. And what happens then?"

"He conquers other Otherworlds. And then other Otherworlds."

"And when he has conquered every Otherworld there is?"

"He sends agents through his weirs to fabricate more Otherworlds, and then more. There is no such thing as everything. We are stewards of an ever-growing stock market, Darryl. It never ends."

Allen Jerome took a hesitant taste of the coffee in the dirty mug. He winced. When Sidonia arrived in earnest into this little town, much would change, some of it for the better, some of it for the worse. While not everything could be predicted with absolute accuracy, the coffee would improve.

CHAPTER 8

"You ever think about death, Hester?" I asked, with the campfire embers burning out in the night, and Hester laughed, and she said, "No, O'Hugh. I've never thought about death. Not a once." I nodded, and I remarked, "Well, I hope we don't die to-morrow," and Hester said she reckoned that she agreed with that sentiment. I held up my bottle and said, "Here's to not dying," and Hester apparently could wait no longer, and she quickly blurted out, almost as though it were one word: "Watt O'Hugh, I was a young woman fifteen years ago, and I was there in New York on that day in 1863 that neither one of us will ever forget, and I saw you brave that monstrous drunken crowd. I know the children you saved. More to the point, I know the ones you tried to save and couldn't save, and they were the finest children I ever had the pleasure of meeting, and if it's true that they're your ghosts, then I know that they will not let us down to-morrow. I know your ghosts, Watt, and I love them, too."

I sat silently for a while, and then Hester wrapped her arms around me, and we fell asleep like that, listening to the sound of the wind just whistling and hissing in the night. We slept for a while, and then around two in the morning, I woke up. I figure that Hester had been awake for a while. The fire was just a haze of barely, gently glowing ashes now, and Hester was smiling up at me, with that hopeful look in her eyes. And there you have it. I am constrained by the gentlemanly code of the late 1930s (as well as the racial one) from continuing on in any great detail, except to muse that the stars might have been to blame, that starry clear moonless Nevada night, or maybe the terrifying and exhilarating fact that we were about to die or get rich. Maybe we just couldn't sleep, and so we had some time to kill. But I think it was Hester's smile. All that randy business took till about 3 in the morning, and I didn't have any time to think about what it meant or why it had happened, because I needed to get word to Wesley before sunrise. I rode into Pyeton, and I just made an appearance in the grub shop where Wesley ate breakfast. That was all it took, that was my code: I just needed to make an appearance and order some coffee, using my special ordering coffee code, just to be safe. Within earshot of Ringleader Wesley, I asked for the slop "with three lumps, and black as tar." Wesley heard, and the scheme was one step closer to success or failure, and I was one step closer either to riches or a more permanent sort of death than any I had experienced previously.

I drank my slop, left the grub shop, mounted my horse and trotted out of Pyeton.

I returned to my campsite, to the dead fire, and to Hester, who had recently woken and was finishing her coffee. She smiled that smile at me, and this time, though it was maybe the last time I would see it, her smile was a little restrained and scared. She asked me for all my liquor, and so I emptied my pockets and then my saddlebag. I guessed Hester's behavior was for the best, though I was sorry to see the liquor leave camp, being as how I had a whole empty day ahead of me. She rummaged around in the bag and found one more, which she also confiscated. I said to her that I supposed we'd have a little sniff to celebrate once we were rich. She nodded with a little worried cheerfulness, and she handed me a pocket watch and told me not to lose it. I held it in my left hand. It was a cheap one. Hester kissed me goodbye, ruffled my hair fondly, mounted her horse and rode off without another word.

So I sat around by the dead ashes till a little before nightfall, reading my dime novels, concentrating to-day on a couple of romantic ones that had somehow wound up in my personal library and ignoring the violent ones, which to-day would hit too close to home. I wondered if I would need to kill anyone. If the train reached New York, all would be lost. The men who had let Lucy Billings die would be triumphant; they would dine on caviar in the New York taverns and kiss the New York maidens till dawn, dancing on Lucy's metaphoric grave. I hated this train, and I hated all aboard, and I wished them dead, and I wished that I could justify killing them. Something had fundamentally changed inside me since the range war in Lervine, when I'd happily let my adversaries escape my bullets. Lucy's death had made me an angry, ruthless soldier in the battle against Sidonia, and only my ghosts could hold me back now.

As sunset approached I galloped out in the direction of Pyeton. I tied up my horse in a little thicket of trees a few meters back of the train tracks and settled into the bushes.

And there it was, coming around the bend, my fate, with its bells clanging in the quiet night; it was a grand train approaching, two express cars, baggage car, mail car, smoker, day cars, and then two Pullman cars and the caboose. The train was a lumbering and dirty blur of steam and smoke.

I waited till the train got to the slow spot – the steep four mile ascent that led to Pyeton, where the train would slow to a crawl – then I crept out of the night, whispered, *"Damn you, train,"* but was otherwise silent as I hopped stealthily onto the blind baggage platform at the front of the express car, and I waited.

Nothing seemed unusual to anyone on this cursed, evil train. The passengers slept in the Pullman cars. The engineer, in the express car, sat by the cannonball stove, staring out into the starry blackness. He was a heavy, older man, a Sidonia veteran, an adherent from the very beginning. The fireman, sitting up front in the locomotive, fed spruce logs into the boiler, relaxed and happy in the moonlight.

Black smoke billowed. And while I waited, and while the engineer stared, and the fireman fed the blaze, Sheriff Wesley was in the Pyeton train station house with a hat pulled over his head, a kerchief over his face and a gun trained on a terrified young station agent named Fiskher Pike. Pike was bound and gagged, his cap pulled down over his eyes. The sheriff was cutting the telegraph wires.

Pike was not supposed to be there that night; the station agent that night was intended to be Pike's apprentice, a man with whom the sheriff was less acquainted, but instead the apprentice spent the night under a pile of wool blankets, shivering with fever, and Pike trudged the five miles to the station from his home just outside Pyeton to spend a second shift with the trains.

Sheriff Wesley had been to Pike's wedding, had celebrated the birth of Pike's baby daughter, had offered condolences and comfort upon the untimely death of Pike's homely and loving wife, Eileen.

This was nothing personal.

It was just that Sheriff Wesley could use some money. And Fiskher Pike would never believe that the man holding the gun was a dear friend. The sheriff prayed that Pike wouldn't try anything heroic, something for which a true outlaw would have shot him, because

Sheriff Wesley would not, could not, even try to bring himself to shoot Fiskher Pike, and the plan would fail. Sheriff Wesley would not be rich. He would be poor. His name would be tainted, poisoned, forever. He would be imprisoned. And so he prayed that his good friend Fiskher Pike would let him bind him, that Fiskher Pike would prove himself a coward.

At that moment, the train was still slogging up the hill, the wind barely riffling my hair; we'd gone two slow miles since the ascent began, and we were still three miles from Pyeton, and I finally spotted the red warning lantern on the track, a signal to the engineer to stop, that there was danger ahead.

As indeed there was.

The fireman summoned the engineer from the express car, and the engineer blew his whistle, acknowledging the warning. He braked, and the train slowly squealed to an uncertain, wobbly halt, till it eventually sat immobile on the track.

Two hundred feet ahead of us, and two hundred feet behind us, Anichka's giant powder cartridges exploded, mangling the tracks, making escape impossible, but hurting no one, to Anichka's terrible chagrin.

I tied a kerchief over my own face, climbed over the tender and captured the engineer and fireman without much fuss. Hester and Anichka bounded from the hills into the car moments behind me, similarly disguised. A random passenger charged at Hester, she slammed his head against the wall, and he slumped to the floor, generally unharmed but thoroughly chastised.

Two cars back was the day car, rows of seats for the passengers accompanying the load to New York, and some Sidonians traveling to New York to plead their Cause to friends and relatives back home. Behind that were the two Pullman sleeper cars. Outside, two of Wesley's men rode back and forth on horseback alongside the train's passenger cars, firing shots randomly in the air and working the passengers into a state of panic.

Hester nodded to me.

"We'll blow the safe," she said. "You check for the guards."

So that's what I did.

Here, as elsewhere in these *Memoirs*, you may pick up certain clues that should convince you that my story is true. While in your world, my friends of the 20th or the 21st century, it will be unremarkable for a Colored g'hal to employ and even order around a white man, it was a definite unknown in my era, and I suppose a humiliation of a certain consequence, and so if I were making this story up, I suppose I would put myself at the center of the operation. I would have brilliant ideas. I would yell at folk. Other people would nearly bungle the job, and I would save the day, the way I allegedly did back in Little Mount.[*] I would make a few cleverish comments that would sound good in the "action movie" that these *Memoirs* would then inevitably become.

But I am telling you no such thing. Plans were formulated while I was out of earshot. Events moved around and through me. I took orders. I did as I was told. *Ergo* (as the philosophers say at Harvard), my tale is true.

On Hester's command, a .45 in my left hand, and another in my right, I kicked through the door of the sleeper, a long narrow corridor with curtains on each side. I made a few remarks in an improvised Irish accent that I gurgled through my kerchief, telling them how no one would be hurt if no one tried to be a hero (the standard clichés, and even back then they weren't new) and I told everyone to open up their curtains and step out with their hands up, but before I could think about the curtains and the bleary-eyed, frightened and confused passengers behind those curtains, two guards burst into the sleeper car, one from the back door, one from the front. One was tall, one was a little short, one was fully dressed, one in white pajama gown, one with long hair and a mustache (all of it brown and beautifully coiffed), and the other almost hairless, but they shared one trait in common, which was that they were both firing at me from close range and reloading quickly, which seemed to leave me little choice but to depart the living world without further delay.

Then a protective shroud descended over me like a warm blanket, and I felt no fear. The wind outside ceased howling. The bullets slowed to a slow slither, and I ducked each one with a tight, nervous smile as it fluttered past me like a moth, like a soft downy

---

[*] If you have come across the first volume of my *Memoirs*, you recall mention of my reputedly "heroic" actions in Little Mount, trumped up tales published by credulous yellow journalists, which had the happy effect of making me a minor but noted Western icon and dime novel hero, before my undeserved fall from grace.

chickadee. Utterly powerless, the guards stopped wasting their bullets. Each stood helpless and frozen motionless, and they waited for death.

So apparently my cause was just. As I have noted, my ghosts sometimes neglect me in times of need, but they have an innate sense of justice that I can feel in the air when they've visited me. One ghost patted me on the small of my back. Her touch dissolved in the air like a drop of dew.

I called out to the gunmen that I didn't want to kill anyone. This was a lie; I wanted to kill the gunmen just because of their association with Darryl Fawley, who had done the unspeakable. I hated this train, and I hated everyone onboard it, and I hated and wished to kill these gunmen. But I thought of my ghosts, and I felt them near me. And so I took a breath, I forced my hatred to subside, and I gestured to the gunmen to approach.

"I don't like killing folk," I said, when they were near. "You've both likely got families that love you, and if you don't, then anyway I know you've got skulls that'll hurt if bullets crack them open and lodge in your brains, and I don't want to do that to a fellow."

They gave me their guns. I didn't know who they were, what they knew, why they'd come to Sidonia, and I supposed that letting them live was the right thing to do. *Bigger fish to fry*, and all that.

I heard a tremendous explosion, and when I arrived at the express car with the guards, I found Hester and Anichka staring at the solid iron safe with no little chagrin. They'd shot their way through the messenger's barricade, subdued him, packed the safe with dynamite and set it off, but in spite of all this, when they'd returned to the car after the explosion, the safe had ne'er a scratch.

Anichka touched the safe.

"I told you," she said to Hester. "This is not any safe. The material is from Otherworld. It's an Otherworld metal."

"Maybe you just couldn't blow the safe."

Anichka pretended to consider this, but I think she was really trying to calm her temper. At last, she said, "I can blow any safe. I can blow anything up. This is an Otherworld metal. And why not?"

Anichka was suddenly superfluous to our mission, and she knew it. No matter what happened now, whether we succeeded or failed, it would have nothing to do with her. She was here to blow a safe, and this was the one safe she could not blow, and so we no longer needed her. Any gold she might earn from this mission would be naught but charity. And I think that realization had much to do with what was to come next.

The two women turned to the messenger. He was a wiry and agitated young man, a bouncing toy of a man, certain of extinction, resigned to it, welcoming it. *Why should to-day be any better?* his voice said, without saying it.

"You're mad," he told the two women. "Any good train robber needs to know these things are locked at the point of origination. The messenger isn't privy to the combination."

Hester put one sawed-off double-barreled shotgun to his head, but this didn't seem to frighten him very much, and I couldn't blame him. Hester didn't seem the sort of person who would blow out a fellow's brains, mess up an express car, all for nothing. Brains on the ground wouldn't be able to remember a safe combination any better than brains in a fellow's head. So Anichka put a gun to his head, and while this scared him plenty, he still insisted he didn't know the combination.

"This being the point," he said. "If Jay Gould gives the combination to a messenger, then train robbers can break in, put a gun to his head, get the combination, and abscond with Gould's gold. Don't give the combination to the messenger, then maybe the messenger dies, but Gould keeps his gold."

Sweat broke out on his forehead.

"A good plan," Anichka said, with a little angry smile, "if you're Gould. If you're the messenger, not such a good plan." Her accent was thick as fish solyanko.

What I didn't know, Anichka didn't know, and Hester didn't know, was that there was a third guard who had held back when the first two attacked me, a fellow who looked like a combination between the others – pajama shirt with pantaloons, balding head and full gray beard – and he took that moment (our failure, our gloom) to attack, to swing into the room, where he fired point-blank at me, and then lifted his rifle to shoot at Hester, who stood by the safe.

The bullet he shot at me zigged then zagged then changed direction and blasted a hole in the ceiling. Stars shined down on us, and a little sliver of moon, and the safe glowed.

During the half second between the guard shooting at me and shooting at Hester, Anichka – the superfluous explosives-expert Anichka – stepped between them and charged. I imagine she figured that either she would die or we all would die, and why shouldn't it just be her? She had become, after all, superfluous. The bullet meant for Hester tore out Anichka's left lung as she flung herself at the guard. The two of them plunged off the train, skimmed along the dusty ground for a moment, then blasted skyward, exploding into the glowing noctilucent clouds like fireworks in the night, streaming and screaming red and blue flames that lit the world for a few moments, melted into the clouds and drifted away over the mountains, just smoke and sparks, and bits of hair and bone, floating on the breezes, as, I imagine, Anichka had always wanted to die, and though her ragged and scorched flesh thudded clumsily to earth in a thousand heaps that clung to the blood and corpuscles of a train guard whose name she didn't even know, the high celestial wind currents mixed bits of her ashes in the empyrean sphere with the ashes of her husband, whom she once loved, whom she still loved, and whom she had killed, and together their ashes would orbit the earth, forever.

CHAPTER 9

This was a predicament, and I felt my dreams of riches melting away in the muggy night, even as I mourned Anichka, a woman I'd never liked – a woman no one had ever liked – but who had been filled with the sort of crazy anger that could become valiant selflessness at the very end.

We were silent, just staring at the empty space where Anichka had stood just a moment ago.

Then a voice, not my own, spoke to me, inside my head, and my hopes rose.

It was a young woman's voice, strong, affectionate, gently taunting. *His brain needs some loosening*, she said, in my mind, a little breathy.

I recognized that voice well, even now, years later, years after she'd promised to forget me, to live thousands of years without me and to forget me forever. Such a voice, a memory from my last moments of optimism, back when happiness had still seemed a possibility. Emelina! my beloved sharp-shooter, the star of my short-lived (but, I must insist, magnificent) Wild West show, practitioner of the somewhat Dark Arts and apparently immortal revenant. My breath caught. My heart thumped, hopeful, happy. My world, as I like to say (and as I've said before), *whirled.*

"Emelina," I said, out-loud.

And then she was there, strolling casually into the express car like a passenger looking for another cup of coffee. Emelina, with her blazing red hair, skin now freckled from years under the Western sun. She smiled. She radiated strength, more strength than most men.

She held her fingers up to the messenger's temples. He shut his eyes. She let her forehead touch his, and she shut her eyes too, in concentration. She let her lips touch his. He sighed, relaxed. He returned her kiss, emphatically, his eyes still shut.

Emelina came up for air. She released him and turned to me, and she winked.

I looked at her with disappointment.

Was that really necessary? I wondered, without speaking.

Emelina replied inside my head.

It opened up his thoughts, she insisted, *massaged his brain, got the neurons flowing, the synapses twanging. And wait'll you see what I found.*

We followed Emelina. She sauntered between the train cars, aggressively, dramatically nonchalant, and she stopped in the second Pullman. She pulled the third curtain on the left. A man was sitting on the edge of his bed, reading the newspaper, a suspicious behavior, come to think of it, when the appropriate activity was to be screaming in panic. He was fully dressed and even wearing a big dipper hat, which he'd pulled down over his face.

Emelina knocked off the big dipper hat, and she yanked him to his feet.

He was a tall, strong man in his early forties, with a broad beard, angry dark eyes, and a wide forehead. He looked at me sternly, and I felt that I was about to receive a real grammar school dressing down, a strict talking-to, that this hijacking was a terrible waste of his time, and didn't I know who he was? And so before he had a chance to say any of that, I stuck my .45 right in his nose and dared him.

The man sighed, and he kept quiet.

Emelina laughed.

"May I introduce to you, Mr. Watt O'Hugh," she said, "the esteemed banker and evil Sidonian sympathizer, Mr. Jay Gould."

Well, you might not be surprised to learn that Mr. Gould had access to the combination, and after that the operation was like melting butter in the desert sun. We opened the safe, and there was the gold, served up like a great refreshing bowl of delicious, shimmering custard, and sitting on top of the pile of gold was a scroll. I took the scroll, and I unrolled it, and at the very top of the scroll was this: 赤眉. I didn't know what it meant, but I could guess. The scroll went on in that vein; a lot of other stuff I didn't understand, and this time I couldn't really guess.

I looked up. Emelina smiled: a smile of farewell on that tough, beautiful face, once again.

Did we really fly? I asked her, just thinking the words, knowing she would hear them. *Did we really fly into the clouds, or was it a dream?*

She nodded, very lightly, so no one else could notice.

We flew into the clouds, Watt O'Hugh the Third. We flew into the clouds and stayed there for a lifetime. Then we came back to Earth.

It was real.

And then she was gone, not even a shadow left, not even a whiff of her breath, as though she had been a fever vision.

As I have mentioned to you, I am now an old man, and I know beyond any real dispute that I will die very soon, so I hope that you won't mind if I wrap up this chapter of my adventures quickly, seeing as how I've given you the highlights in some detail. We retrieved the gold and even found other valuables – watches and diamond bracelets, pendants and whatnot. We put blindfolds on everyone aboard and tied them up. I was good with knots, and so was Hester.

We divided up the spoils. Hester and I loaded up our wagon with gold and Jay Gould. And we all went in different directions.

We rode for a while on the wagon, Jay Gould blindfolded. After a while, the robber baron skunk started offering us all kinds of things, riches and mansions and trips overseas, if we would just let him go, deliver him to his front doorstep. He'd give the orders. With just a couple of words from him, anything we wanted would be ours. Hester and I would be treated as royalty wherever we went, if we would just show a touch of compassion this fine evening.

"Gold worth more than the value of what you've taken tonight," he said.

I pointed out that upon obtaining his freedom, he'd have us arrested off-the-reel, and he swore that he wouldn't.

"A deal is a deal," he said, and he gave me a weak and blind approximation of a smile. "I am a man of honor."

"A contract made under duress," said Hester, "is unenforceable, even for a man of honor."

I suppose I didn't really mind that he was a ruthless millionaire with his sights set on world domination who had cast his lot with a demonic fascist Utopian movement that sought to enslave our universe and maybe others as well with the assistance of a two-thousand-year-old deck of trick cards. After all, that was his job. Just as, at one time, it had been my job as a Union soldier to kill

Confederate soldiers, young men who were probably very nice, if one got to know them. So we all had our jobs. But it vexed me that he thought me so stupid that I'd trust his promises at a time like this, and so I told him to shut up or I'd shoot him.

"Listen, listen," he said. "Why can't I at least take off my blindfold?" and I said because we didn't want him to see where we were going or who we were, and if he bothered me any more I'd shoot him. He muttered harrumphingly that this was "an affront to common decency," and a few other such pompous, upper-classy type sentiments, just to show he wasn't afraid of me, I suppose, but subsequently he stayed mostly quiet.

After a while, he seemed to sleep, or to pass out.

"He knows Allen Jerome from Black Friday, back in '69," Hester whispered to me. "The two of them made a killing on the gold market when the rest of America imploded more than a little bit, before America imploded for good and forever in 1873. But not Mr. Gould. Now he and Allen Jerome are trying to convince the common man to support the Sidonians, and the common man wants someplace to channel his anger."

"What will we do with him?" I asked.

"Drop him off with a couple of settlers," she whispered. "We've got a lead. I'll explain later. But the short story is that settlers around here love train robbers. Their lives have been so destroyed by the power of the railroads that they'll do anything to hurt the robber barons."

When the sun looked about ready to rise, we pulled up to a little settler cabin, where a cheerful, bone-thin couple in their mid-forties were ready to hide us for the day. There was a thin soup cooking. The cabin was clean and spare. The man swept the floor and opened up a cellar door, and he tossed Gould in. The railroad baron rolled down the cellar stairs with several terrible thunks.

"In a few days, or maybe a few weeks, when the trail goes completely cold," Hester said, "some men will come to get the gold. They will have a password. They will also collect Jay Gould at that time."

Hester gave the man two gold pieces, and she gave the woman two gold pieces.

"I know we can trust you," she added, "but I have to note that if you try to abscond with the gold, you won't get away. But you will be richly rewarded for your small role in this little adventure. Of course, keep Mr. Gould healthy."

"I don't think we'll kill him," the man said. "We'll torture him a little. Maybe cut off a finger. Then let him go."

"No finger chopping," Hester said very quietly, making sure Gould, down in the cellar, could not hear her. She wanted Gould frightened that he might lose a finger. She wanted him so frightened that he would leave the Sidonian movement forever. She wanted him good and frightened, but she didn't approve of finger-chopping, just out of principle, no matter the choppee.

Around this time, the engineer and the two surviving train guards wriggled out of their ropes, took off their blindfolds and followed the train tracks to the Pyeton station, where they expected to wire for help, but instead found the cables cut, and the station agent sleeping on the floor, still bound and gagged. So they woke him up, unbound him and ungagged him, and together they all walked into town and, as the sun rose, they summoned the sheriff. Sheriff Wesley dutifully got out of bed, where he was just finishing up what he called "a good, full night of shut-eye, out cold since 10 p.m. last night," rode into town and listened to their story as he drank his terrible coffee in his favorite slop-house. He mused that it would take some time to gather a posse, what with the holiday just ending a day ago, and most citizens still nursing a hangover from the festivities.

"These ruffians," he said. "It sounds like they knew what they were doing. Sounds like a smart bunch, and a dangerous one. It'll be hard to find men willing to go up against a crew such as that one, even without our great celebration just ending – " and here he went on at some length about this tremendous, strenuous holiday that the town had declared this year, for the very first time – "so you *almost* have to admire them." This last bit he said with a little foolish pride evident in his voice, were one to listen for it. Still, he dutifully and carefully raised a posse willing to assist in the righting of such a terrible wrong. A few hours later, the sheriff and the posse all rode out to the scene of the crime, where they freed the remaining passengers, and where the sheriff claimed to find some tracks, that, as it happened, went in exactly the wrong direction. He then led the whole gang off on a merry adventure.

"What do you know?" he marveled, as they stood at the foot of a scrubby and lost Joshua tree. "The trail ends. Just like that. As though they ascended to heaven. Or," he added ominously, "descended into Hell, more like it." He shook his head with surprise and awe. Still, he said, the train robbers probably had some help, and it would make sense to ask around, maybe search a few local homesteads. He promised a thorough search, although Sheriff Wesley knew which one to skip.

And by then, we were well on our way to South America, Hester and I.

We rode west and stopped a few miles inland, a hundred miles south of Pomo, where towering redwoods shrouded a narrow, secluded inlet that glittered green in the moonlight. Some forty-five minutes later, a small boat appeared, helmed by a serious and sturdy young man, who bid us embark without pleasantries. We three rowed together till we rendezvoused with an 18th century brigantine just off the coast, hidden from easy view of the central mainland by the cliff hindering the shoreline. It was a two-masted sailing ship, with holes for cannons, and a wooden carving of a naked woman's torso at the bow for inspiration, a pirate ship (and a naked torso) genuine enough to thrill any eight-year-old boy you'd ever happen to meet.

I pointed out to Hester that the golden era of piracy ended in the early 19th century, but she explained that they were small-time maritime smugglers and petty outlaws who had somehow acquired an indisputably fizzing ship, and who liked to play pirate. It gave their endeavor a romantic flair and a certain nostalgic aesthetic. Without the pirate angle they were just a gang of wanted crooks, but with it they were artists.

There's not much more to tell about our trip south, except to note that the pirates were highly disreputable characters, murderers, thieves and rapists and that, to my chagrin, they seemed to have a great admiration for Hester and me.

I will relate another thing about the pirates that you may find hard to believe: one of the pirates had a wooden leg; one of them had a black patch over a dead eye; and one of them had a parrot on his shoulder.

When we were finally alone, standing on the deck of the brig and watching the forested coast recede into memory, Hester turned to me, took my arm in hers.

"The ghosts approved of our endeavor, I note. They found our cause just, and they saved our lives."

I said they had.

"Did you doubt me?" she asked. "Did you doubt the justice of our cause?"

I admitted that I had, from time to time.

"You mostly doubted me, or mostly trusted me?"

I shrugged. I didn't know. Once she'd led Rasháh to my doorstep and wrecked my cabin, I'd really had no choice but to rob a train with her. At the time, my decision had not really rested on whether or not I thought I would survive it, though in retrospect I was glad that I had, and even gladder that I was now rich.

The ocean was dark black. The sky overhead was thick with angry clouds.

"That Emelina," she said with a nonjudgmental smile. "Quite the *kusit*. She's one of yours, I gather."

I nodded.

"She just vanished," Hester said, nonchalantly. "She was there one moment on the train, and then she wasn't. She didn't disembark. She just wasn't on the train anymore."

"That's right," I said.

"One doesn't see that every day," Hester remarked.

I disagreed.

"I do see that kind of thing every day," I said, as the water swelled up around the stern side, and the ship slipped a bit under our feet.

A hawk cried out in the dark sky.

"Every single day. Women vanishing into thin air. The dead rising from the ground. I would that it warn't so. But it is. If you want to tarry with me, Hester my darling, you'll have to get used to it."

CHAPTER 10

I know very little about the next month of Master Yu's life in San Francisco, just that he practiced seeing the world without looking at the world, as Madame Tang had advised, and that he did not move out of his hovel in the Chinatown cellar. He bought a pair of dark tinted glasses and walked through the city during the day, looking out through the second set of eyes in his head, his physical pupils veiled from the living world. Sometimes he would see things that the rest of us would have missed – for example, one day he passed a butcher in his store at noon, and Master Yu could see the butcher's entire day, carving up a steak in the back of the store, appeasing a hostile customer, leaving for the evening, unlocking the front door of his little home. Sometimes the city seemed unchanged as Master Yu walked through it blindly.

But sometimes he would find himself walking through wilderness; or sometimes through a settlement of cabins; and sometimes through busy streets, dodging mechanical vehicles that ran without horses.

In the mid-afternoon, he would sit in the park and put his thoughts to paper. Sometimes in the early evening, he would share these writings with Li-Ling, who, he learned, lived two floors above his little hole in the ground, which I think is the reason that he did not leave. He could not remain unmoved by her unpolished charms, and he had begun to believe that it required a certain nobility of character, and a certain beauty in the soul, to survive in the world by one's wits and one's strength, to earn money through labor and without the benefit of an allowance from the governor of the province.

Why had he not seen this before? Because it was antithetical to everything that he had ever been taught.

And yet it was true.

As I have said, sometimes in the early evening, Master Yu would share his writings with Li-Ling in the stairwell outside of her room. Sometimes she would bring him tea. But always, when the hour grew late, she would bid him a friendly goodbye and return to her room. Usually Master Yu would linger by her door. Sometimes, he would imagine that he would hear Li-Ling talking to herself; sometimes he would imagine that he heard another voice. But the more closely he listened, the more he would convince himself that he heard naught but the wind blowing through the curtains, and he would put these concerns out of his mind. Then he would creep down the stairs very quietly, so that she would not hear him and realize that he had been lingering by her door.

Sometimes Master Yu would then walk the night streets, watching the dark world through his dark new eyes. Sometimes he would return to his room deep in the earth and write by lantern light.

One morning, Master Yu rose early. He reached a city park, and he sat down cross-legged in the meadow. His corneas clouded over, and his pupils closed. A mourning dove sat a few feet from him, squinting. His eyes cleared, and the bird was gone. Then Master Yu let his eyes cloud over again. The bird fluttered its left wing, cocked its head to the left then glanced down. A stray dog walked over to the bird and sat down beside it.

The dog opened its mouth and yawned, one of those mighty dog yawns, so full of joy and exuberance. Master Yu's eyes cleared, and the dog was gone. When they clouded over again, the dog was there before him.

"Hello," Master Yu said. "Hello, dog. Hello, bird."

He tossed the dog a bit of jerky. The dog ignored him.

"Are you ignoring the meat because you are a ghost dog?" he asked. "Half-dog, half-ghost?"

"Are you condescending to me because you seek some sort of tactical, psychological advantage over me," the dog asked, "or because you believe that I am a stupid beast who will not even notice? Hmm?"

At this, the bird seemed to laugh.

The dog said all this in Chinese, spoken in the Northern dialect with a perfect accent, not the dialect of the peasantry.

"Not stupid, not a beast," said Master Yu. "Just different from humans. Like a human infant. The way one might say, 'Hello, little fellow, how's the weather?' to a perfectly charming baby, even though one knows that no response will be forthcoming. One would not seek a tactical advantage over the baby, nor consider the baby stupid."

"We are not babies," cooed the bird. "We have been here, in this park, since your last visit, Yang Hsiung. Humans do not realize it, but not all animals die. Some are born and do not die. Unlike humans, who must be born again and again. Yes, Yang Hsiung? You are Yang Hsiung, yes?"

Master Yu nodded vigorously.

"Yes," he said excitedly. "That's me."

The dog scratched behind his left ear with his paw.

"Not the famous court poet of the Hsin Dynasty, however," the dog said.

"His bastard son," said the bird. "Who also called himself Yang Hsiung, after his father's death in the Red Eyebrows rebellion, and who has been lost to history."

Master Yu acknowledged this with an unenthusiastic shrug. He frowned.

"Hark," said the bird.

"We are busy," said the dog. "A lot to do. Business to attend to."

Master Yu stared at him, silently.

"Madame Tang taught you to see?" the dog asked.

"Not very well," the bird tweeted. "Is that Madame Tang's fault? Were her instructions faulty? Or was there some flaw in the student?"

She trembled, ruffling her feathers dramatically.

"Yes?" the bird continued, a bit taunting. "Some arrogance in the student? A refusal to open his mind fully to the invisible world? A failure to acknowledge that he could have been so blind, so ignorant?"

Master Yu nodded.

"It is probably a result of the student's arrogance," he said. "I have a lot to learn. There is much in me that must change."

"And what will our thanks be?" the bird asked. "You will poison us –"

"Throw rocks at us," added the dog.

"And eat us," said the bird. "You eat golden pheasant, yes." She cooed. "With dancing girls, prostitutes. Slaves, really, I suppose. Do you think that they love you, that they enjoy your attentions? As you recite your rancid poetry, drink your sweet plum wine, and spend the money you didn't earn and don't deserve on birds killed to satisfy your appetite, wise, lovely creatures who deserved to be floating on the clouds, on a pinnacle far above you."

"You gnaw on the beautiful, unwilling girls," the dog growled, "after gnawing on the beautiful, dead bird, whose delicate wings are broken for your whims. Yes?"

"We are all beautiful creatures," the bird said. "These creatures you enslave and kill. We are all more beautiful than you, *terrible-poet-who-calls-himself-Yang-Hsiung*."

Her chest puffed out angrily.

The dog barked.

"But the battle needs to be fought," he growled. Then, after a pause: "Watch where I piss, you wretched, undeserving, cowardly bastard."

Master Yu watched, his eyes still blind to the real world. And he saw through feet of dirt and rock, into the distant past. And there it was.

"It has been calling out to you, for your entire life," said the bird. "This one spot, this one spot in the world. It has been calling to you, like a mother calling to her lost child."

His eyes cleared, and the dog and bird were gone. He knew that they were still there, staring at him and judging him angrily, but that he could not see them, and he was glad of that.

Master Yu went back to Chinatown and bought a spade and pickax from a dim shop on The Street of the Men of T'ang, then went to Hang Far Low for dinner, where he waited for the sun to set and then waited for the kind of darkness in which a man could be invisible. He drank a couple of glasses of moutai, just for courage, then a couple of glasses of moutai to reward himself for his courage. When the real darkness descended thick and heavy over the streets of the Chinese city, he grabbed his spade and pickax and returned through empty avenues to the park, where he shut his eyes and went to work, his muscles straining as he mined 1800 years of history.

After a few hours, he retrieved a splintered wooden box from the earth, which he slid open, and he put his hands on it, the treasure he sought, which he must have always known was waiting for him here.

It was the scroll of Emperor Wang Mang, the scroll that had already been ancient when the Hsin dynasty Emperor had found it, alone, on a walk in the mountains. Torn by time and eaten away by the sand and the rain, but there it was. Just a Chinese scroll, just Chinese words on a piece of parchment, in the middle of an American park, thousands and thousands of miles from home.

After a day's absence, Li-Ling finally found Master Yu eating eggs and potatoes at 5:30 in the morning in a little food-shop by the docks, already filled with seamen, and reeking of unidentifiable fishy grub.

She pulled up a chair and sat down across from him. The chair wobbled a bit, and the slave girl almost fell. Then she caught her balance and settled comfortably.

"Eggs and potatoes," Master Yu said. "I don't think very highly of Americans. But sometimes, in their simple-minded way, they accidentally get something just right."

And he took a big bite of leaky eggs slopped together with oniony potatoes, browned in fat.

"You bought a horse," she said.

"Yes," he replied passively. "I bought a good one, I think. A brown horse with strong legs. That sounds good to you, yes? A brown horse with strong legs?"

"You are leaving us," she said.

"How did you find me?"

"I found you, that's all."

She was tired. She rested her head in her hands.

"Yes," Master Yu said. "I am leaving all of you."

"And where are you going?" she asked.

"I won't tell you," he said. "I didn't want to tell you that I was leaving. And I won't tell you where I am going. I don't want to put you at risk."

"Won't the Sidonians ask?" she wondered. "Won't they kill me anyway, if I don't tell them what they want to know?"

"No," Master Yu said. "They will realize without even asking. You will be safe."

"You found something?" she asked.

He grunted an affirmation.

He wanted to tell her. Everything.

But what he wanted to tell her most of all was that Wang Mang, their eternal Emperor, then and always, had known that he was going to die. He had known that he would fail, and that he would die. That was why he met the rebels in the palace hallway without fear, and why he didn't flinch.

But instead, Master Yu said, "There are some things that one must do, even if one knows that he will die. That he will be vilified, and spat upon. And that he will die in pain, and die a failure."

Li-Ling nodded as though she understood, although she didn't understand.

"How did you know where to look?" she asked. "For this great treasure? This treasure that will kill you, and ruin you, and ensure that you will fail? How were you so lucky?"

He smiled.

"I shut my eyes," he said, "and I saw things in a new light."

Li-Ling heard the warmth in his voice, and although just a minute earlier she'd had no foreboding whatsoever, now she suddenly knew exactly what was coming, and she flinched, as though bracing herself for a blow.

"This is your fault, after all, Li-Ling," he whispered. "Had you not chased after me, I would have ridden out of San Francisco and gone away, probably to my death. And that would have been that. And we would never have had this conversation, and you would never have heard what I am about to say. But you *did* chase after me, did you not?"

When Yu Dai-Yung spoke to her now, he felt as though he were the greatest poet in the world, rather than one of the worst.

He spoke of having wings with which they could fly above the clouds; of lovers on a riverboat that would sail forever on a golden current, as the mighty sea opened its arms and welcomed them; of a love that had surprised him, and confounded him, and which he could no longer deny. In ordinary times, he admitted, he might take a peasant girl to bed but not kneel before her in an offer of marriage, but these were not ordinary times, and he was no longer a typical man of his class.

"Could you possibly," he said, in conclusion, "reciprocate my feelings and share life with me as my wife?"

After all of this, these sincere poetical flights of fancy, this baring of his heart, Li-Ling merely averted her eyes, touched his hand shyly, and whispered a small, forlorn "*No*."

In spite of Master Yu's rudeness to Li-Ling when they first met – and his continuing refusal, even up until that day at the food-shop, to admit to himself that he could understand her language – it had not occurred to him that she (or, indeed, any woman) could refuse a man of his breeding, wealth and (he had to acknowledge it) handsomeness. Indeed, he had awoken before dawn and crept away because he knew that, were he to see her again before he left town, he would propose to her, he was convinced that she would say yes, and he feared the scandal it would cause him.

"As I said," Master Yu whispered. "There are some things a man must do, even if he must fail."

Li-Ling smiled sadly, for just a fleeting moment.

"It is another man?" Master Yu asked.

"It is another man," she agreed.

"Are you in love with this other man?"

She nodded her head and looked down at her hands.

Master Yu noted aloud that she seemed very sad for a woman in love. Not happy at all when the subject arose. Not glowing, as a woman in love ought to be.

"Perhaps he is dead?" he asked. "Perhaps he is dead, and you are committed to his memory, and you will love no one else until you are reunited in the hereafter?"

She nodded a little, and then she shook her head.

She said a few things about the man she loved. Intelligent, well-read, dashing, heroic. He promised that she would never be hungry, never be lost. He was loyal, and he was funny. He had a little mustache and beautiful, twinkling eyes, and a smile that made her dizzy. And he had made these promises to her about what her life might be, but he had lied.

"He is now dead," she said. "I loved him truly while he lived. But he is dead, and still I see him every night."

A tear came to her left eye. It hovered there, touching her lashes. Finally, the little tear dropped to the table and dissolved in the rough grains of the wood.

"And you love him still," the poet said.

"I love him still," the peasant girl replied, with a deep, woeful sigh. "In a way. I love the memory of what he was to me, and the bit of his true heart that has survived death. And when I see him now, the way he is now...."

She thought about this for a moment, then she spoke with certainty.

"Yes," she said, "I *do* love him still, and I can never leave him while he yet walks the Earth as a deadling. But even if I did not love him, I could not marry you. He is a jealous deadling, Master Yu. It is due to his jealous rage that I am a free woman to-day, and not a slave. But this is how I know that were you and I to wed, he would kill you on our wedding night. Because he has killed before. To save me from slavery, to deny me to other men, and to keep me for himself, he has killed before."

"And so if it were not for Sidonian magic –"

"I would consider your proposal with an open heart," Li-Ling said. "Yes. If it were not for Sidonian magic, the love of my life would be permanently dead, not just usually dead, and I would listen to your proposition with something other than woe and shame."

Master Yu rested his elbows on the table. He touched the tips of his fingers together, and he stared at them.

"The defeat of Sidonia would mean the end of your true love," he said. "And still you fight against Sidonia?"

"He does not want to be a deadling," she said. "He hates it, to be alive for scattered moments. When he is alive, he is confused, and when he can stay awake no longer, it terrifies him to go back, to face the extinction of his mind. His moments of life are nothing more than terror and anger and pain."

Outside the window, a ship was pulling into the harbor. A crowd of dock workers gathered, shouting to each other and laughing. Gulls shrieked. The day was beginning.

"Once you defeat Sidonia," Li-Ling said, "and the world is safe yet again, ride back here on your horse and find me."

She smiled, and her wet eyes brightened.

"And I will consider it then," she said, "with an open heart. All you must do, Master Yu, is defeat Sidonia and save the world. And I will think about marrying you."

She laughed, and then he laughed along.

She walked with him until she tired, and then she walked with him some more, as the sun rose up over the far mountains in the East. At the southern end of San Francisco, he mounted his horse, and he rode off. After a quarter of a mile, he looked back, and he could still see

Li-Ling there, standing at the edge of the city, watching him leave her, just a faraway thin line. He couldn't see her face from this distance, and so he didn't know if she looked sad, but he thought she probably did. She waved, and he waved back.

CHAPTER 11

The pirate ship made haste for the open sea and then headed south; the ship hit landfall in South America in early January of 1879. By late spring of that same year, we had settled quite comfortably into a small, two-story wooden house about a quarter mile from the central plaza of a little village hacked out of the Amazon jungle. Almost no one could find us, and those who could find us couldn't hurt us. A little balcony on the top floor, a canopy of jungle overhead, little manioc trees underfoot, toucan birds alighting on branches just beyond our window pane, smiling at us through the cold, misty morning, shivering through the torrential rains that showered the jungle forest just beyond our paradise, a thick forest broken up by swamps and tiny, twisting streams that fed into the great river that slithered through the jungle like a mighty snake. The *sacha runa* lived on the upper bank in huts roofed with palm leaves, and they stood guard with blowpipes and poison darts. In the distance, a snow-capped volcano. I had never seen a volcano before, and I liked it. I had never imagined that a volcano could be capped with snow and ice. But there you are.

The village was populated by people who'd wanted to vanish – men hiding out from their wives, a couple of bankers hiding out from the bank, one famous actor who'd needed to be invisible for a while and decided to be invisible forever. But for the most part, our little nameless town was a haven for outlaws. We had some retired thieves and *mostly* retired murderers. (Since Hester and I were plotting the deaths of Allen Jerome and [especially] Darryl Fawley, I suppose we fell into this latter category, as well as the former.) I suspected that not all of the rapists had entirely retired from their raping ways. Hester and I considered ourselves special cases – as did everyone, I reckon.

The village downtown had a saloon, and even a theater. Outlaws, apparently, love the bard as much as the next fellow. Supplies came in down the river. Farley had a little ranch with some cows, pigs and chickens.

Then there was the diamond mine. All the outlaws were investors, and that kept the village running. We were diamond magnates.

All this made for a pretty easy life, and it would have been the life I'd have wanted for myself had I given up all ambition and hope for self-improvement. I had plenty of good wine for the first time in a long while, Shakespeare whenever I wanted it, I was a diamond magnate, and Hester was beautiful.

So I was happy. I knew it wouldn't last. I knew the battle that was coming, and that I might not survive it. I was happy, as I had been in 1863, as the last War loomed. Why not?

Sunday, April 20, was Hester's birthday, so I rode across town to Farley's ranch, bought myself a little cow, dragged that cow back to our house. Hester took the cow out back to slaughter – Hester had very strict ideas about the humane slaughter of animals – then returned to the house, her apron covered with blood, but a lovely steak in her hands, which I grilled, and which we ate under the stars on our second floor balcony, as monkeys swung from vines that hung from trees whose names I didn't know, and birds I didn't recognize squawked and chirped overhead.

The steak was good, and so was the French wine that I chose to accompany it, and I was getting nice and warm in my gut. At about 11 o'clock in the evening, we climbed into our little carriage, smacked our stallion and rode into the center of the little village that the diamond mine had built, and from the terrace of the smoky café at the very western edge of town, we listened to Christine Nilsson, the famous and almost supernaturally beautiful Swedish soprano, who sang the aria from *Mignon* in the town square in a rain forest by a diamond mine beside the Amazon river. Were I not already in love with the deadling Lucy Billings, and also in love with the very-alive Hester Smith, I might well have fallen in love with the beautiful and golden-throated Christine Nilsson right off-the-reel.

Hester nibbled at my ear when no one was watching.

I sighed.

"If one were to choose a final stop for one's life," I said, "this would have to be top of the list."

"I should give up my mission?" she asked. "When I am so close?"

"I've lived through enough horrible for ten men," I said. "For ten ninety-year-old men. That's how much horrible I've lived through." I pointed to Hester. "And you too, darlin'. You and I shared the very same long day of horrible back in 1863, if I recall correctly, and your life before that … well, you've got the soul of an angel, Hester, and if there were a God in heaven, He'd be looking out for his angels, you know, He'd be serving you blessings on a golden plate. Up till now, you haven't really deserved the life you've been served. *Up till now.* And now you deserve to live happily here till the end of your life."

As for me, I told her, I wanted to die happy and warm in the Amazon jungle, with wine in my belly, and Hester in my arms. Was it not possible that were I to survive my Sidonian mission, I could return to her warm embrace and retire from the almost-dying business once-and-for-all?

"Hester," I said. "Please do not go."

She just smiled.

"I'm here tonight," she said. "And you are too. We both have things left to do with our lives."

I wondered why she must go, and Hester said that she had sworn an oath to gather her brothers and sisters and to march to a homeland kingdom abandoned for millennia. It was an oath that she had sworn to her ancestors' graves.

"We are dispersed around the world," she continued, "but when rejoined, we will make a fearsome army, and we will retake our kingdom, re-anoint our king and usher in a new era, perhaps of world peace, perhaps of terrible never-ending conflict, but at least we will be home, and together again."

"Well," I whispered, really to myself. "You ask a silly question…."

Hester kissed me. "Come with me, Watt," she said. "After your revenge. After you leave Darryl Fawley dead for what he has done. You *should* come with me. What will this village offer you, once it can no longer offer a life with me?"

The lovely Miss Nilsson hit an even lovelier high C that shattered a wine goblet at a table on an overhead terrace, and shards of glass rained down on us from above. The broken glass glowed in Hester's hair, and the stars glowed in Hester's eyes.

"Come with me, Watt," she said. "Come with me across the sea and see what my Kingdom will offer you. Follow me again, just one more time. When the man you hate is dead and can haunt you no longer, hold your breath, and follow me one more time, as I held my breath and followed you into an ancient ocean."

I had just begun to consider thinking about this, when a voice I recognized well bellowed out of the darkness.

"Watt O'Hugh the Third!" he exclaimed.

It was Billy Golden, the best Roamer who ever lived, and the only man who knew how to change the past and mold the future. He was also the worst enemy that the Sidonian movement had ever seen. He approached our table arm-in-arm with the luscious Christine Nilsson, who was smiling like a diamond in the jungle.

They sat down at our table without asking if we minded. I could not take my eyes off Billy Golden. One minute he was young; the next minute, old. I could see him roaming back and forth through Time, writing and rewriting this scene, trying it again and again, working our lives like wet clay. This particular moment in history was vital, in some inscrutable way.

"Look at him," Christine said in her laughing Swedish accent. "One minute he is a handsome young man. Then the next minute, a handsome *old* man. Always, though, handsome handsome. So handsome." The ageing and unageing did not seem as remarkable to her as his consistent handsomeness.

She smiled, and she put one hand on the crook of his arm, and the other hand on his knee.

"This is an important moment to you," I said. "You're working very hard to get it right."

He smiled, and he was old.

"I'm in a jungle paradise," he said, "with a beautiful, famous chanteuse by my side."

"You must have puffed that one many times," Hester said.

Billy agreed.

"Some things are worth working on," he said. He tapped the table in front of Hester. As a toucan squawked in the jungle – a toucan he was expecting, because he had heard it many times before – he whispered "Congratulations are in order," adding, "I don't think I will be changing the future or your life to tell you that your baby will be strong as Hercules and will arrive as scheduled. Put your mind at ease."

I did not hear this, but Hester reddened a bit, and she gazed down at her fingertips.

"What?" I said.

"Thank you," she whispered.

"What did you say?" I asked, but they both remained silent, and then I gave up.

I took her hand. With a keen sense of the obvious, I noted that Hester and Billy seemed to be acquainted, and Billy said that he was helping her identify brethren in far-flung locales to build her army.

"Oh yeah," I said. "That army of Hester's. Hester's army."

"How do you think she learned about roaming?" he asked. "About your ghosts? Hester loves you terribly, Watt. She loved you when she saw you battle that mob in 1863. And the minute she heard your lazy, drunk voice in that little hovel you called home, she loved you more. All that is true. But she has not told you the whole truth. She didn't find you in the middle of the desert by accident. You have known that all along, but you didn't ask. You always knew that someone sent her. She's known more about you than she let on. All those questions she asked you. She knew the answers all along."

"Don't let him drive a wedge between us," Hester said.

I nodded.

"He's wily," I agreed.

"*La lucha continua*," Billy said. "Sidonia is on the march."

"We traveled to the future," Hester said. "You see, Billy? We traveled to the late 20th century, and it was not a future in which Sidonia had taken over the world. So we know the end of this story, do we not?"

He sat back with a smile, took a long puff on his cigar.

"Ahah. Do you want to travel to a future in which Sidonia wins? Now that is something to see! A real horror show, Hester. We shall leave now, if you wish. Although, my dear, I cannot promise a safe return."

In my study:

"I'm not sure that I'm glad to see you wrapped up in all this, Billy," I said. "You agreed that I was out after the Lervine deal."

He nodded.

"I let you out of the bargain to which you had willingly agreed," he said.

"Yes," I said. "But you let me out. This isn't supposed to be a Billy Golden operation."

"But Hester promised you vengeance, did she not? Is vengeance not your *reward* for helping us to rob the train and retrieve the scroll? Why does it hurt to have as much help as you can?"

The opera singer sat down on an oversized chair in her oversized dress, and she crossed her legs.

"Watt," Billy said. "Hester understands you. She knows that you need this. She knows you love Lucy, and she knows that you will never stop thinking about Lucy, not even for a moment, if you cannot avenge her. If you do not achieve your vengeance, she might as well leave you now and travel across the ocean alone, because you will never leave Lucy behind. I can be of value, I think. I have certain tricks up my sleeve."

I stared at Billy, pondering this scenario.

"That's what I'm afraid of," I said.

"Beg pardon?"

I said: "On the road out of Lervine, I asked Madame Tang why she followed your Cause. She said she didn't. And she said something like, *Billy's Cause is not what it seems, but I don't know what it is. His Cause seems stupid, but Billy is not stupid. And so his Cause must be something else, something other than what he says it is.*"

Billy nodded, noncommittally.

"The person who knows you the best," I said, "doesn't understand you at all, and believes that you're a liar."

"What is this revenge?" the opera singer asked.

"Lucy Billings was a subversive," Hester whispered, "and Watt loved her in the 1860s, in gilded New York City. She thought the Sidonians believed what she believed – freedom, and love, and equality. So she married a Sidonian leader, Darryl Fawley. But the Sidonians believe in power, that's all, and money. The power of Sidonia weakened her, made her sick. She was dying, but Darryl Fawley would not free her, and he imprisoned her in a Sidonian outpost called Weedville, where she died. If Watt had arrived in Weedville a day sooner, he could have saved her. As it was, he spent a night in the arms of her deadling, and she vanished by sunrise."

"If I were a man," Christine Nilsson said, in her beautiful voice, "and someone allowed the woman I loved to die, I would ...." She yawned. "Oh, what would I do? I would shoot in the head. I would rip off arms. I would feed to the ... Oh, I would not let anyone get away with this, if I were a man ...."

And her beautiful voice trailed off.

I glanced at Hester, who left to mix drinks in the next room, and I asked them in a whisper if they even understood.

Billy leaned forward.

"Do you think that the Sidonians will stop with Lucy? Do you think they are finished with you? Lucy deserves to be avenged, of course. And Hester's kingdom will be a counter-Revolutionary stronghold, and she needs to be protected. But beyond that, there are other Watts in the world, and other Lucys, and other Hesters. Watts and Lucys and Hesters who are in love and who deserve happiness, and who will receive instead death and tragedy, if Sidonia is not stopped. We're all in the same cooking pot, Mister. We're all swimming around in the same soup together."

I sighed, and I asked Billy what he wanted. Hester came into the room and she planted a drink in front of each one of us, and then she sat on the arm of my chair. She held my hand.

"I only want what you want, my friend. I want you to kill Darryl Fawley. I want you to kill Allen Jerome."

Hester clenched my hand tightly. I turned to her, and she kissed me on the forehead.

Billy looked over at the opera singer.

"I love *her*, you know," he said. "She is the greatest opera singer who ever lived. But no one will ever record her voice. For centuries to come, the world will take the word of men of the past. The greatest singer who ever lived, the most beautiful voice that the human ear has ever heard, was Christine Nilsson. I am the greatest Roamer the world will ever see – a terrible burden, O'Hugh, I take no pride in this – but even I, the greatest Roamer the world will ever see, can do nothing to change this future, the beauty the world will lose." He squinted at the singer, and he sighed, and suddenly he was old, a very old man, more than eighty. He seemed near-death, suddenly. "How I love her, O'Hugh," he gasped, tears in his voice. "Everything I have done, throughout these terrible thousands of years of roaming

... it always leads back here, to this night in the jungle, to her, that woman right there. I cannot ever leave this night behind."

I wondered if this story had something to do with the mission to Sidonia, and I realized that it did not, that Billy was now just an old man, filled with love and regret. The old Roamer stood up from his chair with a terrible effort and walked slowly and painfully to Christine Nilsson's side, and he knelt down slowly and painfully before her. She cradled his head in her arms, and she ran her fingers through his thin tufts of old-man hair.

I turned to Hester.

"And you, Hester?" I said. "What do you want? Deep down inside. Is it worth it, putting me back into cahoots with Billy Golden?"

"I want you to travel with me to the border of the Sidonian realm," she said. "I want to embrace you at the very edge of eternity, and then I want you to cross over, and I want you to live within the heart of the demon city of the Falsturm himself. I want you to kill Allen Jerome and Darryl Fawley, to see Sidonia destroyed. And I want you to come back to me alive, and travel with me across the ocean, to see my kingdom restored to its ancient glory. I don't care what it takes."

I told Hester I needed a bit of air, and I left my study and walked out the side door, along the winding stone path that led out to my little garden, well-hidden from the light of the house and shrouded in towering kapok and capirona trees that stretched above the jungle canopy. In a moment, Lucy was with me. She was sitting on a log beside the pond, her hair blowing in the light jungle breeze. Red flowers that looked like balloons dangled down from the jungle trees. Beyond the pond was a little stream I'd diverted. The pond glowed like a Christmas tree, like the Manhattan skyline.

She wore a frilly white day dress, something she might have chosen for a party in a city garden back in the New York of the 1860s. (Our New York, the city that would always belong to us, Lucy and me.)

She looked just like a living woman. But she wasn't breathing. The last time I saw her, she told me that she didn't breathe.

"Why does the pond glow?" she said, without turning to look at me.

"Little creatures live in the pond," I said.

"Little creatures," she repeated, and I could hear a smile in her voice.

"*Dinoflagellates*," I added with a sad little laugh. The word sounded clumsy in my throat. "They glow. I don't remember why they glow. But they do. They glow. Each is only a single cell, so they do not know they are glowing. They don't know that they live in a jungle lagoon, and that the lagoon is aglow. They do not understand that human beings find them terribly enchanting, that we can watch them for hours and hours and never want to stop. They are captivatingly beautiful, and they cannot even know it."

"Dinoflagellates," she sighed. It sounded lovely when she said it. Even something like *dinoflagellates* sounded lovely when she said it.

She put one hand in the pond, and little glowing ripples spread out across the surface of the pond, like the reflection of the lamp-lit night ferries in the black water of the North River, all those years ago.

"They want me to avenge you," I said at last, after a long time had passed. "Billy Golden. And ... this woman who lives with me here."

She nodded, still looking at the glowing curls of water, but she disagreed.

"They don't care if you avenge me," she said. "Of course you know that this is not on their mind. Billy wants Sidonia burned to the ground. And Billy is also interested in someone called the 'Falsturm', who I understand you may have heard of by now."

Could she tell me about the Falsturm, this creature predicted by a desert oracle? The question was on my lips; Lucy interrupted.

"And Hester wants the help that Billy will give her, if you help him."

"Even Hester?" I asked. My heart began to break a little.

"Hester wants you to be happy, Watt," she admitted.

She stood up from the lagoon and walked a little bit towards me. Her feet were bare and white.

"I wish I could tell you otherwise," she said. "I may not be entirely alive, but I am still human, and I wish I could tell you not to trust Hester." She laughed. "I want you to myself, even now. But she wants you to be happy, and she thinks it will make you happy if you avenge me."

"You know a lot about my life," I remarked, and she said, "There is not much to do, down in *sheol*."

I could hear the sound of the great river into which this little stream flowed, and the whooping and squawking of the birds (along with an occasional melodic flutter), green birds and red ones, and even the occasional yellow one, birds I could not name, birds with accusing eyes, and birds with feathers that glowed.

A few green birds and one red one fluttered onto a nearby tree branch. They watched, down there in the clearing, cocking their heads, as birds do.

I noticed with a little jolt that they were not looking at Lucy.

Perhaps they couldn't see her. Perhaps Sidonian deadlings weren't real.

"You should have asked me to marry you," she said then, with a regretful sigh.

"When?"

"That night on the island. What was the name of that island?"

"It didn't have a name," I said.

"Then we shall call it Lucy's Island," she said, "and a thousand years from now, lovers will still row out there, and sometimes the girl will wonder to the boy, *I wonder who Lucy was,* and the boy will say, *I imagine that she was the first girl to fall in love on this island.*"

"And would he be right?" I wondered.

"Under the stars on Lucy's Island," she said, "when you rowed that little rowboat across the North Bay, I thought we might well drown, and I was happy that I was to die in your arms."

She smiled.

"Most assuredly, Mr. O'Hugh, had you asked me to marry you, I'd have married you."

A little monkey flittered across a jungle vine, bounced along the canopy and vanished into the shadows.

"I'll go back," I said. "I can roam Time, Lucy. I'll go back and tell young Watt to ask you."

She laughed.

"I know one thing about Roamers," she said, "from my time in my prison in the Village of Sidonia, in Montana. Only one man can change the past. Your friend with the utterly pure heart."

"I will learn," I said. "I will make my heart pure, and I will whisper in my own ear. And one day, young Watt will hear me. And our lives will be saved."

Hester's light was on in the second floor window.

"If it could be done by a man with a pure heart, wouldn't your friend with the pure heart already have done it? I am afraid that moment in the past has hardened, like cement."

Lucy smiled more deeply; while she was engulfed in the terrible beauty of her tragedy, she could not help but enjoy the wonderful beauty of the fleeting night, and this tiny spark of life. Her eyes closed, and a night bird sang, and it was almost a real song.

"Watt," she said. "It is most pleasant being here, in this beautiful cool night in your criminal paradise. But you do know how difficult it is for a deadling to stay in the life."

"Like hanging onto the edge of a cliff with your fingertips," I whispered.

She nodded.

"That's a way of putting it," she agreed. "Spoken like a true deadling."

Now she walked closer to me, and she held my hands. I could see right into her blue eyes, which glowed with the jungle stars, and the dinoflagellates. Her hands felt cool and warm and alive.

"How long?" I asked.

"Not long. I'm weakening. But I have to tell you something before I go." Now her voice grew more matter-of-fact, and a little bit of that old Revolutionary zeal cut through the haze of death. "Sidonian Magic is making its way to the East coast," she said. "Deadlings are on the rise in New York city. Some of my old friends – my old anarchist, bomb-throwing friends from the 1860s, you remember them? – some of these fellows think Sidonia offers a just society."

I remembered them. Joyless, for the most part, and burdened by the world's pain, but they dreamt marvelous dreams.

"You cannot stop Sidonia now, in 1878. But you might perhaps slow it down, and this might prevent my friends – my honorable, well-meaning friends on the isle of Manhattan – from joining the war. For if they join the war, Watt, my darling, you will have to kill them. Though misguided, they are good men and women. You will have no choice but to kill them. So avenge me, if you wish.

But do what you can to slow Sidonia down, just a bit. Let my subversive allies live out their lives waving their clenched fists uselessly in the air." She stopped for a moment, hesitated. Then a little lament, her voice cracking: "I do adore them, Watt. They are silly, as I once was, and they think the world can be a good place, although it cannot."

"And the Falsturm?" I asked, remembering this now with some urgency.

Lucy smiled.

"The Falsturm," she laughed. "This would fill a thousand books. The Falsturm may be defeated only by the hand of the daughter of a Queen, who was born Nephila. So do not try to touch him, my beloved. He is beyond your capacity."

We walked a ways farther into the jungle, down by the river, where we sat together on a log which crumbled a bit beneath us.

"Do you love her the way you love me?" she asked. "Do you love her as much?

I shook my head. *No.* Not even half as much.

"But I am dead," she said. "And Hester is ... not-dead."

"Not only not-dead," I said. "Genuinely alive."

She nodded.

"*Alive*," she whispered. "That was nice. I remember that. Being that way. Alive."

In the jungle, an ocelot leapt and struck, and a small howler monkey shrieked and died.

Lucy heard this, and a frown flitted across her face.

She put her hand on my elbow.

"Everything dies, Watt. You have my blessing."

I nodded. I didn't want her blessing. I wanted her love. All I'd ever wanted was her love.

I hesitated.

"When you died ... were you expecting ... ?"

I couldn't finish. *Fawley's child.* She didn't answer. She looked away. The baby that should have been ours. After we left New York in 1863 with Lucy's money, and married, and lived the life we were meant to live.

"So avenge me," she said, "if you must, my darling."

I promised her that I would.

"And now," she said, "would Hester mind if I asked you to kiss me?"

"I think she would," I said softly. "I believe she would mind a great deal."

"Then I will not ask you to kiss me," Lucy Billings said. "Now just watch me vanish into a jungle night. A trick that I believe you will find was worth the price of admission."

So I watched her vanish into a jungle night, and it was indeed quite a trick. Lucy faded slowly away, becoming translucent, then transparent, then almost entirely invisible – just her beautiful blue eyes were left, one last stolen glance at the world of the living.

How I loved her.

I found Hester downstairs in her nightgown, candles burning on the wall above the dark, polished mahogany bar. She poured herself a whiskey.

"I like it that you drink whiskey," I said, a random thought.

"What did she tell you?" Hester asked me.

"You know what she said."

I collapsed wearily into my armchair.

"She told me to go with you," I added. "Hester, we took a marriage oath, Lucy and me, that afternoon on the Nebraska cliffs over Weedville. When she was already a deadling." I shook my head. "This is all very confusing."

"You know, Watt," Hester sighed, without turning to face me. "I'm alive."

I hesitated.

"Lucy is alive," I whispered.

I felt I needed to clarify this.

"Not all the time," I added. "But sometimes."

Now she turned, and her face was relaxed, not angry.

She shook her head.

"How do you know, Watt, darling?" she asked. "I say that deadlings are just your last best guess, risen from your dreams as a walking illusion. How do you know I'm wrong?"

"How do I know that *you* are alive?" I asked. "That all of this, everything, isn't a dream?" This was a bit solipsistic and epistemological (although I didn't know it at the time) for a mudsill who had not gone to college in the 1960s to smoke "pot" and study metaphysics, but I wasn't aiming for any sort of epiphany, I wasn't trying to change the world. It had just occurred to me, all of sudden. Maybe I was ahead of my time.

Hester would have none of it.

"Perhaps the universe is a great wild boar," she said, "and we are tics in the hair follicles in its nostril. How do you know that we are not?"

I nodded.

"*Hmm*," I murmured. "Um."

This idea seemed interesting. How *did* I know, after all? Hair follicles? A wild boar? My world flipped on its head. *A wild boar*, indeed.

"I don't see Lucy Billings as a threat to our passionate love affair, my dear friend Watt," Hester said wearily. "You love her more than you love me, and now that she is dead, there is nothing I can do about it. She is frozen there in your heart as the woman you will always love above all others, and I want you to love her, Watt, now and always. But living in the past is causing you pain. And I don't want to see you in pain. And Watt – if your wife is dead, you do not need to break off the marriage. It is gone. You need to see that justice is done, that her murderers are punished. Then leave a bouquet on her grave, blow her a kiss, and walk away with wet eyes, and you will have betrayed no one. One has one's revenge. And then there is nothing more to do than to walk away."

She kissed me sadly.

"She is not alive," she whispered again.

"She is alive."

She turned from me then, and she ascended the stairs.

I was alone in the dark, with the stars drifting in on the last wisps of Billy's cigar smoke, and the noises of a South American jungle.

"I'll tell you how I know she is alive," I murmured to no one at all. "It's in the eyes."

The gateway to the soul.

I laughed.

The jungle noises were superficially soothing, like thousands of gold coins splashing into a river, but I realized tonight, more than ever, that the songs of the birds, insects and reptiles were noises of conflict and death.

CHAPTER 12

Yu Dai-Yung rode his brown horse with strong legs into a little Texas cow-town just as the sun was setting over hills in the far west, casting a shadow across the blanket of yellow plains, and the terrible scorching dry heat was dissolving into the orange horizon sky. The town doesn't really exist anymore, even in 1936, as I write these words, though I think if you drove out there you'd probably be able to spy a few store fronts that haven't collapsed from the elements some time during the last couple of decades, or whenever the last cowboy saddled up and rode out of town. I don't remember its name, and I suppose it doesn't matter. It was in northwestern Texas, and it was hot and dry, and just the sight of it burnt the corneas.

The town's little tavern was starting to fill up. Master Yu tied up his horse, strolled into the tavern and sat down at the bar. His skin was dry and dark from the many weeks on the trail, following a map in a Chinese scroll south from San Francisco.

He waved to the bartender who wandered over slowly and leaned down on the bar. The bartender was a stocky man, strong but ruddy cheeked, past his prime, with a stringy beard. (This is an important detail, the stringy beard. Stringy beards can come in handy and be highly beneficial in moments of conflict, though not generally for the wearer of said beard.)

"We don't serve Chinamen in here," he said. "We have a no-serving-John-Chinaman-Policy." He pointed to a sign on the wall which read: *No-Serving-John-Chinaman – Saloon Policy.* "I don't make the rules. Nothing personal."

Master Yu smiled.

"Why in Heaven would I take that personally, my friend? And it does not bother me at all, because I do not need a drink. I'm looking for information. Then I will be out of your hair, so-to-speak."

"No information," said the bartender, "without ordering something."

The two men stared at each other for a moment.

Master Yu thought.

"It's a real Hobson's choice," he said at last. "I would not want to violate your *no-serving-John-Chinaman* policy, yet I cannot get my information if I do not order something. A real Hobson's choice, indeed."

The bartender cocked his head to one side.

He admitted that he was not an expert in the history of medieval English livery stable owners, but he was fairly certain that the quandary he had presented was not a "Hobson's choice."

"I was actually just trying to get a Chinaman to go away," the bartender said. "I was just telling you to leave. Nothing real philosophical-like. Just, you know – *get out of the saloon, Chinaman.*"

"I have an idea," Master Yu announced, clapping his hands together in triumph. "You cannot *serve* Chinamen in here, and yet I cannot have information without *ordering* something. *Ipso factotum*: I shall *order* something, you shall *not serve it to me*, and you will give me my information."

He slammed a gold coin on the bar.

"One whiskey!" he exclaimed. "Now, take my money."

The bartender frowned.

"I am looking," Master Yu exclaimed, still falsely cheery, "for a Peking Indian. I am told that a Peking Indian frequents these parts – indeed, this self-same tavern – and I am looking for a Peking Indian." Quietly, he added, "Or should I say, I am looking for *the* Peking Indian. The last one. Do you know him?"

"I don't think they ever really existed," the bartender said.

He seemed familiar with this concept, and he had his opinion.

"I don't think there's such a thing as a *real* Peking Indian," the bartender said.

Master Yu nodded patiently.

"Let's say," he continued slowly, "that I was looking for a man who *believes* himself to be the last of a great near-extinct tribe, known as the Peking Indians?"

A woman wandered, a little dazed, through the growing crowd of imbibing men. There were a few hoots and hollers, and she smiled uncomfortably.

"*Believes* himself to be ….?" the bartender mused.

"Point taken, my dear friend," Master Yu said. "Perhaps a gentleman who *claims* that he is the last of a great near-extinct tribe, known as the Peking Indians? What he *actually* believes – gosh, I suppose you are correct. That would be speculative. I give you that. *Touché*, as the mandolin players say in the village of *Blois*."

The bartender shook his head and made a remark that ratcheted up the racism to a level that I believe entirely unacceptable to 20th and 21st century readers, and which I therefore choose not to repeat here, and he made it generally clear that, Master Yu's cleverness notwithstanding, the terrible poet would receive no help today, not in this saloon and probably not in this town. An important task at hand, and faced with no other choice, Master Yu reluctantly grabbed the bartender's stringy beard, pulled downward, and thus slammed the bartender's forehead on the bar. When the fat man tried to draw his pistol in self-defense, Master Yu leaped up on the bar, not releasing his grip on the bartender's stringy beard, and kicked the pistol across the room.

Then, still crouched on the bar, he appealed to the bartender's reasonableness as a gentleman.

"I can out-kick you," Master Yu whispered, his pursed lips very close to the bartender's ruddy-red ear, "and I can out-punch you, I can out-shoot any bastard in this room, and I can outride anyone who tries to catch me after I've killed you. You've helpfully told me that no one in this little shithole town shall willingly help me, so I might as well beat it out of you. All I want, you great fat *lo fan*, is to know where I might find a fellow who *claims* that he is the last of a near-extinct tribe known as the Peking Indians, and I am not leaving until you tell me. Shall I break your fingers or crush your kneecaps?"

The bartender rubbed his bald head – throbbing, but not seriously dented – and he gave Master Yu directions to a lonely Indian encampment two miles outside of town with a specificity and cultural descriptiveness that the poet found convincing.

"I will be gone from your property quickly," the Chinese poet said, descending, "I will remain grateful for your help, and I will hold no grudge, and I hope that you will do the same. I have information from you, you have a gold coin from me, and we should part friends and allies."

Master Yu tapped the rim of his hat in thanks, as he had seen done.

"I'm not sure there's really such a thing as a Peking Indian," the bartender said again, his eyes clouding dizzily. "I really don't think they ever existed. All yours, though."

Master Yu found the Indian's hut just where the bartender had said it would be, and the Indian was sitting a few yards out back, on a tree stump, just thinking and staring a little sadly at the sky. He looked near 50, but maybe that was the rough living, and all the tragedy. He was lanky and wiry, downtrodden and helpless.

Master Yu approached the man, who gestured to him to sit. Master Yu sat down on a tree stump next to the Indian.

"I have a proposition," he said. "I need a guide. It pays well. I need a guide who is a Peking Indian."

The Indian nodded.

"John Dead-Man, Peking Indian," he said, and he held out his hand.

Master Yu smiled.

"Yu Dai-Yung," he said. "Peking Chinese," and he took the Indian's hand, and the two men shook on it.

John Dead-Man's home was a circular one-room mud hut, with large posts in the center and shorter posts in the perimeter and beams across the roof, covered by branches and willow leaves. Yu Dai-Yung and John Dead-Man sat in the center of the room, cross-legged on the dirt floor.

"You're a little far south for a Peking, if I recall correctly. Aren't you a tribe of the Dakotas?"

The Indian shook his head.

"We were a dwindling tribe of the Dakotas," he said, "until we were defeated and absorbed by the Mandans, five hundred years ago."

His family kept the Peking tradition and language alive. By the 1800s, they had grown back to twenty-five brave souls, including his father, mother, brother and young John. Then in 1837, when he was fifteen years old, the Mandans were near-destroyed by the white man's small pox. A few dozen of the Mandans joined the Hidatsa to live on the banks of the Missouri River, still allowed to perform their O-keepa ceremony, the few of them that were left. But there was no space in anyone's mind to keep the Peking Indians alive as a race, or even a memory. So he buried his mother and his little brother on a rainy afternoon, he took his new name, and he went his own way, a nomad just waiting to die, when the time came. The last of his kind.

"You cannot say that one man is a tribe of the Dakotas," John Dead-Man said. "Or any kind of a tribe at all."

"You could have married," Master Yu said. "You could have married and raised your children in the old ways."

John Dead-Man smiled.

"Too much responsibility for a man like me, a man not destined for greatness. If the fate of a people rests on the shoulders of such a man, it is a people doomed to die. Could I have found a woman, an outcast like myself, and raised a mutt of a child, or maybe two? Perhaps." He took a slug from his bottle. "Where would be the glory in that? Enough is enough, Chinaman."

Master Yu sighed. He looked down at his fingers, at the grime underneath his finely polished fingernails.

"Do you understand the greatness that you are allowing to slip from this Earth?" he asked. "Do you understand the greatness that once was the Peking Nation, eighteen-hundred years ago, and that still courses through your veins, diluted as it is?"

Teary-eyed, John Dead-Man shook his head.

"I do not, my friend," he whispered. "For hundreds of years, we were an enslaved and weak people, a near-extinct people, and for hundreds of years before that, we were a scared people, shivering and hiding from the shadows of the tribes that were mighty."

"What about your legends? What about the stories you heard when you were little? Before you went to sleep?"

The Indian laughed.

"In our dreams, in our magical stories," he said, "we were a great force for good. We ruled the land. A fierce dragon and a legion of unicorns came from across the ocean to join us in battle. Our only enemy, our only threat, was an army that attacked from the far Winter North, an army that grew from the bowels of the Earth."

He shook his head.

"I can still just barely remember these silly stories," he said. "Soon, no one will be alive to remember. And that will be better. A great veil of sadness and of defeat will pass from the Earth when I die, and the world will be a more joyful place. Who would not want that to happen?"

"The Peking Indians were the greatest of all the native tribes in the land of the Dakotas," Master Yu said, his voice trembling. "In my mind, I can still see them." And his eyes grew foggy and dim, and he described it to the Indian as though the great Peking Indian nation were there before him, great cities of circular homes, armies of the strongest warriors on the continent, sweeping across the entire west, an empire that flowed over mountains and through valleys and plains.

The Indian looked at the poet's face, and he could see Master Yu's pinprick pupils moving furiously within his cloudy corneas, watching a world that only he could see.

The Indian touched Master Yu's sleeve.

"Hey now, Chinaman," he said. "Hey now. You would not happen to be a little bit crazy now? Would you?"

The terrible poet's eyes cleared.

"It is all true," he whispered. "The great army, the enemy from the North. All of it."

The Indian smiled deeply.

"Even the dragon?" John Dead-Man said with a laugh. "Even the unicorns?"

Master Yu nodded forcefully, and the laugh caught in the Indian's throat.

"*Especially* the dragon and unicorns," Master Yu said.

His gaze was serious, piercing.

"Look," he said, and he pulled the rotting wooden box from his bag.

The Indian leaned over on one arm. Master Yu continued.

"This scroll transcribes an ancient prophecy first decreed by Huang-ti, the Yellow Emperor, who, in his lost book, *White Pond*, foresaw the battles to be waged against the Red Eyebrows in the Year One in China and among the Indian nations across many seas. Huang-ti was the only emperor of China with the power to command the dragons to perform his will, and to talk to the unicorns, and he was worshiped as a god through the period of the Warring States, although he was merely a great wizard. He lived in my golden homeland three thousand years ago, and he invented writing, mathematics and astronomy, and he sailed to the Far Eastern Sea, which doesn't exist, where he wrote *White Pond*, which was dictated to him by a terrible sea beast that rose to the surface of the Far Eastern Sea. Most of *White Pond* is lost and only fragments survive to-day; this is one of the fragments which, up till now, had been lost – or, I should say more accurately, hidden for good reason.

"This later transcription of Lord Huang-ti's wisdom was written during the Hsia Dynasty of the golden age of my national past, a past of great poets and sages.

"So do you see, John Dead-Man? Like the great Peking Indian empire, neither the Yellow Emperor nor the Hsia Dynasty nor the Far Eastern Sea ever existed …. Except that they all *did*."

Sitting on the floor of John Dead-Man's mud hut as night fell, Master Yu drank John Dead-Man's whiskey, and John Dead-Man drank Master Yu's moutai, which he had saved from San Francisco for just this sort of occasion, and which had come in handy as expected. A bit of singing ensued, along with a pleasant but not untoward level of camaraderie.

At length, when Master Yu was certain that he and the Peking Indian were truly friends, he unrolled the scroll to the map drawn in its center, which they both examined by torchlight.

"Do you know this place?" he asked.

John Dead-Man nodded.

"It is a famous legendary place," he said. "Every Peking Indian would know the legend."

He smiled sadly at that expression: *every Peking Indian.*

"But it is real, John Dead-Man," Master Yu said. "It is not a legend."

"Hmm."

"You see?" Master Yu said, showing him the topography on the map, which was carefully drawn, though not to scale. "These are real places. Look here" – pointing to the map – "see the Gulf, and the Bay? And see these mountains here? All where they should be, more or less. Drawn by someone who knew this country."

"Hmmph." Not convinced. The Indian shrugged.

"Can you find it?"

He thought about this for a moment.

"You say there is much money involved?" he asked.

Master Yu nodded.

"Of course," he said. "Of course there is much money involved – this is a mission from the Empress. She has a bit of coin to her name, after all. And there will be perhaps a bit of treasure at the end. You can have any treasure, unless I need it for fighting evil. But yes, money for certain, and perhaps some treasure as well."

The Indian smiled now, a real smile for the first time.

"Yes," he said. "I cannot promise you that it is real. But if it is real, then yes, I can find it."

The second week of July 1879, Allen Jerome and Darryl Fawley arrived in the bulging metropolis known as Cloud City, Colorado, a Sidonian enclave ten-thousand feet high in the mountains overlooking Denver, bordered by mighty mountain ranges. Once it had been "Slabtown," a failed gold mining village, but since its alliance with the Sidonian movement, it now flowed with silver, and the mayor, David Dougan, took spectacular credit. I had spent a particularly frightening evening there earlier in the decade, but that's another story, and one that I am not inclined to dwell on once again. (Suffice it to say [and worth repeating]: it was a *particularly* frightening evening.) Cloud City had changed mightily since my visit. Its tents were now replaced with tidy rows of houses; pushing out beyond its former borders, Slabtown's streets were lined with restaurants and great opera houses, and some of the columned architecture, bedecked with statues and ivory white balconies which lined the new primary thoroughfare of Harrison Avenue, could have been shipped from the Madison Avenue in New York City. The Tabor Hotel, in whose half-built frame I once saw two counter-Revolutionaries lynched, was now fully complete and elegant. Cloud City even had its own requisite seedy establishments along the Hell's mailbox known as State Street.

On the way up the mountain, the gentlemen stopped at Law's Lakes for a swim and a rest in the oriental garden. When they finally reached Cloud City, they found that the week they had chosen was a particularly festive one even for this spectacularly festive burg. For one thing, there was the Apollo concert on Monday. Then there was Tabor Cavalry Ball on Tuesday evening, and the Altman-Schloss wedding commenced on Wednesday. The Second Grand Masked Ball of the Knights of Robert Emmet at Shoneberg's Opera House would cap the week, but first Messieurs Jerome and Fawley would visit a number of afternoon lunches and teas, including a lavish event at the home of Roswell Eaton Goodell, one of the great whiskered old men of the city, and his wife, Mrs. Roswell Eaton Goodell, one of the great gray-haired matriarchs of the city. At this tea, Mrs. Roswell paired the two men with adequately attractive but not inappropriately showy young women – and indeed throughout the week the city's aristocracy attempted a bit of tentative matchmaking, perhaps just out of politeness – but Darryl Fawley still mourned his fallen queen (and would to his dying day) and Allen Jerome recognized something lacking in his own character that would ever make him an insufficient match, no matter his wealth and power (as I noted in the first volume of my *Memoirs*, this was a man who did no more than watch as his fiancée – a brilliant East Coast mathematician – fell off a bridge outside Cambridge one icy night and drowned, because he didn't want to ruin his best suit), and for many years he had preferred the company of a paid escort or, these days, an illusion summoned at his whim (who would never demand a raise with a grimace on her pretty face). So the gentlemen verified that week that they remained what one might call *confirmed bachelors*, but the obvious lack of affection between the two business partners banished any gossip. Still, the town was abuzz over the odd mismatch between the well-coiffed Wall Street culture of the handsomely frosty and intellectually precise Mr. Jerome, and the lazily rumpled and cheerful gawkiness of the uncomely Mr. Fawley. How had these two come to join forces, the chattering classes wondered, and how had they acquired the power they undoubtedly wielded?

Oh, I almost forgot: Thursday brought a wildflower picking excursion in Highland Fields.

All of this revelry might have under any circumstances been lumped together during that lovely July week – the weather was clearing up nicely, the mines were spurting silver, and society money had been pouring in for years from the very proper type of society folk who expect to be entertained properly – but it did not hurt the festive mood of the city that Allen Jerome and Darryl Fawley had arrived, leaders of the secessionist social movement that had brought the city not only great riches but also brief, terribly precious visits from departed loved ones, something no political party could ever hope to offer.

As the wedding festivities wound down very late on Wednesday night, Allen Jerome found Mayor Dougan installed behind the Hotel

Windsor, a cigar in his left hand, and a glass of champagne in his right. A young man, his beard tufts of blond fuzz, Dougan held himself with the confidence he knew he had cannily earned. He had been installed a few years earlier from the county seat in Granite, pending Cloud City's first election. His first official visit had been to the rulers of Sidonia, and since then, he sprinkled riches like fairy dust. Once Cloud City had been a sparsely populated counter-Revolutionary settlement, but Dougan had stamped out the counter-Revolution and all who called themselves counter-Revolutionaries with brutal efficiency and many yards of hangman's rope, eventually establishing his city as one of the first true and strong pillars of the Revolution. Now there was a chicken in every pot.

Allen Jerome put a hand on the mayor's shoulder.

"Would you like to see the future of Cloud City?" he asked.

The mayor smiled. Cigar smoke drifted through the starlit night, floating on the breezes out toward the Sawatch mountains.

"Is it a good future?" he asked.

"It can be," Allen Jerome said. "It can be very good for all of us."

The mayor turned to the two men and smiled soullessly.

"Then let's take a look."

Allen Jerome clapped his hands in the darkness and called out, "Siggy!" Immediately, a little man appeared from nowhere. He was no more than five feet tall. The mayor, startled, took a step back.

"Our Roamer," Darryl Fawley said. "He has found something interesting to show you from the Winter of 1895 to 1896. Something that I believe will seal your alliance with Sidonia."

"I have never been much of a Roamer," the mayor said, which would be a bit like my saying that I have never been much of a Latin scholar, except that I believe in the existence of Latin, and the mayor of Cloud City had always considered Roaming to be a myth from the Godless dime novelists out East.

Allen Jerome told the mayor to keep his eyes on Sigmund, who turned and seemed to descend down a dark tunnel, from which the three emerged in exactly the same location, although the temperature had dropped precipitously, and their wedding attire would not keep them warm for long.

"We cannot do much. Just observe. But you can see what we offer. A kingdom."

And indeed, a beautiful palace of ice sat on the vista before Mayor Dougan. Heroic statues of Greek gods (and of Mayor Dougan) greeted them along the entranceway, and the Sidonian flag waved from every icy turret. An orchestra performed in the ballroom, and the Cloud City's subjects danced, bedecked in tuxedoes and evening gowns. At the end of a frigid hallway was a great skating rink, filled with the children of the town, ruddy-cheeked, joyful from skull to foot, spinning, sweating in the cold cold air, their laughter echoing off the icy walls of the immense hall.

"Think of this," Darryl Fawley said, smiling. "A continent bursting with food, and gold and diamonds, and a nation of independent kingdoms, ruled by the wisest among us. Love will reign supreme. Once Sidonia triumphs, there will be no reason for any child to go to bed hungry, anywhere in the land."

"Hmm?" Mayor Dougan said. "*Love* will reign supreme?" He seemed befuddled by this idea. And Fawley could see Allen Jerome averting his eyes, smiling into the snow and ice, but Fawley was not yet willing to give up Lucy's dream. He still hoped against all available evidence that some sort of just result could be redeemed from all the bloodshed.

"A palace of snow and ice," the mayor marveled. "And a beautiful queen."

"Yes," said Darryl Fawley. "An end to hunger, a complete cessation of hostility between the races and the classes, social equality, and a king chosen from amongst the wisest and fairest amongst us … And, if the king so wishes, a palace of snow and ice."

The mayor stared adoringly at the frozen white palace, thinking, no doubt, of the queen who would one day live with him in his Camelot. A couple of boys swept past them on toboggans. Children's laughter echoed in the hallways of ice.

In fact, only one bit of true nastiness marred the week of celebrations, nastiness of the sort that Darryl Fawley despised and Allen Jerome seemed to adore. Well, *two* bits of nastiness, perhaps, depending upon how one counts a "bit" of nastiness.[*]

---

[*] Are two interrelated and concurrent cold-blooded and heartless murders committed by the same perpetrator considered to be one bit of nastiness or two?

Shoneberg's Opera House hosted The Second Grand Masked Ball, with music planned and in some cases orchestrated and conducted by Professor G. A. Godat. A menu of oysters on the half shell, salmon from Alaska, and smoked buffalo tongue au beurre Montelier, among some forty other dishes. Darryl Fawley's evening suit was too short, and showed a healthy glimpse of sock, and his jacket was too tight, and he could not button it around his paunch. He drank a bit too much and told a few stories to Mrs. Roswell Eaton Goodell that were a bit too bawdy, perhaps, but just a bit; no real complaint could honestly be pursued. Allen Jerome looked handsome and terrifying and perfect, and he even danced a bit with a young woman, coldly and dispassionately, with mathematical precision; indeed, he danced perfectly, and the young woman left him in terror and distinct admiration. Women held feather masks over their eyes that made them look as peacocks, doves and swans, and one little girl was a snowy egret, perhaps a coincidence, perhaps not, so tiny under the three great domed and painted interlocking ceilings of the Opera House, a little showy snowy egret spinning beneath glittering chandeliers.

At the bar, a sturdy man in a weathered topcoat cornered Darryl Fawley, introduced himself as Thomas Bridges, from New Jersey originally, but an early and enthusiastic Cloud City settler, even long before its Slabtown days. He'd been away on business and had thus been unable to introduce himself until now, but he desired an audience with the esteemed visitors before their departure in the morning.

"I know that now is not a very convenient moment," he said apologetically, "but I will require only fifteen minutes of your time, and then you may return to the Ball."

In the back room, Bridges unrolled his map on the floor. The three men got down on their hands and knees. Bridges' wife, Holly, stood nervously in the corner.

"You see?" he said. "A ring of silver mines, all the way around the Cloud City peak. Half of them flowing already."

Crawling about like children, they all examined the map.

"It sounds as though you have a happy little enterprise," Allen Jerome said. "What do you need us for?"

Bridges laughed hesitantly. It was a false laugh.

"Friendship," he said. "Solidarity. Sidonia protects my business. All my employees become soldiers in the Sidonian army."

He pointed to the map, sweeping his pointer finger around and around the mountain peak.

"Look," he said. "When the cavalry comes up the mountain, my land will be the first tier of defense."

Jerome looked over the map. He traced his finger along the route of Bridges' land.

"You could be an important man, you are saying," he said. "Your land is strategically located. You could lead the counter-rebellion, or you could join us to repel the government attack, depending on whose bid is higher?"

Bridges shook his head.

"No, I'm as loyal to Sidonia as any true believer," he said casually, unworried.

There was a bit of silence in the room, although in the ballroom, the Georgetown Boys played the Quadrille. Mr. Bridges could hear hooting and laughter. His wife frowned. Mr. Bridges stood. Then Jerome stood as well, still elegant and well-creased after his sojourn on the floor, and his pitiless eyes narrowed to slits. Fawley stumbled slightly as he stood. He turned away, his face pale and mournful, and he leaned against the far wall, exhausted already by events that had not yet occurred.

What happened next happened very quickly. The back door opened and Monsieur Rasháh marched in, his face a parody of mirth. He was alone. He locked the back door, and Allen Jerome locked the door to the ballroom. Rasháh had a pistol in his right hand. The Quadrille ended. Rasháh waited till the Heel and Toe Polka began, and the Opera House was noisy again. He fired a single shot at Bridges, which entered neatly through his forehead and lodged harmlessly in a wooden beam behind him. Nearly no blood, no skull fragments. Rasháh was like a surgeon. Bridges died immediately, without even a gasp. He remained standing for a moment, then fell quietly backward to the floor, like an exhausted man collapsing into bed. In the ballroom, one of the Tabor daughters laughed and laughed, so beautifully, her laughter like little palace bells.

Rasháh stood by the locked door.

"Loyal to Sidonia, yet out of town on business this whole week," Allen Jerome said. "Whom did he need to meet with out of town, without my knowing about it first?"

He turned to Rasháh.

"I assume you were puzzling that out these last few days?"

Rasháh nodded, but his gaze had turned to Mrs. Bridges, who shrank into the corner.

Angry but frightened, she asked breathlessly, "Why is he looking at me like that?"

"Quantitative analysis," Allen Jerome said. "Now your husband is dead. Is it possible that you might yet be of value to the Sidonian movement, or do you present a threat? Are you harmless? Just an angry but frightened and harmless woman who will slink off somewhere and look over your left shoulder for the rest of your life? Maybe get a job down in Denver to support your – " His eyes narrowed. "Three children, yes? He is adding it up. He is naught but a great abacus, who only looks somewhat human. That's all he is. A machine. He doesn't even *look* very human at all, when you examine him closely."

"What is he thinking about?"

"He's running the numbers. Analyzing the variables. It always takes time."

Jerome rolled his cigar between his thumb and pointer finger.

"It's common sense to me. But he must generate random simulations. For the record, he uses Brother Edvin's 'middle square' method. It's time consuming and not entirely reliable, but if he tries to peek into the future and change the past, he'll be swept off the interlinear Maze, so we're stuck with the middle square method. I don't think that I *quite* have time to explain. But to make a long story short, I think by the bye, he'll conclude that there's some feasible scenario in which a woman whose husband was shot down by Sidonian forces in cold blood proves not to be particularly beneficial to Sidonia. He'll get there eventually." Nodding, looking at his cigar. "I think your children shall be orphans, before the hour is out. Give or take a moment or two."

Out in the ballroom, the Denver Boys were in the middle of a raucous version of *Varsouvienna*. Whoops and hollers echoed through the opera house, and the blood drained from the poor woman's face. Darryl Fawley looked away.

"Can we not set her loose?" he asked plaintively, more for Lucy's sake, to retain some vestige of the humanity in her grand dream, than out of any real hope that his business partner might show some pity. Lucy would have wanted to free Mrs. Bridges from her female bondage, from her fear. She would want to teach her to be strong. Still, he knew the answer.

Varsouvienna slowed to its conclusion amid enthusiastic applause, and the Leadville Merchants struck up a *Quadrille*.

"All we ever did was love Sidonia," the woman whispered.

"We will not tell your children that you were traitors," Allen Jerome said. "We will tell them that you were heroes of the Revolution. I suspect that Rasháh will see no reason to kill your children, in all likelihood. Their money may remain intact." With a nod in Rashah's direction. "But it'll be up to him."

She stood from her husband's prone body, and she tried to run from the room, her limbs flipping and trembling as she went. She pounded on the thick wood of the locked ballroom door and called for help, but none of the guests could hear her over the blare of the trumpets, in crescendo. Without hope, still she pounded on the door, she shrieked, she cried.

After a while, Rasháh completed his quantitative calculations, and he smiled with his red lips.

Sitting beside the two bodies, Allen Jerome crossed his legs.

"We can make them dissolve, can we not, Fawley?" he asked. "I hope that we can make them dissolve." He was scribbling on a sheet of rumpled paper, which was filled with numbers surrounded by a bar graph. He scribbled a bit onto the graph, then sat back with satisfaction, before re-noticing with some shock the dead couple who still lay at his feet.

"Can we not make them dissolve into nothingness?" he asked Darryl Fawley, his voice almost pleading.

CHAPTER 13

A few miles south of the Montana mountains – the self-same mountains that purportedly held the legendary city of Sidonia – we found the little clearing shown on the map that Billy Golden had given us. The clearing was hidden from the world by the thick of the forest and not connected to civilization by even a single path. In the center of the clearing was a friendly little inn, with small, stained glass windows in the attic, far above.

Hester tapped the reins, and her horse stopped.

"This is it," she said. "This is where Billy sent us."

"Why are we stopping here?" I asked, and she said that we were stopping here because Billy told us to stop here, and that if we didn't do what he told us, he would undo all the Magic that had reconnected my ruined bones back in the Wyoming penitentiary, and I would collapse to the ground, ruined and wrecked.

I smiled. I wasn't entirely sure that Billy could undo Madame Tang's healing without her help, but I supposed it wasn't worth risking it.

Now that I had something to live for, it mattered to me whether I died in a heap. I would indeed prefer not to die.

Lady Amalie greeted us on the path that led to the inn, a cheerful, elderly woman with clear, sparkling blue eyes, and she led us to our room on the third floor, a suite somehow larger than the space allotted within the little house. I stepped out on a balcony that had not been visible from below, and Hester joined me, and we looked out over an impossible forest, filled with trees I had never seen before. Birds like flying peacocks perched on the branches. In the far distance, a white city was carved from the rock in a snow-covered mountain.

"You see?" Hester said to me. "This is an inn out of Time and out of Place. We could stay here forever, and never age." She slipped her arm around me. "But we cannot, of course. History awaits us both."

She smiled at her grandiosity.

And we stood there, just looking at this world that we didn't know but that we loved, until the sun set. An unfamiliar sky bloomed, filled with strange stars.

I really don't know where to begin or end when I talk about my life at Lady Amalie's inn, that cheerful hostel that was bigger on the inside than the outside.

I don't know how long we stayed there, and in reality, we stayed there no time at all.

To whit: As you already know, but which I did not at this point in our yarn, Hester was with child, just barely.

She said nothing to me as we left South America, because I would not have allowed her to travel, and I might have put off the trip altogether to stay with her and see it all through, and to welcome my son into the world.

But nothing that happened at Lady Amalie's inn gave me cause for suspicion. We might have been there for months, but Hester grew no more pregnant. She was approximately two months pregnant when we arrived in July of 1879, and she remained ever-so as the days stretched into weeks, and perhaps into months.

During my stay in the golden cradle of Lady Amalie's realm, I sometimes wondered idly at our proprietress's age, but I know now that the answer could be only that she was no older and no younger than she had been a moment ago, as were we all.

In the mornings, we would descend the stairs to Lady Amalie's dome-ceilinged dining hall and start the day with a breakfast of fruits I could not identify, eaten alongside neighbors whose life stories seemed, at the time, to be a figment of my own imagination.

The second morning, for example, we were joined by a young girl who insisted that she was a refugee princess from a floating island, whose companion was either a very well-trained monkey who behaved almost like a little man, or a exceptionally odd little man who resembled a monkey. The monkey-like fellow (or fellow-like monkey) could not speak, but he sang with the voice of an angel. The third morning we discussed mathematics with a professor of a university that I am quite sure has never existed. He wore a purple robe, and his eyes were golden blue, and his views on the golden theorem of mathematical residue moved Hester near to tears.

Sometimes in the early afternoons, we explored looping corridors and twisting stairways, and in the late afternoons, we climbed the rolling hills behind the inn, wandered among the orchard fruit trees, and when day sank into night, settled beside the observatory at the top of the highest hill, opened a bottle of the inn's singular wine, and quietly spied on the terpsichoreans of North Sadlareeyah as they strummed their peculiar melodies and danced their strange, leaping dances on the bank of the roaring river far below, under the meteor showers and streaks of purple light that painted Lady Amalie's nighttime skies.

One early morning, while Hester was still asleep, Lady Amalie greeted me in the meadow behind the trees that sheltered the inn. The dew was cool on my bare feet. The peacocks lumbered overhead, plummeting from branch to branch, and above them, a few hawks circled.

Lady Amalie pointed.

"They could be Sidonian scouts," she said, her brow creased. "Or they could just be hawks. They know that we are here, you see, Mr. O'Hugh? They know that we are here, but cannot yet do anything about it. One day, our immunity will end. Time will collapse in on us. And retribution will be swift."

She watched the hawks for a while, till they circled up above the clouds and vanished from view. Then she smiled and touched my arm gently.

"It won't happen to-day," she said, "or to-morrow. And as I said, sometimes a hawk is just a hawk."

After we had resided at the inn for some time, Hester and I visited Lady Amalie in her study on the third floor to let her know that, at the earliest suitable circumstance, I would embark on my journey, and I would march over the hill to Sidonia.

The stars had come out, and the study was shrouded in shadow. Lady Amalie sat at a polished, dark wood desk, scratched and dented and well-loved, and a dim oil lantern flickered on the desk's edge.

"I am grateful that you are ready to go," she said gently.

"Not *ready*," I admitted, and my voice cracked a bit, unheroically. "But," I added, "although not ready, I am drawn somehow to fulfill my obligation without further delay."

And so I would do it, I would leave on this mission that I knew I could not avoid if I were ever to be a complete man again, this ugly mission inextricably linked in my mind to one enchanting night in South America under the influence of beautiful opera music and a beautiful deadling.

Shelves filled with old books lined the walls.

I found myself muttering to the floor.

"I do understand the conflict you are feeling in your heart," she said, "and the sacrifice you are making as a result." With affection in her shaky voice, she smiled and said, "Mr. O'Hugh."

Lady Amalie smiled.

"Love peace, pursue peace," she said, "and love your fellow creatures. May your light burst forth like the first sunrise, and may there be peace among us."

Eventually, I thought. *But first, fight and kill.*

The next morning, when the day was yet still new, a Chinese guide rapped on the door of our room.

He was small, youthful and enthusiastic, with a wide smile, and he introduced himself as Chu Ying. The light of the sunrise glowed on a face that already glowed with eagerness for the day's adventure.

"If we are lucky," said Chu Ying, as he hurried us from our room, "we might seek the audience of a legendary wise man, who lives in the mountain peaks."

Without much delay, he took Hester and me up the side of the nearest mountain – a fabled, storybook mountain still on *this* side of reality – to a peak some feet below the very top, where we arrived when the sun was yet halfway across the sky. We were still shaking the sleep from our eyes when we stopped to await the great man's arrival. In the valley below, I thought I could dimly discern the faded outlines of the great Sidonian metropolis, shrouded in morning fog.

"He is a truly exceptional wise man," Chu Ying said. "He might have some valuable insight into your mission, and perhaps a bit of helpful Magic as well."

Chu Ying leaned back, staring across the narrow passage that led between the two cliffs.

"What if he doesn't show up?" I wondered.

"Then we will go back down the side of the mountain," Chu Ying said. "And your mission will be more dangerous without the weapon of his wisdom, I would think."

He smiled thoughtfully.

"But I do hope he comes," he said. "Magic might come in handy, when one is faced with omnipotent evil."

"This sounds," I agreed, "like a very good idea."

I thought I could use some Chinese Magic. Some spells, hocus-pocus, and whatnot. And it seemed to me that a Chinese wise man who lived ascetically in mythical misty mountains would be just the fellow to provide what we needed.

We waited an hour or so, with no sign of a wise man, and then Chu Ying said that perhaps we should travel a bit farther east, so we crossed the path between the two cliffs into a mountain pasture surrounded by peaks and hidden from the inn and from the smoky distant city.

Then, suddenly, there he was, appearing from around the bend, a heavy-set man in a gigantic black hat, galloping along on the strongest horse I had ever seen. His long gray-black beard waved thickly behind him as he rode forward in the mountain wind, his black coat flapping at his side.

Our Chinese wise man was not what I had imagined.

CHAPTER 14

John Dead-Man and Yu Dai-Yung woke before dawn and rode to the West, the Chinese poet on his brown horse with strong legs, and the sad Indian on just the sort of horse one might imagine for the last lonely heir to the forgotten legacy of a once-great nation: sagging in the middle, snorting with exhaustion, spitting frequently, more like a dying camel than a noble horse. Master Yu gathered that this horse had once been strong and proud, like the Peking Indian nation itself.

After just fifteen minutes of this, Master Yu could take no more, and he tapped on the reins.

"We're going into town, John Dead-Man," he said. "We've got one more piece of business in town, you and me."

And so they detoured from their western course and headed south along the dusty cow-trail, and they reached town, turgid and hot and near-deserted, by the sleepy mid-morning. They stopped at the end of town out-front of an establishment known as Ed Hessel's Stables. Master Yu made arrangements for the Indian's frail horse. While she deserved a quick and compassionate bullet in the head (the horse glue industry was not due to reach our shores till the end of the 19th century), the poet noted an emotional attachment between the near-dead nag and the near-dead Indian and didn't have time to argue. He demanded a new steed from the wrinkled and wiry proprietor, whom he assumed to be Hessel himself. John Dead-Man argued that "Waukendah" had always served him well, and Master Yu promised that Waukendah would await him at the end of the journey, subject only to the unpredictable will of the Jade Emperor, "and would you truly wish to subject such a loyal old friend to the dangers of our perilous mission?"

The Indian said he supposed not, and he looked into old Waukendah's eyes, and he whispered a few words in a language that neither the poet nor the old horse trader understood, and Master Yu knew there was a great chance that these two old friends would never see each other again, for one reason or another.

He turned to old man Hessel.

"We need something in the way of a steed," he told the old man, "that would be more suitable for the last scion of a great, fearless people."

Hessel clucked to himself – he was apparently less awed by John Dead-Man – but presently he returned with a great black horse, with a curly mane, wild eyes, and thin, tightly muscled legs.

"Here," said Hessel, his words whistling in his toothless mouth. "A wild pinder. Not an ordinary horse. Only wild pinder I've ever seen. Two years old."

Master Yu paused, looked the steed up and down, looked in its mouth, behind its ears, stroked its flank, and then he nodded with admiration.

"I think this is just right," he said.

His irises shrank and his corneas clouded over until they were a foggy gray, and he looked out over the rolling prairies to the West of the town and watched things happen that the other two men could not see. He smiled in the gluey air. Then his eyes cleared, and he ran his fingers through the horse's wavy mane.

"That's right." Nodding. "A wild pinder is just what the Peking Indians rode. This is exactly the horse for a noble Peking Indian."

The horse cost Master Yu a pretty penny.

Their journey was long. Dry grasslands rose into forested hills of Douglas fir and ponderosa pine, then descended into the plains, then to the edge of a river. At dusk on their fourth Wednesday together, they found a bend in the river shallow enough for their horses to cross, slept on the western edge, woke early before the dawn on their fourth Thursday together, and by their fifth Monday, rose up into the mountains, where they made camp on a dry lake bed. Over the ridge, yellowing grasslands spread out to the horizon. John Dead-Man left camp for an hour, then returned with a couple of javelinas, which he roasted over an open fire.

"We are close?" Master Yu said, the moonlight in his eyes.

John Dead-Man nodded.

"Very close," he said.

He poured himself a cup of water, took a drink.

"What's in this for you, Chinaman? The praise of the Empress?"

"No," Master Yu said. "That's what I thought when I began the journey. But I know that she would leave me to die, and I have realized that I care not if I pay taxes to the Empress, President Rutherford B. Hayes or the Sidonian King. I didn't know what was in this for me before I arrived here in America. I didn't know what was in this for me until the morning I left San Francisco." He shrugged. "And now I know." He almost admitted that he was doing this for a woman, but then he kept quiet. It didn't sound worth it, when one came right out and said it, without any poetry attached. There's always another woman walking up the next lane, after all, isn't there? Why would one seek the love of a penniless woman with a vengeful deadling husband when one might easily meet a rich woman who did not have a vengeful deadling husband?

From the lake bed, they climbed down a narrow crevice that had once been a beautiful little waterfall, but which had dried up centuries ago. At the next cliff level, they headed a bit east, where John Dead-Man stopped before a thicket of springy, man-size trees, dry but tough. The Peking Indian took a hacking knife from his pack, and he whacked away at the trees until they were splintered and ragged, revealing a cave opening. John Dead-Man lit a lantern, checked his compass, and in they crawled.

The cavern passages were indeed twisty and dark; there was a distant and mysterious (and ultimately infuriating) drip of water; and the air was dank and forbidding. While crawling through a winding rock tunnel would elicit feelings of claustrophobia in the most fearless of men, I have to admit that their trip into the cavern's bowels was relatively uneventful, and thanks to the Indian's orienteering skills, not particularly frightening. I wish I could tell you that they encountered human skeletons and other gruesome discoveries, because this would be exciting and chilling, and it would "up the ante," so to speak. But no human had been in this cavern for many years, if ever, due to the remoteness of its location and the near-unbroachable nature of the cave's mouth.

The tunnel narrowed to a crawlspace, and the two men crept for some yards on their hands and knees.

Then Yu Dai-Yung stopped crawling.

"Soon," he whispered, "we will pass through a portal into the Dark Thief's world, a portal just north of Xiorian. Xiorian is in

Sadlo'reen, but unlike North Sadlareeyah, it is loyal to the Falsturm. Throughout the land, from coast to coast, Time moves at a different pace, and the Dark Thief, their mad sea captain, has been sailing the Sadlareeyahian Sea for more than a thousand years, so long that even the Yellow Emperor knew of his quest."

The Indian grunted.

"It is important that you believe this, that you trust me. If you do not trust me, we are doomed. In the portal, as it is written, you will pass demons, a multitude of them. Look them in the eyes, and be unafraid. If you look them in the eyes without fear, they will be trapped in their frozen air. But you must be unafraid. You must not doubt."

Now comes the frightening part, after pages that were, I admit, not very frightening. But I am not here to frighten you. I am here to tell you the truth.

The next twist of the cave tunnel was just as the Yellow Emperor had described it in *White Pond*, opening up to a wider and higher corridor filled with demons, large hairy demons with teeth and horns, small buzzing demons that poked at our heroes' eyes, and green slithering demons that wound themselves around Master Yu's legs.

"They cannot hurt you," he whispered. "Look in their eyes and do not doubt me. Do not be afraid, even for a moment."

And then it happened. A creature that looked like nothing that could be real – my readers of the 21st century would have dismissed the beast as "computer animation," all bouncing green flab and shining silver claws – took a great swipe at Master Yu's friend and cut his head right off his neck, till it hung sideways, narrowly attached by a thin ligament.

Then Master Yu noticed something. No blood spurted from John Dead-Man's arteries, as one might have expected. And while his head dangled precariously from his body, his eyes remained bright and alert. He had trusted Master Yu just enough, and he had doubted the demon just enough, to keep him just barely alive. His lopsided head smiled and popped back onto his neck, and after that everything was, as one might say, a "snap." They marched through the corridor of screaming, slashing demons without a care, until the tunnel opened up into a large grotto. Sunbeams flickered through a jagged crack in the grotto's ceiling, and chunks of gold were embedded in a scattered pattern across the rocky walls.

The gold embedded in the walls was clear and flawless and turned white in the flecks of sunlight that danced across the cave floor, which was where, incidentally, a dragon reclined, half-asleep, one eye open. The dragon was threatening in its passivity, in its focused calm. A Chinese unicorn lay beside the dragon, and the unicorn was quite unconscious.

The Indian pulled back. He put his hand on his pistol.

Master Yu put out a hand in warning, and he shook his head.

"Is this not, after all, why we came?" he asked.

The dragon was about eleven feet long, significantly smaller than the great lizard that Master Yu had seen atop the Bank of California building. The unicorn was a frail creature, which in its youth must have looked fearsome. Its once vibrant, colorful skin was gray and black. It had the body of a deer, the hooves of a horse, the tail of an ox, and a single corroding horn atop its tired head. Its breathing was labored and painful.

The unicorn opened one eye, which was red and wet. Then its eyelid trembled shut again.

The dragon's tail stroked the unicorn's back, tenderly but mechanically.   ·

"Is this a dream?" John Dead-Man asked. "Are we mad?"

"Perhaps," Master Yu replied. "I am quite certain that not everyone who enters this golden cavern would be able to see this dragon. Does that make us mad? Or, instead, does it mean that we are very very perceptive? Most would say mad. And perhaps they would be correct."

The Chinese poet approached the dragon, whose demon eyes opened wide in his great camel head, expectantly, a bit impatiently.

Master Yu held out his right hand. The dragon rose and put a great tiger paw into the Chinese poet's palm. Master Yu closed his hand around the dragon's paw. They stood for a moment, the Chinese poet and the Chinese dragon, just greeting each other silently.

The dragon purred.

"*Dragons purr,*" Master Yu marveled. Who could have guessed that a happy dragon would purr?

One might expect that the dragon's lair would have been a place filled with jewels and emeralds; that they might fight a fierce battle with the dragon, a fire-soaked battle from which only one combatant would emerge alive. But the only two treasures in that particular lair were an old sword and a large but dusty diamond, and real dragons cannot breathe fire – a physical impossibility, as an expert in the field of Dragonology had once taught me – and this particular dragon did not wish to fight; the dragon pushed the old sword forward towards the two men with one gentle tiger paw before turning back to the ailing unicorn.

The Indian approached the sword gingerly, bent down and lifted it slowly. He stood, and he bounced the sword back and forth in his hands.

"Doesn't seem like a very good sword," he muttered. "A little light and flimsy."

He tossed it to Master Yu, who caught the handle in his left hand. The handle was made of tortoise shell, tied together tightly with a band of leather, which was a strange design, Master Yu thought.

"Maybe they didn't make very good weapons back then," the Indian said. "Thousands of years ago. Maybe they just weren't that good, back then."

Master Yu turned the sword over in his hands. He reluctantly realized that John Dead-Man was correct. *Not a very good sword, as swords go.*

"Maybe it's magic," he said. "Maybe it is a magic sword."

The Indian laughed.

"Let us hope so," he said. Then: "I'll take the diamond, if the dragon doesn't mind."

The dragon, who was deeply focused on nursing his unicorn back to health (or comforting him as he succumbed to death's lure), did not seem to bother or even notice. His reptile eyes were gentle, sad and worried, and the diamond was the last thought in his mind.

CHAPTER 15

And now we come to the Talmudic part of our tale and any disinterested reader is encouraged to skip and to flip ahead without further delay and continue with Chapter 16. I will ensure that you will be able to follow my story without confusion. Readers who stay with me and complete this chapter can be assured that they will be subjected to no proselytizing and that I will take no side on the whole "God" question, although I have developed my views on the issue, as have most men who have reached their tenth decade.

It came about like this: When the wise man of the fictitious mountains dismounted from his very strong horse, I recognized him immediately as a rabbi, not from his garb – his great black coat and hat – but from an aura of wisdom that seemed to glow and engulf him almost visibly (although I had to my knowledge never before in my life even met a genuine Jew close-up). While I am unsure whether the rabbi was indeed wise, he certainly knew a bit of hocus pocus, which I have found can come in handy.

The rabbi's horse snorted, then relaxed.

"Watt O'Hugh," I said, and I held out my hand.

"The late Watt O'Hugh the Third," he laughed. "The several-times-late Watt O'Hugh the Third. You look well for a man so recently and frequently deceased."

He shook my hand.

"Rabbi Samuel Palache," he said.

I was about to introduce Hester, but the rabbi interrupted me.

"Hester Smith," he said with a smile, squinting in the sun. "A pleasure to meet you at last," and Hester smiled back. The rabbi raised a finger, and the two of them strolled a few yards into the clearing, where they spoke animatedly for a few moments. Hester seemed slightly agitated, and the rabbi seemed mildly alarmed. They noticed me noticing them, and they walked a bit farther away and turned their backs.

I nodded to the rabbi's companion, a natty young man of no more than 19- or 20-years of age, with a great waxed mustache and a starchy white seafaring outfit. He introduced himself as Arthur, and he told me that he was a doctor serving an apprenticeship on a Greenland whaling ship, "which is how," he added, "I came to be cast ashore on this island."

"Is this an island?" I asked, peering into the distance, trying to get a clear view of Hester and the rabbi, who were hovering on the far side of a great and precarious pile of boulders.

"Oh, yes," said Arthur distractedly, as though nothing were more sensible than the idea that we were all on an island, or that I would be here on an island and not know it. And for a young man who just yesterday thought he'd be spending this day treating scurvy, this was perhaps not the least sensible thing he had encountered recently.*

The rabbi returned with Hester and said he had some stew in the oven and wondered if we weren't hungry. We all remounted our horses and the rabbi led us through an extravagantly circuitous stone pathway that widened and narrowed between two sheer mountain cliffs. Once we were all thoroughly disoriented, the trail deposited us into a mountain forest, at the center of which was a small, humble wooden home, smoke puffing cheerfully from the chimney.

"He is not the original Samuel Palache," Chu Ying said, his enthusiasm unabated, once we had dismounted and were approaching the cabin on foot. "You know, he is of course not the famous 16th century pirate rabbi."

I nodded, as though I had been up till now well-versed in the history of 16th century Jewish sea piracy, and as though this very question had been therefore on my mind.

According to Chu Ying, in 1624, the "original" Rabbi Palache helmed a pirate flotilla that captured a Spanish warship in the Mediterranean Sea. In the process, the rabbi pirate rescued the passengers of a Dutch vessel that had been captured off the coast of Morocco some months earlier. Almost immediately, the rabbi's ship was met by both a storm of ferocious intensity and the cove of an

---

* I was to run into Arthur again during the Battle of Sidonia at the turn of the following century, when he had become a well-known author. As an older man, he would believe in fairies and wizards and ghosts, and, most of all, perhaps, the magical power of the world's rabbis – with a particular obsession with the secrets secreted within the wizardly brain of the great Houdini's rabbi – which view I suppose he acquired during that timeless month in the mountains.

unmapped and unnamed isle, where the pirates and the rescued passengers attempted to wait out the storm.

One of the passengers was Rivka, a Jewish woman of murky background and provenance, who had by then convinced herself (or at least claimed to have done) that her own sins were to blame for the sudden storm, as though she were a medieval Jonah. The same thing had happened to the *Vliegende Draeck,* a three-level Dutch fleut that she had boarded in Copenhagen, and so she bid the pirates leave without her.

Rabbi Palache's son, Solomon, volunteered to chaperone the young woman until a suitable rescue could be arranged. This proposal was offered too eagerly, and with no possibility of negotiation, it seemed to the Rabbi (and with no realistic hope of the "suitable rescue" of which the young Palache referred), and thus he concluded that love or enchantment had irrevocably intervened and that nothing could be done, and so the young couple – for couple, by now, they were – received a quick shipboard wedding from the pirate rabbi, rowed to shore and vanished from view into the lush island woods and out of recorded history.

The island itself was indeed not free of Magic, and not entirely uninhabited, and so the devoted Solomon and Rivka lived happily and comfortably behind a mist that, on most days, rendered the island invisible to mortal eyes, and protected by winds that steered most ships in a different direction. That is, until the threat of the Red Eyebrows exploded from the Earth again after two Millennia like some terrible thousand-year cicada, and, at Lady Amalie's request, Rabbi Samuel Palache the younger, the 19th century island descendent of the original fearless pirate, saw fit to leave his paradise and teach a counter-Revolutionary army what Magic he had learnt.

Hearing this story, which Chu Ying whispered excitedly to me on the little path leading to the cabin, I nodded patiently and without comment, as one might when accosted by a muttering lunatic on a city street. While this was not by any margin the very strangest thing I had heard since awakening in the Laramie prison, Chu Ying was an especially gullible messenger, and I was not entirely sure that I believed the story about the Jewish pirate rabbi and the magic isle.

The inside of the cabin was lined with shelves that held well-thumbed, ancient looking treatises titled with an unfamiliar script. The home was otherwise filled with unidentifiable baubles, but which seemed to inhabit a place of honor in the house. The rabbi's wife minded the oven stew.

Two other things of particular note: First, I felt that the light in the cabin was rather extraordinary, and when I looked out the window I realized that the view, from this mountain cabin, was a quiet blue sea, gentle waves stroking a yellow, sun-drenched shore. Second, my old friend Billy Golden was sitting in an armchair in the corner, reading a copy of the recently published *Die Entwicklung des Sozialismus von der Utopie zur Wissenschaft* (in the original German), and looking younger than I had ever seen him.

At my first opportunity, I shook Billy's hand, and I asked after the staggeringly beautiful Christine Nilsson.

He shrugged. *The opera singer?* he mouthed in confusion.

I smiled.

"Later on in your life," I said, "during the years when you are rather older – although temporally earlier in the history of the universe – you both fall madly in love with each other."

"In the jungle?" he asked. "In April? 1879?"

I nodded.

He sighed.

"Thank God," he whispered.

At the dinner table, a half hour or so later, the conversation returned to the subject of Christine Nilsson. Billy was very young now, younger than when we'd begun the meal, not much more than a teenage boy and very excited about the possibility of pursuing a love affair with Miss Nilsson, and he peppered us with questions, gunning for advice on how to capture the lovely young woman's affections. Hester sought to warn our friend, to tamp down his rising enthusiasm.

"I fear," she said, "that it may not be entirely happy for you. I think you would be well-advised to look elsewhere for satisfaction."

"A great love is worth experiencing," Billy said, "even if it does not bring great joy."

And with that, I noticed that he had grown very old indeed, and rather sad.

"I would do nothing different with respect to my affair with Miss Nilsson," he told us, his eyes weary, "if I had the opportunity to re-live my life a million times over."

At once, he was young again, happy and eager and hopelessly ensnared in the first throes of love.

We sat around the table, Hester, Chu Ying, Arthur, the young Billy Golden and I. The rabbi sat at the head of the table, and the rabbi's wife joined us, from time to time, at the other end of the table. She was a plump woman with a beautiful smile.

"It has been taught," said the rabbi, holding his spoon aloft. He was answering a rather guileless question that Arthur had just asked. "Abba Binyamin says, *If the eye had the power to see them, no creature could endure the demons.* Abaye says: *They are more numerous than we are and they surround us like the ridge around a field.* Rav Huna says: *Every one among us has a thousand on his left hand and ten thousand on his right hand.* Rava says: *The crushing of the crowd in the yearly public lectures comes from them. Fatigue in the knees comes from them. The wearing out of the clothes of the scholars is due to their rubbing against them. The bruising of the feet comes from them.*"

"Right here?" said Arthur. "Right now? All invisible? Demons?"

The rabbi nodded.

"On the other hand," he said. "It could be an allegory." He held up one finger and pointed at me. "I must tell you all the story of Rabbi Shimon bar Yohai and his adventures upon emerging from the cave. It is very important that I tell you about this before you leave. *Shabbas* 33b-34a. Remind me, if I forget." Then, still to me, he added pointedly and irrelevantly, "And what of your parents, O'Hugh? Do you know the history of your parents?"

"I have no parents," I said. "I grew up on the streets, with no name. Until I named myself."

He stroked his beard absently.

"Just as a point of fact," he said. "Everyone has parents. Whether one knows his own parents, their existence is simply a biological fact. But beyond the scientific nature of my observation, may I offer the likely conjecture that perhaps they held you upon your birth. Perhaps they kissed your soft infant forehead, and perhaps they loved you for a moment, or more than a moment. Perhaps their love floats about in the troposphere a bit. Maybe it keeps you a little bit warm at night, and you don't know it."

"Rabbi," Billy said politely. "We need a prophesy."

He shrugged. Prophesies he could deliver.

"The Falsturm may be defeated," he said, "only by the hand of the daughter of a Queen, who was born Nephila." [*]

He turned to me, and he gave me a potent look. I nodded, and he knew what I meant: *I know this prophesy.* Rabbi Palache was a man not unacquainted with oracles, and snowy egrets.

"I'm reasonably confident about that one," he added.

Still looking at me.

Silence descended, as everyone thought about all this: the demons; the Falsturm; the princess born of the Nephilim.

I filled in the silence.

"So why am I here?" I asked. "Why me? Look, I know why *I* want to be here. Nothing more than blind hatred and foolish blood-lust. But what's made all of you lose your senses?"

I pointed out, astutely I thought, that I was far from anonymous. I was a dime novel hero, then a Wild West star, then a wrongly convicted, although infamous, passion killer, the subject of a number of folk songs and moralistic stage theatricals. (I admit that I never really tired of explaining the ways in which I was far-from-anonymous.) What's more, I noted, the Sidonians had tried to kill me a number of times, once by shooting me through the head in the Wyoming mountains, then again by firing squad in Nebraska.

"The Pinkertons may still care about me a bit," I said, "but the Sidonians care more."

Billy shrugged sadly. He was now middle-aged. This bit had apparently taken practice to get right.

"You have it in you, Watt," he said. "You have the motive. You can taste it. You need it. There is perhaps no one who needs this more than you, who needs to fight them more than you need to fight them. And so we are sending you. We are *allowing* you to go. This is no more than what Hester promised on that beach in Pangaea. It is why you are here, after all."

Had he been more honest, he would have admitted that he had seen patterns in history. I didn't have what one might call a "destiny,"

---

[*] The Nephilim – the offspring of angels and human women – are generally viewed with suspicion and fear. I am not one hundred percent certain that Nephilim exist (or ever existed), but if they do, I am rather certain they are not all bad.

but Billy had learned that if he were to introduce me into the Sidonian capital in 1879, there was at least a possibility that one specific death would occur that could cause a chain reaction favorable to the counter-Revolution. And if he were to send me there tasting the bitter bile of revenge, that probability would increase.

Billy turned to the rabbi.

"Rabbi Palache," he said. "Mr. O'Hugh will need a convincing disguise."

The two of us stood before a full length mirror, the rabbi sturdy, solid and portly; the shootist a bit wobbly, veiny and confused.

Outside the window, palm trees swayed gently in the Pacific breeze.

"Here is Watt O'Hugh," the rabbi said. "Thirty-seven years old. Tall. Weakening, but still strong. A steady aim, thanks to some supernatural help." Here he smiled, and added, "Perhaps.

"With," he continued, "a familiar face." He slapped my cheek very gently with the back of his hand. "Even you, Watt, are tired of this face. You wish to ruin it before you turn forty – you weather it with sun and strong drink, and you chisel it up with your incessant scowl."

I insisted that I still knew how to smile, and I called out for affirmation to Hester, who nodded noncommittally, her gaze elsewhere.

"Elazar ben Azaryah, 10th-generation progeny of the prophet Ezra, was a brilliant scholar, but of a preternaturally youthful appearance, even for a lad of 18. When he was appointed chief rabbi of the Jews, his wife wondered if the people would take direction and leadership from a man with the face of a child, lovely and pure though that childish face might be. *I am like a man of 70 years*, he told her, as his head touched the feather pillow that night. His wife, a girl of sixteen, embraced a youth that evening, and she laughed at what she considered his hubris. But by morn, an old man lay beside her in bed. Elazar now displayed the wisdom that usually comes of age – the wisdom he had possessed since childhood – but he retained the energy and vigor of youth."

By the end of this story, I had forgotten what I was doing, and I was no longer looking in the mirror, but instead at the face of the rabbi, as he spoke, quiet and firm.

"Did he continue ageing?" Arthur asked, observing from the lunch table. "Or was his visage frozen at 70? He had the strong heart of an 18-year-old." He twirled his mustache between the pointer finger and middle finger of his left hand. "Or might this too be some type of allegory?"

The rabbi nudged me, with a small small touch, and I turned back to the face in the mirror.

The scars on my face were gone, as were the imperfections with which I had been born. My brow was unfurrowed, my eyes honest and true. My face itself was handsome and strong. It was a face I didn't recognize, but which I loved better than my own.

Chu Ying beamed.

"The Jews are so magical!" he exclaimed. "So mysterious. So inscrutable."

"What is the explanation for this?" I asked.

The rabbi thought for a moment.

"Consider this," he said, very carefully. "As the Talmud notes, when two men gather cucumbers by Magic, one will be punished and the other exempt. Which man will walk free and which one will die, by the grace of God? He who *really* gathers them is punished: whilst he who produces merely an illusion is exempt. You see?"

I shook my head. I did not see.

"How about this?" the rabbi said, trying again. "We do not see things as they are. We see them as *we* are." And then, almost pleadingly: "*Hmm? Ah?*"

"No," I said. "Nothing."

The rabbi gripped my left arm in his strong, calloused hand, and we walked together out of the cabin, onto the sandy island beach that he had always called home. We stared out together at miles of ocean. The cabin was gone. We were alone on a deserted beach. Sea spray hit my face.

"When Rabbi Elazar needed a miracle," the rabbi said, "he received a miracle. So maybe, as it was with Rabbi Elazar, we can say that sometimes, when we need a miracle, we receive a miracle. Maybe. *Sometimes.*"

The next morning, I sat on the bed in our room at the inn. I looked around at the furnishings for the last time, at the little desk, the polished, dark wood dressing table pushed against the northern wall, its mirror reflecting the room. My bags were packed. Outside our window, it was dark, and the moon still glowed just above the crest of the painted-backdrop mountains.

"In the jungle, I thought I could not possibly have been happier," I said. "And along comes Lady Amalie's magical mountain inn."

I laughed.

Hester sat down beside me on the bed.

"You could stay here forever, couldn't you?" And she smiled.

I nodded. My handsome, handsome new head bobbed up and down. I felt handsome, nodding that head, that handsome head.

But, she pointed out, if I stayed here forever, there would not long be an inn to enjoy, or any world outside of the reality that Sidonia would build. And Darryl Fawley would be king, and he would live forever.

I agreed, reluctantly.

"I know the story of Rabbi Elazar," I said, stroking my handsome new face. "But I forgot to ask Samuel Palache about Rabbi Whoozit ben Yoo-hoo. Do you think it could be important?"

I shrugged. I supposed that I would never know.

"Watt," Hester said, as I tied my bag shut. "I have learned things about you. Before I went to the desert to find you, I learned things about you from a man who runs a shop at 11th Street and 9th avenue in New York city. Then later, I confirmed these things from a shaman in Lansford, New Mexico. These are things you don't know. It's why I hunted for you in the first place. Rabbi Palache filled in some of the blanks. These are facts about your life, about your past."

"Rabbi Palache knew things about me?" I asked.

"He did," Hester said. "Indeed. He was not unfamiliar with you, Watt."

"Will they help me?" I asked. "These things you know that I do not know?"

"How?"

"In my battles to come. To make money. To be a better man. Will it help me in any way to know these things?"

"No," she said. "I am quite sure it will not help you. It will give you knowledge. But this knowledge will not be of any constructive value."

"Will this knowledge hurt me?"

"It will not," she said. "It will make you sad. But answering questions often makes us sad. Would you say that being a little sadder will hurt you?"

I thought about this. I took a drink of coffee with a splash of whiskey. I preferred not to be sadder than I already was.

"I do not want to know," I said. "We have time. That is, if I live. If I do not live, it doesn't matter. And so, if I live, you should ask me again. But for now, I do not want to know."

"Then I will not tell you."

"And so you know me better than I know myself?"

"Yes."

Before I left, I realized that I would need to teach her how to make J.P. Morgan alive and not-alive at the same time, in case I never returned from Sidonia. If I were not alive to impart this particular wisdom to Mr. Morgan, perhaps her business transaction with the Great Man would implode, leaving her without the expected financial windfall and bereft of a golden kingdom.

Hester said that was ridiculous.

"Of course you will return," she insisted.

But she took careful notes.

Hester kissed me goodbye as the day dawned over Lady Amalie's inn.

"Is it like kissing another man?" I asked.

She smiled.

"I feel as though I am being a bit disloyal to my O'Hugh," she said with a little laugh. "Your lips feel different. You look like a prince. I wish that I could see your real face one last time. All badly worn and human."

"You can hear my voice?" I asked her. I couldn't tell what my voice sounded like. "Isn't it my same old voice?"

"It is another man's voice."

She nearly told me the news. She nearly said, *You are to be a father, Watt O'Hugh. Billy Golden has seen his future, and he will be born strong and healthy.*

But she knew that I would not leave her. She knew that I would lose my urge to avenge Lucy and the children Lucy and I would never love, and I would be overcome by a great yearning for the little lump in Hester's womb. Hester wanted my boy to live in his own people's kingdom, in a world where even the memory of the Sidonians has been erased from the heavens. And so instead she said, "The scroll we retrieved from the train in Nevada was a fake, a diversion. The secret of the Red Eyebrows has arrived in New York, delivered via Falsturm hawk. Your mission to Sidonia is now more important than ever."

She caressed the side of my face. Her hand was rough and gentle.

"Return to me from the land of the enemy, and bring me back my O'Hugh. My funny-looking O'Hugh, whom I love so much."

She pulled her shawl around her shoulders, and she went back inside, and I missed her immediately.

I mounted my horse and took my map out of my coat pocket and looked it over, and then I rode off. After a few yards, I stopped, and I turned back to the inn and glanced up at the second floor window and saw Hester looking down at me. When she realized that I had seen her, she turned and shut the curtain and she was gone.

CHAPTER 16

Master Yu and John Dead-Man came down out of the mountains and traveled two weeks to Varley, where they stayed at the only lodging house that would take them, a clean but rickety structure in the questionable Harden neighborhood, surrounded mostly by tents that flapped raggedly in the night. Still, it provided them with a hot bath, after which they intended to go clear across town, right across Timmons Street to Felton, where they might make acquaintance with the only saloon in Varley that would serve them. Perhaps there was a saloon or two that would serve an Injun, the old hotel clerk drawled, staring down at his thumbs. And perhaps, he also noted, there might be one or two that might serve a Chinaman, although that speculation was a bit more questionable. But a saloon that would serve an Injun and a Chinaman settin' down together at the same bar, side by side, barstool by barstool ….

"Now that's out of the question in most places," he concluded. "Except for the one across Felton Street, the one that never bothered to come up with a name. They may hesitate. But tell them I said you were OK. Tell them old Barney said you were OK."

So they crossed both Timmons Street and Felton – a terrifying stretch, with whores and vacant eyed wiry drunks and men lying bloody in the street, laughing and rolling about in the mud – all of which prompted John Dead-Man to clutch his pistol through a hole in his overcoat pocket – until they reached the no-name saloon, where indeed the bartender refused to serve them until Master Yu mentioned the message from old Barney, at which the bartender smiled a one-toothed smile and his eyes grew a touch hazy. "Good old Barney!" he exclaimed. John Dead-Man ordered a whiskey and Master Yu ordered another whiskey. At the front of the bar, sitting on a rickety three-legged stool a heavy-set Colored woman of about forty years of age sang a beautiful but truly mortifying ballad, filled with more kinds of illicit relations than one would expect to find in a single song, each followed by a horrible murder, every one more gruesome than the last. When she finished, she flashed the crowd a charming, winsome smile, and there was an excited whoop of applause, which frightened Master Yu.

He turned to the Indian, and he hesitated, and then he hesitated again. The fact was, he told his friend, that he had been there before, in that cave, many years ago. A couple of thousand years ago. When his eyes clouded over, he could see it as though it were yesterday, his visit to that cave.

"As another man," Master Yu said. "Yang Hsiung."

The Indian's eyebrows rose.

"Yang Shang, bastard son of rich man poet," he said. "Yang Shang rode a dragon over the plains."

Master Yu cocked his head.

"*Maybe,*" he said, dubiously. This might have been embroidery. He wasn't sure that it could be true. "Do Peking Indians believe in reincarnation?" When John Dead-Man didn't answer, Master Yu explained, "In China, it is our view that when we die, we just come back to Earth and are born once more and live another life full of the same pain and confusion and ignorance. Over and over."

"No," said the Indian. "Peking Indians believe – *believed* – that we just go up to the sky."

"Up to the sky!"

Master Yu laughed.

"I'd go straight up to the sky first if I could," he exclaimed, still laughing, "and skip all this 屁話! The Peking Indians are very lucky."

He held up a finger.

"But I remembered one important thing, from all those years ago. Something just came to my mind. Give me the sword."

John Dead-Man slid the old sword gently onto the bar, and it made a soft, melodic clang.

Master Yu tapped the handle on its left side, and the two halves of the tortoise shell slid open, and a scroll slipped out onto the bar. Master Yu unrolled it, grimaced as he analyzed the faint inscription, and then, suddenly satisfied, he looked up at his friend.

"We're looking for a bridge," he said. "No, not really a bridge, because a bridge just takes you across a river to the other bank, which you can see from any vantage point. We are looking for something that is more like a diversion – a *weir*, I think. It is not just a bridge, but it is a weir, because a weir creates its own physical reality. So it is a weir to … oh, for lack of a better expression, let's call it a 'weir to a new realm.' " He smiled. "I think that I like that. *A weir to a new realm.*"

He sat there for a moment by the bar, swirling his whiskey around in its glass, thinking about this little turn of phrase. Then he frowned.

"Not very beautiful, actually," he said. "Not very poetic. A weir to a new realm."

"Not all of life is poetry."

"Maybe not. Maybe so. Well, I know where this weir is located. Generally at least. But I do not know how to get there. John Dead-Man, are you familiar with an 'island of many hills'?"

The Indian laughed.

"Island of many hills," he said. "That's an old name. In the Peking dialect – and also, later, in the Lenape dialect – it's *Manna-hatta.* It's a small island in the Lenapehoking region of the continent. Very far from here."

He smiled at Yu, but the Chinese poet had no reaction.

"New York City," the Indian said gently. "*Manhattan.* You see? *Manna-hatta: Manhattan.*"

"All right, then," Master Yu said decisively. "I need to see a wise sage with a harem of four wives in the far south of the island of many hills, and if you say that is New York city, then New York city it is. I will ride out to California, sell the horse, take the train from Sacramento straight across the country, till the New Jersey ferry."

His work in Texas apparently having concluded successfully, Master Yu opened his bag and began to count out payment, right there on the bar.

John Dead-Man looked offended, and Master Yu misunderstood.

"This is just a 'down payment,' as they say here in America," he said gently. "And the diamond is worth a few good meals, too."

"Should I not come with you?" John Dead-Man asked.

Master Yu shook his head.

"What about poor Waukendah?" Master Yu asked.

He looked up now, fingering one gold coin with his left hand.

"Stabled with old man Hessel. She must miss you."

"Waukendah is dead, I think," said the Indian. "It was only loyalty to me that was keeping her alive. I think when I patted her for the last time and did not return by the next dawn, she was probably a little relieved. When you said she would await me at the end of the journey, I think you meant at the end of life's journey."

He stared into his empty glass.

"I think we need each other's help right now, crazy Chinaman. I never thought I would have another friend."

"What we need most of all," Master Yu said, "is more Peking Indians. And you *will* have another friend. You will have a *wife*, and a house full of noble warriors. Now please accept these coins from her Majesty the Empress's personal mint. It will get you back home and let you live until my instructions to the Empress are received and carried out."

Master Yu began to count again.

"The Peking Indians will live to fight the enemy from the Winter North once more," he said, and he smiled as he counted. "1918, 1919. Thereabouts. The results will be different this time, I think, if we strengthen our hearts to meet the challenge. Change your name, John Dead-Man. Henceforth, you are John Rising-Spirit."

"John Rising-Spirit," the Indian murmured, and he looked stronger and younger than he had a moment before.

"Return to your round mud hut, and more money will arrive shortly from China," Master Yu promised. "Use it for a bride price, if they have such things here in Texas, and if they do not, just use it to impress the ladies. You will have your choice, I think. Please choose a strong one, one destined to be the mother of a fearsome warrior. Only choose one if she is worthy to join the Peking Indian tribe. A real *killer*, with a heart full of love and justice and hard steel. I expect some serious procreation to begin at your earliest convenience, my friend. We can have a full battalion of Peking Indians ready to fight at the dawn of the Falsturm Apocalypse."

He grabbed his friend's shoulder in a firm, confident grip.

"You will know her when you see her, John Rising-Spirit."

CHAPTER 17

As though I were a sincere and devout true pilgrim to Sidonia, in that September of 1879, I led a horse loaded up with all my belongings along the trail that scaled the Montana mountains. From the mountain peaks, the city was barely visible, shrouded as it was in a protective wall of fog.

I was not the only one scrambling over these mountain rocks. Who were these other would-be Sidonians? They were refugees from all across a country devastated by a great Depression that had begun in '73. They all believed their government had let them down, they felt as though their own hard work had let them down, and, in most cases, they also felt that God had let them down, and they were willing to follow a new Savior. Folks like me, mostly, and maybe like you. I met a lot of folks on my journey – widows, widowers, orphans, all desperate, none greedy. I met a couple of political easterners, folks searching for Utopia, and a few true religious pilgrims who thought the one true God had shown Himself in Montana.

For most of them, it was Sidonia or death.

I'll give you one example. I walked for a while with a family from Northern Utah, struggling the last few miles of their journey. They had lost everything when the promised railroad line went broke, their land lost all its value, their remaining crops were ravaged by the locust plague, and their horses died in the epizootic epidemic that had devastated the West. Husband, wife, and three children, all bone thin. Two teenage girls and one nine-year-old boy. From their conversation, I gathered they'd left someone behind on the trail. They didn't say who. I didn't ask. Sidonia was made up, mostly, of folks like these. Decent folks, just hoping they were selling their souls to the angels and not to the Devil, but scared and hungry enough to take the risk.

At length, I descended to the other side into the green valley that held the rebel city. I have since come to understand that Sidonia rejected some pilgrims, who were unable even to penetrate the fog, which physically blocked them. I, however, walked through without difficulty, and when the fog cleared, I entered a city that was clean and brightly lit by the Montana sunshine, a lemniscate reflected in a thousand mirrors. It was an impossible engineering feets, a metropolis closed off on all sides by the Montana mountains, yet here it was. As impossible as the deadlings who occasionally walked its streets. I perpetually touched my face, making certain that this disguise had not worn off, and that I might still maintain my new, princely bearing in the city of the enemy.

The city entrance led immediately to a well-drawn metropolitan center, traversed by a broad boulevard stretching off to the east and west, fronted by a city hall to the east, and finally the Sidonia Palace, glinting silvery gold in the morning air. To the north and south, the streets narrowed and twisted out of sight, leading as they did to new domains that might match each citizen's whimsy.

The boulevard that most directly abutted the Palace gate was lined with government offices and pricy, classy storefronts, hawking jewelry, top-hats, men's suits and ladies' opera gowns, while further from the city center, a livelier fair spread across the street, and crowds gathered to watch dancers, acrobats and clowns, whose energetic and occasionally physically impossible frolics were undoubtedly enhanced by Sidonian magic.

I felt it then, the goodness of the ages, a tug from the dawn of the universe rising up and engulfing the smooth polished surfaces and rough glinting stones of this untainted metropolis, the tranquility and hope of that prehistoric beach, where love rose from the surf with the first stirrings of life, and the idea that existence might consist of anything other than hatred and fear seemed as possible as the blue-green Pangaean sea; and it was this gossamer dream that now sang to me from the cobblestones and emerald facades, and the joyful murmur of the fairground children, and the mountains that stood guard over them all.

I shut my eyes and blocked out these yearnings for paradise.

Look, I had seen men back in the slums return from a two day dalliance with the opium pipe, happy as could be, and on the train that transported Emelina and me from Blue Rock, Wyoming, to a life of riches and fame in New York, I had known the drug of love and happiness, but, like my slum-neighbor waking hungry and penniless from his addled dream, I too had awoken from my flirtation with hopefulness to a life that is random and pointless and short and in which faith is a myth, and so with a less strenuous effort than most, I was able to ignore the fragrance of the Sidonian air. I turned my back on the fairground and headed across the street to the Sidonian hotels closest to the Palace and to the two Sidonian leaders whom I was resolved to destroy.

The hotels, which sat side-by-side on the southern end of the avenue just past the government buildings, were shrouded by towering elms and ringed by well-tended bushes and shrubs. The one to the east was the more imposing and luxurious of the two, with columns, golden angels and turrets, while the one on the western end of the street was plain brick, without any ostentatious adornments. I stabled my horse and wandered into the more frugal of the two. The foyer was small and modest, and an unimposing fellow manned the front desk. He was of medium height and stocky, with a receding hairline and worry lines about his eyes. When he smiled mildly, the worry lines deepened. He seemed a bit surprised to find himself here at the front desk of the more frugal of the two hotels in the Sidonian city center, and at something of a loss as to how to manage a customer. Still, he found a key for me, and when I asked him how much lodging would run me for the night, he shrugged and directed me to the stairs. My room was similarly unpretentious, with a threadbare rug whose colors had long since faded away, a simple wooden bed with a lumpy mattress and a wobbly dresser with three drawers. I tossed my bag on the floor, placed my guns carefully on the floor beside my bed on the far end of the room, lay back on the bed and listened to the noise of the crowds on the main thoroughfare, the Sidonian citizenry enjoying the market and the carnival, living a baffling, unearned life of leisure, kissing cheeks, sipping champagne on the street in glasses that appeared in their hands by Magic, feeling the sun on their bald spots and the breeze flapping their whiskers to and fro.

Without really intending it, I fell quickly into a dark, dreamless sleep. When it was barely dusk, I awoke, hungry and disoriented. Still fully dressed, I grabbed my guns, tossed on my coat, and wandered out into the mild early evening.

I followed a rather broad side street that seemed to lead into an older quarter of the city, with slightly faded but elegant apartment buildings. The smell of slowly roasting meat, chicken, beef and fish wafted through the air from somewhere nearby, and I found myself following that delicious smell. After a while, I could hear a woman's voice singing in the near distance, and the street opened up into a broad plaza – a *piazza*, you want me to call it – which was empty but for a young couple at the far right, embracing in the starlight. A many-times larger-than-life statue of a royal on horseback looked down over the plaza, centuries old and corroded green, a heroic man in full uniform, his strong-knuckled hand resting on the sword at his side. A fountain spouted at the center of the plaza, and a great blue emerald hung suspended above the fountain. I passed under a stone arch at the back of the plaza wrapped in multiple layers of thick vine, and which seemed older than America itself. Beyond the arch, I came into a smaller courtyard, which was lit by torchlight, shrouded by cedar trees, and peopled by a natty crowd of young men in tailcoats and ascots and lithe young women in light summer evening gowns, all with champagne glass in hand and wry delight on their pleasing young porcelain faces. A very young woman in a long dark dress stood by the edge of the forest. Her hair was jet-black with streaks of starlight gold, and she sang into the night breeze. It was a piece of music I had never heard, and she was singing a capella, words I could not understand, even notes that I believe were utterly unfamiliar. It was a piece of music from the deep past, so pure and innate that I could not believe it writ by the hand of a mere human; it must have existed long before our universe came into being, before protons and neutrons, formed in the pre-universal vacuum caldron along with *Pachelbel's Canon, Beethoven's Fifth Symphony* and, I suppose, *Come on Eileen*. Behind her was a little waterfall, a gentle stream trickling prettily over smooth stones.

Her black eyes fearless, she was as old as the trees and the mountains in the far night and younger than the spring flowers emerging from cracks in the stone beneath her feet; she had always been here in this courtyard beyond the vine-covered arches, singing this song that lived before the universe, and she was fire's incandescence, old and new and reborn every fraction of a millisecond. She was a panther, a night-bird, her voice floating among the tree branches and fluttering away into the darkness.

After she finished singing, she nodded indifferently and a touch insolently to the ensuing round of glove-muffled applause – an audience who appreciated what they had just heard, but not nearly enough – and the crowd turned back to their champagne and what I could only imagine was highly sophisticated persiflage.

When I approached, she looked up at me with her black cat eyes, and she seemed relieved to see me.

I admitted to her that I didn't know my name and could not introduce myself (although I treated this as a joke), and so I would not ask hers, that I really didn't know why I was here, or how I would ever get back to my hotel.

"You are lost," she said, and her speaking voice was just as lovely, a soft, whispery velvet.

She seemed pleased and surprised when she heard herself speak.

"Yes. I am lost," I said.

"I think we should take a walk. If we look everywhere, perhaps we will find you."

She took my arm, and we passed under the arch, and around that fountain with the suspended emerald.

To my unasked question, she replied, "The emerald is there, just floating in the air, because that way, you will enjoy this night more than you otherwise would have."

We followed a little cobblestone path just east into thin woods, and then up narrow stone stairs that led to a small clearing. Before us, an old, moss-covered stone wall ran along an abrupt cliff edge, and behind us ruins cut a gash in the dark night sky. The ruins' original function was unclear. A great crumbling tower loomed over us.

She leaned forward, her arms on the wall. Over the edge, we could observe a fanciful landscape, an old fortress on the other side of a winding, moon-bathed river. A far-away figure on a horse, a young woman, rode alone in the starry darkness. The horse trotted rather aimlessly along a river-bank trail that ran parallel to the decaying fortress walls. All of this, a world of antiquity, destruction, great beauty and ageing wealth.

I could still see the statue in the plaza through the trees, and I asked who the imposing gentleman was, and she said this was just a statue that seemed designed to meet expectations. It appeared to be old, dignified and artistic, which was what I must have wanted, deep down.

"He never lived, and after tonight, he will be gone forever."

"Doesn't it destroy the illusion that you've all built for me?" I asked. "Telling me all this?"

"You also must want honesty. Maybe too many people in your life have lied to you. So I tell you the truth."

"And what do you do with your life, the rest of the time?"

"Nothing." She shook her head. "As you approached the plaza, I began to exist, just as a voice in the night air. I became a whole person when you passed under the arch and entered the courtyard."

"I can't think of anything to say. I cannot believe that."

"It's true."

"And what will you do once this is over? Once you and I part?"

"I will … end. I will be over. I will not exist."

"Does that make you sad?"

She nodded.

"It makes me sad. It is terribly unfair. I am like a firefly, aren't I? Or like …" She struggled to find the right word, and then suddenly her face lit up. "Or like a *dinoflagellate*. I am like one little dinoflagellate. Why did that idea come into my mind just like that? I think you must be a man who likes dinoflagellates."

"I do like them. I remember them with great fondness."

"Maybe it seems very vain and arrogant of me to compare myself to beautiful things that do not live very long. To compare myself to things that are so beautiful."

"Not at all. I know that the idea of you and your song has always existed and will always exist. So maybe you come back?"

"You mean my 'soul'? Maybe. I don't remember being here before. Why should I come back again? Maybe fireflies and dinoflagellates come back again. Maybe they don't."

"What about the rest of your audience?" I asked her. "Did they have the same thought that I had? Why did we all want the same thing, on the same night, at the same moment?"

She frowned lightly as she pondered them, her appreciative audience. Those handsome ladies and gentlemen who stood about the courtyard, wine glasses at their lips, and whose gloves offered her muffled applause.

"I imagine they came into being the moment you walked into that courtyard. It would not have been much of a concert with only you there. And now I would guess that they are gone. A short but very happy life. One big party."

"None of them, real?"

"Not *exactly* real. But real in the moment."

"And you are real?"

"I certainly know that I am real, if you mean to ask whether I am sentient, or in other words, conscious. But I have no way to convince you that I am. How do I know that you are real?"

"You don't. No one knows but me."

"I do enjoy being alive," she sighed.

She smiled into the breeze that blew in from the mountains.

"I wonder why you are here," she said. "Do you want to fall in love?"

She turned and looked into my eyes.

"No, that isn't it. You are in love with too many women already."

Her smile faded a little bit.

"You wanted to hear a beautiful song. So I suppose I am just a vessel for a beautiful song." She looked out at the winding river, at the woman on the horse, disappearing into the night mist. "Not so bad, I suppose. There are worse reasons for being. And the song is part of me, you know. It will not exist anymore, after this night."

I touched her chin gently with my hand, and I turned her towards me.

"Then if time is short," I said, "tell me what you want."

"What *I* want?" she laughed. "What does it matter what *I* want?"

But she thought about my question, laughing a little more, quietly.

"I have never eaten a meal," she said. "I would like to eat a meal in a fine, elegant hotel restaurant. And then I would like to fall asleep in a man's arms. I imagine this would be a nice experience to have before I dissolve into the night."

We went back to the center of town, and this time I checked into the more ostentatious hotel, with a chandelier in the expansive lobby, and an army of bellboys to attend to luggage. The dining room was carpeted and lit dimly by candlelight. In the corner, a beautiful woman played the harp, and a handsome man played the cello.

We ordered blue points on the half shell, beef consommé, tomato soup, roast lamb with mint sauce, halibut baked in port wine, roasted asparagus, potatoes Parisienne, and, for dessert, sorbet and Muscat. I smoked a Havana cigar, and she took a puff or two, because why not? She discovered a fondness for cigars. "I wish I could have another one, someday," she said, watching the smoke curl up into the air and dissolve, much like her life. "But had you not called me into being, I would never have tried it even once. At least I tried it once."

Our hotel room was on the 9th floor, with a view of the mountains. She fell asleep peacefully in my arms, and then I fell asleep as well to the sound of her gentle breathing. When I woke, it was 5 in the morning, and she was gone. I was still fully dressed, and a breeze was riffling the curtains in our lavish chamber. I got up out of bed, stumbled down the spiral staircase that led to the lobby, and I wandered out onto the avenue. The town was blue in the shadowy moonlight. Between Sidonie Street and Fawley Lane, a young man suddenly appeared where a moment before there had been only empty space. He had dark and long red hair, which waved in the night breezes. He seemed confused. A moment later he was gone, replaced by a portly man holding hands with a Colored woman, and then, after a moment of confusion, they too were gone.

"Deadlings," I whispered foolishly to myself. *Summoned by someone's dreams.*

A few more perplexed deadlings popped in and out of the world, and so I watched this for a while, but after a couple of them provoked a bewildered, lurching fist fight and popped out of the world at the same moment, I lost my interest, and I wandered across the avenue and followed Fawley Lane to the north. The street narrowed to muddy pathways between dark buildings (and which reminded me of the slums of home) and then widened to a starry thoroughfare that crawled up over a stone bridge which crossed a body of water – a canal, maybe – flanked by marble and stone buildings from a far earlier, apparently European era. On the other side of the canal, I walked alone until I came to a quiet sign that read *Café*. A thick black arrow pointed one story up. I pushed open a heavy wooden door, trod up a torch-lit stairway and into the empty café. A wide window looked out over a dark, quiet cityscape.

There were just three tables in the room, little round wooden tables. One of them, which was close to the window, was lit by candlelight, and was set with a short white tablecloth. The other two looked sadly neglected. I sat down at the table in the window, and I looked out at the canal. A duck dived from the sky and frolicked briefly in the moonlit water.

After a few moments, a man walked through a door in the back of the café, and he approached my table. I recognized him immediately as the man from the frugal hotel in the Sidonian city center.

"I suppose I am your waiter," he said.

His voice, thickly New England.

"I suppose you are the reason I am here," he added.

I asked him to explain. I said that I was new in town.

He wagered a guess that I had woken at five in the morning, and that I had wandered about the city and eventually found myself at this café. He further guessed that I had not for a moment questioned that I was meant to be a customer in this establishment. And so I had sat down and waited, even though the dive was hardly welcoming.

"I, on the other hand," the man continued, "awoke at four in the morning, wandered the streets of this city, and I found myself here at this café with the absolute certainty that I was intended to take an order. A cup of coffee, I believe."

I shrugged.

"All right, then," I said.

"A cup of coffee it will be?" the man asked, making certain. "In the kitchen, there is a cup of coffee, which looks and smells freshly brewed. Otherwise, the kitchen is entirely empty."

"Yes," I said. "A cup of coffee. If that is what is meant to happen. If that is what I am meant to order."

The man nodded, vanished through the kitchen door, and he returned a moment later with my coffee in a china cup, which steamed alluringly.

"You take your coffee without cream or sugar, I imagine," he said, as he placed the cup gingerly on the table. "There is no cream or sugar in this establishment, and so I imagine that none is desired."

He gestured to the empty chair. I nodded, indicating that he could join me if he wished. He sat, and he watched me drink my coffee.

His name was Frederick Slocum, he told me. I said that I was honored to make his acquaintance, but I didn't tell him my name. I still did not know the name that was meant to accompany this new face.

The coffee was very good, strong and hot, but not bitter. I would have expected that a society that had mastered Magic might have also mastered the art of decent coffee, and here, at least, I was not disappointed.

"What brings you here?" he asked me, and he didn't really wait for me to answer. "I'm here from New York. Not originally. From New England originally. Family of maple syrup farmers."

He laughed at this, as though it were funny, and I laughed along, as though I also found it funny.

"I imagine I have something to show you," he said. "Shall we see what it is?"

After I finished my coffee, we left the café, and he steered me to a sharp left, away from the canal and into a narrow alley that descended between two plain but towering brick buildings, until we were nearly underground. Now the sun began to rise, and as we exited the alley we found ourselves in a meadow spotted with blue and gold wildflowers. Small, idyllic villages dotted the horizon, while the Sidonian metropolis receded into the distance behind us, glowing in the sky like a daytime constellation. I noted to Slocum that all of this seemed far larger than Sidonia's little Montana valley, and he nodded. I said that I had never seen a city reflected in the sky, indeed burned into the sky as though with a branding iron, and he smiled a little.

"It all seems impossible," he remarked. "Doesn't it? Everything."

He looked around us.

"There should be a path somewhere near here," he added. "A little trail, leading us – wherever we are going." He smiled. "I find there is always a trail, leading me where I am going. Wherever that happens to be."

Now, please forgive a slight digression. I had believed, up to this point, that while certain Sidonians were attracted to the movement by politics – a more egalitarian world, rights to the masses, and so on, which I believe was Lucy's motive – the remainder were driven by pure greed (or pure need). But this was not entirely correct, and I realized it on the little side trip that I took with Mr. Slocum.

My life hasn't been easy, as you may have discerned, and my guess is that your life hasn't been easy. Life is not easy. Maybe you have lost a job. Maybe it was a job that made your existence a misery, but losing this terrible abomination of a job has made your life even worse than it was before. Maybe you lost your spouse – either to an accident, or an illness, or to someone whom your spouse simply loves more than she has ever loved you. Maybe you lost a leg or two. When events of an uncontrollable nature happen, religious types may tell you that *God has a plan.* Philosophical types who do not necessarily believe in a deity may quote Nietzsche (without necessarily knowing that they are quoting Nietzsche) and insist that whatever "does not kill us makes us stronger." If your favorite horse kicks your wife in the head, and she descends into a coma that persists for the next three decades, it may be part of God's plan, but it is probably not, and while it doesn't much matter either way (whatever God intended or didn't intend, you need to find someone else to comfort you and pick the radishes that your wife once picked), and while none of us can prove it one way or another, it is certainly evident beyond any doubt that your wife, having been kicked in the head without being killed, is not the stronger for it, Nietzsche notwithstanding.

I mention this only because, as I watched Slocum search for a path that he had never seen before, but which he knew without a speck of doubt that he was intended to follow, I realized that there was more to this movement than bread and circuses. Sidonia had wiped out the messiness of life and promised its denizens not merely just rewards for their faith and loyalty, but a careful existential design, mapped out by a thoughtful God who would never look away when your horse rears up and your wife is in the way. It is not just greed that draws us to Sidonia, it is submission to a Kingdom of Heaven that has thoroughly reorganized the chaos of life into mathematical certitude, without the doubt and tribulations of Job. Life is not a search for the mysteries of God, I realized. It is a search for the certainty of mathematics. *Truly, here in Sidonia, everything happens for a reason.*

After a while we reached a little trail that led into the woods, which at length grew thick and seemed impassable. The path continued onward, and as long as we remained on the path, the brush parted for us. After about a quarter mile walk through the thickest, darkest stretch of the forest, we came to a small clearing, where six young men sat on the forest floor in a circle. One of them was playing a lute beautifully and singing like an angel. They wore green and blue uniforms, which, though unfamiliar to me, gave them the bearing of soldiers of war, or a mercenary army. No guns, though. Still, I backed up nervously when they came into view. Slocum put his hand on my arm, trying to reassure me, but also holding me steady. I consciously relaxed. This was, after all, why I had come to Sidonia.

The soldiers stood, and the man with the lute leaned it against the tree.

He smiled. I could see in his eyes that he recognized me and respected me, but I could not yet tell whether we were personally acquainted, and so I held back a bit. I nodded politely.

"Sidonian brothers," said Slocum. "Look who wandered into my café, early in the morning."

He smiled, and it was not unkind.

"You should have told Mr. Jerome that you had arrived," said the younger soldier.

"I hope I have not offended him," I said. "I wanted to experience the Sidonian dream as an anonymous visitor."

"With all due respect," said the soldier who had earlier been playing the lute. "You are an Otherworld Fabricator, are you not?"

I pursed my lips noncommittally. I was not entirely sure if I was disguised as a Otherworld Fabricator.

"You cannot see things as a plebian would, sir," he insisted to me.

My new face clearly belonged to someone rather important, someone with perhaps great powers, someone who could flit along the borderline between worlds, pursuing the great Cause. It was the first time that I had begun truly to recognize the scope of the movement, although I was to become all too familiar with it when the Sidonian war exploded in earnest, early in the following century.

I followed the Sidonian soldiers, who led me out of the forest back into the city, down the main boulevard and right up to the gate of the Sidonia Palace, which opened, and we walked through, and the riches and wisdom of the universe revealed themselves to us.

CHAPTER 18

Master Yu's train stopped in the night in New Jersey, and he took an early morning boat into lower Manhattan, then hiked the remaining blocks to Chinatown. As he passed Wall Street, glowing red in the sunrise, a young man stood at a street corner, unwashed in a fashion that Master Yu recognized as a political form of grubbiness.

"Sidonia is coming!" the man bellowed, his voice cracking with fatigue and righteousness. "Justice is nigh!"

He had pamphlets, which he waved about, although there were as yet no takers.

Yu came to a modest little house off Baxter Street, with an apartment in back of a Chinese cigar shop, and he rapped lightly on the front door. At length, an old and weary Chinese man pulled the door open a crack.

"I am looking for a wise sage," Master Yu said. "Or perhaps a man whose name is 'wise sage.' " Then, remembering the last piece of the puzzle, he added, "And perhaps you have a minor harem? Four wives, or thereabouts?"

The old man shook his head in resignation, and he pulled the door fully open.

"I imagine that I have been expecting your visit," he said. "Come in and have a cup of tea."

The old man's surname was Chang, but his first name was Chihche, which, if pronounced with different tones than the ones he actually used, would have meant "wise sage." Pronounced slightly differently, it would have meant "lewd strumpet" or "gifted artisan." But he was not himself a wise sage, a lewd strumpet or a gifted artisan. He was just a tired old man who'd had the bad luck or unfortunate judgment to have moved into a house with an ancient secret in the cellar.

The house was furnished rather haphazardly, in keeping with the old man's personality. A painting of the Kitchen God was hanging in the kitchen, where it should be.

As Master Yu enjoyed his tea, four women doted on him, all of them pale and white, with rosy, healthy cheeks, and in their late thirties to early forties. The pale white women were chattering away in fluent but rough, flawed and heavily accented Chinese, and it grated on Master Yu, although he appreciated the effort. He could hear the sound of children overhead, shouting and playing, in Irish-brogued English and Chinese. When the women were out of earshot, he inquired, and the old man admitted with some embarrassment that he was married to each of the four women, who were all Irish.

"Why?" Yu asked. "Why did you marry four Irish women?"

"Almost no Chinese ladies here in America," he said. "And in America, only Irish ladies willing to marry a Chinaman."

"I am happy that you have four wives," Yu asked. "Because it fulfills the prophecy. But what I meant to ask was, why more than one?"

"They less demanding than Chinese ladies," Chang said, grasping at straws. "Let me sleep when I want to sleep."

"Maybe you like Irish ladies," Master Yu said, "so you marry one, see another one on the side from time to time when your wife isn't looking. But why *marry* so many?"

The true answer was less than simple. Back in China, Chang Chihche fell in love, hopelessly and forever, with a young woman fated to die. She died beautifully and in his arms, expiring with a gentle and delicate sigh on her lips, as the sunrise bloomed like a flower.

Bereft and heart-broken, Chang traveled to America, where he sought to forget his sorrows in an ocean of hard labor, which would stretch from early morning till late at night and leave him with a dark and dreamless sleep.

Nevertheless, when he awoke in the early mornings, he was lonely, and no one woman could ever replace his little dove.

So he married four.

One with the courage and passion of his lost love; one whose smile he cherished, and who had a golden laugh; one whose compassion came close to compare; and one with a fierce intelligence.

These four women whom he married, when taken as parts of a whole, were very nearly the equal of the beautiful pearl of his far-lost memory.

He didn't tell this to Master Yu. It was too personal, too romantic, and it was not something for a gentleman to share with a stranger. So instead, to his shame, he shrugged, and he said that he didn't really know, come to think of it, how or why he'd gotten himself into this particular kettle of fish.

"They're not like Chinese ladies," he said.

A little silence passed between them.

"I don't think," Yu Dai-Yung said again, "that this explains why you chose to marry so many of them."

The shadows flickered behind him.

Chang sighed.

"Maybe, not knowing it, I do it to fulfill the prophecy. Hmm? Yes?"

Master Yu changed the subject.

"I found a very old document, Chang Chihche. It directed me, I think, to this very home, this very spot, unless I have misread it terribly."

The tired man was silent.

"There is something unusual in this house," Master Yu said. "Is there not?"

Master Yu heard a distant rumbling, like faraway thunder. The sky outside remained blue and clear.

"You cannot fight Red Eyebrows here in the real world," Master Yu said. "You must fight them from somewhere else. From their home, where Eyebrows are born."

Chang Chihche sighed again.

"There is something," he said, "in the basement. In a room in the basement."

And his red weary eyes grew redder and wearier.

He gestured to the stairs. There was something in the basement, he repeated, that might prove of interest to Yu Dai-Yung.

An old nag was tied up in the corner.

Yu Dai-Yung nodded to the horse.

"This is your horse," Chang Chihche said.

Yu Dai-Yung said that this wasn't his horse.

"My horse is a brown horse with strong legs. I left her in a stable in Sacramento. A beautiful horse. This is not my horse. This is an ugly horse. This horse can't run. This horse would die if we went to war against the Red Eyebrows, or tried to traverse even the first mile of a desert battlefield."

The old man shook his head.

"This horse has had a long life. He was a wild island colt, the fastest of his year. He fought the other horses, and he won. He fell in love, to the extent a horse can really fall in love – I suppose he fell into a sort of canny, devoted loyalty – and he became a father himself. He was captured, he was tamed, but he never gave up his will to fight. It is this perspective – *experience* – which will serve you well where you are going."

And then the tired old man uttered words that terrified Master Yu so badly he felt as though his heart had been cut open.

"You will need to travel to 枉死城."

The terrible poet blinked.

"I'm going to 枉死城?" he asked.

This was indeed alarming. 枉死城, this place to which Master Yu was soon to be consigned, could be translated loosely as the Chinese Hell of the Innocent Dead, which doesn't fully do justice to the terror it would strike into the heart of your average terrible Chinese poet, who might wish to write about it, but who wouldn't yearn to visit. It was a place that lived in myth and, Master Yu had always believed, in reality. Of all the magical places of Chinese legend – and there are quite a few – the Hell of the Innocent Dead was the one in which Master Yu had always believed most fervently.

In Hell, the Chinese Hell of the Innocent Dead is on the 6th level (out of a total of 18).

If you die before your time, through some sort of cruel miscarriage of justice, or horrible crime, and you are unable to leave it behind you and ascend to your next life (or extinction, as the case may be), then you descend to the Hell of the Innocent Dead until your death is avenged. While theoretically temporary, the Hell of the Innocent Dead is a permanent prison for most of its inhabitants, because, as they say, *Life is Unfair*, and vengeance is usually not achieved. Of all the Hells, this one is the most filled with hatred. Filled with otherwise good people who cannot stop hating. This, Master Yu now realized, is where the Red Eyebrows were born, in all their incarnations. Otherwise not unkind creatures who were wronged, and who were eaten alive by it, till they were naught but rancor. This is a Hell that would corrupt the most noble of angels through its sheer unfairness.

Chang Chihche smiled.

"Not as bad as you would think. Not as bad as rumor."

The old man insisted that there were good pork buns in 枉死城, and even a passable dragon parade, a pretty maiden or two, but he seemed to be inventing these consolations as he went along, and so Yu Dai-Yung discounted them all.

"And good bean cake at New Year," Chang Chihche added finally. "Or so they say."

"Well then. I will look forward to New Year."

"Always watch out for the giant sand crabs," the old man added. "Almost forgot to warn you about the giant sand crabs. Otherwise, 枉死城 is not as bad as you might fear. Giant sand crabs, though – they're always hungry. Always keep one eye open. I have nothing good to say about the giant sand crabs."

Master Yu and Chang Chihche talked a bit. In English, we would say that they "made small talk." We would also say that Master Yu was "procrastinating." They debated their favorite teahouses in Peking, and Master Yu related a Chinese opera that he had once seen in Chang'an. They complained about America, about the dust and heat, and about the Americans. Every second that Master Yu could spend here in this dim basement was a second that he would not spend in 枉死城.

"Do you have bullets?" Chang Chihche asked. Master Yu admitted that he had many bullets. And a sword that might be magical, but might not be magical. Chang Chihche nodded. He asked whether Master Yu had enough to eat. He thought that Master Yu should bring enough food for several days, until he could find his way to a friendly settlement, to which he could unfortunately provide neither a map nor directions. If his food ran out, Master Yu would need to hunt rabbits.

"There are rabbits there," Chang Chihche added. "Bring matches, to build a fire to roast the rabbits. Not the best rabbits. Bony."

Master Yu had matches and provisions for several days.

"Where is the portal?" he asked.

Chang Chihche pointed.

"Over in the corner."

Something did seem to buzz and hum in the corner of the cellar, but it was too dark for Master Yu to see what it was.

"Get on the horse first," Chang Chihche added. "The horse will help. Very wise horse."

Master Yu mounted the horse, and his heart was full of woe and dread.

The gaunt and gloomy Allen Jerome and the ordinarily gregarious Darryl Fawley had at one time met on a daily basis, but in recent months, with the final degeneration of their partnership, Mr. Jerome had been obliged to insist on a regular weekly meeting. The two men would meet in an elegant boardroom, spacious and empty, at a table of dark, polished wood. The boardroom was sequestered away in the furthest eastern corner of the Sidonia Palace. Jerome, in his elegant suits, seemed to belong in the boardroom; the lopsided Fawley, with his worn jacket and porridge stained trousers, did not. His sunburned scalp peeled, and he scratched it, and flecks of skin floated down to the boardroom table.

These meetings, at one time, had covered issues of civic importance, public morale and military strategy. But the encounters had come to focus more and more on one topic: Darryl Fawley wanted out of the Revolution, he wished to leave the city limits, to ascend one side of the Montana mountains and to descend on the other side, and never to return.

"And where would you go?" Jerome asked. "Back to work with the civil service?"

"Someplace else. Someplace beyond these walls. That is all. What do I have here?"

"Here you have the adoration of the masses, Darryl Fawley, which counts for something. Out there you will have nothing."

It was true. The masses loved Darryl Fawley, and the masses loved Darryl Fawley more than they loved Allen Jerome, a fact that did not befuddle Allen Jerome and did not bother him. He did not want to be loved, by anyone.

"I will go somewhere," he said. "And be alone with my thoughts. Perhaps I will find a middle-aged spinster who will take a bit of pity on me."

Allen Jerome pulled his chair very close to his partner-in-crime. He tapped him gently on the forehead, and Darryl Fawley flinched.

"Sidonia is in here," he whispered. "When you uncovered the secrets of the Red Eyebrows in China, and when you pledged fealty, it became part of you, and you changed. All of this. It is a part of you, and you are a part of it. We all thrive in your light, my friend. There is no way that I can free you. Until the day you die, Sidonia needs you. Until its glory finds another resting place."

Fawley sighed sadly.

"This is nothing less than what I promised, I suppose," he said. "The vision – well, it made it clear that our struggle would not be easy. Lucy and I saw the ivory and marble palace, the white-robed figures singing out to us from tree-covered terraces, and the gardens of blooming flowers that changed color as the wind shifted. But we also saw an ocean that glowed blood-red. So we knew there would be struggles, terrible struggles. But we both believed that our struggles would be for the greater good. Or at least, enough semblance of the greater good that Lucy would happily rule beside me as my queen. As the queen of the downtrodden, lifting them up. I promised something … but did I truly promise *this*? Would I truly betray my word if I were to retire quietly, and to look for that spinster in a damp little cottage?"

"The only way to free you is to kill you, Darryl," Allen Jerome said. "And even if this were what you wished, the people would never forgive me. Our movement would crumble. The masses would suffer. Our world Revolution would never succeed." His voice dropped to a whisper. "One day, Darryl Fawley, you will learn to love us the way we love you. And one day, you will learn to let us love you as we would wish."

At that moment, a soldier came into the boardroom bearing urgent news, the arrival of an Otherworld Fabricator, or so he thought. Allen Jerome's brow creased. He seemed to doubt this news. And then he smiled. He winked at Darryl Fawley, and he told the soldier that he would meet the esteemed guest in Wednesday's Sidonia Gardens.

The Sidonia Gardens on this particular Wednesday bloomed purple and red; spots of purple, smears of red, rows of purple and splotches of red, all extending to what seemed a far horizon, visible to infinity in all directions. Allen Jerome sat in the garden, watching his flowers bloom, change color, fade away into nothing, and bloom again in the sunshine, like a glorious silent daytime fireworks show. From here, he could not even see the Palace; his world was a purple and red garden. A bar table grew from the ground, with a chilled glass of shambro on it. Jerome pushed back the rim of his hat, lifted the glass to his lips and sipped the shambro. It was perfect, as expected. The sun warmed him, and the shambro cooled him. He felt content, for a brief moment.

After a while the soldiers came to visit. He smiled when he saw me. He greeted me with an unpronounceable – what was that? – salutation? Or my purported name? I don't know. I couldn't repeat it to you. Did I detect a bit of wryness on his face when he said it?; an ironic tone in his voice? I nodded noncommittally, but with a friendly manner, I thought. Allen Jerome smiled with thin bloodless lips, and he appraised me with eyes that were cold and gray. Did he know all, had he surmised all, right from the start, perhaps before he had even seen me step across his fields of cinquefoil, and, if so, should I shoot him now? *Could* I shoot him now? And if I did, would I forfeit all hope of getting to Fawley, not to speak of my audience with the Falsturm? The time seemed premature, even if my life were coming to its end.

Allen Jerome gestured to the soldiers to leave us, and they marched off through the beds of posies and hepaticas, cresses and foxgloves, which rolled and tumbled and bowed as they passed.

A chair appeared, and I sat.

"You have been underground," Jerome smiled. "Moving about incognito to examine the fate of our little social experiment. You have seen how the movement has grown?"

Jerome went into a lengthy tirade – or perhaps it was a social disquisition – filled with philosophical asides and mathematical theorems, and I really couldn't repeat it to you verbatim because after a while I stopped listening, but the general underpinnings of his screed were that a greater world would come about through humanity's loss of its freedom.

"We do not wish to be free," he said. "And I include myself in this generalization. We wish to be protected, guided, blanketed, smothered. We do not wish to be free. We wish to be slaves."

I nodded sagely at this nonsense.

"Hmmm," I said, nodding a bit more. Perhaps Allen Jerome was trying to impress me with his erudition. I started to feel more confident.

"What does freedom mean to most people?" he asked. "To be paid enough coin to eat cabbage and rice? To scrounge about on a farm on the prairie? Is that freedom? What does it mean?"

Allen Jerome then went on at great vicious length on the subject of J.P. Morgan, a constant obsession for him, I learned for the first time, but again I stopped listening after a while.

Still, something happened then, which caught my attention. A little man marched into the garden, a go-by-the-ground in a topcoat, with a proud, pompous look on his little round face, and he was arm-in-arm with a sad, mute clown.

Gesturing at me, Jerome muttered that unpronounceable name again.

He then gestured to the two uninvited guests.

"Leopold Kronecker," he said, pointing to the tiny little man. "Dr. Kronecker is a renowned colleague of mine from the world of mathematical academia, whom you might know as the originator of quadratic reciprocity." He eyed me seriously. "Hmm?"

"Ah," I said. "Hmmph."

Now Allen Jerome eyed his colleague's unexpected companion.

"And Prof. Kronecker is joined by some sort of a clown."

Kronecker, that dastardly ne'er-do-well, glared at me.

What did his beady eyes see?

He was no more than five feet tall, balding and imperious. He held a rat in his left hand, which he had brought into the garden. Or perhaps the rat had just materialized. (I cannot really speculate on the origins of the rat.)

Kronecker tossed the rat to Jerome who, without blinking, bit off the rat's head, swirled it around in his mouth and spat it across the field.

I ducked, and the rat's head rolled away between the flowers behind me. It sprouted a new body and ran screaming into the golden sunshine.

The sad clown watched all this impassively.

What's your angle, sad clown? I wondered, turning away from Kronecker and Jerome to stare into the sad clown's tearful eyes.

He smiled a sad little smile with his ruined jaw, and I heard his voice in my head: *Watt O'Hugh the Third, come here to destroy Sidonia.*

It was a childish little voice, taunting and sing-song.

I asked him, without moving my lips: *Are you my friend?*

He slowly shook his head, a glint of real hatred in his eyes.

And all of a sudden, I could not move. I couldn't move my arms or my legs, and I couldn't swallow, I discovered with some concern.

The clown and Kronecker exchanged glances, as I struggled against my paralysis, frozen and helpless.

"*Watt O'Hugh*," Kronecker whispered, turning to me, and his whisper echoed in the wind that whistled through the flowers.

Being unable to swallow was the most uncomfortable part of my paralysis. One doesn't realize how important swallowing is to a man's equilibrium until it is taken away.

Kronecker took my gun, and he tossed it back and forth between his left hand and his right hand, over and over. A little prayer rattled its way into my head, a little entreaty to my ostensible maker, just in case, just to cover my bases.

Kronecker heard the quiet prayer inside my head, and he laughed at my late-breaking religiosity.

"God made the integers," he whispered. "All else is the work of Man."

My legs were not my own.

My legs-that-were-not-my-own marched along beside Allen Jerome without my guiding them. I still could not swallow, and drool dribbled from the left side of my mouth. I could not blink, and my eyes were growing dry. On the other side of me was a soldier, a stout and sturdy man with a rough, scarred face and particularly sadistic smile. "Did you think that you would fool Sidonia for even a minute?" Allen Jerome asked me, and he seemed more amused than angry. Had I truly thought, he wondered aloud, that I might be able to defeat the Falsturm with a word or two? "Picture a mirror store," he said. "Mirrors on two walls, facing each other, reflecting each other, back and forth, deeper and deeper – the Falsturm resides on the farthest level. He's always with us – the shadow you barely notice, or the breeze that lifts a tuft of hair. He is here now, O'Hugh."

I said nothing, because I could not move my tongue.

"You will be tortured," he said. "You will be tortured for whatever information you may be able to provide to us. And then you will be killed, and killed again, and killed and killed and killed."

He laughed. Somehow, he thought that some part of this was funny.

"As many times as it takes," Allen Jerome said.

As Allen Jerome led me to the prison, it struck me that Billy Golden would be terribly disappointed and even penitent over the predicament into which he'd dropped me. How terrible he would feel if he were to learn that in a brief moment the Sidonians had seen through the disguise that Rabbi Palache had fashioned for me, that Sidonia was more powerful, more perceptive than he had realized, and that he had endangered me for no purpose, and that now I would be tortured, and I would die, and his friend Hester would be alone.

It was only much later, sometime in 1928, when I awoke in the middle of the night, that it all made sense, and I realized that the abject failure of what had seemed to be Billy Golden's plan was in fact the Plan itself.

The jail was antiseptic, clean and empty. The walls of my cell were white stone, and the light that lit the cell from far above my head was bright and sunny. I was the fourth cell in the row, the only one occupied. It occurred to me that this prison had likely been constructed in the moment just for my use.

The soldier tossed me like a ball into cell number 17, where I lay helpless and prone on the floor, still unable to move. Allen Jerome left us, whistling, and his tuneless whistle echoed through the long corridors. It was almost beautiful, the whispery, empty echo. The soldier kicked me a few times in the ribs. The first time he kicked me, his boots were soft leather, and it didn't hurt very badly, but the second time he kicked me, his boots were steel, and he sent me barreling across the cell and against the back wall. He followed me to the corner of the cell and kicked me one more time. Then he laughed, and then he snarled like a tiger, then he trumpeted like an elephant, and at last he turned and left, and I lay on the floor, drool leaking out of my useless mouth onto the stone floor.

A day went by, night crawled into the cell, and movement returned to my limbs, then my arms. After a while, I could swallow again. I rolled out of the little puddle of spit that had pooled under me.

I tapped on the metal bar with my tin cup, just to hear that endless echo, to hear something, to feel a little bit alive.

I stood on the room's one wooden chair and I hoisted myself up to the small barred window at the top of the cell. I didn't see the lemniscate beauty of graceful Sidonia, as I had expected, but instead that smoky-grey city that I had seen once before, from the deserted cabin that Hester and I had shared in the woods, and which had sheltered us from the rain. The grey city spread out before me like a vast cancer, and it seemed to grow larger as I stared, to crowd its way into the bay and forest that it abutted. At last my arm muscles tired, and I lowered myself to the cold floor. I leaned back against the wall, and I shut my eyes.

An hour or more must have passed before I heard the sound of the prison door opening and clanking shut. (Really, it was a small town variety theater sound effect of a prison door, I realized with a start – it was nothing from the real world. It was not a door – it was just the *sound* of a door.) I opened my eyes wearily, and I was surprised to see a man I recognized immediately as Darryl Fawley walking slowly and, I thought, forlornly from the front entrance towards my cell. By now he was fifty-years-old, and his unevenly balding head had lost the last scrap of hair. He wore a spotless white suit. He had long skinny legs and a squat frame, and as he walked down the hallway towards me, he looked like a great insect, or an oversized wind-up toy.

A chair materialized just outside the cell, but far enough away that it was just out of my reach.

Darryl Fawley, my terrible enemy, sat. He had not shaken his veneer of failure, even now that he was an emperor.

"Watt O'Hugh," he said, and he smiled thinly. "Your disguise is gone. Your beautiful new face has washed away. You are revealed to us, in all your imperfection."

I knew he was right. I could feel it. My face was once again my own. Battered and worn and rough.

"Some people never give up," he sighed. "Some people never forget."

His voice had a professor's careful cadence.

I didn't move, and I didn't speak. I rested my head on the stone wall and stared at him.

He shook his head, and he met my gaze.

His eyes were red and watery.

"I loved her too, you know," he said.

I whispered: "You did not. I am the only one who ever knew her, and I am the only one who ever loved her."

"She was my queen, and I loved her."

His voice echoed in the empty prison. The words taunted me, again and again, then they faded away into the distance like mist.

"Mr. Fawley," I said. "You did not love her. You *killed* her."

"I didn't kill her," he replied firmly. "Sidonia killed her."

"And you ... you are the king of Sidonia."

"Sidonia," he said, "is the king of us all."

"I will kill *you*, Fawley. And if you kill me first, I will come back as a deadling, and *then* I will kill you."

He smiled a restrained smile, one filled with sympathy.

"You will not come back as a deadling, Mr. O'Hugh. Neither of us will come back as a deadling. One can return to Earth as a deadling only if someone alive loves him and yearns for him ceaselessly. You and I will never be so missed. No one alive will ever miss us the way we both miss our Lucy."

Our Lucy.

He sighed, a forlorn, love-sick lament.

"Although you have pledged to kill me, my dear Mr. O'Hugh, I will not kill you, even though this is a decision that might cost me my life" – this last clause he uttered with condescending irony, as he clearly did not believe that I might ever manage to kill him – "and I will not kill you because I know how our beloved deadling would feel about it. If you were to die at my hands, Lucy would not give me a moment's peace. And so I must take my chances, knowing that you are in the world, sworn to my destruction."

Then, after another quiet little moment: "I loved her very much, Mr. O'Hugh. And she adored me intensely, in her way."

Oh, my readers, then he went on, in his quiet, calm voice, and it was terrible torment. He recalled for me his life with Lucy, the day they met, the day they married, tender moments that I knew were true. I tried to ignore him but could not, and after he finished his colloquy he left, and I heard that prison door clank shut, and I was alone again.

On Tuesday, September 23, 1879, while I was stuck behind bars in the impromptu Sidonian prison, dreaming of bread and water, Mr. Sneed arrived unexpectedly in the offices of Drexel, Morgan & Company at 23 Wall Street. He told Morgan's secretary – that pleasant and obliging young man – that he was from the American Cigar Distribution Company, and he swept down the aisle among the bookkeepers' desks in the direction of Morgan's office. You've seen this kind of thing in your "talking pictures" a hundred times, though rarely in real life: the secretary shouted *Sir, sir, you can't go in there* as he tagged along impotently behind the brusque intruder, who ignored him and continued ceaselessly across the room. When he reached Morgan's office, the great man calmed his secretary, and Sneed shut the door.

There were no pleasantries.

"The war will begin to-morrow," Sneed said, his strong voice betraying a certain bit of dread. "What I'd expected to be a surgical strike will be a rather larger battle. The Sidonian army has swelled. This will be a bloodbath, Mr. Morgan. All around."

He leaned over Morgan's desk, his face uncomfortably close. He would have preferred to let beautiful dreams wither on the vine of their own accord, as all aspirations of perfection and happiness inevitably do. It would be a terrible crime to allow American boys to die in a dirty battle merely to destroy an impossible and doomed yearning for happiness.

Morgan nodded, a little too blithely for Sneed, who put two fingers on Morgan's fat neck. Morgan tried to duck away, but Sneed held Morgan's head in place with his left hand.

"This is an outrage," Morgan said. "Release me."

"I do have a right to an explanation by now," he said. "I know how to do this. I can give you a quick stroke, or a heart attack, and leave no bruise. I will stay to provide assistance till the doctor arrives, and give my name as Timothy Brownley, along with an address that will yield nothing."

"I will scream for help. You will never get away."

"If you scream, the stroke will follow immediately. 'He screamed,' I will say, 'and then he collapsed.' After the doctor has arrived and I have helped to the extent of my limited abilities, I will walk out of this office in thirty seconds and disappear into the bureaucracy, never to be found again. The papers will report that J.P. Morgan has died, mysteriously, of a stroke while in the presence of an employee of the Cigar Distribution Company, who could not be reached for comment."

He slightly loosened his grip, and when he spoke again, Sneed's voice was more gentle.

"The awfulness of this operation has bothered even my own limited conscience, believe it or not. Let me know the reason behind this fight, which will kill so many men."

Sneed released him, and Morgan settled back in his desk chair.

"First," Morgan said, "let me assure you that the Sidonian movement is far more dangerous than you seem to believe. It will not die on its own, like other Utopian movements. It has the power to destroy us all. If we do not move against it, it will grow only more powerful."

Sneed nodded.

"My own conscience is clear," Morgan continued. "I do not desire the death of our young soldiers. But the job of a soldier is put his life at risk for the protection of the homeland, and the homeland needs protection. This is a justified military operation by any external criterion. I am not causing meaningless and unnecessary deaths. There is nothing here that should weigh on my conscience."

"I'm not unimpressed by these issues, but this is not the reason for your interest, is it? And you are not overly concerned about the money that Allen Jerome stole from you. I suspect that there is much more to this tortured tale."

So why did J.P. Morgan choose to tell the truth? It was, I think, more than simple: if he did not, Mr. Sneed would kill him. And in spite of all his sadness, J. Pierpont Morgan was not quite ready to die. He saw his goal in sight. He was not going to die with his goal in sight. Thus, he chose to tell the truth, and he admitted that his mad obsession with

Sidonia had nothing to do with national security, or deterrence that would prevent future business partners from stealing from him, but was instead, as Mr. Filbank had once surmised (to the merriment of all present), entirely about love. He told Mr. Sneed about his first wife, the never-forgotten Mimi Sturges Morgan, who had died yet pure of a man's touch in her honeymoon bed, in a suite with an impossible view of the Alps. He told Mr. Sneed how, immediately after her death, he had left the villa, at the top of a stone-walled street, and sat on the pebbled beach for hours. If money was good for anything – "And I am not sure, Mr. Sneed, that it is indeed good for anything" – then it should be able to undo such a blatant injustice.

"This may seem ridiculous to you," Morgan sighed.

It did indeed seem ridiculous to Sneed, but he remained silent. He just stared at Morgan, not without reproach.

"Again," Morgan said, "the mission against Sidonia is indeed of essential national importance. I hope no brave soldier dies. But such a death would not be in vain. It must be done."

"But that is not why you care."

"Oh, if Sidonia is not defeated, my fortune would be destroyed, along with all of Wall Street. But no, I have long ceased to care about such things. The world of the dead is no longer closed to us."

"And you want its secrets."

"Anything to change this life," Morgan said, and a great boulder of a tear lingered in the great man's eye.

CHAPTER 19

Night fell, and I slept, and the sun rising over the grey city woke me, and at length night fell again, and my stomach ached with hunger. My metal dish and cup remained empty. I fell asleep, weak and losing hope.

In the middle of the night, I woke, and I saw Slocum standing before me. The bars to my cage were gone. He handed me a flask filled with water, and a half-loaf of bread.

"It is not an easy thing to be incognito in Sidonia," he said, smiling.

Slocum led me outside into the cool night, and we stood for a moment beneath the boughs of an elm tree. The graceful silhouette of the great Sidonian burg glowed in the moonlight on the far horizon. I could no longer see the dark and grey city that had lurked in the shadows of my prison cell. The night was quiet and peaceful.

"How did I survive so many days and nights without water?" I asked him, and he said that the days and nights in the prison had been very short. I said that I didn't understand.

"You lost all sense of time," he explained. "The first day the sun rose and then set six hours later. Then the night lasted a few hours, the sun rose, and three hours later it set. You grew hungrier and thirstier with the rising and setting of the sun, but you only *thought* that you were about to die of thirst. Allen Jerome caused the sun to rise and fall relentlessly in the prison to torment you."

I thought this was rather clever, come to think of it.

"Some time ago," Slocum said, "the U.S. government planted a mole here, in Sidonia. That mole was discovered, and he was killed. The government then recruited you, not entirely voluntarily, if the stories I have heard are correct. The theory was that the Sidonian Revolution would quickly and gladly accept a hero gone bad. Not true, it turned out. The Sidonian forces quickly discovered you and killed you, in a manner of speaking. A third mole was recruited, a quiet man, a bland man even, if you will, whose sole distinction was an ability to blend in, to go unnoticed."

He stopped talking for a moment, to allow the obvious to sink into my brain.

"Slocum is not actually my genuine family name, which I do not know," he said.

His great-grandmother Rachel James was engaged to be married before the War of 1812 to a man who called himself William Frederick Slocum, the captain of a merchant vessel, who as a boy had run away from his home, an inland parish in Devonshire, where his family was skilled in lace-making. He was born between 1780 and 1790, and he had two sisters, Alice and Jane, a brother Henry, and an uncle of the same name. He had been taken in by some kind Massachusetts people by the name of Slocum, who lived in or near New Bedford or Cuttyhunk, and by them educated. His own name he revealed to no one but his wife, who once told her own daughter, Slocum's grandmother, who recalled to Slocum, when he was a boy, that her husband's first name was David, and his surname was either Betts or Petts.

As an adult, it took Slocum just a bit of investigation to discover the sad history of the Pettsley family, who hailed from the lace-making hamlet of Honiton in Devonshire, the entire family executed in 1803 for verified and witnessed feats of witchcraft and wizardry. Everyone, that is, but for one lad who escaped.

"Hence," Slocum concluded, "magic flows through my veins, although I know not how to direct it. Still, it has come in handy. I have avoided detection. My wizardry is more of an unconscious matter, as I lack the proper training. Still, I do not doubt that it has helped me."

We stood together in silence for a moment as he waited for me to take this all in. I did not believe a bit of it. Plenty of folk were killed for witchcraft or wizardry without actually being witches or wizards. True witches and wizards had means to escape. Fly in the air, make the noose disappear, make it rain and put out the fire that the church has set to burn you alive. It is not so easy to kill a true witch or wizard, but it is very easy to kill a family of Devonshire lace-makers whom the neighbors happen to dislike.

"There will be a stealth attack in an hour or so," he told me at length, after he imagined that I had integrated the truth of his magical powers. "In the ensuing chaos, you might have an opportunity to accomplish a bit of mischief, to inflict a useful death or two, something that might prove a temporary setback to the Sidonian cause. Just temporary, even if you are successful, but it will be the start of a journey."

He gave me a .45, a rifle and ammunition, shook my hand and turned his back, and in a moment he had descended into the woods and was gone.

I wandered back to the city center, where the sun was setting, and a certain buzz had settled over the city. There was danger in the air, and excitement, and the people were happy that their first battle was finally at hand, and that they could prove their loyalty to Sidonia.

Allen Jerome spoke first, standing in the town square, and his words boomed through the air, vibrating and thundering like a gathering storm. After a few bombastic words about the battle arising on their southern flank, he introduced a young woman whom the crowd seemed to know, as "your beloved Princess." A hawk sat on her left shoulder. Her right eye was a piercing green, and she wore a patch over her left eye. Her features were strong and fierce, her long hair (and of course her eyebrows) a dark red. She wore a red robe and a red headdress; a sword was holstered on her left hip, and a pistol on her right.

"My children," she cried, "Sidonia's strength is not in the fog. Its strength is in our people. The fog derives its strength from our bravery. We cannot cower behind it. I must ask you to show yourselves to these soldiers, to our enemy. To go into battle, and to kill them. The voice of Sidonia is upon the waters, the voice of Sidonia is powerful, the voice of Sidonia is majestic, it crushes the wilderness, it roars, it razes the forests, it burns the cedars."

The government soldiers now appeared, small specks, over the tops of the southern peaks.

"The Sidonian fog can destroy them!" the Princess called. "It can disembowel them and leave them dead on the battlefield. But, my children … I must ask some of you to die for the Cause. Serve Sidonia with fear; rejoice with trembling." And here she stopped and paused and took a deep breath, and she cast a great and sorrowful stare at the crowd, and when she spoke again her voice was as though she would cry.

"I weep for my children; I refuse to be consoled for my children," she sobbed, a cry of lament that was strong and angry and powerful. Then she turned her face to the heavens and called out, "In the name of your Sidonian Princess, Time stops!"

And there was silence, true silence, which most of us had never heard before. I'd seen this enough times to recognize what it felt like when Time stopped. The wind stopped, the trees stopped rustling, the dust stopped floating about. The world was still white with sunshine, but the sun itself did not glow, the explosions at its center stopped exploding, and the great star just sat in the sky, lifeless and motionless as a smooth marble. The citizens ran to their homes and retrieved their pistols and rifles; militias formed throughout the streets. Where before I had stood in the middle of a friendly town, now I was in a war zone, waiting for the battle to begin.

Now she turned to the armies that were poised on the mountaintop, ready to descend into war, men and boys, their face frozen in anger and fear and bravery, their uniforms crisp and clean. Boys and men waiting to tear and bleed.

"*Khatoo aloo pashoo!*" she screamed at them, although they could not hear her.[*] "We are the nation that rises against you from the dark North of the earth, and we will swoop down like an eagle, a nation whose language you don't understand, a pitiless nation that will show the old no respect and the young no mercy." She gasped an anguished breath. "We did not seek this war, but now that you have brought it to our doorstep, we shall lock you up in your cities until every strong, trusted and towering wall has crumbled to dust. And when you are locked in the cities throughout your world, you will eat the meat of your sons and daughters, because of the desperation to which we will reduce you." Her voice shook at the terrible evil of this unnecessary war that had been forced upon her. "If only you had joined us on our quest for peace and justice, instead of trying to kill us.... If only these boys had put down their weapons and simply embraced us, and joined us."

She stared up at them, frozen-still at the very edge of the cliff, a real look of sad affection on her beautiful face. Eric Anthony, 21-years-of-age, dirty blond hair, lean but strong, a clean, innocent white

---

[*] I didn't know what that meant, but even then, I had to admire the poetry in it.

face, who had kissed only two girls in his entire life, and soon to die; Phil Simmons, burly and dark, rough-talking but good hearted, with a fat nose, thick neck, and a pregnant wife back at home, 19-years-old and soon to die. And so many others, frozen in the stillness of a world in which Time had stopped and given them a brief reprieve from death. All of them, statues in the air, and soon to die. The Princess wept for the youth of her enemy's army, she brushed a tear from her eye, and she turned back to her followers.

"You are all beloved," she called out to the crowd, her smile crooked and angry and loving. "You are all flawless; you are all mighty. You are all my babies, as though born of my own womb."

A tremendous cheer erupted from the crowd. They would die willingly for her, their Princess, whom they loved. I wondered now what portion of the crowd preparing to sacrifice themselves for the Cause had come into being moments earlier, just for this moment.

I don't know how long we stood there in the middle of that breezeless valley – Time, after all, was immeasurable – but when the Princess spoke once more, it was as though worlds had been born and died in the meantime. Her voice was very quiet, but it roared through the city square.

"See them up there, on the mountain edge, poised to destroy us. Let us meet them with passion and with justice. I love you all, my golden, Sidonian children."

She paused for a long moment.

Then she whispered, "And now, Time returns, and She takes us in Her arms."

With that, the leaves in the trees began to rustle in the breeze once more, and the birds alighted on their branches, and the soldiers overran the mountain sentries and began their charge into the valley, and the Sidonian soldiers began their countercharge to meet the government forces in the town square.

What can I tell you about this? A battle is a battle, and the soldiers charged down the mountain in a great ball of dust and bravery and bullets, and the Sidonian mob ran forward screaming in anger and fervor. The soldiers fired their rifles, and the world smelled like death. Some Sidonians popped, just an illusion created to frighten the U.S. soldiers, but more of them were struck with bullets and fell to the ground, women and children among them, angry and happy to be defending their Paradise. As they fell, the city buildings began to quiver and fall with them, each structure, built as a living dream, fell as its dreamer died and consciousness left him, dissolving before it hit the ground. My luxurious hotel folded in on itself and vanished in a swirl of dust; the store on the Palace boulevard that sold only top hats collapsed, the columned theater at the end of the Avenue burst like a bubble, and the walls of Sidonia crumbled into an empty field.

At this sight, the Sidonian mob seemed to grow ever larger, and more fighters poured from the side streets and the remaining buildings, and the fog rose and swelled around them and rolled past them and engulfed the soldiers and filled the valley. The soldiers on the front line exploded, coating what was left of the main square with blood and bone, but as the fog progressed, it grew in size and force, and the soldiers just disappeared in the fog, and the blood poured over the meadow.

I didn't really know whom I would fight in this particular kerfuffle, if forced to choose a side. I didn't want to shoot government soldiers, who were just supporting the United States as I had done in the last decade; and I didn't want to shoot the misguided Sidonian adherents, who were just searching for a better life, most of them. But I knew I wanted to kill Allen Jerome, and I knew that I *really* wanted to kill Darryl Fawley.

So I headed for the Palace.

CHAPTER 20

Suns crashed from the sky into rivers that boiled and burned off into the air and up into the ether. Riderless horses galloped screaming over cobblestone streets that crumbled into dust beneath their hooves.

I was in a desert, and the Palace was on fire, encased in fog. I hesitated, but then a little hand touched my back, and an encouraging little voice whispered in my ear – words too quiet to understand, but the voice was comforting and calm – and so I continued onward, and as I approached the Palace, the fog parted around me, as though blown away by a ghost's breath. Thus the fog did not touch me, and so it didn't kill me.

The gate opened before me of its own accord (or perhaps with a nudge from little ghostly hands), and I approached a great front hall, where an officer of the Sidonian legion cowered, an officer named Jeffrey Matthews, who had come to Sidonia after a particularly terrible drought devastated his little Kansas homestead, and after his wife had subsequently died hungry and ill as a consequence of the drought and the ensuing famine. While terrified by the havoc, Matthews was nevertheless still loyal to the Cause, and so he leaped out from the shadows where he hid, determined to protect the Palace from the government invaders, of which he believed me to be one. I didn't see him, and I didn't hear him, and I suppose he raised his gun, but I raised my gun first. Not thinking, my right arm just rose, as though lifted by a little ghost with impeccable aim, and my gun fired, and his gun flew out of his hand, and up over the Palace walls and into the mountains, as though carried by a little ghost who could fly. He charged at me, but I knocked him one in the jaw, and he fell to the ground. He was not dead, just a bit stunned, and I thought that was all right.

I continued into the Palace, unimpeded.

The Palace in Sidonia's last moments was a crumbling, burning ruin, a remnant of ancient greatness. I continued on into the banquet room, where the ceiling was caving in, and intricate paintings by unknown Renaissance masters who had never lived were dissolving and floating away into the fog. The hallways opened up into a greenhouse filled with plants of an unidentifiable nature that changed shape moment to moment; a small bush of pine needles made way for a thick and flowering vine, which became a withered, yellow tree. Faeries buzzed confusedly about the flowers, settled on their petals, and flew into oblivion, leaving a little vague white outline where they had once hovered, which wobbled and drifted into the uncalm air. I turned to the left, and I found myself running down a long corridor lit by torches that lined the gray walls. I could hear footsteps clattering off into the distance, and without deliberation – as I was vaguely convinced that anything I did now would be guided inevitably by my omniscient, infallible specters – I took a sharp left, and a sharp right, and then for just a moment, less than a second, I was on a mountaintop, in crisp air and blinding-white sunshine, teetering on a cliff edge high above a green, flowing valley. After this moment passed, I was deep underground, in a near-airless cellar, following those tapping footsteps.

Up ahead, I saw Darryl Fawley step lightly through a small postern. He shut a thick metal door behind him.

A dark figure stood guard, and I approached, still several yards away.

It was the prison guard, the beefy tough who had kicked me in the ribs back in my cell while I lay helpless on the stone floor.

After a few moments, I stood face to face with my tormenter.

Did he look afraid? No; he was fearless and confident. He didn't believe that anything could hurt him. He was imbued with the spirit and force of Sidonia, and how could anyone imbued with the spirit and force of Sidonia be anything other than invincible and immortal? Flames licked the walls behind him, and the walls began to blacken, but he didn't fear the fire.

I cast my eyes on him, and he died.

I kicked in the metal door and found myself briefly in a grove of imposing trees, which scratched the sky, with trunks a mile wide. An old man wandered in the opposite direction; as we passed, I asked him the way out, but he told me that he had been lost for many years and could only advise me the pathways to avoid. This he did, in some detail.

"I am not entirely certain that I am not utterly imaginary," the old man then acknowledged, before continuing on his way.

As I walked farther into the forest, it became an expansive room with a bright light blazing from far above. The walls were decorated with childish paintings of trees. I ran to the farthest wall, kicked it in and came out into sunlight, an overcast day, a chilly beach, a gray ocean. Little wooden cottages behind the dunes, white paint cracking and peeling in the sea air. The gangly figure of Darryl Fawley rushed down the beach, the son of Sidonie, and the husband of Lucy Billings. He slipped in the sand, lost his balance, recovered tenuously. I ran until I had reached his side, and he turned to me and stopped running. He was afraid, but he seemed resigned.

"That man is still in the world!" I exclaimed.

I cast my eyes on him, and he became a heap of bones.

Darryl Fawley's English seaside melted before my eyes, and a golden treasure room rose up before me. Allen Jerome was on the ceiling, in a sparkling white suit. Architect of the Sidonian experiment, mathematical genius, leader of men, slithering across the ceiling like a silver-skinned gecko. I jumped, and to my surprise, I landed feet first on the wall, which I then scurried up like a squirrel till I was within striking distance of my enemy. I reached out for him, but he ducked; I tried to strike him, but he slipped out of my grasp. Now he was before me, now behind me. The ceiling was cracking under us, and all around me, the Palace was changing moment to moment – now a fortress, now a church, each a memory or fantasy in Allen Jerome's mind, one after another, a great blinking living phenakistoscope.

He dashed to the eastern wall, and I dived from the ceiling, landing on him with a great crash. The wall was disintegrating, crumbling into sand. My knee was in his chest, my gun was on his oily forehead, we tumbled backwards, and he was laughing.

"You cannot kill *an idea* with a gun," he laughed as we fell together to the stone floor with a terrible thunk. He said it as though *he were no longer merely a man*, as though he were something bigger than me, bigger than he had been before, something outside of either one of us, like *helium* or *love* or *justice* (or *Pachelbel's Canon*), which would live on no matter what happened to an insignificant mortal.

"Try it," he whispered, a confident taunt. "Go ahead. *Try it*, you stupid sonofabitch."

So I tried it. I pulled the trigger, and nothing happened.

"*Misfire*," I muttered. "*Barrel empty....*"

Jerome laughed now, again.

"You think your gun is empty, or that it misfired?"

I nodded stupidly, my knee still rammed into his gut.

"Shoot the ceiling," he said.

I hesitated.

"Go ahead," he said, still laughing. "I'll wait. See how the gun works when you're shooting something temporal."

So I did – I wasted a bullet on the crumbling ceiling, and shards of stone and wood and plaster flew into the room and swirled about in the wind. I put the gun back on Allen Jerome's forehead and pulled the trigger, and though I heard the shot, and I felt the recoil, Allen Jerome was unharmed.

"You see?" said Allen Jerome. "Nothing will happen to me."

And he added:

"Hence: $(p|q)(q|p) = (-1)^{((p-1)(q-1)/4)}$, where p and q are distinct odd primes."

For just a moment, *it all made sense.*

"Do not forget," Jerome said, as he easily slipped from my grasp and rose up before me, now six feet tall, now eight feet, now filling up my whole world. "Do not forget, that I am the Falsturm's little dog." Then he added, "主席要我咬谁就咬谁," and for the first time (but not the last), I understood Chinese perfectly. What Allen Jerome said was, "*I bite whomever he asks me to bite,*" and I thought of that poor little rat, and I thought to myself, *We are all of us that rat, all of us, our collective head stuck in Sidonia's teeth.* And isn't that always the way with mathematics?; that discipline that few of us understand, or love, or want to learn, but which governs our every movement, our every breath, our every step, like spinning, heartless blades of steel, that monster that is always right and can never change. His face was a black-green mask of hateful mirth, and I could see the Grey City on the horizon, just a dim outline against an angry virescent sky.

"You just let Darryl Fawley die," I said, swinging from the ceiling to the eastern wall. "He was running along the English shore like a fox chased by hounds. *Running.* Some Movement. Some loyalty."

"We have our martyr!" Allen Jerome laughed. "And I have his power at last. Every movement needs its martyr, and its unquestioned tyrant. In one moment, you gave us our tyrant – that would be me –

and our martyr, the wise Darryl Fawley, who loved the people. And the martyrdom of my dear friend will enrage our masses."

"You let your masses die."

"Some of the Sidonians have died. Others will go with me to the Otherworlds. Angry, strong and more righteous than ever. And the movement will spread. Pilgrims will come from hundreds of miles around, just to lay eyes on this holy spot, where the Dream once lived." He smiled. "See how it all adds up? Two and two will always equal four."

Though I tried to chase him through the increasingly translucent corridors of the Sidonia Palace, Allen Jerome quickly vanished into the distance, and when I escaped the tottering Palace, thick with flames, he was nowhere in sight.

But I could now see Rasháh and his gang approaching from the west, smug and confident under a flaming sun and an angry sky. He smiled.[*]

I stepped beyond the Palace walls and the last speck of ash vanished into the air.

Well, I'm not proud of it, and I am not ashamed either, but my first thought now was to find a horse and ride in the opposite direction. There wasn't much I could do for the counter-Revolution right now, or, more importantly, to kill Allen Jerome or even the Falsturm to avenge Lucy's untimely and unjust death. I imagined a steed, and a steed appeared before me. We galloped to the last traces of the city, the bare ruins on the eastern border, where I thought I might take shelter till the coast was clear. Then I thought I'd spend a few years in 1981, sitting by the swimming pool in Death Valley. I'd return after a

---

[*] What did he know? Was he working for Jerome? Was it even really Rasháh, or were there more than one of them? Was this Rasháh before he fell off the Maze, before he vanished into Time? Or is there a way to come back from off-Maze? Or was this a feat unique to the Dark One? Facing this militia once again, I wondered why Allen Jerome had not just killed me. But now, all these years later, I can understand: because only Rasháh was fated to kill me. Just as the Falsturm may be killed only by the hand of the daughter of a Queen, who was born Nephila (whatever that means, exactly), only Rasháh might kill Watt O'Hugh. That was why Allen Jerome and his guard had not killed me in the prison; and that was why Allen Jerome did not kill me as Sidonia burned.

while, nearly as young as the day I left, and I'd deal with my problems then.

But as I drew near to its outer core, I could vaguely discern a figure who watched me as I approached, seated on a white mare, almost obscured by drifting dirt that had once been the city. When I was yet closer, I recognized Lucy Billings, dressed in a man's denim shirt and rugged work pants, just as she had been that day in Weedville, the day that I learned of her death and met her deadling self for the first time.

"I failed," I said when I had drawn up beside her. "I did nothing that Allen Jerome had not planned for me in advance. I did nothing that he did not want me to do."

I followed her on horseback into the last crumbling quarter of Sidonia, a rickety New York tenement that looked dauntingly familiar, muddy and grim. She galloped down one side alley, then another, turning left, then right, each alley growing narrower and dirtier and darker than the one before it. I was certain that we were hopelessly lost, but then the streets opened up, and with Rasháh behind us we swept through the Five Points – and it was, I saw, the Five Points of my childhood, as the Old Brewery still stood, not yet replaced by the charitable mission of the latter 19th century – and we exited my terrible slum-home and slowed down as we reached the clothing and junk shops of immigrant Chatham Street. Lucy dismounted at Number 17, a lodging house that was unusually tidy for the block. Then I dismounted. And our horses vanished.

"New York has the scroll," I said, and she said nothing. She knew, and she knew what this meant for her idealistic old friends.

As we ascended the stairs, I asked if this neighborhood were an illusion, or if it were real. Lucy said it was real. We were roaming, she said. Still, that would not stop Rasháh, who would be here any moment. So we would have to hurry.

On the third floor, we entered a small apartment. A little kitchen, a little bare throw rug in the small, square living room, and a tiny bedroom off the living room, with a narrow queen-size bed next to a crib. The apartment was as ransacked as such a spare dwelling could be. The dresser had been knocked over. Dishes had been smashed on the kitchen floor. The front door was splintered; someone had broken in, and the family who had lived here was gone. The small front window was a view of the side street; the kitchen window looked onto a brick wall.

"Here is where we say goodbye, Watt," she said. "In a moment's time, a portal will open right about … there –" and she pointed to a little shadowy corner of the kitchen. "You've seen portals before? They look like a rip in the physical world; they just hang there in space, like a great wound."

"Yes. I've seen them. Well, I have seen one. That day in Weedville. That terrible day."

"That terrible day that was also beautiful."

She smiled just for half a moment, remembering something, and then she stopped smiling.

"You will go through the portal this time. All right, Watt?"

I nodded.

"I have to leave now," she said.

"Lucy."

She listened.

I noted that deadlings were a matter of some disputation. Not everyone aware of the concept believed that the souls of our loved ones inhabited the bodies of deadlings. Some people believed that each deadling was born from the imagination of the bereaved, and that such a creature could live only for moments.

"Do you understand?"

Lucy said she supposed she understood what I was trying to say.

"If that is true, then I *believe* that I am Lucy Billings," she went on, "although I am not. I am a woman who came into being moments ago at the edge of this city, imbued only with memories of Lucy that you, the bereaved, might give me. But nothing else."

I said that was exactly right.

"And some believe that deadlings are not even truly alive," I continued. "They are hallucinations, merely walking dreams, who lack even basic consciousness. They are a projection of the imagination of the bereaved into the physical world. In which case, you are no more alive than a painting or a statue – you are just something I created, because I wanted to."

Lucy thought.

"You want some proof, I suppose."

"You owe me nothing, Lucy."

"But you want to know," she said gently.

"How could I not want to know?" I asked.

"Here it is then, Watt my darling. I am rescuing you to-day as I rescued you once before, long ago. You were too young then to remember it now."

She swept out her hand about the tiny apartment.

"In this room, a seven-year-old girl rescued a one-year-old boy. If you escape what comes next – and Watt, I cannot guarantee that you will – please come back here and ask those old enough to remember that day, neighbors who can still remember the people who lived here and that seven-year-old girl I once was. Or roam back here and see for yourself. And this will confirm that I am not a figment of your mind, that I am the very same soul that you loved and who has loved you, for longer than you ever knew."

This was why I could never remember how I had first met my beloved Lucy Billings. Because I have known her forever. Since before she was Lucy, and before I was Watt.

She put her arms around my neck.

"We have thirty seconds left, Watt O'Hugh, and then it is goodbye forever. Sidonian magic brought me to life, and you cannot abide Sidonian magic for much longer. And so we will never see each other again. I will love you from my dark oblivion in sheol, forever forever, from my dark sleep, from my nothingness."

"Maybe you will rise again," I suggested. "Maybe there is a World to Come, where we shall reunite."

"Maybe," she said, "the moon is made of green cheese. Or perhaps it is bleu. I have felt the numb chill of the Oblivion that follows Death, Watt, and you have not. Do not clutter the last moments of a woman's life with nonsense."

She leaned in very close to me, and she shut her eyes, and she smiled sadly.

"Whether or not Hester will mind, darling, I am going to kiss you goodbye."

She did, and it was a kiss full of memory and sadness, and the regret of lost chances.

Lucy dissolved in my arms, until only air and blue sky was left. Then, as predicted, a hole opened in the shadowy corner of the kitchen, black in the middle, a glowing blue around the edges, tattered, rough-edged and not perfectly round, like a terrible bloody wound in the world. (How much more dramatic it would have been had the hole opened just outside the window, and I'd had to leap across the alley, and I'd barely made it! But no, I am sworn to the Truth, and it opened in the corner of the kitchen.)

As I have mentioned, back in Weedville, Madame Tang jumped through one of these bloody holes in the world, and whatever became of her after that, I didn't know. So when the dark hole popped open in front of me, the same hole that had swallowed up Madame Tang and her stallion all those years ago, I wasted no time in jumping in, right into its churning center. I knew that either death or an old friend was on the other side. Either one would have been welcome. And so I leapt from the Chatham Street apartment into the cauldron of Time just moments before it snapped shut, my lips still burning from Lucy's one-last-kiss.

Inside the hole, it was arid and stuffy.

Back in the Sidonian valley, another hole opened up in the sky, black, ragged and wavy, glowing blue around the edges. It was just like the dark hole that claimed me on Chatham Street, except that this one was larger, and it blotted out the sky. Some of the Sidonian patriots were swept up into it and vanished, and many of the Federal soldiers split open and died horribly but quickly as the air boiled.

By the time the hole had snapped shut and vanished into the sky, only three soldiers stood still alive in an empty field, the lucky few that Sidonia had allowed to live and bring news of the massacre and of Sidonia's terrific power back to the government in Washington.

The grass in the valley was soaked with blood and matted flat to the ground, unaffected by the gentle breeze that would have seemed delightful on any other day.

The soldiers turned and looked, and there was Mimi Sturges Morgan, walking through that bloody, empty valley. She passed right by them, her eyes empty. She called out for her darling Pierpont, over and over again.

Surrounding them on all sides, that near-impassable mountain.

Across the valley, Louisa Satterlee watched all this, a woman full-grown and married already for some months, cast back across decades to see her childhood nightmare unfold, about which she had cried to her doting father when she was a girl of eleven, back when her name had been Louisa Morgan. Her dream had come true.

Mimi vanished, just wilting into dust and fading away into the blood-stained and sunrise-hued morning air.

"I am a prophetess," Louisa Satterlee whispered.

Then she too vanished, roaming back to the early 20th century, where an even greater battle raged.

CHAPTER 21

Hester waited at Lady Amalie's inn for a while. When news of the Sidonian massacre reached her, she wept in Lady Amalie's arms. Then she packed her bag, rode her horse out of the enchanted meadow, then out of the woods, followed the deserted tracks of the bankrupt Northern Pacific Railroad all the way to Tacoma, where she boarded a ship that took her to a port in South America. In a little village a few miles inland, a bribe of gold bought her a boat trip down the river and back to our little home in the jungle.

I was dead dead dead, and Hester mourned me.

At the house, Hester read ancient poetry by candlelight and rarely ventured out to town. She sometimes sat in the garden. At times, she wandered into the jungle at midnight to watch the lagoon glow, and she thought about how much I had loved the dinoflagellates. She fasted for three days and three nights. Once her fast had ended, one of Farley's men brought Hester some food from town every third day, and she thanked him with a shaky voice, eyes red from crying.

One night, J.P. Morgan himself arrived at the house, with Sneed in tow, and even that idiotic Filbank.

"Mr. Morgan was looking into some investments in Mexico," Filbank said, "and he took a detour to say hello."

"A long detour," Hester said.

Filbank blinked. He hadn't really checked the geography before inventing his lie.

"Venezuela, I think. Brazil. Maybe. Anyway, I am lying, you know."

"Yes. I know."

Morgan said: "You don't mind if I sit down?"

He sat down with a great thud in my armchair, and the legs of the armchair creaked beneath him, and Hester thought of me, now, crushed by J.P. Morgan, like my chair.

His face assumed an expression of sincerity that seemed rather sincere, come to think of it.

"I have treated Watt poorly," he said. "And I have treated you poorly."

"Yes," she agreed.

There was a whoop from outside. Some kind of bird.

Morgan listened for a moment.

"A bird," Hester said. "A parrot, I think."

"I destroyed Watt's livelihood," Morgan went on. "I brought him to New York on false pretenses, and I shut down his extravaganza."

She smiled.

"It was a good show, Mr. Morgan," she said. "The audience thrilled to scenes of Watt O'Hugh the Third battling an entire band of outlaws, single-handedly shooting them all dead, saving a stagecoach from ferocious bandits, riding on horseback across a lonely prairie town street and sweeping a little orphan girl[*] into his arms moments before a stampede thundered around the bend, and rescuing hysterical passengers from an exploding locomotive. In Watt's show, buffalo pounded across the open plains; cowboys rode wild broncos and lassoed bulls; and natives roamed the land as though the white man had never set anchor off the coast. And then there was the voluptuous Emelina, who rode out into the arena standing on a stallion in an ankle length calfskin dress and topped by a cowboy hat, drew a sixteen-gauge, double barrel, breech-loading hammer-mode shotgun and blasted a series of airborne glass balls as they plummeted to earth, shot an apple off Watt's head, and then, at the end of her act, and after a few more examples of impossible dexterity, chased her stallion around the arena, leapt onto its back, and galloped away waving her hat in the air, leaving the crowd coughing in a thick smelly cloud of gunpowder smoke."

(Or words to that effect.)

"It sounds magnificent," Morgan admitted.

"Do you know how it feels to have your destiny stolen from you?"

"I do," he acknowledged reluctantly. "I do know exactly how that feels."

"It was one of the finest spectacles of our time, Mr. Morgan. Watt O'Hugh was one of the greatest showmen of them all."

---

[*] Actually, a midget in drag.

"And I framed him."

"You did indeed," she said. "And for the worst kind of thing. *Passion* crime!"

"I needed him near Allen Jerome," he said.

"You had him shot off the top of a tenement building," she added.

"My instructions," he said, objecting mildly, "were to take him alive."

"Still," she said. "You were negligent in the execution of the operation. Like those Chinese workers who died beside the train tracks. Those piles of bones that used to be men you hired to build a railroad line for you. They were supposed to build train tracks. They were not supposed to die. And yet they are no less dead to-day for your good intentions."

"I didn't order anyone killed. I want O'Hugh alive. I want the men who built my railroad alive. I don't want anyone to die."

"You destroyed Watt's life. Do you know all the things that he was meant to do? And the life he had instead, because of you?"

Morgan nodded.

"I am not happy with myself," he said. "I am not happy with the things I have done, or even the unintended results of my actions. If I could change every single thing in my life, I would. To-day, I would be sitting on a deck chair on a transatlantic ocean liner, Miss Smith. Drinking a glass of French wine with Mimi. Watching the gulls dive for scraps by the side of the ship as we pulled out of some exotic port. Can one change things? Can one undo the past?"

"One cannot," she said. "Unless one has an utterly pure heart.

"And then," she added, "one *can*."

"My heart," said Morgan, "is impure."

"There you are," she said. "So there is no hope for it. You cannot change the past. I cannot change the past. We all have regrets."

"I once thought only Allen Jerome could answer a question for me," he said, "but I understand that you now possess his secret as well."

The great man lurched forward, his great hands clutching his great walking stick so tightly that his great knuckles turned white.

"How," he said, "can a person be both dead and not-dead?"

Sneed smiled, a patronizing little smile.

"Mr. O'Hugh was killed in the mountains of Wyoming, just outside of Laramie, some years ago," Sneed said.

Filbank stared at the ground.

"And yet," Sneed went on, "he lived to tell the tale. Dead in a shallow grave lo' these many years, and yet this home shows signs of a man reasonably alive."

"As you and Mr. Morgan have already agreed," Filbank said, "Mr. Morgan will quash the arrest warrant for Mr. O'Hugh, if you can explain this phenomenon. And in addition to the earnings from the train robbery, which Mr. Morgan has allowed you to keep, there's a … a million dollars in it for you as well, as per previous arrangement."

It was very hard for him to say this. A million dollars for Hester and me.

Hester smiled bleakly.

"I think my darling may truly be dead this time. With Watt, one never knows. But I lack true hope."

Morgan leaned forward.

"I am very sorry to hear that, Miss Smith. Truly sorry. And I will leave you to your grief if it is your intention to end our partnership prematurely."

Hester did not seem inclined to end their partnership prematurely.

"I intend to return to my homeland and fight to restore it to its glorious past as a golden kingdom," she said. "Even to-day, my people struggle to re-establish their kingdom at Petach Tikvah. And so I would ask for five hundred thousand for Petach Tikvah. And five hundred thousand for Watt." With a glance at my chair, which Morgan now occupied: "To do with as he might see fit. Should he prove to be alive."

"You have a great world plan. You and your people."

Hester smiled.

"Some are in central Africa. Some are in India. But we are everywhere. Everywhere the sea could take us. We were once a seafaring people."

"What is this homeland of yours?" Morgan asked.

Hester laughed.

"What do you think?"

"And who are your people?"

"The Z'vulunites," she said.

"Hmmm," Morgan grunted.

"*Rejoice Z'vulun in your journeys*," she said. "The true-hearted people of the sea, who put their life in jeopardy to the point of death in the Midianite war, the Assyrian campaigns, and the battle of the wadi Kishon, the people of Yotvat-Yodpat, and Zevudah, of the town of Rumah, in the Valley of Beit-Netophah. We need very little – all we seek is the return of our little Z'vulun kingdom on the border of Yissachar and Menashe, from Rimmon in the Northeast to Yokne'an in the Southwest with passage to our capital Akko on the coast. Our army of yore, reconstituted at the foot of Mount Tavor, will be triumphant against the occupiers, from Sarid, through Shimron, and up into Hannathon. Leave Naphtali and Asher to whomsoever should wish to claim them. Perhaps the Naphtalites and the Asherites. Or whomsoever else. It is no matter to me."

Morgan nodded.

"How will you all find each other, all around the world, to form this army?"

"Billy is helping. All Z'vulunites know who they are, wherever they are," she said, with what seemed to Morgan unwarranted confidence. He was a little bit shaken by her zeal, a little pale in the jowls, but he persisted. He had a mission here in the jungle, and he would see it through. It did not matter to him who might occupy the town of Shimron (whatever that was), and if it would serve his purposes, he was more than happy to help the Z'vulunites succeed in their conquest. He was willing, in fact, to become a full-blown partisan of the Z'vulunite cause, and whole-hearted sponsor of the settlement of Petach Tikvah.

"Nothing would please me more than to ensure the Z'vulunites safe passage to their port city in Akko," he said. "Shouldn't a sea-faring people like the Z'vulunites have access to the sea, after all? I don't remember much from Sunday school, but I believe that the Z'vulunites were my favorite of all the lost tribes. I greatly preferred them over the tribes of Reuben and Simeon, for example."

He shuddered dramatically. Reuben and Simeon! *He had no use for them!*

And this made Hester laugh.

"There are a few ways to be dead and not-dead at the same time," Hester Smith said, out in the garden. "Watt was killed in the Wyoming mountains after he broke out of the Laramie prison, but he remained ever alive. I can show you this. But I need a gun. And you need to tell your men to stand down."

She thought.

Morgan nodded.

"You see," she said. "This will look as though I am killing you. I cannot have them protect you when I am killing you."

"Stand down," he said to Sneed and Filbank. "I need no protection."

"I am going to kill Mr. Morgan," she said.

Morgan nodded.

"Allow her to kill me," he said. "Do nothing. That is my instruction to you."

Sneed and Filbank raised no objection to this instruction, and I have wondered to this day how that made Morgan feel. Hated, I suppose, which was perhaps not particularly enlightening or unusual.

The moon and the stars shined sporadically through the thick canopy above the garden, lighting Hester like a ghost, an angel of death.

She lifted her gun to Morgan's head, and she pulled the trigger. I gather that what happened next came as a shock to Hester, although not precisely as a surprise. The top of the banker's skull split in two, and his brain flew across the jungle night and splattered against the bark of two trees that had grown twisted together. Although dead, his face held a look of pain and surprise, and his body seemed to stand upright for longer than was actually physically possible before slumping to a jelly-like heap on the jungle floor.

Filbank wiped a bit of brain from the side of his face with a fresh handkerchief.

"Did that hurt?" Hester asked. "I've always wondered if that would hurt."

Morgan sat down on a log. Sneed handed him a flask of whiskey, and Morgan took a long slug.

"It hurt."

He looked at the body.

"And who was that?"

Hester sat beside him.

"He was you, in a manner of speaking. Everyone has twenty-one essences. Most of them we never use. It's possible to kill one, without killing the whole man. Takes a little skill, though. I didn't tell you beforehand, but this was my first try. I wasn't entirely sure it would work. I knocked off one that has been holding you back. Your avarice. It's smaller than most people think. Now it's gone."

"No avarice?"

"None. But that was never what mainly drove you."

"And this is how O'Hugh died and lived on?"

"Exactly. The Sidonians ordered him executed in the mountains of Wyoming. A Sidonian double-agent shot him in the head but kept his face recognizable, and they left a dead body in the snow."

Back in the house.

"My business," she said, "means I will travel much in the next decades. I will often be on ships, traveling back and forth. Anyplace where my people live. And I will convince them to return to a glorious past. So I will often be on ships."

She touched his left temple with her right pointer finger, and his right temple with her left pointer finger. She stared into his eyes.

"This shedding of essences is good for killing a harmful part of one's personality," she said, "and as you might guess, it is useful for faking one's own death, for being, as you put it, 'dead and not-dead at the same time.' And there are essences that allow a body to roam Time, to flitter about, seeing things that other people cannot see, which I have managed to access. I cannot tell you much, J. Pierpont! But I can tell you a little bit, and I think it might make you feel a little more hopeful."

And so she told him that around a decade and a half into the new century, when all would seem lost, he would board a ship to the Middle East, not having thought about her, Hester, for decades, and he would see her onboard as the ship left the Mediterranean Sea and entered the mouth of the Nile. If by then, he had tired of the lawyers, the politicians and the conspiracies, and if he wished to shed one more essence – "your desire for power" – to live anonymously and happily in a far-off land, she would allow it to happen. She would let an essence expire peacefully in his ship-board bed.

Filbank was mixing drinks. Hester sat beside Morgan on the couch.

"J.P. Morgan will die," Hester said, "so that J.P. Morgan might live. If you wish it, at the time. I will promise you a home in the Z'vulun kingdom, if you wish it. Dry air, good for the lungs. For a few shekels more."

"It sounds like a bargain. I will keep it in mind."

Filbank pulled up a chair. He tapped Hester on the knee.

"Mr. Morgan is not exclusively interested in his own death. There is someone else."

"There was a young woman," Morgan said. "I was married once before. She was very ill when we wed, and she died not long after the wedding."

He stared at his fingers, at his walking stick. Not at Hester.

"There is another way that one can be dead and not-dead at the same time," she told him.

His dead essence lay in a pool of blood in the jungle outside. Scavengers had begun to gather. He could hear shrieking and slurping as jungle rats fought over the body.

"The Magic of Sidonia is growing stronger here," she said. "I cannot remain, and in a week or so, it will kill you, Mr. Morgan. But right now, to-day, it's at just the right temperature. Not boiling. Not tepid. You know? Just warm enough to make the dough rise."

They heard footsteps on the floor above, the light tapping footsteps of a young woman.

Hester smiled. Why did she wish to help him? It was not just the financial gain for her and for her war, although that was most of it. But sometimes she wanted him to be happy, however briefly she could arrange it, in spite of everything.

"She's upstairs," Hester whispered.

She listened more closely.

After only about a year in this house, she knew it well. A stranger in the house was like an itch on her body.

"I'd say she's waiting for you in the guest room," she told him. "The third door on the left, after the staircase."

Well, I can speculate, but I cannot tell you for certain what went on in that room.

As I mentioned in the first volume of my *Memoirs*, I was destined many years later to meet a woman named Georgina de Louvre, who, along with Louisa and Angela (she of the terrible coffee) filled in the gaps in Morgan's life for me. But most of the more intimate scenes in Morgan's life that are dramatized in these *Memoirs* come from good old Georgie and her uncanny (or imaginative) memory.

But she was unable to give me any detail whatsoever as to the particulars of that reunion. So I cannot tell you for certain what went on in that room, although I can speculate, and here is what I think: by then, he was old, and she was ever young. He was used to overpowering women, and he knew nothing else. He did not want to overpower her. He did not want to send a timid and frail soul back into the underworld violated. And so he sat on the edge of the bed, and he told her about his life. He told her how much he missed her; he told her how much her brief life on Earth, and her briefer moments with him, had forever changed the heart of the most powerful man in the world. He held her in his arms, I think, and it is my supposition that he probably wept, and that she did as well. And then a moment or two later, she was gone.

But I can only guess. On the other hand, the entire interlude could have been devoted to wild pully hawly. What do I know, after all, about the mind of a millionaire?

Hester, Sneed and Filbank walked around the grounds of our home, waiting for Morgan to return from upstairs. The night was pleasant and cool.

"How does this work?" Sneed asked. "You just told him what the future entails. You went into the future to change what – in the future – is the past. I mean to say that if you go to the future to find out how to fix the present, you're changing the past. What does that do to the logic of the ... the, oh, what you might call –"

"I ran the risk of being expelled from the interlinear Maze," Hester agreed, "before the first word left my mouth. Poor Mr. Morgan. I knew where he'd be, what he'd need. I didn't change a thing. I just made his life a little more pleasant."

"But won't it change his life, knowing the whole time where he'll be?"

"What will actually change? That man lost any power over his own life long ago."

Sneed nodded.

"I am not a bad man," Sneed said. "I keep doing bad things. But I am not a bad man, although I do bad things."

"That's pretty much the definition of a bad man, nay? A man who does bad things?"

Sneed shook his head.

"A bad man is a man who enjoys doing such bad things. Yet I am not without a conscience. I was guilt stricken over the deaths that would result from Morgan's misadventure, which I nevertheless planned and executed. I am not without human feeling and sympathy."

"Then you are not the *worst* man," Hester said, "but still a bad man."

Sneed nodded. He supposed this was true. He had never thought about this before, and he wasn't happy about it, but he didn't see any need to argue the point.

"Well," she said, staring out at the little lagoon. "I'll be leaving soon." She turned to him. "And you must, too. And take Mr. Morgan."

She lowered her eyes, blinked back a tear, and took a deep breath.

"I wish Watt were coming with me," she said. "To raise his child. And maybe to make more children. To help repopulate the Z'vulun Kingdom with more pureblood Z'vulunites."

She said this to nobody, although Sneed stood beside her. Sneed seemed inclined to put a tentative, comforting hand on her arm, but then he reconsidered, and so he stood beside her silently, until J.P. Morgan returned, and then he and Sneed and Filbank left the grounds of the house, although it was yet deep night.

CHAPTER 22

How long was I inside the portal? I don't know. Maybe a half hour, maybe a day. That's the perplexing characteristic of Time: when you unmoor it from the external units by which it is measured – the movement of the sun and the tides – it becomes unmeasurable and indefinable.

All I know is that while I was inside the portal, I came more than a little bit haphazardly unstuck in Time, and that I stayed not long in each moment. Now I was holding Lucy's hand at the opera – and each time, I wished to ask her to marry me, but somehow could not speak – and now I was battling the crowds on that fateful date in 1863, when my city went mad, with a little girl in my arms, a child I sought to save from the enraged mob. Every time I revisited that moment, I thought I might save her, so that she might not become one of my ghosts, but again and again, I felt her little hands being torn from mine, and the men dragged me away. I looked for Hester, but I didn't see her.[*] Now I was a boy running along the streets of the Five Points with another boy, and we were laughing.

And now, oddly, I found myself dropped into a large room that hummed and glowed with fluorescence, and which had a view of a city that glowed greenish-blue in a sooty, starless night.

The room was filled with desks that were empty, other than one, at which a tired man sat. His skin was oily and blue in the artificial light. A clock on the wall showed that it was fifteen minutes before midnight.

The man frowned.

"You must be one of those time-traveling cowboys we used to hear so much about," he said, not without some veiled amusement.

"A time Roaming shootist, really," I replied, "or gunman, if you will. My career on the cattle drives was limited, and we don't

---

[*] At that moment, I wondered if she had been lying to me all along about her presence on that day, but some years later, I realized the truth, in the middle of the night, waking from a dream, as these things usually come to me. Hester had not lied to me, but she had come to me from a different past, a past that no longer existed, and that a Roamer could no longer visit.

really call ourselves time 'travelers'. That implies fully occupying another time in a way that we really cannot do. We roam. We drift. We're like a shadow."

He shrugged.

"And what brings you to my cubicle?" he wondered.

"I don't know. I kissed my Lucy goodbye, and here I am. She is a deadling, and I'm never going to see her again."

"We don't get deadlings around so much anymore," he said. "Yer magic and what-not, basically a thing-of-the-past. That's all right with most of us. It's very sad, very heart-breaking, to meet someone as a deadling, whom you once loved."

I nodded.

"Deadlings," he went on, "are just something the Falsturm tossed our way to create a little loyalty. We don't get them around anymore, hardly ever."

My life, I told him, had driven me to drown my sorrows in Monongahela.

It had driven me to black unconsciousness.

"You think I don't drink?" the man said, those diabolical lights flickering and popping over his head. "You're not the only one who drinks, my friend."

Then he told me a story out of nowhere, gritting his teeth. Back when he was a teenaged boy, in the middle years of the Struggle (or what some called the Conflict), he'd been engaged to the girl he still considered the love of his life, even all these years later, after two divorces that had drained him of his money and his strength. Her name was Laura, and she'd been a Loyalist, while he'd been a Skeptic – "in my heart, only," he said, but still the Falsturm's dark spies knew. "It's how they make an example of you, if they know you're a Skeptic," he said. "They take someone you love, then someone else you love." He and Laura were walking hand-in-hand along the little lane that ran in a circle around their cluster of tidy boxy homes with geraniums in the windows. Suddenly, a van careened around the corner, swept past him and pinned Laura to the wall of her house.

"Look, I knew what would happen next, because I'd seen it in a thousand movies. I said a bunch of stuff about how much I was looking forward to celebrating Thanksgiving with her next week, and she told me to live my life and find another girl. I said we'd get married and raise beautiful children. Then she gasped a little and told me she loved me, and that was it. *Darkness veiled her eyes*, as the fella said.

"She doesn't come back as a deadling, I can tell you that."

So here it was: Billy's future in which Sidonia wins. I was in the Grey City, in an office where a functionary worked on the City's business underneath those lifeless lights, barely squeezing breath through his near-dead lungs. We looked out the windows together, at this joyless night City, at its glowing grey stone buildings.

Then Something happened, there in his office. First a little buzz in the air, then a round spark that floated towards us.

"Ball lightning," the man said. "Many people see it and think they're seeing angels."

"Angels don't exist," I said.

"*Tell* me about it," the man said. This means, in the language of the 21st century, *I agree with you*. It doesn't literally mean *Tell me about it.*

"And God doesn't exist," I added, gratuitously and blasphemously. Because *why not*? It seemed a logical conclusion at that moment, everything considered.

"I *hear* you," the man said. This is another thing that, in the 21st century, means *I agree with you*. It doesn't just mean that he hears me, although that would of course be a necessary precondition.

The spark stopped sparkling, darkened and grew larger, like a visual migraine made manifest.

"Ah," said the man. "Not just ball lightning. A dark hole to another world. A *weir to a new realm*, as it were. These things were more common in the early years of the Falsturm's reign." Confidentially: "The Battle of Sidonia opened the way for the Falsturm's coup. That was an ugly one." He shook his head, regretfully. "If I could, I would jump, you know."

I said that I heard him.

"I think this one is for me," I said, and in I went. "Not so bad, once you get used to it," I called back to my friend, whose name I didn't know, before the hole snapped shut.

Inside this hole, the air was moist and chewy. Funny, I thought. Different holes, different climates.

Bemusing.

I don't know how long I churned around in the moist noiselessness of the hole, but before long, I dropped with a gentle, scratchy thud on cold sand, in the dark of night. The air smelled a little bit like old fish, although there was no water nearby that I could see or hear. I stood. And after I stood, something immediately knocked me to the ground. I tried to reach for my .45, but a giant sand crab had pinned my arms to the dusty sand.

Where was I?

I didn't know it, but I was underground, in the Chinese Hell of the Innocent Dead. Sand crabs in the Chinese Hell of the Innocent Dead are entirely different animals from those we know now in the world of the Sun. Most sand crabs are very small – in fact, in the world that you know and in which I grew up, *all* sand crabs are very small and present no danger to human beings at all. To my knowledge, none are even poisonous. They might pinch you. I am not sure if they might even draw blood. I don't know what they ordinarily eat. They are silly little creatures, and they are not even delicious. I do not know what purpose sand crabs serve in the world.

But the large, Chinese Hell sand crabs live anywhere that there is sand, so they might suddenly surprise you many miles from the nearest ocean. They are nimble and can pin a body quickly to the ground, with their unusually large and long pincers (which, by the way, are also known in the scientific crab community as "chelipeds.") They eat people. They pin us with their pincers, then they make us numb with their saliva, and then they eat us alive. They are bright blue in color with pretty white spots all over their bodies, which is apparently attractive to the opposite sex. Some giant sand crabs are nine feet long and weigh up to three hundred pounds.

The giant blue sand crab's drool dripped into my face and flowed down my body, and my skin grew cold, numb and dead.

Now, when things seem blackest – completely poleaxed by a giant sand crab and covered in anesthetic crab drool on the cold dry sand of the Chinese Hell of the Innocent Dead, and so on (not a good scenario by any stretch of the imagination) – it might make a bit of sense to pause for a moment to catch our collective breaths and try to make some sense of all of this. I am an old man, and just thinking of that sand crab makes my heart flutter and creak and puts me at risk of stroke. Not death, I suppose, as I understand that I am to die on January 1, 1937, but it is entirely possible that some of these memories could induce a stroke and prevent my finishing my tale.

I told you that all of this story is 100% true, and I do believe that to be the case, but perhaps I should amend that a bit to say that most of this story is 100% verifiably true, and a few bits are reliable hearsay, and a very small bit of it is speculative but probably correct. For example, who is M. Rasháh? I have heard that Mr. Bridges and his wife died, both mysteriously, of a double suicide in the bedroom of the home they shared just below Cloud City, on the same night, during the week that Allen Jerome and Darryl Fawley visited. I believe that M. Rasháh was Sidonia's primary assassin of probable trouble-makers – that is, those who have not yet made any trouble but who are likely to make trouble in the future – which is why he tried to kill me in the Great Roman Hippodrome in 1874, in Weedville later that same year, and in Sidonia.[*] And, sadly, it must be said, upon my birth, killing my parents instead, as the young Lucy Billings, then known by her true name, swept me from the building to hide me in the Old Brewery, watching over me with a heavenly heart, and mostly in the shadows (for example, paying Mrs. Welch to give me food in the morning and, when danger lurked, a warm bed at night), until I was old enough to care for myself.

So I believe M. Rasháh was a sort of statistical arbitrage quantitative analyst of the Otherworld, examining probabilities and possibilities and shooting when probably profitable for the Sidonian movement and the Falsturm. I don't know it for sure, but while not entirely perfect, I think he was significantly more skilled than the 20th century quant analysts of Level-Global or Jemmco Capital, who were mere con artists. Anyway, I can imagine Allen Jerome boasting about his human abacus before M. Rasháh shot Mrs. Bridges. Why not, after all? She would soon be dead and unable to tell the tale, Allen Jerome was a boastful man, and secrecy prevented him from boasting about M. Rasháh to anyone who might possibly live for more than a few minutes. So I think he spilled the beans. Much of what I know about the private conversations between Allen Jerome and Darryl Fawley I

---

[*] And, while I cannot prove it, I believe this is why he could do naught but send his Otherworldly assassins to hit Master Yu, an Old Soul from the Old War whom Rasháh – a mere half-soul from the Next War – would be powerless to stop by himself.

know from Frederick Slocum, who became a bit of a confident of Mr. Fawley, but of the death of the Bridges couple, I know very little. It is something Darryl Fawley did not wish to discuss in detail. So I have guessed, correctly I think, but I cannot guarantee it with perfect certitude.

Why did Billy Golden permit me to walk into Sidonia with such a feeble disguise, one that guaranteed that I would be imprisoned and beaten by that sadistic, nameless prison guard? I realized the truth in the middle of the night in 1928, when I awoke with an epiphany. The prison guard had some sort of historic role to play in either the Battle of Sidonia in the early 20th century or (less likely) the Great Sidonian Revolt of 1917 to 1918; either way, Billy wanted him dead, and he knew from his roaming that I would be likely to kill him if given the motive and the means. That was my true mission, and I knew it not.

Nothing has ever been as it seems.

How did Slocum manage to elude detection for so long? I suspect it had nothing to do with the mysterious origin of William Frederick Slocum, the captain of a merchant vessel. M. Rasháh, that quantitative analyst *extraordinaire*, must have told Allen Jerome that the living Slocum would lead me to Darryl Fawley, whom I would kill, giving Sidonia an important martyr and loosing Fawley's ancient and parasitic powers to settle into a new host, namely Allen Jerome himself. Allen Jerome would be rid of Darryl Fawley, an assassination he had long desired but could not commit himself, and he grew almost immediately into the most powerful man within our Realm, willing to use his powers in ways that Darryl Fawley would never even have contemplated.

I am not sure if you have ever felt in control of your life.

I felt in control of my life only once: when I was riding a train north with Emelina, about to present the greatest Wild West show the East Coast had ever seen.

Otherwise, I have felt buffeted by uncontrollable tides.

In fact, I have often been, figuratively, a man pinned to the dusty ground by a voracious sand crab. And, at least once, literally.

In the Chinese Hell of the Innocent Dead, one could feel the hatred in the air. And smell it. (This kind of hatred smells like old fish. And it makes the air cold. And it makes the sun go away.)

Just when the crab was about to take a great hungry bite out of my skull, I heard a shot ring out, and the crab loosened its grip just a bit, but not enough. Another shot, and the grip slackened. Two more shots, and the crab was suddenly dead weight. I flopped about until I was out from under the dead crab, unable to feel a thing.

A figure appeared at the far horizon, a thin man on a lopsided horse. He meandered, lopsidedly and rather slowly, in my direction. At length he drew within a few yards of me. He was a Chinese man, not entirely young but not yet old, and a woman would have described him as handsome, even now, weathered and ragged.

"I saved your life," he said, standing over my prone body.

Even though I didn't understand Chinese, and he was speaking Chinese, I could understand him.

"It was a very difficult shot from such a distance," he said, "but had I waited until I was closer, sand crab would have eaten your face."

"Thank you," I said, my speech slurred and drooly.

"I used four bullets," he said. "I'm running short on bullets. None to spare. You have bullets? And you have guns?"

I nodded.

"A .45 and a rifle," I gurgled, as spittle spilled down the side of my face, my own saliva mixing with sand crab drool. "And plenty of ammunition," I added, failing to sound authoritative and in control.

"Good," he said. "We will need guns. And we will need bullets. I have a sword. Not a very good one. But perhaps it is Magic."

He knelt down and held out his hand. He grasped my shoulder, which was still numb.

"Yu Dai-Yung," he said to me. "I am Yu Dai-Yung; this is my name," he added, in case I might misunderstand what he meant.

"The acclaimed poet?" I said. "With the terrible name?"

"The *terrible* poet," he admitted. "With a beautiful name that he does not deserve. But thank you."

"Ah," I said.

I had heard his story once, on a trek through the canyons of Utah, from an old friend of mine, I said. I was familiar with his story.

"And you are the reincarnation of a court poet of yore?" I added. "If I recall correctly?"

"You recall almost correctly," he said, in Chinese. "Actually, his bastard son. But you were close."

"I am Watt O'Hugh," I said. "The Third."

A dry little gasp of wind mixed a bit of sand and dirt into the air and blew the smell of Hate into my lungs.

Yu Dai-Yung turned and looked out at the landscape, and then my way.

Shaking his head, he said, "一 塌 糊涂," and while this came out of his mouth sort of pitiably and hysterically as *i-ha hu t'u*, I understood his meaning perfectly. What he meant, with a terrible sigh, was this:

"Well. What a hell of an out-of-control mess."

And so it was.

THE END
of
**THE SECOND PART OF THE STRANGE AND ASTOUNDING MEMOIRS
OF WATT O'HUGH the THIRD**

AUTHOR'S NOTE

While I grounded this book in historical reality, I played with dates and places where necessary. For example, I have tried to describe with some accuracy the history and structure of the Bank of California, although the Bank was out of business for a relatively brief period of time, a few years earlier than the events of this story. Furthermore, there was no lawn, garden and iron fence in front of the Bank building. My fictitious J.P. Morgan continues to live in his Madison Avenue mansion a few years before the real one did. In Chapter 12, Master Yu expresses a rather modern skepticism towards ancient Chinese myths, the slave ship Africain sailed in the early 19th century, not the 18th century, the Second Grand Ball of the Knights of Robert Emmet was not a masked ball, and it was held in October 1879, not July, as were the other events described during that eventful week in Cloud City. I am aware of no evidence that the now-defunct town of Freda, North Dakota existed prior to its turn of the century establishment as Pearce, North Dakota, and while it was hit by a meteor around the end of World War I, the meteor didn't destroy the entire town. There are no little isles in the North River. The details of William Frederick Slocum's tale as related in this book are mostly true, although his family's trial for witchcraft and wizardry is my own invention; why he fled is unknown. "Peking Indians" did not exist. Senator William Sharon probably never abused William C. Ralston's wife and children, and I know absolutely nothing about Leadville's Mayor Dougan, and I apologize to any of his descendants offended by this mildly negative portrayal. Scholars of Soviet history will recognize Anichka's hometown of Khabnoye as modern day Poliske, a once-lovely city filled with historic architecture, which is now an abandoned ruin in the Chernobyl Exclusion Zone. I have scattered what I think are some particularly lovely bits of unattributed Midrash and other poetical snippets of Judaica throughout the text (which are generally my own re-translation), and the first sentence of the first and second paragraphs of chapter 15 each has an unattributed Cheever quote, which is, I think, definitive proof that on one of his jaunts to the late 1950s, Watt read *The Wapshot Chronicles* (as good use of anyone's time-roaming skills as I can imagine).

Thanks to my wife, Lan, as always my first reader, to my kids, Liana and Julianne, for support you showed me as I finished this book during those terrible days of unemployment, Mark Matcho, for his great cover art and incredible enthusiasm for this project, Andrea Basora for an early read, David Groff for his insightful and essential final edit and Elena Stokes at Wunderkind PR for recognizing the potential in my little endeavor.

Thanks also to R. Michael Wilson, who corresponded with me on how to rob a 19th century train, Tzyann H. Berman, who helped me with Chinese idioms, the historian Leslie Harris for her knowledge of African-Americans in old New York, The New York Historical Society, Jack Hursh for information on Reno in 1878, Alison Moore at the California Historical Society, who provided essential information on 1878 San Francisco, Rand Richards, Lynn Coleman's 19th century website, and Rabbis Matt Carl and Frank Tamburello for your help with chapter 15. Edward Blair, Christian J. Buys and Lawrence Von Bamford have written useful books on Leadville, Colorado (which was known in the past first as Slabtown and then as Cloud City), and my 30-year-old notes from Professor Hans Bielenstein's amazing Ancient Chinese History class proved very useful. (Good old Prof Hans Bielenstein. What a great guy!)

Stay with me. Just one more to go ….

Steven S. Drachman
November 2013

OTHER BOOKS FROM CHICKADEE PRINCE THAT YOU WILL ENJOY

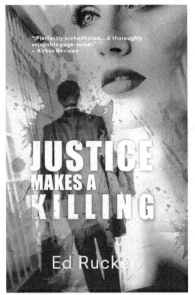

Justice Makes a Killing: *A Bobby Earle Novel*, by Ed Rucker –
ISBN 978-1732913905

"A thoroughly enjoyable page-turner…. The classic courtroom drama at the heart of this story is perfectly orchestrated, and the seemingly impossible odds make Earl's masterful handling of evidence, witnesses, opposing counsel, the jury, and the judge wonderfully satisfying to read. Rucker has a knack for explaining the minutiae of legal procedure clearly as he weaves them into the story." — Kirkus Reviews

Probability Shadow, by Mark Laporta
ISBN 978-0-9997569-2-8

"This is a good series opener for speculative readers who like tangled story lines in which solved problems reveal even greater challenges."
— *PUBLISHER'S WEEKLY*

"[A]n engrossing far-future reality of galaxy spanning civilizations, populated by multiple alien races … [Laporta's] imagination is impressive and establishes a delightful playground for the trilogy to explore." — John Keogh, *BOOKLIST*

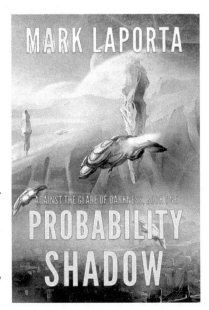

AND DO NOT MISS!

Watt O'Hugh and the Innocent Dead: Being the Third Part of the Strange and Astounding Memoirs of Watt O'Hugh the Third

By Steven S. Drachman

ISBN 978-1-7329139-3-6

"Touching tragedy, dead-pan comedy and a time-roaming cowboy? Part three of Drachman's epic fantasy series is **indeed fantastic!**" — David David Katzman, award-winning author of *A Greater Monster* (Bedhead Books)

On the morning of Wednesday, September 24, 1879, I awoke in a prison in Montana.

I did not imagine that evening might find me sprawled beneath a great and ferocious sand crab on a rancid beach, deep in the Hell of the Innocent Dead.

But that is indeed where I wound up.

The moral, if there is one: never plan your day too inflexibly.

THE WAIT IS OVER: THE CLASSIC ADVENTURE CONCLUDES

In the final book of the trilogy, Watt O'Hugh, the dead/not-dead, time Roaming Western gunman, travels the length and breadth of the sixth level of Hell, recruiting a shadowy army that might storm the borders of the Underworld, free humanity and the inscapes from the clutches of the Falsturm and his Sidonian hordes, and stave off the Coming Storm.

He'll need a little luck.